THE
LAST
PILGRIM

THE
LAST
PILGRIM

The Tommy Bergmann Series

GARD SVEEN
Translated by Steven T. Murray

Previously published as *Den siste pilgrimen* by Vigmostad og Bjørke in 2013 in Norway. Translated from Norwegian by Steven T. Murray. First published in English by AmazonCrossing in 2016.

Published by AmazonCrossing, Seattle

www.apub.com

Amazon, the Amazon logo, and AmazonCrossing are trademarks of Amazon.com, Inc., or its affiliates.

ISBN-13: 9781503937116
ISBN-10: 1503937119

Cover design by David Drummond

Printed in the United States of America

PROLOGUE

Whitsunday, June 8, 2003
Carl Oscar Krogh's Residence
Dr. Holms Vei
Oslo, Norway

Only when she had parked in front of the large timbered house did the young housekeeper realize that the gate up by the road had not been closed. Even so, she remained sitting in her car for almost a minute to finish listening to a song on the radio. As the song faded out she turned off the radio, got out of the car, and looked back up the paved driveway.

The wrought-iron gate stood wide open, and she hadn't opened it when she drove in.

It's never left open, she thought.

One thing she'd learned after almost a year of having Carl Oscar Krogh on her client list was that he was a stickler on that point. The first question he'd asked her when she arrived was whether she'd remembered to close the gate behind her. And the same reminder was always repeated as she left for the day: "You *must* remember to close the gate behind you."

And the dog, she thought. *Where's the dog?*

The frisky English setter, which still scared her a little, hadn't barked or yanked on its chain in the backyard. The dog always made its presence known, excited to go out for the day's long walk as soon as she got out of her car.

The housekeeper turned toward the house. She slammed the car door, a little too hard. The metallic thunk rang in her ears before everything went quiet around her, quieter than before. *And so much warmer,* she thought. The sudden heat wave that had descended upon the city yesterday no longer seemed pleasant, but unbearable.

After she had rung the doorbell twice, there was no longer any doubt.

Something was wrong.

She had a creepy feeling that somebody had quite recently—only a few minutes ago—stood on the stairs just as she was now. Someone who didn't belong there.

She rang the doorbell again.

"Herr Krogh," she called out. "Carl Oscar?"

Finally she put her hand on the heavy door handle. Locked. As she turned around, she silently cursed this huge, lonely property and the tall spruce trees forming a windbreak that blocked any view from outside. It was as though she was all alone in the world. Not a soul would hear her if she shouted.

She walked slowly around the side of the house. She stopped at the kitchen window, put her hands on the windowpane, and peered inside. Empty. Then she continued past the library down the flagstone path that led to the terrace in the rear. She moved cautiously, trying to make as little noise as possible. When she was three feet from the corner of the house, she stopped and ran her hand along the corner beam, which was warm from the blazing sun. Normally she would have waved off the bugs buzzing in front of her face, but now she didn't even notice them. She was concentrating on staring straight ahead, which somehow calmed her. She scarcely noticed the city spread out far below and the zigzag pattern of white boats as they silently sliced across the fjord.

She rounded the corner of the house and noticed the white curtains billowing out of the terrace doorway.

Something flickered at the edge of her field of vision, something on the flagstones by the lawn furniture. A pool of red fanned out beneath the dead body of the dog. The black-and-white spotted throat gaped up at her. The blood looked as though it had hardly begun to congeal.

She considered running back to her car, but her legs propelled her toward the terrace.

As she moved slowly toward the billowing curtains, she silently prayed to God to watch over her.

She sidestepped the dead dog and entered the living room. In the middle of the floor lay what had once been Carl Oscar Krogh. Even his eyes were gone, chopped up like jellyfish.

How could they? she thought. *How could anyone do such a thing to another human being?*

CHAPTER 1

Monday, May 28, 1945
Jørstadmoen POW Camp
Former Stalag 303
Lillehammer, Norway

Captain Kaj Holt of the Norwegian Resistance movement Milorg stopped at the parade ground. He studied the barracks arranged in front of him for a moment. Then he turned around and looked toward the gate through which he had entered, as though to assure himself that it wasn't too late to turn back.

Wasn't it true that you should never ask a question if you didn't want to know the answer? Maybe it was best not to know and instead resign yourself to the way things were, as normal people did, and get on with your life. The only problem was that he no longer had any life to get on with. The war would not let him go.

"It would've been best if they'd caught you too," said Kaj Holt quietly to himself. That was what his wife had said.

A few minutes later, he had simply walked out the door, abandoning everything that had kept him alive for the past five years: his wife, his child, all of it. The first night he slept outside had felt like liberation.

He shook off the memories and pulled out the interrogation orders from the side pocket of his uniform jacket. He spread out the paper and read the words he himself had entered into the blanks on the form. *Hauptsturmführer Peter Waldhorst. Security Police (SIPO) Division IV. Foreign Service Post Lillehammer.* At the bottom of the page was Holt's own signature. Although a handful of people knew that he was in Lillehammer, no one knew why he was there. That was best for the time being. Not many people knew that a group of German officers had been transferred to this camp, which still housed a large number of Soviet prisoners of war.

Division IV, he thought. The Gestapo's official name sounded innocent enough. So typically German to create a hell concealed by bureaucracy.

From farther up the valley came a powerful crash of thunder, unusual for late spring in Norway.

Kaj Holt carefully folded up the interrogation orders and put them back in his pocket. The heavy rain had already begun to soak through his uniform. He jogged toward the building in front of him, but instead of going inside he stopped on the steps under the eaves, wanting to postpone everything for a few more minutes. He fished out a Swedish cigarette from his breast pocket; soon almost everything he owned would be Swedish. The nicotine calmed him down, slowing his pulse, which had been pumping hard since he came through the gate.

Like a deluge, Kaj Holt thought as he watched the torrents of water striking the hill and ricocheting back into the air, frothing and foaming. The sight reminded him that the Creator Himself had once wanted to drown them all for their sins, because no one, absolutely *no one*, was free of sin. Holt himself had killed people who still, even after it was all over, haunted him every night: young people, old people, parents, even a young mother who was only nineteen years old. Her baby had begun to scream as soon as Holt started down the stairs. He could still hear the crying through the flimsy door and down the stairwell; he could still see the baby lying alone in its crib, while the mother, still a child herself, lay in a pool of blood in the hall.

No one is free of guilt.

Isn't that the truth? he thought. He ought to jot it down on a scrap of paper and save it with all the other scraps he'd scribbled on over the last five years, saving them for what he imagined would become his memoirs, assuming anyone cared. If he even made it out alive—wasn't that what he'd been thinking? And had he really left without taking all those notes with him? The thought hadn't occurred to him until now. He had to get hold of those notes. He hadn't planned that far ahead when he'd simply walked out on his wife and child and vanished out of their lives ten days ago, on the seventeenth of May too, the first Independence Day celebrated in freedom since 1939. He'd hidden the notes in a shoe box and put the box in an old "America trunk" full of discarded clothes in the attic of what had once been his home. And that was where all that stuff would remain if he never returned home.

Holt gave a start at the sudden sound of a jeep rounding the corner at terrific speed. It ground to a halt right in front of the stairs where he was standing. The young American driver leaned his head back, lost in his own world, as he chewed his gum.

When Kaj Holt had almost finished his cigarette, the door next to him opened. Two men stepped out and stopped short; they obviously hadn't noticed the sudden change in the weather. One was American, a captain like Holt himself, and the other was in civvies. The civilian bumped into Holt as they passed and muttered "sorry" in Swedish. The American captain gave Holt a brusque nod before they went down the steps. The captain said "Get back in" when the driver jumped out to open the door on the passenger side. The civilian, who had a remarkably childish face, turned to give Holt a long look before he got in the car. A smile seemed to tug at his lips beneath the wet brim of his hat.

Holt watched the car as it vanished among the trees; he had a feeling he'd seen that childish face somewhere before. *No,* he thought. He must be imagining things. Usually he would have reacted to the fact that a Swedish civilian was here with an American officer, but today he thought no more about it. The liberation of Norway had created such chaos that almost nothing surprised him anymore.

He dropped the cigarette on the ground and turned around. The German imperial eagle above the wheel with the swastika inside was still imprinted on the wired glass of the entry door. The sight gave him a momentary jolt, and he stopped with his hand on the door handle.

The hair of the British lieutenant seated behind the improvised counter was thick, black, and shiny. He looked as if he'd sat behind a desk for the duration of the war and now had emerged to take over the country from the Germans. Beside him stood an armed British MP with a supercilious look on his face. The Englishmen had been here less than a month, but they acted like they owned the country, as did the Americans. He didn't especially like the Yanks, but it was the English for whom he'd developed an odd distaste. They didn't feel a need to proclaim to all the world that they were the victors—they just assumed everybody knew it. If anyone had told this to Kaj Holt just a few weeks ago—that he'd end up wishing the damned Brits would go home—well, he would have thought they were out of their minds. As crazy as a person got from lying mutely under the floorboards of a little girl's room in an apartment on Valkyriegata in Oslo while listening to the Gestapo breathing across the room.

Holt pulled the interrogation orders out of his jacket pocket. A corner of the paper had gotten wet and ripped a bit. The British officer took the paper but kept his eyes fixed on Holt, as if he were some kind of idiot. Then he sighed in resignation and smoothed out the sheet of paper. Holt chewed on the insides of his cheeks, suppressing a stupid remark about the English. The lieutenant signed his initials and handed the orders back to him. A British MP corporal strode ahead of him down the basement stairs. A musty smell hovered over the dark basement corridor, causing Holt to gasp for air.

A young Milorg soldier was standing guard outside the room where Peter Waldhorst was being held. The young man snapped to attention, but Holt waved his hand dismissively, then grunted a few words to the corporal and watched him retreat the same way he had come. Holt turned around. The stairway at that end of the basement had been blocked off with wide, rough planks. He ran his hand through his hair and tried to ignore the fact that he was underground—confined in a dark, damp basement with only one way out—but the slight trembling of his hand gave him away.

He brushed past the Milorg youth and reached for the door handle. The light from the narrow basement window hurt his eyes, the stench assaulting him, and for a moment he couldn't see what was in the room. After a few seconds he made out the contours of a man lying curled up in the corner by the window.

Holt stopped in the doorway, noting the surprise, even astonishment he felt at seeing a German lying on a rough concrete floor. He'd been beaten severely.

He glanced over at the young Milorg soldier, who was fiddling with the barrel of the Schmeisser MP 40 submachine gun he held in front of his chest. Holt noticed that his eyes had a panicked expression and his face was pale. The boy finally left, closing the door behind him.

When the German heard footsteps coming across the floor and drowning out the sound of the rain outside, he put his hands over his head, slowly. Clearly that was as fast as he could manage. One arm seemed to be painfully stiff. It was dark in the corner and hard to see clearly, but the German seemed to be weeping. Yep, no doubt about it. *You devil,* he thought. *You're a damned bastard who deserves every single kick you get.* A moment later, his anger vanished, and Holt cursed himself for such thoughts.

"*Hauptsturmführer* Waldhorst?" he said quietly.

The German didn't reply. He kept his hands over his head. If he covered his chest or groin, they would kick him in the head. And then he would definitely end up dead.

"Peter Waldhorst?"

A sound. A kind of yes.

"*Möchten Sie nach Hause fahren?*" Holt asked. *Do you want to go home?*

Peter Waldhorst gave a low laugh.

"I'm probably not going anywhere."

"I have enough contacts to get you home," said Holt. He wasn't sure whether that was true. But Waldhorst didn't have to know that. If the situation was bad enough, he would be shot.

Kaj Holt repeated the question that no one in Peter Waldhorst's condition could resist.

"Do you want to go home?"

There was a long pause. The sound of the rain on the basement window had decreased somewhat, as though the clouds were about to lift.

"I have a little daughter," said Waldhorst at last.

"Don't we all have a little daughter?" said Holt.

"I've seen her only once."

The rain began hammering on the little basement window again.

"Who are you?" Waldhorst asked.

Holt didn't answer. The raw stench of the cellar threatened to overpower him for a few seconds, making him feel as though he were back under the floorboards on Valkyriegata. He dug his nails into his palm.

"Tell me who you are," said Waldhorst again, this time in perfect Norwegian. Kaj Holt froze. For some reason he couldn't stand hearing Germans speak Norwegian, especially when they spoke it as well as Waldhorst did. It was as if these Germans wanted to say, "We are like you, and you are like us, so let's lay down our weapons and live as brothers."

"Holt. Kaj Holt."

Waldhorst made a sound.

"The man the angels protected," he said in a low voice. "So that's what you look like."

Holt had heard that the Germans had nicknamed him the Angel. It didn't matter. He didn't believe in angels; he didn't even believe in himself any longer. The Germans had tried to rip him apart for a week before they suddenly tossed him out on the street. Maybe someone was watching over him after all. Maybe he should have believed in something greater than himself. It didn't matter anymore.

"Are you thirsty, *Hauptsturmführer*?"

"I can't . . ." Waldhorst removed his hands from his face and spat a bloody clot onto the floor. "Drink . . ."

Holt went out into the hall. "Bring some water." The Milorg soldier looked even more scared than he had a few minutes before. The sound of things breaking could be heard down the hall, behind a closed door. "Now!" Holt shouted, to snap the young man out of his unresponsive state. "And see if you can find some gauze bandages or a handkerchief, or some damn thing like that."

Back in the room Holt fished a pack of cigarettes out of his pocket. He found two that weren't soaked, lit one, and handed it to Waldhorst.

The German tried to raise himself up on his elbow, but gave up at once. His young face contorted in pain, but not a sound escaped his lips. Holt looked around the room. There were two chairs in one corner, one of which lay on its side due to a broken leg. Holt thought he ought to talk to the Red Cross representatives in the camp but quickly rejected that idea. Should he defend a German? A Gestapo officer?

He dragged over the chair that was still intact, pulled Peter Waldhorst up onto it, and stuck the cigarette between his lips. Waldhorst took a deep drag before he took out the cigarette with his left hand and touched two fingers to his bloody mouth. His right arm must have been dislocated or broken. Holt told himself to stop thinking about it. Waldhorst had only gotten what he deserved. He'd been given a good old-fashioned beating, and who hadn't? The Germans had been no different. The first hours of an interrogation were nothing—if you didn't know better, you'd almost think you'd wound up in some sort of coffee klatsch, but after a few hours of silence, they'd told Kaj Holt that his own mother wouldn't recognize his body. "My mother's dead," he'd replied. That had made them as mad as rabid dogs. And now he stood here facing this young Gestapo officer, thinking what a waste it had all been. All those years, all the pain, his own meaningless survival. Holt had been tortured because a twist of fate had caused the Germans to mistake him for some other Resistance fighter. But torture wasn't the worst of it. The worst thing was lying underneath the floor, as though in a coffin—a living corpse—unable to do anything but wait.

"So," said Waldhorst, tossing his half-smoked cigarette to the floor. "Why are you being so friendly to me?"

Holt took the pack of cigarettes out of his pocket again, lit a new one off Waldhorst's, and threw the butt on the rough concrete floor.

"As I understand it, you were in Oslo in 1940, right?"

"If you already know that, why do you ask?"

"I can't find any documents confirming your presence there during that time. You worked in intelligence for the Abwehr?"

Holt interpreted Waldhorst's grimace as confirmation.

"Who told you that?" Waldhorst asked.

"A man who's not going to live much longer," said Holt. "Don't worry about it."

"I stopped worrying a long time ago," said Waldhorst.

"Well, if you don't want to end up like him, I suggest you cooperate with me."

The two men stared at each other for a long moment. Then Waldhorst shut his eyes and nodded.

"There's something I don't understand," said Holt, taking a long drag on his cigarette. "And I think . . . you're the only one who can help me with . . . this thing."

"There's always something a person can't understand," Waldhorst said softly.

"Autumn of '42 . . ." Holt said, maybe more to himself than to *Hauptsturmführer* Waldhorst. Then he had to stop because his voice failed him for a moment. He cleared his throat once, then twice, but it didn't help.

The two men stared at each other for what seemed an eternity.

"Not a good autumn," Peter Waldhorst said at last.

Holt could see from Waldhorst's expression that he knew what the question would be. And what the answer was. The mere thought of it was enough to make him weep. But not here, not now. What kind of a victor would he be if he started crying at the loser's feet?

"We had a . . . serpent at our breast that fall, a traitor . . ." Holt said. "A young man named Gudbrand Svendstuen, I'm sure you know about that . . . but I think . . ."

He opened his mouth to ask the question, but then changed his mind.

"You think that Svendstuen was the wrong man?" Waldhorst asked, as if reading Holt's mind.

Holt nodded.

"Was he?"

"I can't tell you."

"Then I can't help you either," said Holt.

"So be it," said Waldhorst. "Maybe I'll make it, who knows?"

There was a pause during which neither of them spoke when the Milorg solider returned with the water and bandages.

Holt considered his options. He'd made a mistake by coming here. And another mistake by not having anything concrete to offer Waldhorst. The truth was that the peace had been usurped by non-Norwegians, so there was really nothing he could do for a man like Waldhorst.

"It was stupid of you to transfer to the Gestapo," Holt said. "I hope you get to see your daughter again."

Waldhorst's expression remained impassive. The dried blood covered his face like a mask. Holt had no more threats he could wield, and Waldhorst had been beaten up enough as it was. He turned on his heel and walked the few steps to the door.

"Have you ever been to Spain?" Waldhorst asked in a low voice when Holt had put his hand on the door handle. "To the province of Galicia?"

Holt turned around.

Peter Waldhorst sat with his head bowed. His injured arm hung limp, while the other rested in his lap. The light from the basement window cast a long shadow from the German officer's body across the concrete floor.

"To a town with a famous cathedral?"

"To Spain, Galicia, a cathedral? What are you talking about?" Holt shook his head. He had no idea what the man meant.

Waldhorst raised his good arm and looked up with a sad smile on his lips, as if he felt sorry for the man facing him.

"I'm sure you know the name of the town I'm thinking of," said Waldhorst. "And when you remember it, you should ask yourself: Who goes to places like that, Herr Holt?"

But Holt had already whispered the answer to himself.

CHAPTER 2

Friday, May 16, 2003
Police Headquarters
Oslo, Norway

Tommy Bergmann had often wondered how good his judgment was. His choice to work overtime in the Criminal Division on the night of the sixteenth of May—the night before Independence Day—should have been proof enough. It was traditionally one of the shittiest days to work, so police HQ was full of rookies and guys like himself who naively believed they could save the city from perdition. Moreover, they were willing to sacrifice their already marginalized personal lives, so that people living a proper life—even a proper family life—could take full advantage of the holiday. Whenever other people talked about not having enough time, Bergmann always felt they were speaking a foreign language. After Hege left, he had more time on his hands than he would ever need. His only vacation plans—if you could even call it such—were to ride herd on a handball team of twelve-year-old girls in Göteborg for a week in July.

Oh well, he thought, pushing open the door to the roof terrace. *At least I'm not on the graveyard shift. And I can use the money. So I guess I'm not a complete idiot.*

Besides, he was sure he was going to win the swing shift's bet regarding the cause of the first fatality on their shift. Bergmann knew that if there was an unnatural death during the swing shift, it was bound to be suicide. Monsen, who was the duty officer this evening, had wagered two hundred kroner on the same basic combination he always did: new immigrants and some sort of deadly weapon.

Bergmann had stopped being bothered by Monsen's infantile racism and his own inability to stop participating in these wagers. He sat down at one of the green plastic tables out on the terrace under the awning. Life seemed better out here than in the break room. With its blue linoleum and outdated leather sofas, it made even the biggest optimist feel disillusioned. The sight of the city spread out before him gave him a strange sense of calm.

He leaned back in the chair, closed his eyes, and allowed the sun to warm his face for the first time in ages. For a few minutes he managed the impossible: to think of nothing at all. Only the sounds of the city filled his head. Then a tiny unconscious thought at the back of his mind disturbed his calm. Hege. Her hair, which turned almost white in the summertime, her turquoise eyes and brown skin. The salt he had licked from her body one afternoon in a cool white hotel room in a Tuscan village whose name he could no longer recall.

That summer when everything was going to be all right again. That summer when he had told himself, and really meant it: never again.

But when they had returned home, he had beat her up again. He'd simply whacked her two, three, four times. He no longer remembered why. Undoubtedly she'd said something, something that made him snap, as only she could, making him feel small with just a few words. It happened only once, only one single time after he'd promised to stop. But it was one time too many. No, it was several times too many. He couldn't recall how many times. He didn't want to remember anything about what he'd done to her. He only wanted to remember that he mustn't ever fall in love with another woman who was so much better looking than he was. As Hege was.

"Goddamn you, Tommy Bergmann," he muttered.

The red double door to his left slammed shut.

He didn't open his eyes.

The familiar voice of an old bastard, hoarse from smoking: Dramstad from the Robbery Division, who had nothing better to do on weekends than waste his life down here at HQ.

"Some fucking amazing weather, isn't it?" said Dramstad, who according to scuttlebutt managed to live up to his name most days in the week—the man did like his drams.

Bergmann grunted in reply and cursed himself for having thought about Hege.

"Yep, it's some weather, all right," Dramstad muttered to himself. *No,* Bergmann thought, opening his eyes wide, letting in a bit too much of the sharp sunlight. *This is suicide weather.* But he didn't say a word. He let old Dramstad stand there thinking the weather was just fine.

Bergmann had just returned to his office to finish up a couple of old reports that miraculously quiet evening when Monsen's number appeared on the display on his cell phone.

Monsen cleared his throat. His voice was almost hesitant when he said his name, and Bergmann was reasonably sure he was going to win the modest pot from the bet.

A few hundred-krone bills would come in handy, he thought as he swung his legs down from his desk, his gaze fixed on one of the highrises up on Enerhaugen.

"Some students have found a bunch of old bones."

There was a pause. Bergmann felt a frown crease his face.

"A ways into the Nordmarka forest," said Monsen, naming the region in Oslo's north end popular with residents for hiking and skiing.

"What sort of bones?" Bergmann asked.

He straightened up and put his left hand over his ear to block out the city noise coming in the open window.

"Well, human ones, of course," said Monsen.

"Human bones? You sure it wasn't some old mutt they found?"

Monsen snorted and Bergmann could hear him lighting a smoke at the other end of the line. He took his time. Bergmann could imagine him, maybe running his finger between his collar and his fat neck with the cigarette dangling from his lip.

"It would have to have been a damned big dog," said Monsen. "No, they're pretty sure they're human bones."

"Don't tell me they're medical students."

"Bingo," said Monsen. "Four of them, even. You're going to have to go up there."

Bergmann closed his eyes.

He didn't want to go back into the woods. He'd seen a dead body in a forest in 1988, and that had almost done him in.

But they're old bones, he thought, grabbing his car keys from the desk. *I should be able to handle a few old bones.*

CHAPTER 3

Tuesday, May 29, 1945
Restaurant at the Hotel Cecil
Stockholm, Sweden

Kaj Holt fixed his gaze on a couple of young girls strolling along the sidewalk on the other side of the street. They stopped to look in a milliner's shop window. One of them pointed at something, and the other, a stunning brunette, laughed and put her hand to her mouth. Holt imagined the scent of cheap perfume, maybe lily of the valley, enveloping her. Her hands looked delicate and small, and for a few seconds he envisioned them gripped hard around his naked back. Perhaps she could have given him something to live for, dragged him back to the real world. But what would a girl like that want with a man like him?

He looked away, directing his attention back to Håkan Nordenstam across the table from him. He nodded from time to time, but otherwise let his Swedish lunch partner ramble on. Something about an Englishman they had investigated during the war. An utterly innocuous case, one of no consequence, which he had clearly brought up just to avoid talking about the important things, the dangerous things, such as the fact that German intelligence operatives had managed to make it over the border just a few days before everything fell apart for the Germans. Nordenstam seemed to be afraid that Holt might ask him the obvious question: Where were they now? Had anyone here helped them? Put them on a ship to Portugal or Spain or even farther afield, to countries whose names he scarcely knew?

The war, Kaj Holt thought. It had been less than a month since the liberation, and he still awoke each morning thinking that the war was still on. He still carried a cyanide capsule in his jacket pocket, the little Colt Llama in a garter around his calf beneath his wide trouser legs, and a silencer in his coat pocket, in case he ever woke up to the sound of boots at his door. *Yes,* he thought. *This war will never end.* As he carefully wiped his mouth with the napkin—real linen—he recalled how during the war he had always felt guilty when he was here at the Cecil, in this beautiful city. He had been overwhelmed by those damned feelings of guilt every time he had made it across the border to Stockholm, where he was given new orders and enjoyed a couple of weeks' R & R. Because he knew that when he went back across the border, he'd be met with the news that yet another of his best friends had been killed. He felt guilty because he'd survived the longest years in Norway's history. Some people said that the greatest honor in war was to survive, but now, a few weeks after the liberation, Holt thought that such talk sounded false. There was only one honor in war, and that was to *die,* the way so many had died. They had all been better human beings than he was, with real lives to return to. But here he sat, the survivor. And what had he used his freedom for but to leave everything behind, including his wife and child?

Did I really just leave? he wondered. He stared distractedly at his own hand. A big scar ran across it—almost white among the stiff black hairs—and he was suddenly unable to remember how he had gotten it. For a few seconds he felt as though nothing bad had happened, not the war, nothing at all. Then the thought of Agnes struck him like a bolt of lightning. So young, far too young. If only he'd been able to save Agnes, the war would at least have had a scrap of meaning. And it was all his fault. To think that he could have been so infinitely blind, so boundlessly naïve.

Holt's musings were interrupted by Nordenstam's voice, and the Swede's hand gripped his arm lightly.

"What is it?" he said, leaning across the table. "Kaj. *Look* at me."

"Waldhorst," said Holt.

"Peter Waldhorst?" Nordenstam said in a low voice.

Holt nodded, more to himself than in answer to the question. He should have responded to the fact that Nordenstam clearly knew who Peter Waldhorst was, but he didn't bother. He was no longer surprised at all the information the Swedes had acquired.

Holt averted his gaze and turned to look out the window at the brunette again. She was strolling happy and carefree down the street, arm in arm with her girlfriend. Nordenstam took a cigarette from the silver case he always carried in his inside pocket, tapped it lightly on the lid, and lit it. Holt watched him surreptitiously. Nordenstam was a true friend of Norway, far more so than his superior at the Swedish military intelligence organization, the C-Bureau, whom he was going to meet tomorrow. For an instant Holt wished that he himself were Swedish. How much easier it would be to carry on after the war, raising a few pigs in the forest or some such thing.

Nordenstam held out the open cigarette case to Holt.

"Peter Waldhorst . . . what about him?" he asked as he lit Holt's cigarette.

"Oh, nothing really. He's locked up in Jørstadmoen. I paid him a visit and he . . . asked me a question."

For a second Holt thought he might have revealed too much. But no, there was no reason to hold back. Nordenstam would understand, if anyone would. *And how could I have known?* Holt thought. How could anyone have known, or even have suspected?

Nordenstam blew a smoke ring toward the ceiling. The sound of the piano across the room competed with the constant stream of voices around them.

"He asked *you* a question?" he said.

Holt didn't reply. He just stared at Nordenstam's classic features, noting the hint of boyish optimism in his eyes, a look that suggested he was utterly unaffected by the innate evil in people. He had a sudden impulse to smash his handsome face with a sledgehammer, just to watch it dissolve into a mess of bone, blood, and brain matter, and then to dump the pulverized man on his wife's doorstep, so that she would understand what had taken place on the other side of the border.

Holt shook off the grotesque thought as a wave of nausea rose up in his throat. One of these days, he was going to lose his grip on reality for good.

"Isn't the food coming soon?" he said absently, as if they had never started this conversation.

"I thought you were going to ask me questions, Kaj." Nordenstam fixed his gaze on him. The piano player finished a number to muted applause from one of the tables, and a lively group yelled something in Swedish, which was followed by laughter.

"Have you been to Spain?" Holt asked. "To Galicia?"

Nordenstam shook his head, then smiled. "What's this about, Kaj?"

"I went to Lillehammer to get an answer to a question. I didn't get it. But I was asked whether I knew the name of a town in Galicia, a town with a famous cathedral."

Nordenstam frowned. Either he was bored with this conversation or he was worried about what might come of it. Holt no longer cared.

"I have no idea what you're talking about," he said.

Holt pulled a pen out of his suit pocket. From the piano came the first notes of "The Jazz Boy," a song that the Nazis back home had hated intensely. A smile formed almost imperceptibly on his lips as he wrote the words on a napkin. He carefully folded it up and pushed it slowly over to Nordenstam.

"So," said Holt. "I'd like to get an answer from Waldhorst about the thing with Gudbrand. I think he was the wrong man."

Nordenstam's expression turned somber. It took him several seconds to gather his thoughts. Then he unfolded the napkin.

"That may be some sort of answer," said Holt. "Who goes to places like that?" He nodded toward the napkin that Nordenstam held in his hand.

Nordenstam folded it up and stubbed out his half-smoked cigarette. He tried to meet Holt's gaze, but Holt looked away. In the reflection of the windowpane, he saw Nordenstam put the napkin in the inside pocket of his suit coat.

"What is this, Kaj?" he asked, a sympathetic look on his face. "What has got into you, my friend? Where is the Kaj I used to know? Are you letting a Gestapo officer pull your leg?"

Holt didn't reply, but instead let his gaze sweep the premises, only stopping when he noticed that one of the men in the lively party a couple of tables over looked familiar. Very familiar, in fact.

No, he thought to himself. *I can't keep doing this.* In his mind he could still hear Peter Waldhorst's voice and see his brown eyes under those thick black eyebrows. Maybe it was just his imagination, a final dastardly trick from that condemned, conniving German. Holt felt like he could no longer tell what was true or false, as though he were on a carousel going round and round, surrounded by dead people. Agnes, Hvitosten, the young mother he had killed, Gudbrand—all spun in his head, almost driving him mad.

"Let me get you a girl tonight, Kaj. What do you say? You need to relax a little."

He shook his head. For a second he wanted to grab Nordenstam by his lapels and shout, "Don't you have any idea what Waldhorst was talking about?"

"Where are you staying tonight?" Nordenstam asked.

"At the apartment. On Rindögatan."

Nordenstam nodded as his eyes followed a young girl across the room.

"You've got to unwind a little," he repeated and smiled, exposing his perfect white teeth.

A plate was set down in front of Holt with a thud. Finally.

"Later," said Nordenstam, "you and I are going to *have some fun*, aren't we?" He began to laugh. Holt couldn't help joining in. He knew exactly what Nordenstam meant by *have some fun*.

"I'm going to take you to a hell of a place that'll make you forget all about these interrogation games, all right?"

Holt had already forgotten, at least he thought he had. He cut into his meat almost brutally, knowing that he hadn't had a decent meal in days, not to mention enough sleep.

"Tonight we're going to live a little!" said Nordenstam.

Holt nodded and thought, *Yes, tonight I'm going to live it up*. If only to disprove what his own wife had told him just a few days before: "It would've been best if they'd caught you too." Just as she had the first time she'd told him she'd lost him.

He had said yes again. That it was probably for the best. She had stood there holding the girl in her arms, a child he hadn't managed to develop any feelings for. He wasn't even glad that he'd survived and could be a father to her.

"The only thing that will make you happy," she'd said, clutching their daughter even tighter as if the child belonged to her alone, "is to follow the others, the dead, all the way home."

He had walked away without a word. There was nothing left to say.

Kaj Holt put down the silverware on the damask tablecloth and surveyed the room as though for the first time: the crowd, the smiling faces, the cigarette smoke beneath the ceiling, the singer's white tuxedo, the behind of a young woman on her way across the restaurant to the ladies' room, the gazes that followed her, the ripple of the magenta fabric over her buttocks.

"Håkan . . . I don't want to live any longer," he said bluntly.

In a daze, he saw himself at Jørstadmoen. When he'd stood out on the steps after the interrogation and filled his lungs with fresh air, he was no longer sure whether it had even happened. Whether he had really held Peter Waldhorst's head in his hands and screamed at him. Screamed that it couldn't be true. That it was all lies.

"Don't say that," said Nordenstam.

Then, a split second later, a familiar face popped up at the periphery of Holt's vision. He turned around. *Yes,* he thought, *it's definitely him.* Across the restaurant, at a corner table by the band, sat the civilian from Jørstadmoen. He sat there alone with that childish face of his, looking as if he'd been waiting all afternoon for Holt to look his way.

What was he doing here?

Who was he?

Their eyes met. A couple crossing the room broke their contact for a moment. When they had passed, the civilian gave him a friendly smile and a curt nod, and raised his glass in a toast.

"Kaj, what is it?" said Nordenstam, gripping Holt's arm once more.

"Nothing," he whispered.

"Something's wrong," said Nordenstam.

"Do you know who that is?" Holt asked. A group of people walking past them momentarily cut off the view of the table where the civilian sat. They stopped and talked to one of the waiters, then continued on their way.

Nordenstam turned in the direction Holt had indicated.

"I've seen that man before," said Holt. "Yesterday at Jørstadmoen. But . . . before that too."

Nordenstam turned back to Holt and frowned.

"What man, Kaj? I don't understand."

Holt glanced back at the table over in the corner. He blinked. His pulse seemed to stop.

The table was empty.

It was obvious that no one had been sitting there. The tablecloth was fresh and the utensils hadn't been moved. A waiter was showing a party of four to that table.

"But—" Holt sprang up from his chair, knocking over his glass, which rolled off the table and smashed on the floor.

The restaurant fell silent. The band paused for a few seconds, staring in Holt's direction, and the waiters froze.

Holt felt the room spinning; only the table in the corner stood still. Round and round, tablecloths, glasses, laughter, clinking, "The Jazz Boy," glamorous women, matches being lit, crystals in the chandeliers. The man was sitting there again. Holt was sure that their eyes met, that the man was looking straight through him, right at everything he knew.

A second later he was gone.

"He's sitting over there!" Holt was shouting now, oblivious to the oppressive silence in the large room. And again: "He's sitting right there!"

"It's okay," Holt heard from somewhere far away. "It's okay."

The next thing he knew, hands were gripping his shoulders, he was waving his arms, and the floor vanished beneath him.

Nordenstam's face hovering above him turned into the childish face of the man from Lillehammer. Although Nordenstam's lips were moving, Holt heard nothing. Overhead it was pitch dark, and to the left he felt a long, thin stream of air. He shut his eyes and took a few weak breaths. Each time he inhaled his chest touched the floorboards above him. He ran as quietly as he could down the stairs, the child screaming behind him.

Once they were out on the street, he turned to Nordenstam and whispered, "How can anyone live in a world like this?"

CHAPTER 4

Friday, May 16, 2003
Nordmarka
Oslo, Norway

Tommy Bergmann stopped on the path and looked up. Above him all was green and blue. He closed his eyes for a few seconds and felt his pulse hammering through his body. No matter how absurd it might seem, it had been good to get out of the city, if only for a while. If only to look at some old bones.

He snorted to himself and fished a cigarette out of his breast pocket. Then he turned around slowly, studying the interplay of the trees with the evening light, or maybe it was the other way around. Voices. *Yes,* he thought. Beyond the soughing of the treetops, he could hear voices off to the left. He looked up and saw red-and-white crime-scene tape fluttering about thirty or forty yards farther up the path.

He started walking again but was more worn out than he felt he ought to be. Soon he would hardly be able to keep up with the laziest girls on the handball team. This spring he'd noticed that he could no longer hold his own with the top athletes when they took their warm-up runs, and he'd long since given up on the 15-15 intervals.

A strip of crime-scene tape had been wrapped around a tree trunk to the left of the wide path. Bergmann turned onto a much narrower, slightly overgrown path. A piece of tape had been tied every ten yards to mark the way to the location of the bones.

Georg Abrahamsen and a colleague were already there. He was trying to put up a white tent over an area Bergmann first thought looked like nothing more than ferns and moss. A heavy battery-powered light lay on the ground, illuminating the work of the crime-scene techs. A few feet away, two uniformed men stood talking in low voices with one of the students. The boy kept running his hand through his hair as he spoke. Another tent had been put up a little ways behind them. Two girls and a boy sat on the ground, staring into space.

"Damn," said Abrahamsen, "how many times have we run past this very spot?" He motioned toward the wide path where Bergmann had just been walking.

"Speak for yourself," said Bergmann as he stuck another cigarette between his lips. He should have stopped smoking long ago if he wanted to keep up with the girls, but he kept putting it off. And tonight wasn't a great time to start a new and better life.

"Shit. Don't go starting a forest fire up here," he heard someone say behind him.

Leif Monsen, the watch commander of Kripo, the Criminal Police, came huffing and puffing through the lingonberry bushes not far from where Bergmann himself had entered the clearing. His red face was a good match for the setting sun shining through the spruce trees.

"This is the *shits*," said Monsen, and "shit" was about the strongest swearword Monsen ever used. Although he smoked like a chimney and was an almost pathological racist, he was a God-fearing man who seldom saw a need to pepper his comments with curses. Bergmann had once thought Monsen smoked so much because he wanted to meet his maker sooner than he would have done otherwise.

"So, no pool winnings for any of us," he said to Bergmann with a nod toward Abrahamsen.

Bergmann didn't reply, but instead studied Abrahamsen as he and his colleague gave up on their attempt to set up the tent. Abrahamsen squatted down and began carefully removing the top layer of peat from a patch of ground in front of him. Bergmann thought he could see the outline of a brownish skull under Abrahamsen's latex gloves. He took two steps forward, and Monsen followed suit.

"Look like some pretty old bones, don't they?" said Monsen as he pulled out his pouch of tobacco.

"Yep," said Bergmann.

"You know," said Monsen, reaching for the lighter that Bergmann handed him, "this miserable excuse for a criminal division investigates an average of one point three dead bodies every blessed day . . ." He looked at Abrahamsen, who was now down on his knees, digging deeper into the heath with his bare hands. "And I'll be darned if we don't end up having to deal with a bunch of old soup bones too."

"You've got your students over there," Bergmann said, nodding in greeting toward Abrahamsen. One of the girls was gesticulating as she talked to the uniforms. It would probably be a long time before those four students went camping again.

"No, we ought to leave this sort of insanity to the rich folks on Brynsallé." Monsen hawked and shot a clot of phlegm onto the heath before taking a deep drag on his hand-rolled smoke.

It didn't take much for Monsen's bitterness to surface. Bergmann had thought many a time that he had a point. People had a habit of getting killed outside office hours, and then it always turned out the way Monsen said it did. The Kripo officers were the ones who had to work all through the night for no extra pay, wading through blood and tending to abused women and half-dead children, until the station opened for business again at eight the next morning.

"Well," said Abrahamsen. "No matter what you think of the rich folks who live on Brynsallé, I'm not going to dig anymore until I get some support from them."

"Oh?" Monsen seemed surprised for once.

"Well," replied Abrahamsen. "I'm not going to risk having that skull fall apart in my hands." He took his cell phone out of his pocket.

"Well," said Monsen in an attempt to imitate Abrahamsen. "If these bones and that skull have been lying there for over twenty-five years, all we have to do is transfer this case ASAP, and then *they*'ll have to figure out what to do about them."

Five minutes later Monsen was gone.

An hour and a half later, the students had left and another couple of uniforms had arrived. Getting a statement from them hadn't taken much time. They'd just been hammering in the last tent peg when they struck something in the dirt and pulled up a bone. A human bone, probably a leg bone. Since they were probably more familiar with human leg bones than anyone else at the scene, there was little cause to doubt that they were right.

Bergmann had put on a pair of gloves and was following Abrahamsen's instructions. He shivered as he ran his hand over the forearm bones, which now lay exposed. An apparently complete skeleton lay buried here among the earth and stones. The chest cavity had collapsed, but apart from that the remains were fairly intact. With the exception of the hole in the forehead, that is.

"The permafrost pressed the skeleton up to the surface," said Abrahamsen. "The bones have been here for years."

Bergmann shook his head and wiped his forehead with the back of his hand.

"That's why we bury people six feet under, you know. Just imagine what a hell of a mess it would be if you managed to outlive your mother-in-law, only to have her rise up from the damned ground a year later."

Bergmann was hardly listening any longer. He felt dizzy as he got up off his knees and stood staring down at the two forearm bones, which lay across what was left of the rib cage. The odor of the forest floor made him feel sick. He tore off his plastic gloves and stuck a cigarette in his mouth. How long had they been out here working on this? An hour? He cocked his head to one side as he always did when lighting a smoke, but stopped just before the lighter flame reached the cigarette.

The angle of the battery-powered light cast a sharp glow on the end of the forearm, or maybe it was the hand. Bergmann saw something flash down in the dirt.

He took the unlit cigarette from his mouth and held it almost listlessly between his fingers.

"Georg," he said in a low voice, dropping the cigarette to the ground. Putting his gloves back on, he knelt down and began to dig carefully around what must have been the left hand. He removed the last bits of dirt from around the brown, porous finger bones.

Hanging on the half-rotten ring finger was a dull ring.

A gold ring.

A wedding ring.

Tommy Bergmann felt another chill run through his body as he picked up the remnants of the hand.

"Don't do that," said Abrahamsen behind him.

Bergmann ignored him. It was too late anyway. Besides, the bones didn't break. He slipped the ring on his own finger and held it up to the sky. After three tries he managed to make out the letters on the engraving.

YOURS FOREVER. GUSTAV.

CHAPTER 5

Early Wednesday Morning, May 30, 1945
Berns Restaurant, Large Salon
Stockholm, Sweden

Kaj Holt had no idea where he was when he was rudely awakened by a hand shaking him lightly by the shoulder. All the lights were on in the large, long room, and there was no music coming from the stage. He was reclining rather than sitting, and a thundering headache was the only sign that he was still alive. For a moment it seemed like the huge, gleaming chandeliers on the ceiling were falling toward him. But there was no sound, absolutely none. And nothing could penetrate his headache, not even the thought of lying beneath the floorboards on Valkyriegata, or the fear of not having identification papers on him.

"The gentleman will have to leave," said a voice above him.

Holt automatically straightened up, tipping the chair over backward. The hand gripped his shoulder again. He had a sudden desire to lash out around him, but reason prevailed. Maybe it was the clinking of glasses somewhere in the room, or the sound of laughter—friendly, not jeering—coming from somewhere else.

Images from the night before flashed across his mind's eye. The faces, the laughter, a woman on his lap, her fragrance, the taste of her.

Nordenstam's suntanned face and white teeth, the pats on his back. The words "It's over now, it's all over."

But where am I? Holt thought, glancing around the room. *Where is everybody?*

"Sorry," he heard himself say. Then he was suddenly standing out on the street with his suit coat over his arm, holding his hat between his thumb and index finger. Carefully, as if to ensure that his head wouldn't fall off, he looked up at the sky, relieved to see that an almost invisible rain was falling from the darkness above him. He checked his watch several times, but was unable to make sense of its hands.

After he'd stood there long enough to get soaked, someone behind him said that a cab was coming. All he could manage was a grunt in reply. A pair of headlights appeared down the street.

"To Gärdet," he said softly to himself. His mind was starting to clear, but he still couldn't remember anything about the night before. It was as if his short-term memory had been wiped clean.

"What address?"

"Rindögatan."

Holt took the sleeping pills out of his pocket, counted them, then counted them again.

He wondered whether there were enough.

"Quiet," Holt whispered. His hands were shaking as he counted the sleeping pills in his hand one more time. Seven. That wasn't enough.

"Quiet . . ." he said again, surprised at how loud it sounded.

The next thing he remembered was kneeling in front of the fountain in the middle of Karlaplan, drinking water out of his hand. He swallowed one, two, three sleeping pills. He stood up, swaying, as if he expected to fall asleep and tumble into the water, drown, disappear forever.

But nothing happened. He reached for his hip flask in his inside pocket, but it was gone. He swore to himself a couple of times, soaked by the rain falling quietly from the black sky.

The fountain was turned off, and there were no sounds apart from the faint hiss of the occasional car. Holt didn't know how he had found the right street, but it didn't matter. He was now staggering up Rindögatan, he was sure of it. He wandered past his building and headed across the street, spinning around as a taxi came out of nowhere and almost ran him down. He thought he had a girlfriend on the next block with whom he'd spent a few nights the year before. He wished that summer had never come to an end. That he could have stayed and slept with her every single night. That the war could have lasted forever, but that he would no longer have had to be part of it.

He found the doorbell automatically. The fourth button from the bottom felt like the right one.

"I want you," he said when she answered. He didn't even know if he meant it. In fact, he didn't mean it. But he repeated the words anyway: "I want you." He was almost incomprehensible.

"Come back when you're sober, Kaj. You're waking up the whole street."

"Well, shit," he said. He didn't even remember her name. He laughed at himself. Seconds later, he felt tears welling up in his eyes. He leaned down and felt the contours of the pistol under his pants leg. *My little friend,* he thought. *My little friend.*

"Do you know what time it is? I'm going to call the cops, Kaj. Go home and sleep it off, all right?"

She hung up.

Holt leaned against the glass door. A moment later, his shoes were covered with vomit.

"This can't be happening," he said quietly to himself. He sat down on the granite steps, getting the seat of his pants all wet. "Tell me it isn't true . . . dear God . . ."

Back at his own building, he looked down at the vomit on his shoes through his tears. "I don't even know why I'm crying," he muttered to himself. "It just feels so damn good. Better than it's ever felt before."

Moving like a sleepwalker, he went up the stairs without even turning on the light in the stairwell.

The tiny strip of paper he had fastened to the bottom of the front door and the threshold had fallen to the floor in the hall.

He tripped over his own feet.

He crawled over to the bed and flopped down on top of the bedspread.

Nothing was real anymore. Not even the face of the man who stood looking down at him with that indescribably calm expression.

Finally, Holt thought. *Finally you're here.* He couldn't even manage to say the words to the face hovering above him. *What are you doing here?* He thought he should have screamed the words, just to scare him off. *What are you doing here?* His legs felt like they'd been sawed off. He knew the little pistol was down around his ankle somewhere, he could just barely feel it, but he couldn't get up. The man—the same man with the childish face and the soft features, almost like a girl's—took the pistol out of his garter. He gave a wry smile as he looked down at Holt.

"Oh Kaj, oh Kaj," he said, running his finger over the threading on the muzzle. His accent was hardly noticeable. Holt knew that he had seen this man before. It was the childish face of the civilian from Jørstadmoen. In the pocket of the coat draped over the back of the chair the man found the silencer. As if Holt had planned it all himself.

All right, Holt thought. *So I guess I wasn't meant to survive.* What was it he'd said to Waldhorst? "Don't we all have a little daughter?" Holt tried fleetingly to remember his own little daughter's smell, but he couldn't do it. He started crying again despite himself. He didn't want the man leaning over him to think that he, Captain Kaj Holt, was afraid of taking a bullet to the head.

If he hadn't been so drunk, so overwhelmed by sleep, so sad, then . . . he didn't know . . . then he would have used his bare hands to kill the man hovering over him.

The man had a faint smile on his lips. It may have been that smile that made Holt get up as though he'd never had a drop of alcohol in his life.

"If I'm going to die, I'll die by my own hand," he whispered. The childish face must have been surprised at that, because he seemed caught off guard when Holt slugged him in the kidneys with his left hand. He doubled over silently and then took a step back, tipping over the chair next to the wall. Holt waited just a second, a single second too long. The floor seemed sloped, the wall was slanted, the ceiling was caving in—wasn't it? That fucking guy would be pissing blood for the rest of the summer, and Holt laughed at the thought. *I'm laughing, you hear me, baby face?*

A second too long, he realized when it was already too late.

Baby Face's head-butt must have punctured a lung. His sternum felt like it gave way, but no sound came out of Holt's mouth. When he lay back down on the bed, it was like he'd never gotten up.

Holt closed his eyes and thought, *It's going to be like coming home.*

CHAPTER 6

Early Saturday Morning, May 17, 2003
Nordmarka
Oslo, Norway

A heavy fog had settled over the forest in the last half hour, clinging to the black spruce trees like dust. An owl screeched somewhere over Tommy Bergmann's head as he stood looking at the white vapor rising up from the piss drenching the cold moss. He buttoned up his fly and listened to the silence all around him. For a moment there wasn't a sound; everyone—including the newly arrived officers from the Kripo crime-scene team, Georg Abrahamsen, and the two uniformed cops from the Majorstua police station who had arrived late that night—had fallen silent.

A crackle from the uniforms' portable radio broke the silence. For a moment Bergmann caught himself missing the camaraderie and cooperation of life on patrol. As investigators, they worked as a team, but deep down they all knew it was every man for himself.

They hadn't made much progress in the past few hours, and none of them were even close to being able to answer the question they were all asking themselves: Who was Gustav? The only thing they knew for sure was that the first skeleton they had uncovered was a woman who had been married or at least engaged to this Gustav. One of the Kripo guys thought he could tell at a glance that there were definitely more bodies in the grave. Bergmann didn't go for that sort of overconfidence, but if that were the case, it might give them a better idea what had become of Gustav.

He went back down the path and studied the scene before him. The white tent was now up. It was illuminated by one battery-powered light on the outside and three on the inside. The two uniforms stood outside, each with a headlamp. The glaring beams cut through the treetops like air defense searchlights before they turned their heads, and then the light swept over the tree trunks. Bergmann was blinded for a few seconds. When his sight returned, he noticed a pair of deer eyes deep in the forest. Caught in the headlamp's light beam, the animal froze as if petrified.

"Tommy!" Abrahamsen's voice cut through the night. The eyes in the forest vanished, and Bergmann could hear the frightened flight of the deer through the heath.

The light fanned over the ground in front of him, and he began walking slowly toward the tent. Abrahamsen stood in the opening, peering out into the darkness as though unable to see anything at all in the abrupt transition from the light.

"You have to see this," he said.

"See what?" Bergmann asked, stepping past Abrahamsen, who held the tent flap open for him. It felt as though all the oxygen inside the tent had been used up. Five men were standing or squatting around the excavated area, which was now about six square feet. Bergmann looked first at the remains of the woman, his gaze moving from the skull with the hole in it to the rib cage, hips, femurs, and tibias. The feet appeared to be crushed.

Then he looked to the right.

Abrahamsen nodded somberly. He was dressed all in white, and a big digital camera hung over his stomach.

"So, that must be Gustav," said Bergmann, pointing to the preliminary excavation they'd done next to the woman. Another skull had come into view, but this one lay more deeply buried in the dirt. The skeleton was positioned on its left side. The rib cage was almost intact. The rest of the body had not yet been exposed.

"Yes, but that's not all," said one of the Kripo men. Bergmann gazed at the man, a white-haired, self-appointed senior investigator whose name he could never remember. He carefully removed his heavy steel-framed glasses and wiped them with his shirtsleeve. Then he put them back on just as carefully.

"Come here," he said, waving over Bergmann and Abrahamsen. Bergmann approached reluctantly. The older man squatted down, and Bergmann did the same. The Kripo man held a ruler. Abrahamsen leaned so far over them that he almost fell into the grave. For the first time that night, Bergmann felt an intense desire to throw up. Maybe it was only the rotten smell of damp earth and gnawed human bones. Or maybe the sight had dredged up the memory of the first time he'd seen a corpse: a battered young woman he had found in a garbage bag in the woods fifteen years before.

The Kripo man poked tentatively at the rib cage, which looked like it was filled with dark soil.

"There," he said, pointing. "Between those two ribs there."

There was a flash above Bergmann's head, and the beam of a flashlight lit the end of the yellow ruler. He still didn't see anything noteworthy, apart from the ribs.

The Kripo man rapped lightly with the ruler again. Bergmann felt the hairs on his arms rise and the oxygen leave his lungs. For a moment he felt like he was tipping over the edge.

"What the hell?" said Abrahamsen, standing next to Bergmann. Then he said what both of them were thinking: "There aren't two bodies down there. There are three."

Bergmann stared, his eyes wide. A fifth hand was visible in the dirt inside the rib cage. Slowly he counted the fingers on the little hand, which looked as though it was clenched into a fist. A little fist with tiny fingers.

"So," he whispered to himself, "there's a child on the bottom."

Abrahamsen said something that Bergmann didn't catch. He felt his colleague's hand on his back.

"Well, I'll be damned," said Abrahamsen.

Bergmann was filled with an emotion he'd never felt before, a kind of déjà vu. As though he knew that the child who lay at the bottom of this grave had stood exactly where he himself had stood when he'd seen the deer's eyes through the trees.

"A child," he said into thin air. "Somebody killed a child."

CHAPTER 7

Wednesday, May 30, 1945
Rindögatan 42
Gärdet
Stockholm, Sweden

Detective Inspector Gösta Persson's stomach growled as he stood straddle-legged on the sidewalk in front of Rindögatan 42. He gazed up at the pale-yellow brick facade. A face disappeared behind the curtain in the tall window on the second floor. A light drizzle fell from the steel-gray sky, and it soon covered the lenses of his glasses. He searched his pocket for a clean cloth to wipe them off.

If only he could stop this growling in his stomach. Persson was a man who made few demands on life as long as he got three square meals a day at regular hours. But that was essential. So if he didn't get lunch soon, he was going to explode. He nodded curtly to the officer who was standing guard at the entrance. Ruin his lunch? For what? A dead Norwegian? He almost chuckled to himself as he scanned the mailboxes inside the vestibule. There were still plenty of Norwegians in the world, even after this damned war. But lunch? Lunch was what made the world go round, and he'd been on his way to lunch when the damn phone rang.

Persson had just grabbed his hat from the coat rack and reached for the door handle when the phone on his massive teak desk began ringing. For a few seconds he had deliberated over whether to pick up, but being a man of ambition, he lifted the receiver to his ear instead of sneaking off to lunch. The watch commander had informed him that one of Stockholm's ten radio cruisers had reported a suspicious death at Rindögatan 42 in Gärdet. The whole thing could have waited until after lunch, had the zealous watch commander not clarified that the apartment was owned by the Norwegian legation in Stockholm. And something like that couldn't very well be ignored, could it? Persson could still hear the watch commander's voice ringing in his ears. He had big plans for his career—maybe he would even make station chief one day—so this lamentable fatality definitely couldn't be ignored.

What are these Norwegians supposed to be good for? Persson wondered as he paused on the third-floor landing. Sweat had soaked into the brim of his hat. No lunch and now he was drenched with sweat. And on top of all that, these goddamned Norwegians. Nothing but trouble from them for five long years, hassles and more hassles. If it wasn't the Finns drinking and fighting and stabbing each other, then it was the Norwegians. No, he damned sure missed the good old days when law and order had reigned in Scandinavia. Persson summoned what motivation he could find and hauled his bulk up the last thirteen steps.

A uniformed officer, a young kid Persson had never seen before, stood outside the open door of the fourth-floor apartment. He was about to say something, but Persson motioned dismissively and stepped over the threshold. He didn't want anyone spoiling his first impression of the deceased. He'd stopped trusting anything else years ago. In the kitchen another officer sat talking in a low voice to a trembling woman who was weeping softly, her face buried in her hands. Persson nodded to the officer, an old acquaintance, and put his finger to his lips. Then he stepped past the kitchen doorway and went down the hall toward the living room.

The body lay on the bed in the bedroom, and even Persson had to admit it was a sad sight. In his stiff right hand the deceased held a pistol that Persson recognized as a Colt Llama. The barrel was pointing at the ceiling. He had an appalling hole in the middle of his forehead. Black blood had congealed over half his face and left huge stains on the white pillow. The Norwegian's eyes stared in the same direction as the pistol that had blown him into history. A faint odor of old vomit filled the room. Persson stood for a moment observing the man before him. He sighed a couple of times, as he always did when some unpleasant thought tickled the back of his mind. Then he took a couple of steps and began rummaging through the pockets of the coat hanging over the back of the chair by the door. The only thing of interest—aside from Kaj Holt's ID card, which had been issued two weeks before—was a rather fat wallet. Persson quickly counted the bills, then studied the photo of the deceased on the ID card. The inspector scratched his head. He recalled what it was he'd reacted to and walked over toward the bed. He gave the man in the bed a quick look. The frozen expression on Holt's face made him shudder. Persson had witnessed similar scenes many times before, but that didn't make it any easier.

Quite right, he thought, taking a ballpoint pen out of his pocket. The thought that had festered ever since he first glimpsed the Spanish-made miniature Colt pistol was now scintillatingly clear. Persson poked at the muzzle with the cap of the ballpoint. It had obviously been tapped so a silencer could be screwed on. But where in the world was the silencer? And it was highly unlikely that anyone would use one to commit suicide.

Persson inspected Holt's skull. Besides, the distance between the gun and the bullet hole simply seemed too great for him to have been certain to hit the right spot. People who took their own lives with firearms most often put the weapon in their mouth because then there was no way out, no room for remorse. Those who put the gun to their temple were most likely to change their minds while pulling the trigger, with the result that they ended up with a less accurate wound than the one poor Holt had in his forehead. Not to mention that it would be much more effective to hold the pistol to the temple at an angle, pointing toward the back of the head. A man like Kaj Holt should have known that.

As if that weren't enough, Detective Inspector Persson knew that the neighbors would most likely have woken up when a nine-millimeter projectile that broke the sound barrier made its way into Holt's skull. But with a silencer those same people would have probably just turned over in bed and continued sleeping.

Persson went around to the other side of the bed to study Holt from the other side. He looked blue and ashen gray in the cold light coming in the bedroom window. Persson set his hat cautiously on the nightstand and pulled out his handkerchief to wipe his bald pate. Then he lay down on the floor and looked underneath the bed. He got back up with some effort and put his hand on the right side of Holt's skull. He tried to lift his head carefully, but the rigid neck resisted. Finally he managed to produce a gap between the hair and the pillow. And quite right, there was no exit hole. The bullet was still inside Holt's head. A silencer would have reduced the bullet's velocity so that it wouldn't have penetrated all the way through the skull.

Damn it, Persson thought as his stomach growled again, even worse than earlier. He would eat his damn hat if it turned out that poor Kaj Holt had really committed suicide.

Persson cursed himself as he headed back down the hall to the kitchen. *Why did I have to pick up that damn telephone?* He pictured himself back in the office, deliberating over whether to take the call.

Before he reached the kitchen he made a detour to the entry hall and knelt down to inspect the doorframe. There were no marks to suggest a break-in. Ergo, the door must not have been locked—or else someone had a key. Or Holt could have come in with the killer, or let in someone he knew. It was that simple and that difficult.

Provided he didn't fall for the idea that Holt had taken his own life. But Persson knew himself too well for that. He'd been in the apartment only a few minutes, and already he could sense that something was amiss. And he was not a man to let it go.

Captain Kaj Holt, Persson thought, getting up from his knees with a grunt. The officer who still stood in the hallway offered a helping hand, but he waved him off. Detective Inspector Persson may have been too fat for his own good, but he could still stand up on his own.

He leaned in the doorway and met the uncertain gaze of the young officer.

"So you talked to the neighbors, am I right?"

The country boy gave a nod.

"And nobody heard a thing?" Persson wiped the sweat from his head again and recalled that his hat was still lying next to Kaj Holt's shattered skull in the bedroom.

"That's right," said the officer. "No one was home next door, but across—"

"It doesn't matter," Persson broke in.

In the kitchen he managed to calm down the crying woman enough that he was able to get some reasonable answers out of her. Persson learned that she was twenty-five years old and that she lived on the next block. She claimed that she'd had a relationship with Kaj Holt until a few months before, but she no longer wanted to keep seeing him after she found out he was going to be a father. And that he was married.

"No, of course not," said Inspector Persson.

The young woman wiped away a tear. The last she'd shed for him, Persson hoped.

"And he rang your doorbell last night?"

She nodded. Then she began to fiddle with her hat lying on the kitchen table.

"Did you get the impression that he was . . . how should I put it . . . depressed?"

"I think so, maybe. Kaj was like that a lot."

"Like what?" Persson asked.

"Depressed," she said.

"I see. But you didn't let him in."

"No, he sounded really drunk."

"And so you went to work today?"

"No. I was sick."

Persson scrutinized the woman. She didn't look very sick. Maybe Holt wasn't the only one she had that sort of relationship with.

"And you came over to check on him?"

"He sounded so sad," said the young woman, bursting into tears again.

Right, Persson thought. *Sad people are always the ones who commit suicide. That's just the way it is.*

"And the door was open?"

The woman nodded. Persson reached out his hand to touch her shoulder, but changed his mind. Instead he stood up without a word and went back to the bedroom to get his hat. He stood for a long while gazing at the dead captain. *This is just too terrible,* he said to himself. *A wife and a kid and everything.*

Out in the living room he picked up a note lying on the coffee table. He held it gingerly by the top corner.

Sorry. Kaj.

He put it back on the table and went out to the hall.

"Run downstairs to the patrol car, get hold of the station, and ask them to call the Norwegian legation for me," he told the officer.

If nothing else, he needed them to identify the dead man. They might as well do that right away, even though it wasn't really necessary. The man on the bed was clearly the same as the man in the photo on his ID card.

The rookie cop rushed down the stairs at once.

"And pick up something for me to eat," Persson called after him.

Back in the living room he sat down on the sofa next to the coffee table.

After Holt's girlfriend had left the apartment with the other officer, he went over to the end table and turned on the Silver Super 2 short-wave radio. It was set to Aachen. Zarah Leander's voice filled the room. Persson thought his ears were deceiving him. Had the Americans gotten the station back up and running? Was that really possible?

And that damned Nazi whore, he thought. *That goddamned Nazi whore.*

Even so he hummed along as he fished a cigarette out of the pack that the officer must have left lying on the table.

"Don't tell me adieu. Only auf Wiedersehen."

CHAPTER 8

Saturday, May 17, 2003
Nordmarka
Oslo, Norway

All the details were accentuated with a sharp clarity in the gray light. Tommy Bergmann cast a final glance at the three skeletons, which now lay in the daylight under the thin white fabric of the tent. *Is this all a human being is?* he wondered, gazing at the skulls' gaping holes where the eyes, nose, and mouth should be. He felt uncertain and clumsy as he confronted this sight, but it seemed there was nothing more for him to do. It had been twenty-four hours since he'd last slept, and twelve hours of digging hadn't given him and his colleagues anything more to go on other than the poor wedding ring. The only thing that was clear was that the two adults had been shot in the head; no immediate cause of death had been determined for the child. Bergmann leaned over the excavation and held his hand over the little brownish head. According to the forensic team the child must have been seven or eight years old. Its mother was undoubtedly the woman with the gold ring—which promised her the eternal fidelity of this Gustav—who lay beside the child and grimaced up at the roof of the tent. But as to the identity of the third person, nobody in the tent had any theory, except for vague assumptions that it might be Gustav himself, or maybe Gustav's wife's lover. Twelve hours of digging had yielded only one ring; if the third person was indeed Gustav, he should have had a ring too. Which was why Bergmann had proposed the theory of a lover.

But as the sun broke through the morning mist, Bergmann knew that he could no longer think clearly enough to solve this mystery. He should have gone home hours ago. And even though spending Independence Day all alone in a three-room apartment on Lambertseter might not have been what he was dreaming of, his only alternative was to spend his day off with three old skeletons deep in the forests of Nordmarka. And he certainly had no intention of doing that.

But the thought of the child bothers the hell out of me, he mused as he stepped out of the tent. The clicking of a dozen cameras filled the air. Bergmann looked up, momentarily the subject of the insatiable and tireless press chasing a juicy murder story. He exchanged a few words with one of the reporters, who looked like he'd been freezing in the woods for a couple of hours. Bergmann offered a few vague clichés and referred all the reporters to the police spokesperson. Then he headed for home, taking the narrow path lined with huge spruce trees.

After a few minutes he stopped and turned around, peering through the forest. He thought he'd seen something move out of the corner of his eye.

No, he told himself. The bright sunshine gave him a confidence that he'd lacked the night before.

"Gustav," Bergmann murmured as he descended the main path. He stopped and wiped the sweat from the back of his neck. What had happened up there?

CHAPTER 9

Wednesday, May 30, 1945
Rindögatan 42
Gärdet
Stockholm, Sweden

Detective Inspector Gösta Persson had sternly asked not to be disturbed as he ate lunch. But there was a knock on the kitchen door before he was even halfway through his sandwich. He got up. There was another knock, but Persson just stood there staring into space. *How can they play Zarah Leander?* he wondered, though he had long since turned off the radio in the living room, partly because he couldn't stand that woman, and partly because he always ate his meals in silence.

There was a third knock on the door.

Persson stood by the kitchen window looking out at the backyard.

"Come in," he said finally, but he didn't turn around when the door opened. Instead he stared at a skinny birch tree out in the yard that looked just as dead as the Norwegian in the bedroom.

Someone behind him cleared his throat.

"This is Ms. Fredriksen from the Norwegian legation," said the rookie officer.

"Next time don't order a ham sandwich for me," said Persson, wiping his fingers on a paper napkin. "If there is a next time."

Slowly he turned around. The woman facing him was young, undoubtedly one of those who had escaped over the border a year or two ago, then rapidly found a job for herself at the legation, which apparently never had enough people. Her gaze was determined, almost challenging. She was the sort of woman Persson would have kept his distance from if he'd been younger.

"I'm actually not supposed to let you in here," said Persson.

"This residence belongs to the Norwegian state," said the young woman, cocking her head in such a way that he thought her hat might fall off.

"This is a crime scene," said Persson.

There was a pause.

"So was he murdered?" she said at last, a bit too loudly, so that her words echoed in the empty corridor behind her.

Persson sighed.

"There are some indications that he was, yes." *But I'm not going to confirm it until I'm certain I won't be dragged into the case,* he thought.

He reached out his enormous hand and engulfed the woman's pale little hand in his.

"Gösta Persson," he said firmly. "Detective Inspector."

The woman maintained her intense stare. Persson was the one who looked away first.

"Karen Eline Fredriksen. Secretary."

He took his notebook out of his inside coat pocket and jotted down her personal information.

"Soon to be Krogh," she said.

Persson looked up from his notebook.

"Excuse me?"

"Soon to be Krogh," she said. "I'm getting married in a month."

"Congratulations," said Persson, studying her face for a moment. Strange how Karen Eline Fredriksen thought it important to stress that she was getting married. Her loose-fitting coat made him think she might be pregnant.

A future husband both blessed and damned, Persson thought, putting his notebook and pen back in his pocket. With a hand lightly on her back, he ushered her out of the kitchen, down the dark hallway, through the sparsely furnished living room, and into the bedroom. He gave her no warning of what she would see when he opened the door.

Karen Fredriksen instantly covered her face with her hands as she murmured Kaj Holt's name.

"Did you know him well?" asked the inspector after Karen had wiped her face with a handkerchief she took from her expensive handbag.

It was a long time before she answered. She stared out of the window, seemingly unaware that Persson had asked her a question.

He opened his mouth to ask her again, but she beat him to it.

"Yes. He . . . he was here several times. I mean, he lived here . . . the last year, year and a half . . . he . . . worked at the legation, I mean—"

"So you're saying you knew him?"

"Yes."

"And this is Kaj Holt?"

Persson pointed at the man on the bed, who by now had turned almost blue.

A single mascara-stained tear ran down her cheek. Then she pulled herself together and her expression changed, as though it were hardly unexpected that one of her colleagues had been found dead. Persson couldn't put his finger on it, but something about her behavior gave him the feeling that she'd been prepared for something like this. It was as if she'd already known it when the phone rang at the Norwegian legation.

Persson gestured toward the door leading to the living room.

Then Karen did something entirely unexpected. She walked slowly over to Kaj Holt's dead body, reached out her left hand, and stroked the hair on the right side of his head. Then she stroked the cheek that wasn't covered with blood.

"I'm sorry," she said as they walked back to the kitchen and sat down at the table. "He has . . . he recently had a daughter, and his wife . . ." She let the sentence ebb away.

"I understand," said Persson. So he'd recently had a daughter. Why then would he take his life just now?

"Kaj was suicidal," said Karen, as if reading his mind. She touched the kitchen table with her gloved right hand. Persson watched her, thinking how much more beautiful she was than his wife. Her corn-yellow hair and blue eyes made her look like an angel, or like a model who appeared in advertisements. Her black hat hid her eyes when she looked down for a moment.

"So you think he could have committed suicide?" Persson asked.

Karen Eline Fredriksen looked him in the eye. Her crimson lips parted.

"That's for you to determine. I just wanted you to know that Kaj had been deeply . . . depressed this past year. The war took a great toll on him."

She held his eyes with hers. Once again it was Persson who had to look away first. He nodded to himself. Her explanation sounded plausible.

"Tell me, does this look like his handwriting?"

Persson handed her the note.

Karen looked at the paper for a long while.

"It could be. But I can't say for sure."

A good thing you said that, Persson thought.

"I'd like to take a look at something that we know is his handwriting . . . Do you have anything at the legation that Holt wrote? A letter or something?"

"I don't really think . . ." Karen wiped her hand over her forehead, and her gaze slid toward the kitchen window, where a fly was bumping against the glass.

"I just want to be completely sure," said Persson.

Karen nodded.

"I can assure you this will stay between the two of us. Have you notified Oslo that he was found dead?"

"I, or rather the legation, will let his wife know," said Karen. "If that's all . . ." She got up abruptly and straightened her beige coat.

"I'll phone you about a letter or anything else you might have with Holt's handwriting."

"All right," she said and extended her hand. He nodded when she asked if she could leave.

Persson underlined Ms. Karen Eline Fredriksen's name twice in his notebook after he walked her to the front door. Then he wrote carefully, as if the paper were resisting the word *suicidal*. He thought, *Why didn't you tell me the truth?*

He stood and watched the ambulance personnel as they placed Kaj Holt on a stretcher. They had wrapped his head in a bandage. When they moved into the stairwell, Persson was still standing in the middle of the living room, looking through the doorway into the bedroom at the empty bed where the body had lain. The blood on the pillowcase had turned black.

He went through the apartment one more time. But there was nothing that might help him, no papers or folders, not even a newspaper. Only a set of sheets, some towels, and a Bible in the drawer of the nightstand, as if it were a hotel.

Persson finally ended up in the cramped, narrow kitchen. The fly buzzed over by the window, bumping repeatedly against the windowpane. Persson walked across the linoleum floor, took a dirty glass from the sink, and waited until the fly landed on the windowsill. Then he put the glass upside down over the fly. He closed his eyes. The blue irises of Karen Eline Fredriksen's eyes were all he saw.

Who sent you here? he wondered.

CHAPTER 10

Monday, May 19, 2003
Police Headquarters
Oslo, Norway

Tommy Bergmann pressed his forehead against the windowpane as he waited for a callback from Kripo. Far below on Åkebergveien the crowds looked like tiny Lego people, and the cars like the Matchbox versions he'd had as a child. He looked up toward the high-rises on Enerhaugen hill. They had always looked so misplaced in the center of town. He'd never been able to get used to the sight of them outside his office windows. The only thing he liked about them was that Hege had lived in a studio apartment there when he first met her. If there was one summer in his life he had nothing but good memories from, it was the summer when they met. The sweltering apartment, the light nights, a life that seemed as though it would never end, and the almost dreamlike feeling that everything was a little too good to be true.

That was many years ago now, he told himself. Another life, another time. The image of him and Hege in that narrow bed of hers up on Enerhaugen was replaced by Hege lying on the bathroom floor at

Lambertseter and whispering, "Please don't kill me." He mouthed the words to himself: *Don't kill me, Tommy, please don't kill me.*

He slapped himself lightly on the cheeks and looked at his wrist-watch to get his mind off Hege. He was counting down the hours until it was time for handball practice and hoping that Sara's mother would show up. Her eyes, her laugh, and the joie de vivre she radiated always made him feel normal somehow. He imagined that she might be able to give him the peace of mind he seldom—or rather, never—felt. A sense of calm that might tell him it wasn't dangerous to be loved. Wasn't that what Hege had told him once? "You act as if you don't want to be loved, as if it's dangerous to let someone love you." In recent weeks he had even begun to fantasize about whether something might work out between them. *Good Lord,* he thought now, *how naïve and pathetic.* He didn't even know her name, or whether she was single. He'd barely spoken to her, just exchanged a few pleasantries a couple of times a week over the past six months. No doubt she believed he was just like other men. That was what Hege had believed.

He checked his watch one more time as he tried to recall the details of Sara's nameless mother's face. Then he forced himself to turn his attention back to his work. He enlarged the picture of the inside of the gold ring on his computer screen. He studied the engraving letter by letter for what must have been the tenth time that day, as though hoping to discover something new.

Yours forever. Gustav.

Who was Gustav? Bergmann wondered. *And how long will it take before the guy at Kripo calls me back?*

No one was going to make any headway on this case until Kripo decided to send him the entire missing-persons list. It was their domain, and they guarded it well.

No matter why those three people were murdered up there in Nordmarka, someone must have reported them missing, most likely shortly after they were killed. At first Bergmann, as well as everyone else, had thought the three bodies were a family. But if so, why wasn't the other adult wearing a ring? Bergmann did not think that it was Gustav lying there beside his wife. But that was as far as anyone on the seventh floor of police headquarters had gotten with the case. Since the case was undeniably an old one, Bergmann knew he'd soon be ordered to drop the case anyway.

"Finally," he said when the phone rang. He'd been waiting so long that he'd just about given up hope that the missing-persons list might give him any leads.

The man's voice on the other end sounded nasal and self-important. Bergmann managed to control himself. For once he needed Kripo more than they needed him.

"There's not a single active missing-persons search before 1988," the man said. "And you know what that means," he added. "Not a single open case . . ."

"Okay," Bergmann said, feeling like a child. Like everyone else in the department, he knew that the police functioned like any ordinary bureaucracy. The main goal was to put out the big fires first, then search for an excuse to file away the rest. The maximum statute of limitations was twenty-five years.

"There have been 1,121 missing persons since 1934. But you can forget about any of them before 1988," the man said.

Bergmann repressed an urge to spew out a torrent of curses. How many times did this guy have to drum the rules into his head?

When the Kripo man hung up, Bergmann went upstairs to the cafeteria and stepped out on the roof terrace in an attempt to clear his head. He quickly polished off two smokes. Those skeletons had been out in Nordmarka a long time; a few more minutes wouldn't matter.

When he came in from the terrace, he had three new e-mails waiting for him: one from HR, reminding him about the upcoming summer party; a newsletter; and a message from Kripo with an Excel file attached.

Bergmann said a silent prayer before he opened the spreadsheet. The list was longer than he would have thought, but at least the reports were arranged chronologically. Some clever soul had thought to include a comments field, which made it easier to tell the cases apart. A few terse keywords about each case plus a case number were better than nothing. Bergmann, who had only worked on a couple of missing-persons cases before, had heard that people who went missing during the war were usually declared dead in accordance with an interim law. But after 1947 many who'd been presumed dead were put back on the missing-persons list. In a worst-case scenario, the three people in Nordmarka might have been officially declared dead after that date. Could that be right? Bergmann paused for a second before he picked up the phone, but then changed his mind and put it back down.

He sat staring at the spreadsheet for a while. They were looking for three people who had vanished simultaneously in Nordmarka, unless they'd been brought from somewhere else and buried in the same grave. But that sounded too improbable. How could the three bodies have been transported so far into the forest? So he had to look for three people who'd been reported missing at the same time. How old were the remains? What was it that Forensics had said? Bergmann paged through the reports, even though he knew the answer. When would it have been most likely for three people to be executed in Norway, deep in the forest? It must have been during the German occupation. Forensics had said they couldn't make such an old case a priority. Or maybe Reuter had put those words in their mouths. Bergmann knew it was only a matter of time before the case would be shelved. Not even the press would give a damn. If they acted true to form, they'd forget all about it in a few days' time. Unless the deaths turned out to be a big story for some reason.

He scrolled slowly down the screen. All manner of miseries flickered before his eyes. People who undoubtedly had committed suicide or been murdered, children who had never had a chance to grow up. He stopped around 1950 just to be on the safe side.

After half an hour he'd found nothing that matched what he was looking for. There were plenty of children who had gone missing during the war, but none in Nordmarka. He stared at the letters on the screen until they melted together. An idea was trying to take shape in his head, but he couldn't pin it down.

Shit, he thought. *It can't be that difficult.*

For a while he just sat staring out the window. The calm of early summer, the bright blue sky over the apartment towers on Enerhaugen, the soundless rustling of the foliage in the trees—all of it was making him depressed.

He got up from his desk chair and headed one floor up to the cafeteria. He bought himself a soggy baguette and went out on the terrace again. Just as he heard the door slam behind him, he figured out what was nagging at him. He put the cigarette back in the pack and tore open the red door, almost tripping over a man coming out.

"Sorry," Bergmann muttered, sticking the baguette under his arm. He jogged past the elevator and dashed down the stairs to his office. *There,* he thought, tossing the baguette into the wastebasket under his desk.

He stared at three names glowing on the screen. They hadn't been reported missing in Nordmarka, or even in Oslo, but in Hurum. There was nothing in the comments field but the words "Hurum countryside?" next to the name of a missing woman, Agnes Gerner. The other two were listed in different columns, separated by other, unrelated missing persons. It had to be them. He scrolled up and down the spreadsheet to make sure there weren't three other people who'd been reported missing the same day. *No,* he said to himself. These three were the only ones who'd been reported missing on precisely the same day, September 28, 1942.

Bergmann scanned the spreadsheet.

```
Cecilia Lande, born March 16, 1934

Agnes Gerner, born June 19, 1918

Johanne Caspersen, born November 5, 1915
```

He fumbled for something to write with, inadvertently pushing a stack of case files onto the floor. He shoved them out of the way with his foot.

Two women in their twenties and a little girl. Shot at point-blank range.

He moved his pen over the names he had written down, double-checking them to be on the safe side. He printed out two copies of the Excel spreadsheet and found an empty file folder. He wrote "NORDMARKA" on it in big block letters.

Now it feels like a real case, he thought, inserting several printouts of pictures of the remains. The three skulls had names. The only problem was that the only skull he could positively identify at the moment was the small one.

"Cecilia Lande," Bergmann said quietly as he studied the photo of the skull on the screen. It was the only one that was intact after all these years in the ground. The two adult skulls were so cracked that they needed to be glued back together, but nobody'd had time to do that yet. The crime scene techs guessed that the two skulls had been shattered because they'd been shot in the head. But there was no entry hole in the smallest skull.

Cecilia, Bergmann thought, staring at the gaping eye sockets of what had once been a child. *You were only eight years old.* He studied the photos, thirty of them altogether, taken from different angles so that he almost had a 360-degree view of the head.

No hole or projectiles inside.

Then something occurred to him.

Were you buried alive?

CHAPTER 11

Thursday, May 31, 1945
The Stable
Östermalm Police District
Stockholm, Sweden

Someone knocked on the door of Detective Inspector Gösta Persson's office. Persson recognized the station chief's characteristic knock and thought he'd just barge in without waiting for a go-ahead as he usually did. So Persson remained sitting with Kaj Holt's case file in his lap and his feet on the desk, staring out the ancient windows. Another rainy day. *It'll probably be nicer this weekend,* thought Persson as he swung his legs down from the massive hardwood desk. The station chief still hadn't entered, which was very unlike him. Persson wasn't stupid. He guessed that the chief must have people with him that he wanted to impress.

"Come in," he said, straightening his tie.

The heavy door slowly opened.

Persson put Holt's case file down on the almost empty desktop. The chief tentatively approached across the old plank floor. Two men entered behind him.

"Well, Gösta, my man," said the station chief, but then he seemed to have a mental block. He stopped a couple of steps from the desk.

Persson raised his eyebrows in anticipation. The chief's tone revealed a feigned camaraderie that did not suit him. Persson reckoned that it was the man next to him who was making the chief uneasy. He was a tanned, tall fellow about Persson's age, maybe a little younger, in a much too expensive suit and an overcoat that must have cost what Persson made in a month. The other man wore the same type of coat, and if Persson were to guess, he was no more than twenty years old. Judging by his childlike face, he would have had no problem fitting in with any middle school class. He made no attempt at a greeting, just looked around the room with his soaking wet hat on.

"Well, Gösta. What exactly happened to that Norwegian . . . Holt?" asked the chief, nodding at the case file on the desk.

Persson sighed.

"Who knows?" he said.

The taller of the two men behind the chief took a couple of steps across the floor and held out his hand to Persson, who made a move to get up and gave him a limp handshake. Although he only introduced himself as Håkan Nordenstam, Persson had already figured out who this man was and what he wanted, someone with an interest in making Holt's death seem like nothing but a suicide, if not, indeed, the person who had killed the depressed Norwegian. The man with the baby face stood by the bookcase. He gave a slight nod when he noticed Persson watch him pick up a black ivory elephant. For an instant it looked as though he might drop it on the floor. His eyes met Persson's and he smiled. Without averting his gaze he set the elephant statue back on the bookshelf.

"Well . . . I had lunch with Kaj on Tuesday," said Nordenstam. "And he was very . . . depressed."

"So you believe that he took his own life?" asked Persson.

Nordenstam waved dismissively, apparently completely oblivious to Persson's tone of voice, which held a hint of sarcasm. Enough to make the chief look even more uncomfortable than he already was.

"Yes. That's the conclusion we have reached as well," said the chief. "With the statements of the legation and Nordenstam. And they are weighty statements . . ."

"I—" Persson began.

Nordenstam held up his hand and took his newly lit Sibir cigarette out of his mouth.

"Kaj Holt . . . worked for us, Detective Inspector Persson."

"For *us*?" Persson said.

Baby Face sat down on the desk.

"For the C-Bureau. So you see . . ." Nordenstam attempted a smile, the kind one might give a child who didn't quite understand what was being said.

"Which means . . ." If Persson had had any doubts before, they were now gone.

Nordenstam took a deep breath as he rubbed the back of his hand over his prominent, smooth-shaven chin.

"Kaj Holt"—he paused for effect—"was involved with all the Allied forces."

Persson nodded.

"He had also made contact with some . . . Soviet agents here in town."

"So we don't want to . . ." the chief began, fixing his gaze on Persson.

"Provoke them unnecessarily," said Nordenstam.

Persson and Nordenstam sat gauging each other for what seemed like an eternity. The silence was only broken when a car outside downshifted and drove through a puddle on the street.

"So, where did you go on Tuesday?" Persson said at last. "You and Holt. Was it enjoyable?"

The chief cleared his throat. Then he coughed and slid his reading glasses even farther down the tip of his nose. Persson stared back at him.

"Let me just say that we've decided to take over the case," said Nordenstam, trying for a genial tone in an apparent effort to smooth over the tension that now filled the room. "We'd like to take your report with us. Then we'll take care of the rest. By the way, we were at the Cecil and stayed afterward for a little . . . private visit"—he winked—"and finished up at Berns. Have a nice afternoon, Inspector." Nordenstam stubbed out his cigarette in the crystal ashtray on the desk. Then he looked at Persson and smiled one last time, the same trusting smile Persson didn't quite know how to interpret, except that he couldn't think of anything to say.

The three men left the room in reverse order to the way they had entered.

The chief stopped in the doorway and gave Persson a look that could not be misunderstood. Then he slammed the door behind him.

Only then did Detective Inspector Persson notice how hard his heart was pounding. The blood was throbbing behind his brow, from one ear to the other, like an arc through his head. He took his handkerchief from the breast pocket of his suit jacket and wiped his almost completely bald pate. With trembling hands he took his comb out of the other inside pocket and brushed the few strands he still had on his head. Then he surveyed his office, the finest in the whole building, even nicer than the chief's. It had a mahogany bookcase, a little elephant statue he had inherited from his predecessor, and a small sitting area with elegant leather furniture; an oil painting from when the building was new in 1738 hung next to the door.

Persson took in the entire office, then turned and stared at the solemn black-and-white portrait of King Gustav V that hung in a gilt frame. Should he, Detective Inspector Gösta Persson, give up all this and more for a dead Norwegian?

He closed his eyes for a moment and knew that this would be a matter between God and himself. Only he, the detective inspector of Stockholm's seventh police district, would ever know that poor Kaj Holt should have been autopsied, and that the apartment should have been sealed right away. The weapon should have been sent to the crime lab, and all walls, door handles, cutlery, and windowsills should have been dusted for fingerprints.

He quickly pulled out the top drawer of his desk and took out the overpriced Caran d'Ache fountain pen he'd received from his father-in-law on his fortieth birthday. Then he took out a report form from one of the three file boxes on his desk. Normally he did not fill out the forms himself, but God help him if he had the stomach to order someone else to do it in this case. If he was going to deny the obvious truth, he had to do the job himself.

The inspector entered yesterday's date in the top right corner. "May 30, 1945. Captain Kaj Holt found dead at Rindögatan 42. Examination of the scene points to suicide as the probable cause of death. Witness statements confirm this." Persson opened the case file and studied the note with the words "Sorry. Kaj." Then he wrote a couple of sentences about the testimonies of the apparently irresponsible girlfriend and Karen Eline Fredriksen from the Norwegian legation. He scribbled his signature at the bottom and slapped the folder shut.

His hand no longer trembled as he replaced the cap on the fountain pen. Persson closed his eyes and saw himself standing in the kitchen at Rindögatan 42 and staring at the sad little birch tree in the backyard. *Don't tell me adieu,* he thought.

He opened the case file one last time and gazed impassively at what he'd just written. He wondered fleetingly how he, of all people, had ended up in such a situation. The terse report was patently false, yet he felt only a twinge of guilt, as if his own career were worth more than seeking justice for a dead man who had apparently been murdered.

Quickly, before there was time to change his mind, he grabbed the file folder, strode across the old, tilting floor, and placed it in the anteroom. The secretary glanced at him over her typewriter. Persson raised an eyebrow at her and gave her a wan smile. Then he hurried down the corridor, past the investigators' offices, and into the men's room.

He'd long ago lost count of how many times he'd washed his hands in near boiling-hot water. Persson stared at himself in the mirror. The day before, he'd looked fresh and rested, as if he'd spent the weekend out on his boat. But now?

He whispered quietly to his own reflection, "Forgive me, for I know well what I have done."

CHAPTER 12

Tommy Bergmann pulled up the photo of the gold ring on the screen.

Yours forever. Gustav.

Then he clicked ahead to the photos of the two adult skulls, which were positioned on a metal table at the Institute of Forensic Medicine.

So which of them had been Gustav's forever? he wondered. Agnes Gerner or Johanne Caspersen?

Judging by their ages, it was most likely that Johanne was Gustav's chosen one. And Cecilia's mother. But why hadn't she taken his name? Could Gustav's wife have survived, perhaps along with Gustav himself?

Bergmann sighed with resignation. It was all a huge mess, a labyrinthine jumble. He was going to have to start from scratch.

He phoned the archive, but hung up before anyone could answer. It was no use. If the case files still existed, they wouldn't be here in this building, or even in the backup archive. He decided instead to try and find something in the National Registry. He typed in the names, one by one. No hits. He cross-checked "Gustav" with the surnames of the two women. Nothing. Not a single damned hit. People always boasted about how great the system was, but there were plenty of gaps in the records before 1947. Maybe it didn't really matter—if you were dead, you could neither commit crimes nor pay taxes, so the tax authority and the justice system didn't give a damn who you used to be, or when you were born. But it seemed that nobody had bothered to demand that these three be officially reported dead after the war, or they would have been on the missing-persons list. That could mean several things. The family might have wanted to believe they were still alive. But it was more likely that no one in their families, if any were still alive after the war, cared enough about them to bother reporting that they were dead. There were only two reasons to have missing persons declared dead: to achieve a sense of peace so the survivors could get on with their lives, or to get hold of their money.

Yet someone had reported them missing in the first place. That was a start. It was most likely this Gustav who had reported the woman with the ring missing. The problem was how to track down this illustrious Gustav's last name without having to phone every person in Norway named either Gerner or Caspersen.

He got up from his chair and patted all his coat pockets. No tobacco pouch. He swore softly, unable to recall where he had left it. *On the roof terrace,* he thought. He'd put the pouch down on one of the tables up there.

Just as he took hold of the door handle, the phone on his desk rang. He hesitated a moment and then went back to check the display. It was someone from the archive calling him back. He ignored it and opened his web browser instead. It might be worth a try—certainly better than loafing on the roof terrace. He typed "Agnes Gerner" in the search field. Then he quickly shut his eyes, as if hoping for a miracle when he opened them again.

Nothing. Not a single hit.

Then he typed in "Johanne Caspersen."

Nothing. Next he tried Gustav with the last names of the two women.

Finally "Cecilia Lande."

"Did you mean Cecilie Lande?" the search engine responded.

"No," said Bergmann out loud. "I did not mean Cecilie Lande."

Once again the phone rang. He picked it up as he stared at the text on the screen.

"I saw you had called?" said the voice on the other end. Bergmann recognized the woman from some summer party he'd attended.

"Yeah" was all he said.

"Did you call to ask me something?"

"I'm working on a case from 1942," he said, keeping his voice neutral.

She gave a short laugh. "Tommy . . ."

He didn't reply.

"What sort of case?" she asked.

"The three bodies that were found in Nordmarka."

"The National Archives," she said.

"The National Archives?"

"Yeah, the Oslo archive has merged with the National Archives at Sognsvann."

"Damn!" he exclaimed. "Of course, of course."

"Excuse me?" she said, but he put the receiver gently back in the cradle.

Of course, he thought. *Why didn't I think of that?* Cecilia Lande. He hadn't yet tried her last name with Gustav. It was worth a try.

He typed the name "Gustav Lande" in the Google search field.

He closed his eyes. He could clearly smell the dug-up dirt from Nordmarka; he could see the child's hand sticking up between the ribs of the second woman, either Agnes or Johanne.

He opened his eyes and looked at the screen.

Four hits. Four little hits. But the name was right.

"Bingo."

So this Gustav had been Gustav Lande, and he was the father of Cecilia Lande. That must be the way it fit together. And he must have been married to one of the two women.

Bergmann studied the list. Four hits weren't much, but they were a hell of a lot better than none. As he clicked on the first link, he sat for a while as though petrified.

Gustav Lande (1905-1944). Businessman and primary stockholder in Knaben Molybdenum Mines, Inc., and Nasjonal Samling (NS) patron. Committed suicide in July 1944. Known for his close association with the Occupation forces. Source: Torgeir Moberg, *Those Who Played the Enemy's Game* (1980).

CHAPTER 13

Thursday, May 31, 1945
The Stable
Östermalm Police District
Stockholm, Sweden

He was already at the door when he changed his mind. What had he just done? Detective Inspector Gösta Persson paused for a few seconds on the threshold, clutching the brim of his hat in his fingers. A hard rain was pouring onto the sidewalk. It made the choice easy.

I'm not even hungry anymore, Persson thought, turning on his heel and heading inside. He strode down the corridor with determined steps, looking straight ahead without nodding or greeting the people he passed. By the time he reached the anteroom, sweat had settled around his collar and under his cuffs; his face was undoubtedly flushed because his blood pressure had spiked.

"Do you have the Holt file?" he asked, leaning on the counter with all his weight, which creaked under him.

The secretary stopped typing, turned halfway toward him, and regarded him over the rim of her glasses.

"Yes . . ." she said in a hesitant tone of voice, as if Persson were an idiot.

He motioned with his hand, which prompted her to pick up the light-green document folder next to her. Persson took it without a word and unfastened the thick cord around the folder. He paged carefully through the few documents, starting from the back, and quietly exhaled when he found the note that Holt had supposedly written before he took his life. Nordenstam would have a hard time removing it unseen before the entire file was formally transferred to the C-Bureau. Persson studied the handwriting. If he'd had any sense he would have gone back to Rindögatan and collected all the ballpoint pens to examine them for fingerprints and check whether one was left where Holt might have set it down after writing those two words.

Instead he told his secretary, "Find Holt's wife's address in Oslo."

"But—" She looked crestfallen.

"Call and find out. I'll wait in the office."

"His wife? Call her?"

Persson thought it over. He pictured Karen Eline Fredriksen's eyes, the tucks in her blouse, the budding cleavage between her young breasts. He could still smell the scent of her perfume. He didn't give a shit that Nordenstam or the baby face he'd had with him had sent Karen Eline Fredriksen to Holt's apartment.

He leaned over the counter again. Once more it threatened to collapse.

"Call the secretary at the Norwegian legation, *not* Ms. Fredriksen," he said quietly, "and ask for Holt's last address in Oslo. Just say we need it for our report on Kaj Holt's tragic suicide, nothing more."

"Okay, I can do that."

"Great," said Persson, "and when you've got the address, give it to me." He took the document folder with him and fished out a brown envelope from the shelf. As he turned to go back to his office, he felt the secretary's gaze upon him.

Once inside, he stopped and leaned against the closed door for a couple of minutes until his heart stopped racing. If she called the station chief, he was done for, there was no doubt about it. He tried to eavesdrop for a while, but the double door made it impossible to hear anything but unintelligible mumbling.

Finally he moved away from the door. He found a bottle of liquor in the filing cabinet beneath his desk. He couldn't recall the last time he'd needed it. Reimersholms bitters stung like cat piss. With his hip flask in hand, he went over to the bookcase, where the man with the baby face had stood playing with the elephant statue. Persson picked it up the way Baby Face had done, turned toward his desk, and saw the scene as it had played out less than an hour before. He jumped when someone knocked on his door, nearly dropping both the elephant and the flask. He hurriedly set both items on the bookshelf and strode over to the windows before he called out "Come in!" as gruffly as he could.

He heard the clack of the secretary's heels crossing the floor behind him, but he didn't turn around. Instead he studied the lousy weather outside and followed the slim lines of a patrol car that glistened in the heavy rain.

"Did you find the address?" he asked.

"Yes," she said. "I jotted it down for you."

"Just leave it on the desk."

Her footsteps stopped in the middle of the room.

Persson still didn't turn around.

He heard her make a faint sound, but that was all. Finally she moved toward the door, stopped, turned around again, and then exited the office.

Persson copied Holt's address onto the brown envelope and carefully inserted the note that said "Sorry. Kaj." as though it were the most fragile thing in the world. One day everyone would know that he, Detective Inspector Gösta Persson, had sent this evidence to Holt's widow. For now that would have to suffice. At least he had done what little he could.

Before leaving the office, he finished off the bitters in his hip flask. He wasn't going to do any more work today anyway.

"I'll take this downstairs myself," he announced in the anteroom, then left before his secretary had a chance to object. He rushed down the spiral staircase to the basement as if the Devil himself were on his heels.

"You're lucky, you just made it," said the mailroom boy.

Persson muttered some response. He needed all the luck he could get today. He wanted to get out of here. He'd never liked the basement.

"To Norway, huh?" the boy said, glancing up at Persson, who managed to return the boy's feigned smile despite the stab he felt in his chest. With his own eyes Persson watched the boy feed the envelope into the postage meter, stamp it twice, and then put it into the burlap sack beside him.

"Yep, you're lucky, all right," the boy said again, hefting the sack onto his back. The outside doors behind him opened and a postal service driver appeared next to a Volvo with its trunk open.

Yep, Persson said to himself. *It helps to have a little luck.*

He stood out on the loading dock as the sack was loaded into the back of the van. The double doors of the van slammed. Persson watched until it disappeared around the corner.

CHAPTER 14

Monday, May 19, 2003
National Archives
Oslo, Norway

The parking lot at Sognsvann was barely half-full. Tommy Bergmann parked his brand-new service vehicle as close to the footpath as possible. He briefly studied the building through the trees before he took the printout from the passenger seat, rolled down the window, and lit a smoke. Somebody had to be the first to break the no-smoking rule in this damned car.

A mild breeze blew in from the Nordmarka woods, and the pale-green leaves on the nearby birch trees rustled. Then the wind died out and the leaves stopped moving, drooping as if summer were over before it had even started.

Gustav Lande, Bergmann said to himself, looking down at the piece of paper in his lap. All four hits on the Internet had been more or less similar and originated from a website called the Norwegian War Encyclopedia. All the articles referred to the same author, a well-known figure by the name of Professor Torgeir Moberg. He read the text several times as he puffed on his cigarette, trying to put together what little he knew. In September 1942 someone killed the wife and child of the

Nazi Gustav Lande, along with another woman. Almost two years later Gustav Lande took his own life.

All right, Bergmann thought. *Not much to go on.* But he couldn't stop thinking about that little girl. It seemed clear that she'd been buried alive. Why were the two women shot in the head, but not the girl? Had the person who killed them simply tossed the child into the grave, clinging to her mother?

He shook off the thought and looked at the printout from the missing-persons list again.

```
Cecilia Lande, born March 16, 1934.

Agnes Gerner, born June 19, 1918.

Johanne Caspersen, born November 5, 1915.
```

Yes, he thought, *Caspersen was probably the mother.* She must have been. He had decided not to speculate as to which of the two women was the mother until he had proof, but he couldn't help himself.

The man behind the counter looked as if he didn't appreciate people showing up unannounced at the National Archives.

"You need to make an appointment," he said. "We get a lot of requests, and we can't just . . ."

The man, whose name was Rolf according to his nametag, let the sentence die out.

"Look, Rolf," said Bergmann. "I'm sure the two of us can agree on an appointment time . . . say, right about now."

Rolf merely sighed when Bergmann held up his police badge and laid the printout on the counter along with a copy of a newspaper article about the three skeletons found in Nordmarka. Rolf pursed his lips several times as he studied the names before him.

"September 1942," said Bergmann.

Rolf sighed again, scratching the sparse beard he'd managed to grow. Bergmann tried to stay calm by looking out the big picture windows off the lobby.

"Well," said Rolf, "the old case files are probably in the records for the Oslo and Aker Police Department, because the city and Aker County's departments were combined during the Occupation." Then he muttered something that Bergmann didn't catch and began pounding away at the keyboard. He stared at the screen with an annoyed expression on his face. "Let's see . . . maybe you'll get lucky," he said, smiling in a way that Bergmann chose not to interpret. "They could have been shredded."

You're the one who'd be lucky if they haven't been shredded, thought Bergmann.

"Come with me," Rolf said at last. "Looks like this is your lucky day."

Bergmann didn't say a word as he followed him over to the elevators. Down in the basement Rolf led him to a seating area and disappeared into a vast sea of rolling stacks. Yesterday's *Dagbladet* dated Sunday, May 18, lay on the low table in front of him. Bergmann recognized the scene in the right column of the front page. The photo had been taken late in the evening on May 16. The white tent illuminated the dark forest, and two figures in white tech overalls stood outside. Bergmann glanced at the caption and "mystery in the woods" caught his eye. He put down the paper without turning to the story inside.

The archivist came back ten minutes later, more sullen than before, if that were possible.

"You have to read them here," he said, placing an old beige file folder on the table.

For a few minutes Bergmann simply sat there with his hand on top of the old folder. Then he removed the white string holding it together. Inside were three separate files, which he spread out on the table. The top one was from the combined Oslo and Aker Police Department, the second from the National Police, and the last one from the Oslo

Police Presidium. The stamp on the cover page revealed that the case had been closed on April 15, 1944, three months before Gustav Lande committed suicide.

He put all the folders back in their original order and opened the top one. The first document was the missing-persons report. It gave him a few answers, but unfortunately raised even more questions.

Police Officer Ragnar Dahl, Vinderen Police Station.

Cecilia Lande, Johanne Caspersen, and Agnes Margaretha Gerner were reported missing at 11:55 p.m. on September 28, 1942. All three individuals live at Tuengen Allé 10C. Reported by Gustav Lande of Knaben Molybdenum Mines, Inc., born: March 8, 1905, status: widower, residence: as above. Engaged to Agnes M. Gerner. Ms. Gerner has special permission from the Higher SS and Police Leader North to be on the street from 8:00 p.m. to 5:00 a.m. The housekeeper, Johanne Caspersen, does not and is therefore subject to the curfew.

So Gustav Lande was a widower, and neither of the women was Cecilia Lande's mother. And he was engaged to Agnes Gerner, not Johanne Caspersen. Bergmann felt relieved at having overcome the first hurdle on a path he knew would present many more. Gustav Lande's first wife, Cecilia's mother, was dead, and Agnes was his new fiancée. It was no more complicated than that. But it did nothing to change the fact that the child was dead.

The next document was a brief report from the following day, September 29, 1942.

A search was instigated around Lande's summer house at Rødtangen on the Hurum peninsula. According to Lande, who was on a business trip to Berlin and returned to Oslo

*late in the evening on September 28, Agnes G. was supposed
to help Johanne C. (Lande's housekeeper) close up the summer
house at Rødtangen for the winter on Sunday, September 27.
According to witnesses nobody was in the house that weekend.
Canvassing on September 29 at Rødtangen and interviews
with Lande's neighbors at Vinderen produced no further information. Lande's car, a 1939 black Mercedes-Benz 170V, was
not found. List of witnesses questioned is attached.*

Bergmann skimmed over the witness list, which consisted of the
names of only those who had been questioned during the canvassing
out in Rødtangen and about ten people who resided on Lande's street.

At the bottom of the file was a sheet of paper that had obviously
served as the basis for the investigation that took place the next day,
Wednesday, September 30, 1942. Bergmann carefully read through the
descriptions of the two women and child. Only one thing caught his
attention. Cecilia Lande, born: March 16, 1934, height: 4'1", blue eyes
and dark-blonde hair, had a congenital hip defect that "gave her a characteristic limping gait." Bergmann pictured the girl up in Nordmarka.
Maybe whoever had killed her knew that she wouldn't be able to run
away. Maybe she'd been forced to watch as Agnes and the housekeeper
were shot.

Next, he opened a worn light-blue folder containing paper of better quality. From the documents inside, he learned that the National
Police had investigated the case under orders from Sipo, the German
Security Police, dated September 30, 1942. The introductory report
stated that the National Police could not rule out the likelihood that
Lande's collaboration with Norway's pro-Nazi Reichskommissariat
Norwegen made his family a target for the Resistance movement's terrorist actions. On the previous Friday the Resistance had liquidated
one of Gustav Lande's most trusted men. The National Police also

mentioned that both his fiancée, Agnes Gerner, and the housekeeper, Johanne Caspersen, were active members of Vidkun Quisling's Nasjonal Samling, or NS, Norway's fascist National Unity Party. The next report stated that a number of presumed Resistance men had been brought in to the Nazis' provisional HQ at Møllergata 19 on October first and second. Two of them were later transferred to the Gestapo's HQ at Victoria Terrasse for interrogation by Sipo.

As Bergmann continued leafing through the folder, he came upon transcripts of the interrogations from Møllergata 19, but none from Victoria Terrasse. The transcripts seemed to be of no interest, apart from the fact that one of the alleged Resistance men had committed suicide by jumping from the fourth floor of the Møllergata police station. Gustav Lande's car had been found on Madserud Allé, nowhere near Nordmarka, on Thursday, October 1, 1942, but an examination of the car, the testimony of witnesses living on that street, and a search of the area all proved fruitless. The final document in the file indicated that the National Police had closed its own preliminary investigation into the case, citing the parallel investigation being conducted by the Oslo and Aker Police Department.

Bergmann said a silent prayer before he opened the third and final folder. It didn't help much. There was only a single sheet of paper indicating that the case was closed on April 15, 1944. It was signed by Detective Inspector G. Lid and stamped by the Oslo Police Presidium.

There were no photos in any of the folders. *I need to know what they looked like,* he thought. Why had Gustav Lande's car shown up on Madserud Allé? The three of them were killed an hour north in Nordmarka when they were thought to be on their way south to Hurum, and the car they had supposedly used had been found halfway between the two places in the neighborhood of Skøyen. Bergmann was probably as baffled as the detectives investigating during the war must have been.

He sat for half an hour copying information from the sections of the reports he thought were most relevant. He decided to drive to Rødtangen on the Hurum peninsula as soon as possible to get a sense for the summer house's surroundings. And photos. He had to find photos of them.

"Newspapers," he said when he returned the folder. "Have you got any?"

Rolf pointed at several evening papers lying on the counter.

Bergmann tapped his finger lightly on the file folder in front of him to indicate he meant archived newspapers.

"The National Library," Rolf said. "They close at seven."

Bergmann looked up at the white clock on the wall and decided to leave the National Library till the next day. He'd rather make it to handball warm-up on time, which started in half an hour.

Although the tempo of the warm-up run had been leisurely, Bergmann had to lie down on the floor of the gym when they were done. This gave the entire Girls 12 team a chance to tease him. He stared up at the ceiling and cursed his old childhood friend Erlend Dybdahl, who had talked him into signing up as assistant coach three years ago.

A year later Erlend got a plum manager's job with the Asian subsidiary of the IT firm he worked for, and moved to Singapore with his talented daughter and the rest of his family. The coaching situation at the club had deteriorated as a result, and Bergmann had had no choice but to promote himself to head coach. He had appointed the top man at the time, Arne Drabløs—whom Dybdahl had secretly nicknamed Hopeless—as assistant coach. But Hopeless did have one strong point. He was in damned great shape. So even though he could hardly tell a handball from a medicine ball, he played handball admirably. Over the years Bergmann and Erlend had played on teams together and finally ended up on junior varsity for Oppsal. Although Erlend was the big star, Tommy Bergmann was close behind.

Bergmann was big and tall, a rough-cut block of granite when he was in his prime, and well suited to clearing the field for the backs. He was so big that the goalies of the younger opposing teams would creep inside the goal net and shut their eyes whenever he was about to take a shot. Then he tore a ligament in his left knee during his military service, which was enough to make him give up handball, even after a successful operation. In any case he lacked Erlend's talent and would never have been more than a reserve on the A-team's bench. By that time he was so fed up with handball that he doubted he would ever pick up a ball again.

But as he lay on the floor of the Klemetsrud gym almost twenty years after he'd given up playing, he thanked his lucky stars for this unpaid job that filled his free time. It cleared his head three or four times a week and kept his body more or less in shape. Plus the sight of these girls, no matter whether they won or lost, made him believe the world was a good place in spite of everything.

"Come here," a girl's voice said above him. Tommy had put his arm over his face to rub the sweat out of his eyes. He took a couple of deep breaths and his pulse slowed to an acceptable rate. He looked up to see Sara smiling down at him as she held out her hand. The expression in her eyes reminded him of her mother, who was from the Maghreb. Algeria or Morocco, Bergmann guessed.

He took Sara's hand, a bit embarrassed that he almost felt like her father whenever she was nearby. When she had joined the team in the fall of last year, she had been one of the worst players, fluttering about like a baby bird. Bergmann had reached a low point last fall and winter, but he'd kept his spirits up by taking Sara under his wing and vowing to turn her into a better player. By now she had improved enough to score a goal once in a while. In addition, the brief conversations he had with her mother, insignificant as they were, had given him a reason to live.

"I thought you were supposed to be a good player," said Sara, smiling just the way her mother did.

"I am good," said Bergmann. "I'm just terribly out of shape. There's a difference."

"I'm sure," she said, pulling him up before she ran over to Arne Drabløs. He stood near one of the goals, fumbling with a ball net along with a couple of the girls. Bergmann drank a full bottle of water as he followed Sara with his eyes. Sometimes he thought that he ought to ask her whether her mother was single, just blurt it out in the gym: "I've never seen your father. Is your mother single or what?" In a weak moment he'd told some of the parents at the Easter Cup in Larvik that he'd just broken up with his longtime partner and had no plans for the Easter holiday. Only later did he recall that one of the girls' mothers knew Sara's mother well.

He took his whistle out of the bag and blew it to gather the team. He knew Erlend's training regimen by heart. It was not all that different from the regimen they'd trained under twenty, thirty years before. Shoulder warm-up, ball handling, feints, shooting practice combined with goalkeeper training, and finally position play. Drabløs took care of the last half hour of practice today, a sprint that was supposed to give the girls a competitive edge, something Bergmann was happy to skip.

As he watched the girls practicing position play, he thought about the three people who had met their maker in Nordmarka during the war. Not even the thought that Sara's mother might appear at any moment could blot out the images he had conjured of the way Cecilia Lande might have been killed. A shot struck the goal post, and two girls got into an argument. One of them had apparently tackled the other one while Bergmann wasn't looking. When he finished calming them down, he saw Sara's mother standing on the sideline with the father of one of the Pakistani girls on the team. Her thick black curls were pulled back with a big dark hair tie. The father said something that made her laugh, and Bergmann felt a twinge of jealousy. Yet a warmth spread through his body, the rotten feeling associated with his twelve-year relationship with Hege dissipating every time Sara's mother laughed or looked his way.

Ignoring the practice altogether, he moved closer to her. They exchanged a glance and a quick smile while the girls gathered up the balls and handed in their numbered jerseys to Drabløs. She continued talking to the Pakistani man and another father who had joined them. Something about school, it sounded like, or summer vacation. Bergmann sat down on the bench next to them and stared quite openly. If he liked her, he liked her, and that was all there was to it. She was wearing a white blouse, tight jeans, and a pair of flat leather sandals. It was a completely ordinary outfit, but one that still made him feel like a middle school kid for several minutes.

As he told the girls about what had worked well—and not so well—in their position practice today, he imagined Sara's mother without her feather-light white blouse. He pictured her thin, tan arms, and her fine hands stroking his chest. One of the girls asked him a question, something about an underarm shield, but he wasn't paying attention anymore, and the girls began to giggle. Finally he started to laugh too.

"Sorry, I'm kind of exhausted today. See you on Wednesday, girls. Arne will take over now."

Arne Drabløs launched into an overly enthusiastic pep talk about the hard work that awaited them. Bergmann checked his cell phone as he cast surreptitious glances at Sara and her mother. She ruffled her daughter's hair. Sara turned away with a resigned "Mamma . . ." before she changed out of her handball shoes and put on her jogging shoes. Then she took off after the other girls leaving the gym.

"I'm a little overprotective, right?" her mother said to Bergmann, hitching her large expensive-looking shoulder bag more securely onto her shoulder.

"I don't know about that," he said. "She's starting to show real confidence on the field."

"I'm glad." She raised her hands to her head and pulled out her hair tie. "You're very good with them."

They walked out of the gym together. A gust of wind swept across the sidewalk, blowing her hair in every direction.

"Oh my goodness," she said, laughing to herself. Bergmann looked on as she gathered her unruly curls back into the hair tie. He wished they could just stand there like that all evening. That she would keep smiling at him, her dark eyes flashing like mica, and that his relationship with Hege had never happened.

"So, time to fix dinner," she said, heading for the stairs that led up to the shopping center.

"Oh right, dinner . . ." he said almost to himself as he followed her. He might as well take that way to the parking lot.

"If you're stopping at the ICA supermarket, maybe I could get some cooking tips from you," she said when they reached the top of the stairs.

Bergmann began to laugh.

"I don't think you want to know what I have for dinner. Besides, I've already eaten. Two hot dogs at the Exxon station on Lambertseter."

"Is it that bad?" she asked, pausing in front of the entrance to the shopping center. She cocked her head to one side.

"Extra bad today," he said.

"My name is Hadja, by the way." She held out her hand to him. It was soft and warm.

"Tommy."

"I know," she said, smiling again. "I'll see you on Wednesday."

Don't go, he thought as she disappeared inside.

CHAPTER 15

Friday, June 1, 1945
The Stable
Östermalm Police District
Stockholm, Sweden

Detective Inspector Gösta Persson had had an intense headache all morning. Only now, after a long lunch, did it seem to be abating, slowly but surely. The only thing he'd been able to think about all day was the envelope containing Kaj Holt's presumed suicide note. His wife would receive it today or tomorrow, Persson was sure.

In less than an hour he wouldn't have to give it any more thought. By then he and his wife would be sitting in the lounge of their boat, sailing out of Blasieholm Quay, on their way to her family's summer house in the archipelago. Persson could hardly wait; a weekend out there would make everything okay. Absolutely everything. The images of Kaj Holt's head would be erased from his consciousness. The scent of Karen Eline Fredriksen's perfume would fade from his memory, along with her ice-blue eyes and deep-red lips. As would the thought of who had sent her over to tell him that Holt couldn't wait to take his own life. Nor would he have to give any more thought to the baby-faced guy who'd been in his office, the man who had threatened to drop his expensive elephant statue on the floor. All these thoughts would vanish out there on the island with his first cold morning dip, his wife on the pier waving, a cigarette in her hand, smiling at his childish antics in the water. No, he simply couldn't wait to be reborn out there among the islets and skerries, to be awakened by screeching gulls, the sunlight playing over the old linen curtains.

He was abruptly jolted out of his daydreams. He stared at the door. Wasn't that where the sound was coming from? He quickly lowered his feet off the teak desk.

"Come in," he said.

His secretary opened the door and took a step into his office. Then to his surprise she lowered her gaze. *Well,* Persson thought, *that might not be so strange.* He had specifically asked her not to disturb him before he was ready to leave for the day, and especially not to route any phone calls to him.

"Your wife is on the phone," the secretary said, looking at the floor.

Persson stifled his irritation. All right. She was a good person, his wife. They had never had children, but he couldn't blame her for that. And now they were both too old. But they still had each other.

"Fine," he said, looking at his secretary, who continued staring at the floor. It seemed odd for her to be standing like that.

But it didn't matter. He tried to force himself to stop worrying about the envelope. It wasn't important. Nordenstam would never find it. If Holt's wife did anything with it, he'd have to deal with the conse-quences, but he was man enough to take responsibility for his actions. He had to be.

"Put the call through," Persson told her. Her face lit up, as though with relief. "And leave the door open," he added as she was about to close it. He was feeling magnanimous now that the week was nearly over. It had been a terrible week, to be honest.

"A bunch of blouses were delivered here . . . Couldn't you have surprised me for once?" his wife said on the phone. "And pick up something good for dinner, will you? I called the butcher at Östermalm Market. He knows what to give you."

"Östermalm Market," Persson repeated. "All right, dear. So Willy Ohlson knows what to give me?" He laughed with relief into the phone.

He tore off his overcoat in the middle of the sidewalk and draped it over his arm as he turned the corner onto Östermalmstorg an hour later. Persson felt great, better than he could remember feeling in a long time. The sun even looked like it was breaking through the clouds.

The market square was swarming with people—old and young and worn-out office workers like himself. A new produce shipment must have just come in. He started to cross the teeming square, hardly noticing when someone bumped into him from behind. Then a violent pain exploded in his back and chest, and he realized that his head was about to slam onto the granite paving stones, that the crowds behind him were inadvertently going to trample him, that the warm wetness in his suit was his own blood, that his life would be over in a few seconds because everything inside him was falling out of a crater on the left side of his back.

By the time he hit the ground, he was already dead. The people behind him stumbled over his body. Somebody began screaming loudly in the sun-filled square, as if that might bring Detective Inspector Gösta Persson back to life.

CHAPTER 16

Tuesday, May 20, 2003
National Library
Oslo, Norway

As the tram accelerated through the intersection of Drammensveien and Frederiks Gate, Tommy Bergmann lost his balance for a second, deep in thought about Hadja. *Hadja,* he murmured to himself. He replayed the scene in his mind's eye, the two of them standing outside the entrance to the Mortensrud Shopping Center. Why hadn't he taken advantage of the opportunity? *What opportunity?* he thought. He was imagining things. Assuming she was single and even interested in him. What was he actually after? He needed help. Hadn't Bent, his old colleague from the uniformed police, told him just that? "You're going to need help before you can move on, Tommy," he'd said.

He pushed it all aside—Hadja, her laughter, her eyes, and her hair, Hege, Bent, and everything else, all that old shit—and turned his thoughts to the case. That was why he was heading to the National Library, not to lose himself in daydreams. He had a job to do: to find out what had happened to that little girl and those two women during the war. Why hadn't Cecilia been shot in the head like the others? The tram braked abruptly and he lost his balance again, as if he'd never been on a tram in his life.

He was surprised at the library's impressive newspaper collection and how easy it was to navigate through the material. Only ten minutes after entering the building, he was sitting at one of the microfilm screens in the reading room, scrolling through all the newspapers published during the war. The September 30, 1942, issue of the *Aftenposten* provided the faces he was looking for. The front page featured a two-column article about the three missing females.

The first picture was of Gustav Lande's fiancée. Agnes was a very beautiful young woman with classic features and her dark hair done like a pinup model's. Her eyebrows were slightly arched, and her eyelashes looked so full that they hardly needed mascara. "Agnes Gerner, twenty-four years old," the caption said.

Next to it was a photo of Cecilia Lande, Gustav Lande's daughter. She had a lovely open expression, her smile directed at the professional photographer but probably intended for whoever was standing behind him. She had a heart-shaped face and two dark braids with a big white bow at the end of each one. He could see a dimple in her left cheek, but none on the right. She was missing one of her canine teeth. If Agnes Gerner looked like a woman that men would kill for, Cecilia Lande looked like a child for whom anyone would take a bullet.

To the right of little Cecilia was the housekeeper, Johanne Caspersen. Bergmann tried to enlarge the page but couldn't. The picture was of such poor quality that she would have been difficult to recognize in real life. She had a rather plain face, birdlike and so pale as to appear almost transparent. Or maybe it was just the low resolution of the image that was tricking him into thinking that.

Bergmann read through the text a couple of times, in his characteristic halting way. He studied Cecilia's features and thought of her skull with the gaping black eye sockets. *Who did this to you?* he wondered. *And were they the ones who parked the car on Madserud Allé?*

He sat there for a while, staring at her picture without focusing. Then he began to skim a few other articles in the paper—ads for rationed soap, announcements from National Police headquarters, tributes to Norwegian soldiers at the front.

He scrolled farther down to the next page. At first he read the article without understanding what he was reading. But something in the introduction struck him as familiar, reminding him of something he'd recently seen.

> *The National Police are conducting an all-out investigation into the assassination on September 25 of Torfinn Rolborg, a research director at Knaben Molybdenum Mines, Inc. Still being sought is a blonde woman in her twenties or thirties, thought to have blue eyes although she was wearing glasses, with a beauty mark on her left upper lip. There is a reward of 25,000 kroner for information leading to the conviction of the perpetrator.*

Twenty-five thousand kroner must have been a huge sum of money during the war, Bergmann thought.

Then he remembered.

Knaben Molybdenum Mines, Inc. was owned by Gustav Lande.

First one of his managers was killed, then a few days later his small family was summarily executed.

CHAPTER 17

Friday, May 23, 2003
Police Headquarters
Oslo, Norway

It was an unusually warm Friday morning, and Tommy Bergmann still had no answer to why someone had murdered Gustav Lande's fiancée, daughter, and maid in September 1942. But he no longer needed to find an answer—not to why or more importantly *who* had killed them. The minimal knowledge he had acquired about molybdenum was no longer of any use. As he sat in the weekly status meeting of the Violent and Sex Crimes Division, Bergmann felt that all his work in the past week had been wasted. Fredrik Reuter had just told the group what Bergmann had known since early that morning, namely that a decades-old triple homicide could not be given priority, and that Kripo would now be taking over the investigation—which all those present knew was only a euphemism for shelving the case altogether.

Bergmann felt depressed, but that might just have been because Hadja hadn't shown up for her daughter's practice on Wednesday. He'd stood outside the gym for several minutes watching Sara and the other girls heading home, in the hope that she would appear. He had even sat down on the steps to the shopping center and waited for the next subway train. When she wasn't on that one either, he waited for a couple of buses, and then for the next train. At last he had asked himself what the hell he was doing and gone home. *Forget about her,* he'd told himself as he stood in the shower. *Forget all about Hadja.*

He stared at the second hand on the wall clock. He hated to let things go, and he could swear that there was a connection between the three murders in Nordmarka and the death of the research director at the molybdenum company. But it didn't matter now. This was 2003, after all, and according to Fredrik Reuter the state had plenty of things to spend its precious time on other than three old skeletons found buried in the forest. And no one could really blame him for thinking that way. The Violent and Sex Crimes Division consisted of about sixty investigators—or at least that was the official figure that appeared in every publication about the division's manpower. If he subtracted the five or six vacancies the division had to allow for because the police were constantly underfunded, there were probably fifty-five detectives at any one time. Of these about ten were usually out sick. And when he subtracted another fifteen detectives who only worked on sex-crime cases—including rape, incest, sexual abuse of minors, and all the other deviant activities that human sexuality could imagine—that brought the total down to thirty detectives. These select few, no more than in an elementary school class, had to handle all the city's murders, attempted murders, and incidents that fell under the rather meaningless rubric of "aggravated assault."

Reuter paced restlessly back and forth in front of the screen. Words were coming out of his mouth, but Bergmann was unable to grasp what he was talking about. Even the images on the screen showing the murder of an Ethiopian woman in a studio apartment four weeks ago meant nothing to him. He glanced at the faces of those sitting at the table. Sometimes he felt like he had no colleagues at all. It was every man for himself, with nobody to lean on. Maybe that was the way he wanted it. That was the way the job had to be done.

After a few minutes he picked up yesterday's *Dagbladet*, which lay on top of the case folder he'd brought with him. Not much had happened over the Independence Day holiday, apart from the routine drunkenness and violence, and it seemed that everyone who'd been knocked down or beaten up had survived with no serious injuries. So the skeletal remains discovered in the forest of Nordmarka were the big story. "Mystery in the Woods" senior crime reporter Frank Krokhol had dubbed the case, unless some rookie reporter on the crime desk had come up with that headline.

Krokhol and his colleagues had managed to squeeze four whole pages out of the case. One of the photos showed Abrahamsen and the Kripo techs scratching their heads as they looked down into a hole in the ground. The next two pages were full of pictures of the three missing females: Agnes Gerner, Cecilia Lande, and Johanne Caspersen. Krokhol had clearly been smart enough to think along the same lines as Bergmann, even without phoning him as he usually did. For the umpteenth time Bergmann studied the three faces in the photos that had appeared in the *Aftenposten* of September 30, 1942. At the bottom of the page was an appeal to anyone who knew anything about the victims or the case in general to call in or send old Krokhol an e-mail.

Good luck, Bergmann thought, casting a glance at Reuter, who was in the midst of a thunderous oration claiming that they would find the devil who did this while pointing at the image of the woman who had been stabbed. If they weren't even capable of tracking down a murderer who had struck only four weeks ago, how in the world would they manage to find a perpetrator from more than sixty years back?

Bergmann knew it would be almost impossible to untangle such an old case. Usually, he would have put it behind him and focused on making inroads on the pile he had waiting in his inbox. But he couldn't stop thinking about the little girl and wondering how she had died. There was nothing puzzling about how the two grown women had been killed. Agnes Gerner had been shot directly in the forehead at point-blank range, while Johanne Caspersen looked to have been shot from the side, directly in the temple. Agnes had been buried with the projectile inside her head, a 7.65mm Browning, and Johanne had an exit hole on the left side of her skull, at the same height as what was assumed to be the entry wound. The bullet—also a 7.65mm Browning—had been found a few feet behind the grave.

But that's all just conjecture, in the best-case scenario, Bergmann thought. He looked up at Reuter, pretending to follow the discussion in the room, but as the meeting continued, he skimmed through the final report he had written to accompany the evidence they were sending to Kripo. He perused the text, which was clinical and bureaucratic. Three females murdered more than sixty years ago. Back then they were three human beings; now they were nothing more than names, and almost no one in Norway knew anything about them. Bergmann had managed to get hold of one of the sixty-five people in the country named Gerner, who was able to tell him a little about Agnes. But it hadn't been much help. He only learned that Agnes Gerner had belonged to his branch of the family, but that her family had moved to England in the late twenties. All of them except the father, who'd died young, had been Nazis. The rest of the family seldom—or rather, never—mentioned them. Agnes and her sister had moved back to Norway before the war, but they had been ostracized, both because they were Nazis and because Agnes's father had an ongoing dispute with other family members. The old man considered the whole thing a tragedy, but he said that was how things go when you pick the wrong side. Agnes's sister had married a German and might be living down in Oslo if she was still alive. The mother died in England just after the war.

Frank Krokhol and his friends in the press had succeeded in digging up a few people from Hadeland province who were said to be related to Johanne Caspersen, but they seemed mainly interested in getting their names in the paper. Krokhol had also found out that Gustav Lande had hanged himself one July day in 1944, leaving a huge inheritance to his brother. The brother died twenty years later, and his children refused to talk to the press. They had referred Bergmann to a lawyer the one time he'd phoned them. *No doubt they wanted nothing to do with the subject,* he thought.

The room exploded with the sound of laughter and scraping chairs, and Bergmann looked up in confusion. He couldn't figure out what was going on, as if he weren't on the same planet as the thirty other people in the room. Somebody opened a window and a summer breeze blew in. Outside the air was shimmering in a cloudless sky. He thought this was the kind of day everyone dreamed about all winter long. One of those days that Cecilia Lande would never experience again.

Bergmann looked down at the newspaper and concentrated on the photo from the missing-persons article in the *Aftenposten* of September 30, 1942. If he ever had a child, he pictured she'd be like Cecilia. With the same braids, the same dimple on her left cheek, the same fine eyebrows.

That evening, Hadja didn't show up at practice. Nor did Sara. Bergmann was usually in a good mood at practice, but he was morose and uncommunicative that night. The girls noticed and didn't play well. It was a warm, summerlike Friday evening, and none of them really wanted to be there. He probably should have sent them down to the beach to go swimming, but instead he decided to wrap up early so Drabløs could take them on a run. As they disappeared around the corner, Bergmann stood outside wondering where Sara and Hadja lived. He dismissed the thought and hurried off to his car.

Back home at his apartment he turned on the record player and lay down on the floor of the living room. When side one of his old Joni Mitchell record was over, he listened to the sounds coming from outdoors. A cricket bat hit a ball out on the blacktop between the apartment buildings. Shouts in a mixture of Norwegian and Punjabi echoed off the walls.

Bergmann's thoughts had turned from Hadja and her curly hair in the wind outside the gym to Hege. He had run into her by chance on the street in late April, and they had acted like they hardly knew each other. Her huge belly made her look like a completely different person, but her skin had burned against his cheek, just as it had the first time she touched him.

He repeated her words just as she had spoken them, with something he interpreted as warmth in her voice, as if she still liked him and always would.

"How are you, anyway?"

CHAPTER 18

Whitsunday, June 8, 2003
Sofiemyr Gym
Oppegård
Oslo, Norway

Some bright handball geniuses in Oslo had come up with the idea of holding a local minitournament for the teams that weren't going to travel south to Tønsberg for the big Whitsun Cup. For Tommy Bergmann the decision had come as a relief. Now he wouldn't have to wonder what he was going to do over the three-day weekend. There were limits to how many shifts he could take at Kripo without seeming socially dysfunctional.

The team's best player, Isabelle, was from an affluent family, and she and her parents would be heading out to their newly built cabin in Kragerø for the weekend. She usually saved the team on their worst days, and today looked like it was going to be one of those days. Without Isabelle the other girls seemed like they'd given up before even getting going. Only ten minutes into their first match against Kolbotn's second-string team, they'd let in seven goals and only scored one themselves. When Kolbotn scored an eighth goal, Bergmann went to the officials and asked for a timeout.

He patted the goalie, Aatifa, on the back and said that she was doing well. Then he gathered the girls in a circle on the sideline.

"Have you decided to go on vacation early, girls?"

"They're just so good," said Sara, squirting water from a sports bottle into her mouth. Privately Bergmann ranked her as the second best on the team. Sara held his gaze for a second and gave him a quick wink, as though she knew what he thought about her mother.

"They're not that good. We're just not playing well. You have to move those legs, girls, and get your arms up. Don't just stand there watching . . . Aatifa isn't getting any help at all. And remember, we've beaten these girls before."

"But without Isabelle—" began one of the girls.

"That's life," said Bergmann. "You can't count on anyone else to do the job. Today you've got to do it yourselves, okay?"

He decided to attach Sara to Kolbotn's best player, which worked fine, in a way. Before halftime, Kolbotn scored only two more times, while Martine slammed in four goals and made an assist on the fifth.

Just before the referee blew his whistle to start the second half, Bergmann saw a familiar figure appear in the end-zone bleachers. Hadja pushed her sunglasses up on top of her head and searched for some parents she knew in the bleachers below. When she waved at him, he realized how much he'd missed the sight of her. He had to restrain himself from breaking into a smile. She found a seat near the bottom of the bleachers behind Kolbotn's goal next to Martine's mother, who was one of the parents Bergmann had confided in about his bachelor status during the Easter Cup last spring.

The Klemetsrud team managed to keep up with Kolbotn—more or less—during the second half. But Bergmann was paying almost more attention to what was going on behind Kolbotn's goal than the game. The match ended in a respectable loss, and he gave the girls a half-hour break. The parents in the stands were replaced by the parents of two other teams. Bergmann discreetly kept an eye out for Hadja, but she was lost in the crowd somewhere. He went out the side door of the gym to enjoy the sunshine for a few minutes. He considered going over to the main entrance, where a large group of people were likely soaking up the sun between matches, but instead walked the opposite way, around the back of the gym. He sat down on the ground and leaned against the wall, trying to clear his mind.

When he was halfway through his cigarette, he heard footsteps approaching.

"So this is where you're hiding."

Hadja came up to him with an almost apologetic smile and removed her sunglasses before sitting down next to him.

"Can I bum one off of you? I just can't manage to quit altogether."

He studied her fingers as she pulled a cigarette out of the pack. Her hand seemed to be attached a little crooked to her forearm, and her nails looked white against her glowing olive skin. He imagined that she left her hand on his a little longer than necessary when he lit her cigarette.

"Did you get your hot dogs for lunch already?" she asked, fidgeting with her sunglasses. "At the kiosk?" She nodded toward the entrance to the gym.

Bergmann couldn't help but laugh.

"I only eat lunch at gas stations," he said.

"Oh, I forgot," she said, taking a drag.

"Have you been on vacation? You're so tan."

Hadja smiled. "Yes, I've been in Morocco. I got home yesterday. Sara's been staying with her aunt . . . She probably missed some practices."

She smiled again, and Bergmann thought that as long as Hadja kept smiling at him like that, Sara could miss as many sessions as she liked.

"Visiting family there?"

"In a way," she said. Her face took on a serious expression. "Yes, you could probably say that . . . Papa . . ." She stopped and seemed to ponder what to say as she took another drag. "It wasn't very worthwhile, to tell the truth . . . It's a long story. I probably shouldn't have gone at all."

"All right—" Bergmann said as his cell phone rang. He stood up slowly and took it out of the pocket of his shorts. He stared at the familiar number of the dispatch switchboard for a few seconds.

"Bad news?" Hadja asked.

"Probably," he said. Their eyes locked for a moment as he raised the phone to his ear.

"This is Karlsvik, in Dispatch," said the voice on the other end of the line.

Something in Karlsvik's tone made Bergmann look at Hadja.

"Yes?"

"Well, Monsen called and asked me . . ." He paused. "A guy apparently got knocked off up on Dr. Holms Vei," he said. "Among other things. Apparently it's damned . . ."

"Damned what?"

"Damned awful."

"So, who was it?"

"Monsen from Kripo thinks it's a . . . a Carl Oscar Krogh."

"*A* Carl Oscar Krogh?" Bergmann said, thinking, *All hell is going to break loose. And Leif fucking Monsen is tossing the grenade right in my lap.*

"Well, I've never heard of the guy, but Monsen . . ." said Karlsvik. He let the sentence die out.

You idiot, Bergmann thought.

"Anyway. It's a madhouse up there. The housekeeper found the old man. Reuter's on his way up from Strömstad, down in Sweden, and he asked Monsen—"

"The housekeeper?" Bergmann broke in. He looked back at Hadja.

Karlsvik cleared his throat. Then he said something about a stabbing.

At first Bergmann thought he'd misunderstood.

"At least fifty stab wounds?" he repeated quietly.

"His eyes are gone," said Karlsvik.

Bergmann shut his own eyes.

"I've got to go," he said to Hadja.

She frowned.

"Is it *that* bad?" she said.

"You'll have to pretend you didn't hear anything I said until the news hits the papers."

He held out the pack of cigarettes to her. She shook her head.

"That's enough for today," she said, getting up. Bergmann lit himself another, took a deep drag, and exhaled hard through his nose.

"Can you find Drabløs for me?" he asked, looking at the clock. "Tell him I have to go back to work, and he has to take charge of the last two games. He can call me if he needs to, but it would have to be really important."

Hadja nodded.

"It was so nice to see you again," she said.

CHAPTER 19

Thursday, August 24, 1939
Seven Oaks Court
Kent, Great Britain

If anyone had asked her how many shades of green there were in the world, she would have told them to go to Westerham Ponds and try to count them. Agnes Gerner turned around one last time to gaze down the path lined with willow trees. She could see the water glittering amid the foliage in the distance. Bess was waiting for her at the top of the path. She knew what she would see up there, a vast infinity of green beauty. The rolling landscape would stretch before them, glowing with oxeye daisies and Scottish bluebells and all sorts of butterflies, and far off on the horizon they'd be able to glimpse Seven Oaks Court, the red-brick manor house where she had spent so much of the last six months.

"Beautiful, isn't it?" she heard someone say behind her. Christopher Bratchard had walked a few steps ahead of her on the way back. A gentleman never walked behind a lady in skirts going up a stairway or a slope of any kind.

Agnes turned to face him. He was staring at her again, as if searching for something—possibly a sign that his feelings were reciprocated.

Feelings that an agent handler was forbidden to have. Especially a married one.

It had been his suggestion that they spend the day out in God's country, as he called it, on this final day of their last week at Seven Oaks Court. All her instincts had warned her against being out here alone with him, several miles from anyone else. But what could she do? After all, she had placed her life in this man's hands.

Very few people knew what had become of her in recent months, and even fewer what she was doing here. Some days even she hardly knew. Less than a year ago it had appeared to be a conscious decision, but it could just as easily be considered a coincidence.

She had attended a reception at the Norwegian embassy for an occasion she could no longer recall, and during the social hour she expressed an honest observation about her own mother. After her Norwegian father's death her mother had married a British lord who was threatened with bankruptcy. This man, whom she hated intensely, was a leading supporter of the detestable fascist Oswald Mosley, a fact that distressed her half-British heart. Even worse, her sister in Oslo seemed to have adopted the same outlook as her new stepfather and her mother.

That evening Agnes had met an attaché from the British embassy in Oslo, who insisted on being addressed as Richard. Later that night, she and her girlfriend, whose father held a high-level post as a diplomat at the embassy, ended up in a newly opened French restaurant in Mayfair with the attaché and some of his friends from Magdalen College in Oxford. She fell hard for him. When he insisted on accompanying her home in a cab after she had imbibed far too much champagne, she wouldn't have been surprised if they'd ended up in bed together. But instead of making a pass, he had merely kissed her hand as they stood on the stoop. When she, slightly bewildered, finally managed to get the key in the door, he cleared his throat and asked if they could meet the next day.

Christopher Bratchard now held out his arm to her, even though Agnes had no problem walking on the neatly groomed path. She was rescued by Bess, who emerged from the surrounding woods, racing at full speed with her tongue hanging out of her mouth. She cut between them and ran up the path toward Seven Oaks Court. Bratchard smiled and dropped his arm. *How I love that dog,* Agnes thought. The only thing she didn't understand was why Christopher had insisted that she bring Bess along for the three weeks down here. Her mother had bought an English setter puppy for her right after her father died. It was practically the only good thing she could say about her.

"If only life could be like this forever," Christopher said. He set down his gray field sack, took out a handkerchief from his tweed jacket, and wiped his forehead. Even in this heat he refused to remove his hat.

Agnes mumbled something in reply, keeping her eye on Bess, who was waiting at the top of the hill. Up there, she recalled, they would pass through a grove of oak trees before they emerged into the meadow. From there it would be less than a half hour back to Seven Oaks Court.

Just before they reached the hilltop, Bratchard fortunately began cross-checking her to make sure she remembered where and when she was supposed to meet her contact in Oslo.

"He'll recognize you," said Bratchard. It sounded as if he wanted to add, "Don't you worry your pretty little head about it."

When they reached the top of the hill, they found Bess lying in the shade of a tree. Agnes called to her, wondering how the two of them would get along back home in Oslo. Was Oslo her home? No place was really home anymore.

Bess came over to them, wagging her tail as she circled them. Bratchard stopped again and pulled something out of his field sack. The folding spade that hung off the sack rapped on the gravel path. When he looked up, she'd expected Bratchard to give her that usual half-flirtatious smile of his, but his expression was serious. His chiseled features only further emphasized that this was not meant to be amusing.

Agnes looked down at his hand, and he opened it.

It was a little red ball, a dog's toy.

They stood there looking at each other.

"Here, Bess!" Bratchard called, kneeling down. The dog came running, tail wagging.

What is he doing? Agnes wondered.

Bratchard stood up and threw the ball as far as he could down the path toward the grove, and the dog took off after it.

"Come on," said Bratchard without looking at Agnes.

They'd only walked a few steps when the dog came racing back to Bratchard with the ball in her mouth and dropped it in front of him. He picked it up and threw it into the grove once more. They kept walking. Agnes didn't mind. It was only a whim, nothing more. Seven Oaks Court would soon come into view, and she would go straight to her room and rest until dinner. Tomorrow she would be sitting on the train back to London.

Just before they entered the grove, where the dog was hunting for the ball, Agnes saw Christopher take something else out of his field sack.

The sun seemed to vanish from the sky when she saw what he was holding. A big Webley revolver.

"When we enter the grove," he said, nodding straight ahead, "you have to shoot the dog."

Agnes opened her mouth, but nothing came out. The ground seemed to sway beneath her.

"I don't think I . . ." she said softly.

Bratchard didn't say a word. He held out the revolver to her. She had shot three pigs in her life, only to prove that she could, but . . . the man was insane.

"If you don't do it, I will," he said.

They looked at each other until the dog came back. The only thought Agnes had was that she couldn't start crying.

As Bratchard held out his left hand to take the ball from the dog, he shoved the revolver into Agnes's right hand. The knurled grip felt cold, and her wrist almost gave way with the weight of the heavy steel. A Webley would stop a charging bull dead in its tracks in a split second. Agnes turned to look at the skinny English setter chasing the ball that Bratchard had just thrown.

Their eyes met. His lips were pressed tight, and the shadow of his hat brim had turned his face gray.

"It's too late, Agnes. You can't leave the service."

Agnes bit the inside of her cheek. *He's going to kill me,* she thought. Once more the dog came back.

She felt her legs go weak under her as she bent down to give Bess one last hug. She'd thought she would have her for ten or twelve years, until she got married and had kids. A happy life, as happy as she could be.

Bess looked at her as though expecting a reward, then looked at Bratchard. Agnes patted her one last time. Seconds later the dog took off into the grove.

Agnes followed. Fine rays of sunlight sliced through the dark-green foliage. Bess was rooting around for the ball in some ferns.

"Sit," said Bratchard, standing right behind her about five yards from the dog. Agnes murmured a silent prayer.

Bess sat and looked up at Agnes with her head tilted to one side. *Papa, oh Papa,* she thought, *please forgive me.*

She took a step forward, then one more. Bess remained still, but she had cocked her head even more, as if to say, "What are you doing?" Agnes was nauseated by the smell of the moist earth. She heard the sound of rotten leaves from last winter under her shoes. Nothing else, not even birdsong.

The dog's narrow head was in her sights. The revolver no longer felt heavy, and her hand was steady. A thought ran through her mind. *I must be sick. Really sick.*

"Now!" Bratchard whispered. "Don't think. You must *never* think. Then you'll find out how long a second is."

The boom of the Webley unleashed chaos in the treetops. What sounded like thousands of birds shrieked in fright overhead and they took flight all at once, fleeing the hell below.

Half of the setter's long, handsome head was smashed, and a torrent of blood—bright red like that of the pigs'—gushed out from what was left of its mouth. Bess stared at her with her undamaged eye, then dropped to the ground.

Agnes lowered the revolver.

"Give her one more," Bratchard said in a low voice. "She's still alive."

Agnes took a step forward. Her own mouth felt like it was full of blood, and a metallic taste ran down her throat, into her stomach, sickening her. She gulped once, twice. Then she raised the revolver and shot away the rest of the dog's head. *Don't cry, don't ever cry,* she urged herself. Never cry. That was what her mother had taught her when she was a girl: "You must never cry when someone can see you, Agnes, never."

Bratchard took the revolver from her hand. He nodded to himself, watching her intently.

"You're crazy," she said softly, closing her eyes. But no tears ran down her cheek.

He whispered something, but she didn't hear him. She tilted her head back and stared up through the branches above them. All the birds were gone; perhaps they would never come back.

"What did you say?" she whispered.

His hand was suddenly heavy on her shoulder. He squeezed hard, as if he wanted to crush her with his bare hand.

"It'll happen in just a few weeks. Maybe only a matter of days."

"And then?" Agnes asked.

"When Hitler crosses the border into Poland, that will be it. If Norway is ever going to have any honor again, we must declare war on Germany."

Agnes said nothing. The blood in her mouth now had a sweet taste that made her think of candy. That blood was a good thing.

"And then only the crazy people will survive what lies ahead," he told her.

"Let me go," she said. "Let me go, you bastard."

Bratchard took her face in his hands and turned her head toward the dog's ruined body.

"Only the insane," he said and let her go.

She felt him shove something into her left hand. The spade.

"Now bury her."

CHAPTER 20

Whitsunday, June 8, 2003
Carl Oscar Krogh's Residence
Dr. Holms Vei
Oslo, Norway

Tommy Bergmann tried to regain his balance by planting his legs a little farther apart and gripping his cell phone a little tighter. With stiff fingers he pressed the speed-dial number for Dispatch.

"I need you two to go block off the street," he said to the two uniforms who had followed him like children, their faces pale. Neither of them had ever seen anything like this before. But Bergmann had, and it may have been that recollection that had knocked the air out of him.

"Now!" Bergmann said. "And maintain radio silence."

The marching boots tramped back through the living room. He didn't bother yelling at them about destroying the crime scene. They'd already stomped around like elephants in there, totally ignoring regulations.

Bergmann stepped around the deceased and went out on the terrace where the dog lay. It looked like it was staring at him with its brown eyes. He followed the tether across the yard with his gaze. A white butterfly fluttered over by the fence. He watched it until it vanished from sight.

He felt sick to his stomach as he reentered the room. It had been years since the last time, but that made no difference. He felt the blood drain from his head and cursed himself for not getting enough sleep last night. The young housekeeper stood in the middle of the Persian carpet, crying in her hands. She'd been standing like that ever since he'd entered the house. The knees of her jeans were bloody. She must have fallen somehow.

In the middle of the floor lay real-estate mogul and former minister of trade Carl Oscar Krogh. His throat was sliced open and his head pulled back at an almost right angle to his skinny old body. His light-blue tennis shirt was dark with blood except for a small area at the bottom. The smell of urine and excrement filled the room. His face was completely chopped up as if a bird had pecked at him. His eyes were a gelatinous mass mixed with blood and the remains of what must have been his eyelids. Bergmann could only trust the housekeeper's statement that it was actually Carl Oscar Krogh.

But the worst part was the man's chest. Krogh must have been stabbed multiple times in and around the heart. The left side of his rib cage was a mass of bloody pulp. A surprisingly small knife lay on the floor beside Krogh's left hand.

Bergmann managed to make it to the guest toilet in the hall. As he bent over the toilet bowl, he thought of what Hadja had said as he left the Sofiemyr gym: "It was so nice to see you again." If he'd only been smart enough to turn off his phone on his day off.

When he was finished vomiting he noticed that the white washstand was pink. He was holding on to the faucet, not even thinking that he might have destroyed evidence. He looked straight into the mirror. Exactly the way the perp must have done only a few minutes before. Less than ten, maybe only five. Maybe the housekeeper had even crossed paths with him on her way up here. The hand towel next to the washstand had spots of newly dried blood. There was blood on the walls, even the impression of a hand. The killer must have leaned against the wall. Maybe even he had gotten dizzy from the sight of all that blood. Maybe in a moment of clarity he had realized the insanity of what he had done.

Bergmann heard a sound behind him. In the mirror he saw the door slowly open.

A pale, scared face appeared.

The housekeeper screamed.

She was clearly just as surprised to see Bergmann as he was at the sight of her.

Thank God, he thought.

Her face was contorted with fright and she kept on screaming. She pointed at the bloody handprints on the white wall.

Then she stopped abruptly. Almost as if someone had slashed her throat too.

"The knife," she said so softly he could hardly hear her. "You have to look at the knife."

CHAPTER 21

Sunday, September 3, 1939
King's Cross Station
London, Great Britain

Agnes Gerner's final thought as the train began to move was that she would always hate the man who stood motionless on the platform.

Christopher Bratchard stared vacantly ahead in the white light coming through the glass ceiling. Maybe he was embarrassed that he had shown up here at ten minutes to midnight. Maybe his expression was no different than that of everyone around him. Embittered and sad about what was now inevitable. How right he had been on that last day in Kent. There was no turning back. Britain could no longer retreat.

Now may God bless you all. She whispered the words from Chamberlain's radio speech that morning to herself, meeting Bratchard's gaze. A second later his face was gone, replaced by strangers waving handkerchiefs, some of whom were running along the platform, waving and crying.

Agnes gave a start when the sliding door of the compartment opened. The elderly conductor gave her a quick smile and heaved a suitcase onto the overhead rack. A woman about her age nodded briefly to the men in the compartment and sat down across from her. After exchanging some polite chitchat about how warm the weather was today, Agnes went back to staring out the window to avoid getting into a real conversation. *I hate you, Christopher Bratchard,* she thought, recalling Bess in her mind's eye, the shattered head, the open skull, the eye that still stared at her as though the dog couldn't understand how she could do such a thing.

She could barely make out the vaulted roof over the departure platform at King's Cross. He was still somewhere inside, and she wondered how long his aftershave would sting her cheek. She thought of his words in her ear. His bad breath, which he tried to camouflage with mouthwash. His unabashed lust for her. Even Christopher, her own control officer. On his own initiative he'd accompanied her to the door of the train, as if he were her fiancé. As if he would whisper the words "I'll wait for you" in her ear and run along with the train like so many of the others, or at least walk, wave, do something, anything at all. But no, he had stood motionless and stared into space with his hands in the pockets of his heavy tweed jacket, even though the weather was much too warm for it. The most violent, sultry storms had thundered down upon them all weekend, as if the Lord Himself were casting His wrath upon the world and Chamberlain in particular.

All six people in the compartment, four men and two women, looked grim, as though they'd just been informed that they'd contracted some fatal disease. Two of the men were middle aged, much older than those who were in danger of being drafted to the front. They spoke together in low tones about Chamberlain's speech earlier that day. The other two men, about Agnes's age, stared vacantly into space. Agnes noticed how exhausted she was. But never in her life would she be able to fall asleep in these seats, and the sleeping compartment farther back in the train had sold out long ago. She would sleep when she boarded the ferry tomorrow morning. She had booked a berth on the last ferry to Norway, the *MS Leda*, from Port of Tyne to Bergen.

She had never been to Bergen before. Although she was Norwegian, she had hardly been outside Oslo. She closed her eyes, trying to concentrate on the metallic clacking of the wheels over the tracks, the *click-clack, click-clack* sound, the steady rocking of her body.

When she opened her eyes, she saw that they were already deep in the countryside. Had she really slept? Only an occasional light passed by, like a tracer bullet over a battlefield, revealing a beautiful rolling landscape outside the windows.

She fixed her gaze on the young woman facing her, who cast her eyes down and began brushing something off her skirt. Her dark curls hid half her face. She seemed to be afraid that someone would recognize her.

Agnes went back to looking out the window after she found her pack of cigarettes in her handbag. The train began slowing down, and she reasoned that they must be approaching a town because there were more and more lights. Only then, as if she were waking from a dream, did Agnes hear what the men in the compartment were saying. "It's war," they said. "Now we're really at war."

That's what Bratchard meant, Agnes thought, letting the man next to her light her cigarette. If war came to Norway, she would have to be prepared to die. She would probably never return to England. The sound of the air brakes whined beneath the carriage.

She'd been trained for this. She knew that the job she'd volunteered for could mean the end for her. Still, for several fumbling seconds, that realization felt surprising. That was why Bratchard had pulled her close and forced her into a hug, whispering in her ear as a last farewell, "May God have mercy on your soul."

CHAPTER 22

Whitsunday, June 8, 2003
Carl Oscar Krogh's Residence
Dr. Holms Vei
Oslo, Norway

Tommy Bergmann tried to avoid looking at Carl Oscar Krogh for too long. He was lying more or less midway between two big Persian carpets. The pool of blood had reached one of them, and a little puddle of deep red had started to soak into the rug. A wheeled walker stood over by the sofa, and a cane lay on the floor between the open terrace door and Krogh's body. Bergmann tried to imagine the course of events. The perp had obviously gone around the house and come in through the terrace door, and Krogh had clearly attempted to flee in the other direction, toward the front door or the telephone in the hall. According to what Bergmann had read about Carl Oscar Krogh, he'd been a real hardnose in his day, but both the walker and the cane proved that he'd become physically feeble.

"Was the door locked?" he asked the housekeeper, who was shuffling along beside him. She too looked as though all the blood had drained from her body.

"Yes, it was," she said. "I think he must have tried to get to the chest of drawers, to press the security alarm. Or maybe to his cell phone, which he keeps in the same drawer."

"Wasn't he supposed to wear the alarm around his neck?" Bergmann asked.

A tear ran down her cheek.

"He said he didn't need it. He said it was for old people, not an eighty-five-year-old like himself. And he only carried his cell phone around for a couple of hours in the evening. He accepted the walker to stop his son and daughter from nagging, as he said. But he never used it, even though his hip is . . . had gotten quite frail."

"But how spry was he really?" Bergmann asked, though he could guess the answer.

"He got around all right. But he spent all his energy on the dog," she said. "It wore him out. A man of his age shouldn't have a setter. But he still went out walking with the dog . . . Although I was the one who usually took him out."

"I understand," said Bergmann as he knelt down next to Krogh.

"Did you make these marks in the blood?"

The housekeeper nodded, though the round bloodstains on her knees made the question superfluous.

"What happened?"

"I . . . just couldn't stand up any longer."

Bergmann nodded and leaned over to look at the knife, which lay in the blood next to Krogh.

A swastika. Even though the medium-sized knife was covered in blood, the swastika in the middle of the shaft was unmistakable. He glanced at the old man's body.

Who could have done it? Bergmann wondered. A Nazi? A neo-Nazi?

The swastika formed the center of a diamond he knew he had seen somewhere before. He racked his memory for a few seconds, then remembered, relieved that his brain still seemed to be functioning in this slaughterhouse.

"*Hitlerjugend,*" he muttered to himself with a nod. "The Hitler Youth." He'd seen a couple of those knives confiscated from neo-Nazis many years ago.

In the distance he heard a car door slam. Then another. Familiar voices were approaching—Monsen, Abrahamsen.

"Hitler?" said the housekeeper softly.

"You didn't see this," he said, turning to look at her. She was staring into space.

"Booties, put 'em on," Abrahamsen said disapprovingly from over by the door.

"That's my vomit in the crapper down the hall," Bergmann said.

He expected some snide remark about vomiting from Abrahamsen, but he didn't say a word.

Monsen's eyes widened. Bergmann had never seen him respond like that before. Even Abrahamsen appeared to be almost paralyzed for a moment.

"Fredrik's on his way up from the cabin," Monsen said quietly.

"Damn," said Abrahamsen. "The old man."

"The gate was open," said the housekeeper.

Monsen and Bergmann looked at each other.

"What do you mean?" Monsen asked. Bergmann could hear that for once he'd been caught off balance.

"The gate up by the road, it's never open. But today it was," the woman said.

"Nobody touch that gate," Abrahamsen said, turning on his heel. "Don't *anyone* touch that gate." He pulled one of his rolling flight cases out the front door, which slammed after him in the draft from the open terrace door.

"Find a blanket to put over him," Bergmann told Monsen, as if he were the chief of Kripo and not vice versa.

Three-quarters of an hour later the team leader told the uniforms to run up and down the street with questionnaires. They were short of investigators. Whitsunday was a particularly bad time to be murdered; everybody knew that. Only Easter was worse. Not only were there hardly any people at work down at police headquarters, it was also hard to get hold of any witnesses. Especially in this part of town, high up on Holmenkollen ridge, where almost everyone who could crawl or walk had taken off for their cabins as soon as school let out.

Bergmann was in the master bedroom on the third floor when Fredrik Reuter came walking across the forecourt. He waved to Reuter, then turned his attention to a dusty photograph of Krogh holding hands with his wife.

Out in the hall he took off his blue latex gloves as he took one last look at the rooms on that floor, which consisted of an office, four bedrooms, and a bathroom. Everything was painstakingly neat, and Bergmann was fairly sure that almost nothing had been touched since Krogh's wife had died the year before. It looked as though Krogh himself had hardly been up there. Maybe he'd never made it up the stairs.

Most likely the perp hadn't set foot on the third floor either. A large room lined with green wallpaper and heavy hardwood bookshelves that had probably been Krogh's office looked completely untouched.

No, Bergmann thought, *Carl Oscar Krogh was not killed by someone who was out for money.* This was not a burglar who had been surprised to find anyone at home. And he'd bet that Krogh was not the victim of a random madman. No, old Krogh had been subjected to such extreme violence that they were probably dealing with a killer who had a strong personal motive.

Down in the living room, Reuter leaned against the wall, watching Abrahamsen and his team examine the crime scene. One of the assistants looked through the photos on the camera while talking to another tech in a low voice.

Reuter didn't turn around when Bergmann entered the room.

"Holy shit," he said to himself. Then to Abrahamsen: "He really looks terrible. Get Forensics to patch him up for the relatives. They have to do a clean job. Got that, Georg?"

Abrahamsen was standing in the terrace doorway looking out at the view.

"Did you hear what I said, Georg?"

"It won't be easy," he said without turning around.

"This isn't good," said Monsen as he came back in. "This is definitely not good." He sounded like a boy who had smashed his mother's porcelain plates.

"Check whether there are any lunatics on the loose at the moment," said Reuter, looking around for Bergmann. His face was red as a lobster from too much sun over the holiday. A shiny circle on top of his head looked to have been particularly exposed. He looked downright exhausted in his worn sandals, old T-shirt, and shorts, which had surely fit better ten years ago.

"Have you got a smoke?" he asked, reaching out to Bergmann. He looked skeptically at Bergmann's exercise outfit, then began waving his fingers. "I've got to have a smoke, Tommy." His cell phone rang in his pants pocket. Reuter let the phone ring till it stopped.

Abrahamsen could be heard speaking into a voice recorder. "The head has been almost separated from the body, apparently with a knife. The murder must have taken place with great force, so the perpetrator was probably male." He held up the knife and went on. "The murder weapon is covered with coagulated blood, tissue remnants, and bone splinters on both the blade and shaft. From what I can see, the words

Blut und Ehre are engraved horizontally on the blade in cursive script." He angled it toward the light from the window. "Vertically R2 M M7/2 1937. Solingen . . ."

"Solingen?" Bergmann asked.

"Solingen," Abrahamsen replied. "Who doesn't have a Solingen knife in his kitchen drawer?"

"Shut up," said Reuter from out on the terrace. "Just shut up, all right?"

Bergmann couldn't recall ever having seen him so pale. He shook his head as he fiddled with his phone.

"The Hitler Youth, right?" Bergmann said at last.

Abrahamsen nodded, noticeably reticent after Reuter's outburst.

"Put it in a bag," said Reuter as he came back in from the terrace. He put the cell phone back in his shorts. Then he raised his voice. "How many of you have seen this?"

"Only the two of us, and Bent, the housekeeper, the officer who arrived first, and the other one, his partner," Bergmann said.

"Okay," said Reuter. "All of you! Everyone in here."

Five minutes later, the living room was full of people, in violation of every regulation.

Reuter, whose face had taken on a deep-red flush, said, "Everything, absolutely everything that occurs within these four walls today and in the days to come, must remain within these walls or well inside police headquarters. Those of you who haven't seen the murder weapon—don't even ask. Those of you who *have* seen it, speak only to me about it, or if necessary with each other in my presence. Is that understood?"

Bergmann figured that everyone in the room felt the same way he did. This case was already a total mess. And Detective Inspector Fredrik Reuter was on the verge of losing control.

After everyone had left the room, Reuter stood there holding the plastic bag with the knife.

"Come here," he said to Bergmann. He pointed at the shaft. Then he glanced over at Carl Oscar Krogh. The blood from his slashed throat had begun to turn black. "Covered in prints," said Reuter. "What does that tell you?"

"That the perp's a real nutcase," said Bergmann.

"Or he doesn't give a damn if he's caught," said Reuter.

CHAPTER 23

Tuesday, June 10, 2003
Police Headquarters
Oslo, Norway

Tommy Bergmann leafed through the newspaper. *Dagbladet* had devoted ten whole pages to Krogh, which he thought was inevitable. On Sunday afternoon some idiot in one of the patrol cars had mentioned Krogh's name over the police radio, and then the whole media circus had begun. He hadn't expected anything less. But this wasn't going to turn out well. Maybe he shouldn't blame people for flying off the handle. And if they'd known what he and a dozen other detectives and uniforms knew, there would have been no chance of saving the situation. Krogh was a former trade minister and a prominent figure in the majority party after the war. Bergmann read in his obituary, "One of the nation builders of Norway has been brutally and senselessly taken from us."

He looked up when Fredrik Reuter raised his voice. Everyone in the room turned to look in the same direction. Reuter paused for dramatic effect as a photo of Krogh's body at the crime scene appeared on the screen behind him.

"The boss is the only one who will speak to the press. Not a word from the rest of us."

"Only Papa," said Halgeir Sørvaag, making a note to himself. "That's perfectly fine with me."

"I'll be taking charge of the investigation," said Reuter. "Halgeir's and Tommy's teams will join forces for this one."

Sørvaag heaved a big sigh. He and Bergmann held equal positions as team leaders, but Sørvaag was more ambitious than Bergmann, who had never really understood why he had been named a team leader in the first place. He worked best alone, or with one other person, if need be. He now earned more money than he had before, but he spent too much time supervising four other people—people he didn't always get along with. The fact that Reuter was taking charge of this case was a breach of all organizational protocols and would result in the worst possible leadership within the police force. But Bergmann had seen this happen before. The chief of the Criminal Division simply needed to show that he was a man of action. Although everyone knew that an investigation always suffered under such decisions, it played well in the media. Unlike Sørvaag, Bergmann actually felt slightly relieved by the fact that he wouldn't be in charge of this case. It would give him the freedom he craved. Twenty-four hours had already been pretty much wasted because Krogh had met his maker on Whitsunday. Only now, almost forty-eight hours later, had they managed to gather a full staff. And potential witnesses and those who knew the victim had only just returned from their country homes and trips abroad.

A new photo of Krogh appeared on the screen. It was from a newspaper interview conducted only four weeks ago in connection with a VE Day commemoration taking place somewhere in town May 8. Bergmann saw that it had been taken from the terrace where he himself had stood only two days before. Reuter had added a few bullet points to the image. "A little background information about Krogh for those who'd been born after 1975," he'd explained. Reuter would probably also feel compelled to give them a lecture on the Second World War, describing who the villains and heroes were, and how they were connected. That was something Reuter had taught Bergmann when he came over from the uniformed police. Without villains there would be no heroes. Apparently it was as simple as that.

"Any thoughts?" Reuter asked the room. "Everything is of interest. There are no stupid questions." He squeezed the bridge of his nose and briefly closed his eyes in a way that made Bergmann think he'd prefer not to open them again until the day was over.

"The preliminary autopsy report," Sørvaag said as he leaned across the table and held out a file folder. He grinned, briefly showing his crooked teeth. "I'll never understand what the hell is so interesting about a person's last meal or when he ate it, considering that his head was chopped off," he said.

Reuter didn't bother contradicting him. He merely held out his right hand in a peremptory manner.

"We need to find out who butchered Carl Oscar Krogh on Whitsunday," said Sørvaag, "and the only thing Forensics seems to care about is what was in the guy's stomach. Have any of you ever solved a homicide based on the fact that the poor devil had eggs and bacon a couple of hours before he was killed?"

Sørvaag dropped the folder on the table.

"Why don't we try for a more constructive approach." Reuter's voice suggested that he was getting annoyed. If Sørvaag kept this up, he might kiss the whole Krogh case good-bye.

"There has to be a connection," said Bergmann. "We haven't found anything else related to Krogh. No disputes, no debts, not a fucking thing."

"Connection?" said Reuter, rubbing his face, which could have been described as boyish if not for the fine lines around his eyes. "What sort of connection?" He glared at his soggy baguette and reluctantly took a bite.

"Two weeks ago, we found the skeletons of two women and a child up in the woods—"

"What are you getting at?" asked Reuter, waving his hand at Bergmann.

"And two weeks later, Krogh is killed—by someone who must hate him so intensely that he gouges out the old man's eyes, hacks his chest to pieces, and practically decapitates him. I think the perp is somehow related to Agnes, Johanne, or Cecilia. Someone with a Hitler Youth knife."

"Okay. That's a start. But how, damn it?" said Reuter.

"Yes, what's the motive for killing Krogh?" said a newly hired whippersnapper from Sørvaag's team. Bergmann couldn't recall his name, but he was growing increasingly annoyed with his tendency to ask smartass questions.

Sørvaag raised his hand, wanting to attract even more attention than usual.

"What if the perp is a Nazi?" he said.

"There aren't any Nazis," said Reuter.

"A neo-Nazi who bought a Hitler Youth knife on the Internet," said Sørvaag.

"Forget it," said Bergmann. "Even if some crazy neo-Nazi hated Krogh because he killed Nazis during the war, most of them today would rather direct their anger at foreigners. Don't you agree?"

"How old does someone have to be to kill another person?" said Reuter.

Sørvaag grinned.

"What are you talking about?"

"Just think about it," said Reuter. "Those three individuals up in Nordmarka were most likely liquidated during the war, right? What if Krogh knew who killed them, and the murderer were still alive?"

"And now he's killed Krogh?"

"Improbable but still possible," said Bergmann.

"It might not be as crazy as it sounds." Reuter raised his coffee cup toward Sørvaag, as though awaiting a response. Sørvaag frowned. Reuter continued. "Well, if Krogh lived to be eighty-plus years old, then whoever killed those three people could still be alive. Someone of Krogh's own age who was naturally strong and still in good health could have killed him."

"But why now?" said Bergmann, directing the query more to himself than to his colleagues.

"Maybe Krogh had called up the guy," said Reuter. "Maybe he threatened him after the skeletons were found."

"It's possible," said Sørvaag.

Reuter ignored him and turned to Bergmann.

"Tommy, I want you to put together a bio of the old man and give it to me first thing in the morning. The rest of you need to do some good, old-fashioned detective work," he said. He pulled up one last image, which outlined specific tasks for each team member. Then he clapped his hands, as he usually did, like some sort of amateur handball coach.

Bergmann muttered as he stared at the preliminary profile of the perp that Reuter had requested from Kripo: "MO suggests psychosis, rage, excessive violence."

"This isn't just some coincidence," he said, looking up at Reuter. "I think you may be onto something."

"Get me Krogh's phone records from the last three weeks. I want every single person he called to be thoroughly checked out," Reuter demanded.

What if the killer is back? thought Bergmann. *What if he really is back?*

CHAPTER 24

Tuesday, June 10, 2003
Bygdøy
Oslo, Norway

Back when Tommy Bergmann was attending the police academy, he thought the term "tactical investigation" sounded impressive. Sixteen years later, he wasn't so convinced. In reality it was simply a matter of making basic observations, at least on paper. Reuter had taught him that a tactical investigation usually involved no more than two circles of suspects. It was rare for someone to be killed by a complete stranger. So the starting point in cases involving an unknown perpetrator and absolutely zero witnesses was often simply a question of identifying all the individuals who'd had any sort of relationship with the victim, specifically close family members and friends. If the killer—most often a man—couldn't be found among that circle, then it was necessary to draw up a new one comprised of distant relatives, colleagues, and acquaintances.

For an eighty-five-year-old man, there weren't many people to include in either circle. With the exception of children, grandchildren, or great-grandchildren, most of them were dead.

Carl Oscar Krogh had two children. His son lived in the United States, and Bergmann had talked to him twice. He had at least been able to confirm what he'd suspected. Krogh had no friends left, or at least none that the son knew about. And Krogh's wife had died a year ago.

He was now talking to the daughter, Bente Bull-Krogh, but she hadn't been able to tell him much more than he already knew. The conversation wasn't going well. She had stopped to cry and stare off into space several times. Now he was sitting on her terrace, waiting for her to collect herself enough to go on speaking. He'd called her on Sunday afternoon, but hadn't been able to reach her until close to midnight. In addition to this enormous house in Bygdøy and a couple of other properties in Norway, she and her husband owned a vineyard and horse ranch outside Ronda, Spain, where she spent long periods every year. It was no doubt a beautiful place, but the cellular coverage down there was clearly nothing to brag about.

Bergmann shifted his gaze from the woman to the terrace door, where the Filipino maid was standing. She motioned discreetly toward the glass on the teak table in front of Bergmann. He shook his head. He'd had enough iced tea.

"Please forgive me," said Bente. "It's just so . . . unbelievable."

Normally Bergmann didn't have much sympathy for people who were born with a silver spoon in their mouths. But right now he felt genuinely sorry for Bente Bull-Krogh. He didn't envy anyone having to identify a father who had been so horribly mutilated.

"No apologies necessary," he said.

Bente looked at him as she wiped her mascara-streaked cheeks, which made her look older than she actually was. She fumbled for her designer sunglasses on the table.

They'd already gone over everything, but Bergmann was not a man given to carelessness. An eighty-five-year-old was bound to have secrets, dark rooms that no one but he might know about, or at least spaces that he didn't want others to find.

"So he never had anyone else?" asked Bergmann. "Your father?"

"What do you mean?" she asked in a low voice.

"I know this may seem inappropriate right now, but are you sure that he never had a relationship with another woman?"

Bente put on her sunglasses and turned her face away.

"What does that have to do with anything?"

"The murder . . ." said Bergmann. "It's the sort of killing we often see in cases of extreme jealousy."

She shook her head.

"Good Lord. Father was eighty-five. To be honest—"

"He wasn't always eighty-five," said Bergmann. "And he seemed to be quite a handsome man in his day. Or am I mistaken?"

A wan smile appeared on Bente's face. It quickly vanished, and then she started crying again.

Bergmann waited. He studied the house and the grounds, trying to guess how much the place was worth. Every time he found himself in such places, he felt an almost insurmountable chasm between himself and the people sitting across from him. It was probably normal to cough up fifteen to twenty million kroner for a house in this part of town. But where he came from—in Tveita, one of the city's biggest housing projects—a thousand kroner was still a lot of money. He'd had the only bedroom in his family's apartment. He was proud of where he came from and thought that the people who lived there were generally happy. But at moments like this, he realized it was people like Bente Bull-Krogh and her husband who held all the cards in Norway and that the wealth was ending up in fewer and fewer hands.

"It's strange you should mention it," said Bente. "No, I'm sure it's nothing . . ." Again she gave him a sad smile. Then she uttered a laugh that she tried to hide behind her hand.

"What do you mean?" asked Bergmann.

"You asked whether my father ever had anyone else."

Bergmann sat up straight.

"I remember now that my mother once thought he was having an affair. Father was up in the mountains, hunting for grouse, and . . . the phone rang, and my mother answered, but no one said anything. She could just hear somebody breathing."

"What did she think?" he asked quietly. "Did she feel threatened?"

Bente shook her head.

"No. I'm not sure. Mother simply hung up. I wasn't home that night, but in the morning she told me at breakfast that she thought a woman had tried to call my father. She asked me if I thought Father was the type of man to have a mistress."

"A woman?" asked Bergmann.

"It was just a feeling that Mother had. The two of us were very close. Oh God. This would have destroyed her, to have Father killed this way . . ."

Bente took off her sunglasses and buried her face in her hands.

Bergmann looked down at his notes. "An affair?" he wrote in big letters, followed by "his mistress's husband?"

"Do you remember when this happened?"

"It was during exam week of my senior year in high school," she replied at once. This was clearly something she'd thought about over the years.

"So that must have been in . . . 1964?" said Bergmann. He recalled that she'd been born in December of 1945.

She shook her head.

"No, 1963. I graduated the year before."

"So your mother thought it was a woman on the phone?"

"She said she could tell it was a woman by the way she was breathing. That's what I remember her saying. It's something another woman would know."

"Okay," said Bergmann.

"But what does this have to do with my father? I mean, this isn't the basis of your investigation, is it?"

"No," he said. "But did this happen more than once?"

"No."

Bente took a deep breath as she tried to compose herself. She quickly put her sunglasses back on.

"I think you're lying," said Bergmann.

"About what?"

"About the phone calls."

Bente looked away. "It went on for years," she said. Her voice was so low that it was almost drowned out by the motorboats on the fjord.

"Always at the same time? A woman, most likely, who phoned your home at the same time for several years?"

"Always when he was away hunting grouse."

"And when did he do that?"

"In September," said Bente.

September, thought Bergmann. *The two women and the little girl were killed in September.*

"Always on the same day?"

"What are you getting at? No, no, I don't remember . . ."

"Was it in early or late September?"

She sighed in resignation. "I think it was late in the month."

"So how long did this go on?"

"Several years, I think. Father stopped going off to hunt grouse. But it was never discussed."

"I see," said Bergmann.

"Mother didn't want to talk about it. As I said . . . She thought he had another woman, somebody who might have been a little crazy or jealous, or something. I didn't want to think about it. So, why would this be important?"

"I'm afraid I can't say," replied Bergmann. The truth was that he had no concrete idea why it might be significant. Except for the time of year, which could just be coincidental. He nonetheless drew a circle around the word "September" with his ballpoint pen.

"So do you have any leads in the investigation, or . . ." She didn't finish her sentence.

"I can tell you in confidence that we are fairly certain his death has something to do with the war, though I wouldn't rule out other possibilities. Do you understand?"

"Yes, I understand," she said.

"Do you recall hearing about the three skeletons that were found in Nordmarka? Three females, the youngest of whom was only a child, who were killed in 1942. Did you read about it in the papers?"

Bente nodded. She turned to look out at the fjord, as if seeking solace from the shimmering blue water.

"Did your father ever mention anything about this to you? About them being killed during the war?"

She shook her head and pushed her sunglasses back in place.

"Why are you asking me about that?" she said. "Does it have something to do with Father?"

"I don't know," said Bergmann. "But he was a very prominent figure in the Resistance, and he may have known what happened back then."

"I see."

"Do you know when they were killed?" he asked.

Bente shook her head.

"In September."

She stared out at the fjord from behind her sunglasses for what seemed like a long time.

"I think the person who knows the most about Father and the war is that man at the university, you know . . ."

"Moberg," said Bergmann. "Torgeir Moberg."

She nodded.

"He probably knows more about Father than my brother or I or even my mother ever knew."

"Which of the old Resistance fighters was he most involved with?"

"I think only one of them is still alive. I know that Father visited him in the nursing home recently. I remember him talking about it . . ." Again Bente buried her face in her hands.

Bingo, thought Bergmann.

"Do you recall his name?"

She lowered her hands.

"Kolstad. Marius Kolstad."

"Do you know which nursing home?"

Bente reached for her glass. Bergmann stared at the golden liquid and her red lips.

"Somewhere on the east side of town."

She set down her glass.

"Okay," he said. "Where exactly on the east side?"

He studied the gold chain around her wrist, thinking that the woman sitting across from him had probably never set foot on the east side.

"I don't remember. Is it important? Do you think Kolstad might know something?"

"I don't know. But it's worth finding out. Drabantby or farther east?"

Bente sighed heavily.

"I don't . . . I'm not very familiar with that part of town, but it wasn't downtown, I'm positive about that."

Bergmann closed his eyes for a moment, trying to recall the hospitals he knew. But it didn't really matter. At least he had a name. It wouldn't be hard to find out where Marius Kolstad lived.

"Langerud?" suggested Bergmann.

"That's a handball team," said Bente. "I remember that from the old days, from the seventies."

"Oppsal?" said Bergmann. "Does he live in Oppsal?"

"Yes," she said in a low voice. "That's what I remember Father saying. Oppsal."

Bergmann glanced at his watch. He had the overwhelming and unmistakable feeling that he'd found a lead he should follow.

This was exactly what he'd been hoping for.

CHAPTER 25

Wednesday, September 6, 1939
Majorstua
Oslo, Norway

The sound of the ship's planks being ripped apart sliced through her head, growing so loud that soon she could hear nothing else. Before Agnes Gerner could even scream, she was floating in the water beneath the massive ship, her long white nightgown swirling around her body. She watched as the ship slowly disappeared into the distance, even though the huge propeller had stopped. Below she heard a muted thudding. Agnes turned over in the water, noting that she had barely enough oxygen in her lungs, and looked down into a swarm of tube-shaped U-boats gliding along the sea bottom, illuminated by a glaring light from above. To her left she saw a person sinking down through the water. It was the Jewish girl from the cabin. As she slid naked toward the bottom, Agnes tried to grab the girl's chalk-white hand, but she couldn't even lift her own arm. The girl's black hair danced in the water until she disappeared.

Agnes opened her eyes. She saw only a white ceiling above her, no water. The room told her nothing. She had no idea where in the world she was.

For several seconds she drifted in and out of the dream, swimming down through the water, but finding nothing. Then she awoke to the sound of children playing nearby. After a few minutes she got up and closed the bedroom door. The alarm clock on the white-painted night-stand showed that she had less than an hour until her appointment at the hair salon.

She walked through the apartment, which was as unfamiliar to her as her own mother. The bathroom floor felt cold, so she placed a towel under her feet before brushing her shoulder-length hair. *I could definitely use a haircut,* she thought and smiled. Back in the bedroom she took out one of the cyanide capsules from the false bottom in her suitcase, wrapped it in toilet paper, and then stuck it in her purse. It seemed improbable that she'd ever have to use it, so improbable that she didn't even consider it a real possibility. As long as Norway remained neutral, she probably wouldn't have to risk her life for this job. Yet she nonetheless chose to follow her own rule—or rather, Christopher Bratchard's rule—to carry a capsule with her wherever she went. *He must have indoctrinated me very thoroughly,* she thought.

At the tram stop she thought once more about how absurd it all seemed. An appointment had been made in her name for twelve o'clock. "All right," she murmured quietly.

At precisely 11:55 she opened the door of Helge K. Moen's hair salon. It was quite a large salon for such a small city. It would have been better suited to London than Oslo. She went over to the reception desk to give her name. While the man seated behind the desk—whom she assumed was Moen—checked the appointment book, Agnes discreetly surveyed the premises. Six chairs were lined up in front of a big mirror, half of which were occupied. There were seven people in the salon. Four customers, counting herself, and three hairdressers. She supposed that behind the desk was a back area with an office and a bathroom, as well as a door leading to a stairwell. Places with only one exit were dicey. She didn't need anyone in the service to tell her that.

Agnes sat down in one of the chairs next to the windows facing the passageway and leafed through a copy of *Aftenposten*. Occasionally she looked up to study the hairdressers as they glided around the chairs. They wore white smocks that made them look more like doctors or nurses than people who curled and cut hair.

"I don't think I've seen you here before, have I, miss?" said the middle-aged man who now ushered her to a chair in the middle of the row.

"Gerner," she said. "Agnes Gerner."

The man nodded and shook her hand. "Helge K. Moen."

His eyes radiated a calm that made her feel like she was just an ordinary customer.

"Gerner?" he said.

"My father emigrated to England ten years ago."

Moen nodded but didn't comment. He began cutting her hair without asking how she might like it. He was going a little shorter than she'd intended, although she actually hadn't given it much thought.

Agnes studied the salon in the mirror, which covered the entire wall, though there wasn't much to see aside from the empty chairs and people rushing past outside. A few minutes later, two ladies who appeared to be about her age came in, sat down, and crossed their legs to wait for their appointments. They seemed to have all the time in the world. And all the money they could ever want. After Moen had been working for ten minutes or so, Agnes took a magazine from the table in front of the mirror and began looking at photos of people from Paris. Parisians seemed to live in a completely different world, a world filled with joy and beauty, where no one wished to hurt anyone else.

When Moen was done, a young assistant appeared with a standing hair dryer and curlers in a cart on wheels. As he began setting her hair, Agnes studied a photo of the movie star Gary Cooper in the magazine she was holding on her lap, which was now scattered with snips of her hair.

She suddenly froze, fixing her gaze on Gary Cooper's strained expression in the black-and-white photo. Her fingers gripped the magazine. The assistant paused with a curler in each hand, uncertain what was going on.

She raised her eyes and looked in the mirror. And there on her right she saw what had caused her to react. She must have let down her guard during the past few minutes, because she'd stopped paying attention to who came and went. As the assistant continued putting curlers in her hair, Agnes fixed her gaze on the man seated among the women. He was reading *Aftenposten*, his hat resting on one knee, ignoring Agnes and everyone else around him.

What on earth is he doing here? thought Agnes. *This is a hair salon for women.* As the man leafed through the newspaper, he ran his hand over his black hair, which was combed back from his face. He was slightly older than her, with a receding hairline. Agnes tried to assume a calm expression, though she knew she wasn't successful.

"All right now," said the assistant, positioning the standing hair dryer over her head. Abruptly it began droning so loudly in her ears that she could barely concentrate. The man reading the newspaper got up and looked right at Agnes in the mirror. She felt almost naked as she sat there with her hair in curlers and the big dryer over her head. The man's expression didn't change. He merely took his coat from the rack and nodded to Moen sitting behind the counter. As he opened the door, he put on his charcoal-gray hat.

Agnes felt the blood rise to her cheeks as she watched the man walk off down the passageway. Then he was gone. She slipped her hand out from under the black salon cape. How long was this going to take?

"Excuse me," she said, grabbing the assistant's arm. "I have to leave."

He stared at her, uncomprehending.

Five minutes later she was finally out of the chair. Moen escorted her to the reception counter, wrote out a receipt, tore off her part, and placed it in an oblong white envelope made from good quality paper.

"Here you are, miss. We look forward to seeing you again soon."

His broad face seemed hardly able to contain his delight. He gave her a wink, but managed not to smile.

Agnes found herself frowning. She didn't like her hairdo, and the smell of hairspray was going to make her faint if she didn't get some fresh air at once.

"See you next time," she murmured, reluctantly accepting the envelope.

It was liberating to step outside. The air in the passageway still held a hint of summer. As she walked off in the same direction the man had gone, she felt Moen watching her. Where had he gone? A small crowd was bustling about the nearby square, and she stopped to survey the people, trams, and cabs at the intersection. There were lots of men wearing hats, and Agnes kept thinking she saw the man from the salon.

But he wasn't there.

She pulled the brim of her hat lower to shade her face from the sun.

"Ms. Gerner," a man's voice said right behind her.

She turned around.

"I just wanted to see how you reacted," the man from the salon said, holding a pack of Craven A cigarettes out to her.

She shook her head.

As they stood there, staring at each other, Agnes waited for him to say something more. The man wore a serious, closed expression, as if he would never in the world reveal even the smallest secret about himself or anyone close to him. He was not handsome, but there was a gentle, conciliatory look to his face.

"Holt," he said. "Kaj Holt." He raised his hat and then held out a powerful-looking hand with stubby fingers.

Agnes didn't feel the need to introduce herself as they shook hands. He already knew her name.

"Christopher recommends you highly." Holt lit a cigarette.

"Christopher?" she couldn't help saying. An image of Bess's head, half shot off, flashed through her mind, and she felt Bratchard's aftershave stinging her cheek.

"Magdalen College, Oxford," said Holt. "That's where we met. But that was a long time ago."

"Oh, Magdalen," she said. "Half the service seems to have met each other there."

"Are you hungry?"

Kaj Holt had already stepped out into the street to flag down a cab.

A short while later, Agnes found herself seated at the Grand Café, devouring two open-faced sandwiches. How many years had it been since she had last been here? She could hardly remember. Ten or eleven, maybe more. As Holt talked, she cast a glance at the nearby Parliament building and Eidsvolls Plass. *I was a child the last time I was here,* she thought. *And my parents were still married.* For a moment she felt once again like the carefree ten-year-old girl she had once been. She heard her father's laughter echoing in the room. That was how he laughed when business was good. At such times, nothing in the world could sour his mood.

"But why there?" she asked, looking at Holt. He blew out a match and offered her the flat red packet of cigarettes. Although she declined again, she liked him much better now than when he'd offered her a cigarette an hour ago.

"Helge is a friend."

"A hair salon?" she said, more sarcastically than she'd intended.

Holt gave her an almost imperceptible smile, as if she were a child.

"Give me the receipt," he said, holding out his hand. Reluctantly she handed over the envelope.

Holt opened it and took out the receipt.

"Helge's is going to be one of your dead drops," he said in a low voice, holding the envelope between his thumb and index finger. "Once a week you'll go there to have your hair curled or cut or whatever it is you women do. For now, your appointment will be every Wednesday. If I want to contact you, my message to you will be with the receipt. All the hairdressers escort their customers to the reception desk for payment. The receipt is always placed in an open envelope, like this one. Helge will always be your hairdresser. Do you understand? If you ever go to the salon and Helge isn't there, cancel the appointment at once. Okay?"

Agnes nodded hesitantly.

"Helge is one of us, my dear," Holt whispered, leaning forward. Agnes could barely hear him in the hubbub of the crowded room. He placed his hand on hers and gave it a squeeze. "Come on. We have an appointment at two o'clock."

A few minutes later, Agnes sat down on a sofa in a third-floor office just around the corner from the Grand. As she stirred her tea without letting the spoon touch the china cup, she listened to the strange Englishman who sat behind the massive desk in front of her. He seemed to be repeating much of what Kaj Holt had just said—perhaps they had agreed beforehand what to tell her.

"Christopher Bratchard speaks very highly of you, Ms. Gerner." Archibald Lafton gave her a suitably discreet smile and loosened his tie. His shiny pate gleamed with sweat as he bent over his desk. Agnes cast a quick glance at Holt, who was sitting in a chair near the window next to another Englishman. She'd been ushered briskly through the reception area, which looked as if it belonged to an ordinary import firm with its advertising posters for cotton products and spinning machines and a young secretary who didn't look as if she'd harm a fly. More offices lined the corridor, indicating that Holt may have been telling the truth when he told her that Dominion Textile was a legitimate company. However, the boss, Archibald Lafton, was also head of the British intelligence service here in Oslo.

"The Germans are already here," said Lafton. "They've been here since last autumn. Here in town, and in Bergen, Haugesund, and Narvik as well. They arrive as fish merchants. They run import firms and act as trade attachés at the embassy. A few of our own have also been recruited—and it happened on British soil."

He picked up a cigar cutter from his desk and cut a slender cigar, studying it intently as he did so, as if it were something the Abwehr had smuggled into his office.

"Really?" said Agnes.

"One is a friend of Christopher's, by the way. But that's classified information, my dear. You didn't hear it from me, at any rate. It's too painful for the top brass to talk about. My point is that they're a pack of sly devils, those Germans."

Lafton stuck the unlit cigar in his mouth and leaned across the desk.

"They're like foxes, Ms. Gerner," he said, his voice subdued. "They don't yet have a large presence here in Oslo, not enough to put the British firms in town under surveillance, hardly even enough to keep an eye on the embassy. No, right now they're working on the Norwegian authorities. But in a few months' time, there will be more of them. They're like foxes, and the fox is a wily hunter. It can even play dead to lure its prey closer. And poor Christopher had the shock of his life when we sank our claws into his friend. But you never heard me say that. Never."

A pause ensued. Holt was staring into space. Maybe he knew about Christopher's friend. Maybe he didn't. Was that why Christopher's mood had gotten progressively worse? Was he about to be drawn into the trap himself? Regardless, Agnes had not come to Oslo to listen to Lafton's animal analogies.

"What sort of assignment are you planning for me?"

Lafton lit a match and set the flame to the end of his cigar. He puffed on it a few times, his expression impassive, as if no one else were in the room. Agnes felt Holt looking at her and she turned to meet his gaze.

"You'll be given your orders by Kaj and his subordinates. We like to use Norwegians who have a soft spot in their hearts for the British Empire. I'm sure you've realized that. But let me say this: given your appearance, there will be no lack of assignments for you, Ms. Gerner."

"What did he mean by that?" Agnes asked Holt when they were back out on the street.

"You probably won't see Lafton again. Only me and a few others. So don't worry about it. It's a sign of trust, you see. Lafton wanted to meet you personally. He invited you to his office because you come with the best references from London. If he says things you don't like . . . well, you'll just have to put up with it. In my opinion he takes too many risks and talks a little too much. He shouldn't have invited us to his office at all. I've hardly ever been there myself. I don't like it, but what can I do? He's my boss."

They rounded the corner of the Grand and walked past the window table where they'd dined a short time ago. Agnes paused in the middle of the crowd moving along the sidewalk. Holt continued on a few paces before he noticed that she'd stopped.

He held out his arm to her.

"I'd like you to meet the person you'll be reporting to directly."

"I thought you were my boss," Agnes said, unenthusiastic about the prospect of meeting anyone else that day. But she caught up to Holt anyway and continued walking.

Holt broke into a smile, making his eyes look like a child's for a moment.

They stopped outside the Horn building, which had been built after she left Oslo and was now Norway's tallest building. Holt excused himself and went inside the menswear shop while Agnes looked up at the imposing edifice. At the very top she saw a sign with the words Metro-Goldwyn-Mayer. *It's too tall for this town,* she thought.

The Floris café on the third floor was almost full. The steady buzz of voices filled the room, the ringing of a cash register competed with the laughter coming from a nearby table, and cigarette smoke hovered like a dim fog below the expensive hardwood ceiling. Holt gripped her shoulder as he led her toward a row of tables near the window.

In the far corner sat a young man with dark-blond hair who appeared to be close to her own age. A notebook lay open in front of him, filled with what looked like lecture notes. He was eating a piece of cake with a silver fork. Next to him on the table was a small stack of worn books.

Holt cleared his throat. The young man looked up at them in bewilderment. Then a disarming smile spread across his face. Agnes felt herself blush.

"Agnes, this is the Pilgrim," whispered Holt, barely audible above the hum of voices.

At first glance, the Pilgrim looked more like a boy scout than an intelligence agent. His suit looked like something he might have worn for his confirmation. But the blue eyes beneath his finely etched brows left no doubt that he'd been around the block a few times. And when he smiled, all traces of boyish innocence vanished. As Agnes sat down across from him, she barely heard Holt ask her what she'd like to order.

"Just a cup of coffee," she heard herself say.

The Pilgrim, she thought as the man packed up his books and notebook with an apologetic but confident smile. *What sort of cover name is that?* She cast a glance outside at the street, not because she was interested in the crowds or the cars driving past, but to restrain a strong urge to find a mirror. She felt that her hair was more wavy than she liked, even though her hat hid most of her hair. She silently cursed Moen and his salon, as well as Lafton's yellowed horse teeth and his poorly disguised insinuation that she was going to spend her time in Oslo sleeping with men and not sitting across from them, as she was now. As an equal.

"So. What have they told you about the situation here in Oslo?" asked the Pilgrim. He surveyed the room and finally settled his gaze on Holt, who was now standing at the counter.

"Almost nothing," she told him. What Lafton had said was hardly worth mentioning. Or even remembering.

"He's a real strange guy, our friend down the street," said the Pilgrim. He seemed like the sort of person who smiled as often as he could, and his teeth—unlike Lafton's—were perfect. As perfect as only the teeth of a dentist's child could be. She tried to find fault with his face, looking for something out of proportion or any tiny flaw, but she couldn't find a thing.

Agnes merely nodded. She could think of nothing to say. For the umpteenth time, she cursed herself for having allowed herself to be recruited into the service. To be bowled over like this, by a boy like him!

"The Pilgrim studied in Germany," said Holt when he returned. "An engineer. Wasn't that what you wanted to be?"

The Pilgrim nodded and ran his hand through his hair.

"You wouldn't believe what's going on in that country," he said. His expression remained neutral as he reached across the table and took a cigarette from Holt's pack. He stared distractedly out the window, seeming to disappear into himself, to thoughts he would never share with anyone else.

When Holt left half an hour later, Agnes was still none the wiser. Holt and the Pilgrim had mostly talked cryptically about people she didn't know.

She and the Pilgrim remained seated at the table and watched Holt walk off down the street.

"Tell me one thing. I . . ." she began. But she didn't know what she was trying to say.

The Pilgrim kept on staring out the window at the reversed letters of the café's sign.

"Let's take a walk," he said.

They walked slowly up Akersgata until they finally came to Vår Frelsers cemetery, which was deserted. The trees surrounding feminist and politician Gina Krog's tombstone swayed in the wind. "I think we'll soon be ratcheting up to Operation Charlie level," said the Pilgrim. "That means you'll refer to Kaj only as Number 1, and to yourself as Number 13. We can keep on this way. Lafton may have already breached protocol."

I don't want to be Number 13, Agnes thought.

"Only my boss, Number 1, knows who belongs to which cells and how many of us there are," said the Pilgrim. "In case the worst comes to pass. That's all you need to know. For the time being, I'm your only contact."

"How did you . . ." Agnes sat down on the nearest bench. She didn't want to know.

They sat there for a while, looking at each other. As if they were both thinking, *What are we doing here?*

"You're not the only one here," said the Pilgrim at last. "But I'm sure you know that."

She nodded as she studied the bust of Gina Krog. It was a relief to evade his eyes, even though all she really wanted to do was stare at him.

"Try not to kill each other."

She laughed quietly.

"What's your real name?" she asked.

The Pilgrim didn't answer. Instead, he took another cigarette out of the pack that Holt had left behind at the café. After struggling to light it in the wind, he took out a stack of papers from his briefcase and set them on the bench next to her.

She didn't need to pick them up to know what they said.

On top was a flyer promoting the Nasjonal Samling. The yellow sun cross against a red background was unmistakable. The Pilgrim pointed to the address at the bottom.

Next he pulled out a newspaper clipping. An attorney she'd never heard of was looking for a typist and a secretary. Agnes put both papers in her purse without asking any questions.

"Tomorrow you'll go and join the Party. Your sister is already a member. After that, you'll call and apply for one of the two open positions in the office of Supreme Court Advocate Wilhelmsen. Then you'll start going to the Rainbow Club, preferably every evening. Any questions?"

"What's your real name?" she merely said.

Their eyes met. She could clearly see the black ring around the dark-blue iris of his eyes. A faint smile played over his face. He took out the pack of Craven A's and offered her one. Agnes felt her fingers tremble as she raised the cigarette to her lips. For a moment the smoke threatened to choke her.

"The Pilgrim," he said in a low voice. "Just the Pilgrim."

CHAPTER 26

Tuesday, June 10, 2003
Oppsal
Oslo, Norway

The traffic light changed to green. Tommy Bergmann heard the car behind him honk, but kept on reading the documents on his lap. When the car honked again, he shifted into first and pulled into the closest bus bay. He had three printouts from the Web and several copies of newspaper articles from the past decade. So far that was all he'd been able to dig up on Krogh. And that might have been intentional. From his research, Bergmann gathered that Krogh had never provided any biographical information about himself, participated in any debates, or written a single article about the war. According to a newspaper interview from 1999, which was linked to one of the Internet articles, Krogh left postwar commentary to others. He described himself as a simple man, first and foremost an engineer who was also interested in business and politics. He was not a historian, nor a man who judged others who had made different choices than he had during the war.

The three articles Bergmann had found all referred to books written by Torgeir Moberg, a well-known historian who was possibly the leading expert on the war. According to Moberg, Krogh had been a member of Milorg, the Norwegian Resistance, from 1941 to 1945, and a British SIS agent in Oslo even before the war broke out, until he was exposed by the Gestapo in the fall of 1942. He managed to flee to Sweden under dramatic circumstances, but in March 1943 was sent back to Norway, where he was presumed to have been behind a number of liquidations, including the death of Gudbrand Svendstuen, whom the Brits claimed had betrayed Krogh and his cell to the Nazis. Krogh later became a leading figure in the Norwegian Resistance community in Stockholm, and he also spent long periods of time in London.

Bergmann's reading was once again interrupted by honking. The driver of the 69 bus was waving his arms at him, as if they were in the middle of a traffic jam in Karachi and not the outskirts of Oslo.

"Marius Kolstad," Bergmann muttered. "I need to find Marius Kolstad."

Standing outside the high-rise building that housed the Oppsal nursing home, Bergmann tried to recall the last time he had been here. It had been years ago—maybe even a decade—when he was still on patrol duty. He turned around to survey the nearby apartment buildings and the shopping center, which he remembered as being old and worn out, but which had been so completely modernized that he felt like a stranger here, in his own part of town.

As he went inside, he silently vowed never to end up in a nursing home, not even if he could have a private room and wine at dinner. The mere smell of the place was enough to make him want to leave. A hospital was different because it held the hope of life, side by side with death. Here the stale smell merely underscored the fact that no one was ever going to get out alive. Few things scared him more than the thought of a lingering death in a place like this. It was better to die the way his mother had, even though she'd died far too early. Three weeks from diagnosis to death was just enough time to put things in order and try for some sort of closure.

He showed his ID to the young woman sitting at the reception desk. An old man passed behind him, and Bergmann turned to look over his shoulder, noting the gnarled, bluish knuckles of the man's hands, trembling slightly, as he held on to the walker.

"I'd like to speak to Marius Kolstad," said Bergmann.

"Kolstad? Let's see now . . ." She gave him a practiced and professional smile that made Bergmann feel a bit better. And her perfume smelled wonderful. "May I ask what it's about? I mean . . ." She pointed at his ID. Bergmann noticed that her nails were bitten to the quick, and he found himself appreciating this flaw in her otherwise perfect appearance.

"It's about a homicide case," he said.

The nurse, whose nametag identified her as Lise, gave him a perplexed look. He nodded to emphasize that he was serious.

"Well . . ." she said. "That's a little shocking. I . . ."

"It's important that I speak with him. I can get a warrant, if . . ."

She suddenly looked relieved.

"Oh, that's right," she said, her eyes on her computer screen. "Kolstad is at the Ullevål Hospital. He was transferred there yesterday. I forgot all about it. He took a turn for the worse two nights ago."

Bergman felt his pulse quicken at the thought that Kolstad might slip through his fingers. Maybe he was already dead.

"Do you keep a list of visitors?" he asked.

She reached for a blue folder.

Bergmann took the folder and sat down on one of the blue chairs lined up against the wall.

It only took him about five minutes to find Carl Oscar Krogh's name.

On May 20, four days after the three skeletons were found, Krogh had paid a visit to Marius Kolstad, his old comrade in the Resistance.

CHAPTER 27

Tuesday, June 10, 2003
Ullevål Hospital
Oslo, Norway

Sitting in the corridor outside the intensive care unit, Bergmann tried to keep his eyes on the newly waxed linoleum floor. Even though Hege worked in the Gastroenterological Surgery Department, he was still afraid that she might come around the corner at any moment. He didn't want to run into her. He didn't want to know anything about her new life. He should have come to grips with things by now, but he hadn't. *Never again,* he thought.

A door clicked open and Bergmann jumped at the sound. A male nurse came out, turned left, and headed briskly down the corridor.

He stared at the white double doors ahead of him, each of which had a round window like a porthole. Finally he sighed loudly, glanced at his watch, and opened the case file he'd brought along.

Krogh had liquidated Gudbrand Svendstuen in March 1943. Did Svendstuen have any descendants? He was about to take his cell phone from his inside pocket when the doors opened again.

"Inspector Bergmann?" said a dark-haired woman in a white coat who now stood in the doorway. Two nurses were conversing quietly behind her. An elderly woman sat in a chair next to the wall. Judging by her body language, she seemed to be trying to hide the fact that she was crying. One of the nurses knelt down beside her.

Bergmann silently prayed that Marius Kolstad was still alive.

The woman in the white coat had a pleasantly firm handshake as she introduced herself as the attending physician.

"One of them, at any rate," she said with a smile. She told Bergmann that he was in luck because Kolstad was awake.

The door closed behind them. Everything seemed to move twice as fast in the ICU than out in the hall. The nurses walked quickly, their faces somber, halfway on the path between life and death.

The old man was lying in bed, the only patient in a semiprivate room, with an oxygen mask on the pillow next to him. His face was more yellow than white, but his skin lacked the leathery texture that many other old people had when they were dying. His skin was stretched tight over his skull and cheekbones, thin as rice paper and just as transparent, though with a scattering of liver spots. His veins were thin and dark blue, and he had dark circles under his eyes. A tube in one nostril was supplying him with oxygen, and an IV had been inserted in his gaunt arm, which lay on top of the covers. Despite every indication that Marius Kolstad was on the verge of dying, his eyes gleamed bright blue, as if he were still a young boy with his whole life ahead of him.

Without moving his head, Kolstad looked up at Bergmann as he leaned over him.

"Do you smoke?" Kolstad asked Bergmann. His voice was raspy, and there was a gurgling sound from deep in his throat, as if dark tar were bubbling up.

Bergmann nodded.

"Keep on smoking," said Kolstad. "It doesn't hurt nearly as much as they say. They give you a lot of morphine. And it's completely legal, even for a policeman."

Kolstad gasped for breath and reached for the oxygen mask, but quickly gave up. Bergman moved to pick it up, but Kolstad waved him away.

Bergmann pulled up a chair and sat down.

"It's about Carl Oscar. Am I right?" said Kolstad quietly.

Bergmann nodded. The old man turned his head so he could look him in the eye.

"A god-awful turn of events," said Kolstad.

If you only knew, Bergmann thought.

"Why would anyone kill Carl Oscar?" Kolstad said as he once again reached for the oxygen mask. Bergmann looked at his bony fingers, noting how similar they were to the skeletal hand of Agnes Gerner.

The old man took his time filling what was left of his lungs with oxygen. Bergmann hoped that Kolstad wouldn't die right in front of him.

"The dead . . ." said Kolstad with his eyes closed. "The dead tell no tales." He opened his eyes.

"No," said Bergmann, not sure what he meant by his own response.

"So it was a bad scene up there? At his place?"

Kolstad coughed for a long time, his throat gurgling.

Bergmann hesitated. Was there any real risk? Kolstad could die at any moment.

"Krogh . . . was killed with a knife," he said.

Kolstad closed his eyes again. He seemed exhausted. Maybe this was all too much for him.

"A knife?" he whispered, breathing harder.

"A Hitler Youth knife," said Bergmann.

Marius Kolstad lay motionless, seeming not to comprehend what he'd just heard.

Bergmann was starting to think this was pointless. Kolstad had nothing to say. He looked around the room and then out the window.

The sight of the green leaves of the birch tree gave him a sudden urge to be outside in the fresh air.

"So they finally got him, those bastards. They got him too," said Kolstad, his eyes still closed.

"What do you mean?" asked Bergmann, leaning forward on his chair, but it was no use. Kolstad seemed to have dozed off again. Yet something was going on inside that head of his.

"The dead tell no tales," Kolstad repeated. "Did you know that?"

Bergmann glanced discreetly at the clock on the wall. Kolstad was talking nonsense. That was all.

"Carl Oscar . . . fell apart after Karen died."

"His wife?"

Kolstad nodded. Bergmann jotted something down in his notebook. Then neither of them spoke for a moment. The only sound in the room was the faint hissing of the ventilation system and a muted thud from out in the corridor.

"What did you mean when you said 'those bastards'?" asked Bergmann. "The Germans?" He turned the page in his notebook and wrote down "bastards" followed by "Germans" and two exclamation marks.

Kolstad cautiously moved his arm with the IV. Then he tilted his head slightly in what looked like a nod.

The Germans, thought Bergmann. That seemed a bit implausible. Anyone could have purchased a Hitler Youth knife on the Internet.

"I understand that Krogh came to visit you on May 20. Is that right?' he said. "Did he mention anything about the three bodies that were discovered in Nordmarka?"

"What three bodies?" said Kolstad. Then, before Bergmann could say anything, "Oh, yes, right. Those three." Those few words seemed to have cost him more effort than he possessed, and his head sank into the big white pillow. Kolstad lay there gasping for breath, but he didn't reach for the extra oxygen that the mask would give him.

When the old man had regained control of his breathing, Bergmann asked, "So you don't know anything about them?"

"No," he rasped. "They might have been Germans, for all I know . . . They were capable of anything."

Kolstad's eyes fell shut. He lay so still that only the EKG monitor indicated that he was actually still alive. Bergmann didn't understand Kolstad's last remark. Why would the Germans have killed a woman who was engaged to a prominent Norwegian Nazi?

"What did the two of you talk about?" Bergmann asked. "You and Krogh."

"The war," whispered Kolstad. "What else would we talk about? We never talked about anything but the war."

Bergmann was about to respond, but Kolstad spoke first.

"But it was just the same old stuff . . . Carl Oscar didn't mention anything that might help you. I just don't understand it. Why would anyone . . ."

Kolstad's voice faded, and his head sank even deeper into the pillow. Bergmann watched the glucose drip from the bag on the stand next to the bed and flow through the tube into the arm of this living skeleton. He studied the man's face. The steady heartbeat on the EKG indicated he was asleep.

Bergmann decided to leave. There wasn't much more he could do here.

But before he could get up, he felt Kolstad's cold hand on his arm. His grip was firm. There was still strength in the old man's fingers.

"There's only one thing about the war that still bothers me. I've made peace with all the rest." Kolstad spoke so quietly that Bergmann had to lean forward to hear him.

"Kaj."

"Kaj?"

"If only you could find out what happened to Kaj."

Kolstad began coughing, and the EKG surged.

"The Germans got him. I think those bastards got him in the end. And now they got Carl Oscar too." Kolstad gripped Bergmann's arm with amazing force. "Kaj," he said again.

"Kaj who?" asked Bergmann.

"Carl Oscar and I went to Stockholm when we heard that Kaj had been found dead."

Bergmann nodded, keeping his gaze fixed on Kolstad, who now closed his eyes.

"We tried everything, but they stopped us at every turn." His fingers released their hold on Bergmann's arm, but the EKG was still beeping rapidly. Under the white hospital gown, Bergmann could see the sensor attached to the left side of Kolstad's chest.

"What . . . ?"

Kolstad opened his eyes, gasped for breath, and motioned for the oxygen mask. Bergmann handed it to him.

"Who is Kaj?" he asked, his voice louder than he'd intended.

"Kaj spelled with a *j*, not an *i*," said Kolstad. "Remember that. Kaj."

"Okay. Kaj with a *j*."

Kolstad put his hand on the oxygen mask, shook his head, and opened his eyes wide. The EKG emitted a shrill sound that Bergmann knew was a distress signal. He pulled the cord for the nurse, silently cursing. *Who is this Kaj?* he wondered.

Kolstad suddenly seemed to have taken in enough oxygen and removed the mask from his face. His eyes filled with tears, and he raised his hand to touch the solitary tear that spilled from his left eye.

"What makes me so sad," Kolstad said, "is that nobody remembers Kaj anymore." He held out his wrinkled hand toward Bergmann. "Nobody," he repeated. "And he was the best, you know. No one was greater than Kaj. Not even Carl Oscar. Or Max."

Bergmann was about to speak when the door opened.

"You'll have to leave now. We can't have him getting upset," the nurse said sternly, as if Bergmann were trying to kill the old man.

Kolstad held up his hand toward her, tugging at the stand with the IV drip, and grimaced.

"Leave us alone," he said to her. "Please."

"I'm staying here," said the nurse.

Kolstad motioned for Bergmann to lean close. His voice was now nearly inaudible.

"Those fucking Swedes made us drop the case. Carl Oscar said there was something fishy about the whole thing. Something didn't seem right. We went to Stockholm a few days after Kaj's body was found. We were strongly warned not to proceed any further. Carl Oscar took it hard. Kaj's death, I mean. Very hard."

Kolstad closed his eyes, and a whistling, gurgling sound came from his throat. It didn't take a doctor to understand what the EKG was showing. The old man's pulse was more rapid than his heart could stand. Another nurse came into the room.

"You need to leave now," said the first nurse without even looking at him.

"But I have to find out what he's talking about!" he practically shouted.

The doctor who had escorted Bergmann into the room earlier had now returned and was staring at him with wide eyes, as if she'd taken some sort of stimulant and was on her third shift.

"Out," said the doctor. "Out. Now."

There was hardly a soul in sight outside what was once the biggest hospital in northern Europe. Only one poor man in a wheelchair who was trying to roll a cigarette. Bergmann took out his own cigarettes and went over to sit on a bench in the little green park near the front entrance. After a couple of drags he felt calmer. His thoughts were consumed by one thing: the name he'd written down in his notebook. Kaj.

In the supermarket later that afternoon, Bergmann filled his cart with too many items, in an unconscious attempt to hide how lonely he felt. As he approached the checkout stand, he wondered who he was trying to fool—himself or the young cashier. Maybe he wanted her to think that he had more waiting for him at home than the little notebook burning a hole in his pocket.

Back at his apartment, he emptied a can of stew into a saucepan, set it on the stove, and turned on his PC. He left the rest of the groceries in the front hall. He'd bought more than he'd ever be able to eat, so what did it matter whether he put the food in the fridge, since he'd be throwing most of it out anyway. He wondered fleetingly who would sit at his bedside when he found himself on his deathbed like Marius Kolstad, but quickly dismissed the thought.

He typed "Kaj Second World War" into the search field.

The screen filled with hits.

"Kaj Holt, 1913–1945." That had to be him.

```
Holt died under mysterious circumstances
in Stockholm in May 1945. When Carl Oscar
Krogh had to flee for his life to Sweden
in the fall of 1942, Holt was the only
remaining link in Oslo between Milorg,
the British intelligence service, the
Osvald Group, and the Norwegian legation
in Stockholm. Kaj Holt was Krogh's
superior in Oslo.
```

Bergmann's interview with Kolstad hadn't been a waste of time, after all. That first line smelled fishy—given that Kolstad had told him that he and Krogh had been prevented from investigating Holt's death—but Kaj Holt might just be his ticket to finding Krogh's killer. But what did they have to do with the three females in Nordmarka? It couldn't be a coincidence. Bergmann didn't believe in coincidences.

The few times in his life he'd allowed himself to do so, everything had gone to hell.

He scrolled down. Then back up.

Something had stuck in his mind.

```
Kaj Holt was Krogh's superior in Oslo.
```

Somewhere in his apartment a phone was ringing.

He tried to ignore it, but finally went to grab it in the hall. He held the phone in his hand as it continued to ring. The call was from Bent, and he didn't feel like talking to him. He didn't want to talk to anybody just then. Not even Hadja.

The ringing stopped. Bergmann went back to his computer, but he took the cell with him.

"Kaj Holt," he read aloud in an attempt to forget about Bent's call.

Could there be a connection between Krogh's murder and Holt's death? It was a long shot, but not impossible. Krogh had tried to investigate what happened to Holt, and . . .

His cell started ringing again.

Bergmann uttered a loud curse. Bent wasn't the type to give up easily. If he switched off his phone, Bent would soon be knocking at the door.

He pressed the answer button, albeit reluctantly.

"How's it going?" said Bent. "Still at work?"

He sounded friendly, as if he wanted to reestablish a good rapport. They'd hardly spoken since Hege had moved out.

"Sort of," said Bergmann.

"Out in the field?"

"No," said Bergmann with a sigh. "At home. Working on a case."

He glanced around the living room. It looked as if nothing had been touched since Hege left. She hadn't taken a single thing with her. Not so much as a book or any of the lithographs on the walls. It was like a museum, with objects from a bygone era, everything covered by a fine layer of dust.

"Hungry?" asked Bent.

"Hmm . . ." said Bergmann, only now noticing the smell of burnt stew coming from the kitchen.

"We're going to eat in an hour," said Bent. "Maiken is making tapas. Then we can have a few beers out on the terrace."

Bergmann fixed his eyes on the computer screen. "Carl Oscar Krogh," he read. But he couldn't concentrate.

"It'd be nice to see you, Tommy. And you could finally meet Maiken."

What should he say? Bergmann had very few friends left. In two years he'd be forty, and he'd been scraping bottom so long that he could hardly remember anything but loneliness. He rubbed his face. Images from the past flashed through his mind. They'd spent a lot of time together, he and Hege and Bent and his first wife, Marianne. Damn. He and Bent went back a long way, seventeen or eighteen years, since their police academy days. They shared a history. Maybe Bent didn't judge him after all. Bergmann felt a pang of guilt because he'd never sought help, as Bent had urged him to do. Violence was part of their profession, of course, but not something you took home with you. Wasn't that what Bent had once said?

An hour later Bergmann was standing at the door of a newly remodeled old house on Steinliveien, a ten-minute walk from his own apartment, a bottle of wine in hand. One of the many that Hege had left behind.

A woman opened the door. She had long brown hair pinned up on top of her head. He was surprised by how young she looked, but quickly realized she must be Maiken. She had a limp handshake and didn't say her name when he introduced himself. Bergmann felt like he could tell what she was thinking. She probably already knew what sort of man he was. She invited him in but seemed distant, and he wondered whether she and

Bent might have argued about whether to have him over for dinner or not. Only when Bent came down the stairs did Bergmann feel welcome. Bent smiled as if he meant it, giving him a hug and a couple of pats on the back, and said it was good to see him again. Maiken seemed to thaw out a bit when she saw the warm reception Bent gave him. Bergmann noticed how the bulge of her stomach under her tight top didn't really match the rest of her toned body and realized she must be pregnant.

"Nice place," said Bergmann as he followed Bent into the living room. It was such a huge contrast to his own apartment that he didn't feel like he could ask how they could afford it.

"Damn, it's really good to see you, Tommy." Bent put his strong, sinewy arm around his friend's shoulder. Then he showed Bergmann the flagstone terrace, which looked like it was straight out of an interior design magazine. There was not a thing out of place; the matching flowers and coordinated furniture suggested that the owners knew what they were doing. Only Bent himself didn't seem to fit in. Ever since joining the special-ops unit, he'd started looking like an ordinary thug, just like all his colleagues. He'd let his hair grow out, he was unshaven, and his arms were covered with tattoos—probably fake, but still. Only his smile and the devil-may-care look in his eye remained unchanged. Bergmann didn't know how he could stand the life of a cop, but when he thought about it, maybe it was no worse than his own job as a detective.

They ate their tapas out on the shady terrace. Bent kept the conversation going. Maiken was pleasant enough, but maintained an almost formal distance from the whole situation. Although she was attractive, Bergmann couldn't see what had made Bent leave Marianne and their son for her. He didn't think she seemed especially bright, but he realized he'd underestimated her when she explained that she'd just taken a job as head nurse at Aker University Hospital, and it wasn't the best of times to be pregnant.

"Nurses," said Bent, taking her hand. "What would we do without them?"

You're right, thought Bergmann. *What would we do without them?*

Bent told a few anecdotes from their days as patrol officers and with the SWAT team, and that put all of them at ease. Bergmann thought it was a good thing that Bent hadn't told Maiken everything they'd been through together. Let sleeping dogs lie, so to speak. How Bergmann was actually doing was a topic they all carefully avoided.

An hour later, Maiken finished off her San Pellegrino and went inside to rest.

Once they'd cleared the table, Bent came back out with a couple of beers. For a while they talked about all the usual things—former colleagues, a recent case that Bent had worked on, and a little about Carl Oscar Krogh. It was a superficial and stilted exchange by two men who knew each other far too well to be chatting about work, but Bergmann didn't mind that they were circling around what was actually important.

Then, just as Bergmann was about to light another cigarette, Bent said, "So, have you talked to Hege lately?"

Bergmann paused with his thumb on his lighter.

"No," he said, and lit the cigarette.

Bent pulled his long hair back in a ponytail, then let it fall loose again. He nodded.

"Well, she's been over here a few times, with that new guy of hers. Just so you know."

"I see," said Bergmann.

"She's doing fine," said Bent.

Bergmann didn't reply. *Aren't you going to ask how I'm doing?* he wondered. Then he shook his head. Self-pity was seldom pretty, especially from someone who was solely to blame. He suddenly got the feeling that Bent had invited him over just so he could tell him that he was planning to remain friends with Hege.

"I guess I'd better be getting home," he said, unable to bear this any longer. The next thing Bent would say was that he should see a therapist.

"You'll have to accept that we're friends," said Bent. "Me and Hege."

Bergmann sighed in resignation.

"That's not how I meant it," said Bent.

"It's getting late," said Bergmann. "I've got a lot of work to do."

"What exactly is waiting for you at home?" asked Bent.

Bergmann didn't know what to say.

"You can't keep living like this, Tommy."

They drank their beer in silence. Bergmann imagined they were both wishing the same thing—that everything would go back to the way it was before, that Bergmann had never beaten up Hege, that Bent had never met another woman.

Bent eventually went into the kitchen and began filling the dishwasher, but Bergmann couldn't bring himself to leave. Bent was right. What was waiting for him at home?

"How about one for the road?" said Bent when he came back. The soft light of dusk had settled over the garden. The trees cast long shadows over the lawn, and the faint roar of traffic on the E6 mingled with the chirping of willow warblers in the birch trees. A rare evening calm had descended upon the city.

He took the can of Heineken Bent handed him and decided to forget about Hege for the moment.

"Have you ever heard of a guy from the war named Kaj Holt?" he asked as Bent sat down.

Bent shook his head.

Bergmann told him what little he knew about Holt. Bent listened in silence.

"Maybe I'm just imagining there's a connection," said Bergmann.

"I don't know," said Bent. "But I do know one thing that might help you. Fredrik Reuter is good pals with a guy in the National Police in Stockholm, real top brass as far as I can tell. A man who could definitely pull a few strings."

They toasted this potential lead, no matter how slim it might be, and Bergmann stayed a while longer, until it was almost dark. A few times he thought to himself that maybe he would be happy again someday—or at least as happy as he'd ever be. And a few times over the course of the evening he had an urge to go to Maiken and say, "I'm not like that. I'm not the kind of man people have told you I am."

When he got home, he stood in the entryway without switching on the light. *Maybe if I just stand still long enough, she won't have gone away,* he thought.

After five minutes or so, he turned on the light and went to brush his teeth. When he turned off the water, he heard his cell phone ping out in the entryway.

For a moment he thought it might be Hege. Finally he shook his head and opened the text.

```
Hi, Tommy. Just wanted to say that you're
doing a great job with the girls. Sara
is looking forward to Göteborg, hardly
talks about anything else. ☺ Here's a
wild idea: Do you have plans for tomorrow
evening? All this talk of dinner . . .
If not, I get off work at 7. How about
dinner after practice, between 8 and
8:30? So we could get to know each other
a little better? Hadja
```

CHAPTER 28

Friday, May 7, 1942
The Rainbow Club
Klingenberggata
Oslo, Norway

The maître d' navigated through a sea of Germans and Norwegian Nazis as he escorted Agnes Gerner to a table on the lowest tier of the club facing the dance floor. Although it was becoming increasingly difficult to find loyal Norwegians at the Rainbow Club, it was still one of the few places where both sides could gather and feel they were on relatively neutral ground. *The damn Germans have been here for more than two years,* Agnes thought, *and what use have I been to anybody?*

She smiled at the maître d' as he pulled out a chair for her, addressing her as "my dear Ms. Gerner," with emphasis on the word "miss." Helge Schreiner, the Supreme Court Advocate—a title he'd acquired under Nazi rule—placed his hand on hers and assured her for the umpteenth time that she was the most beautiful woman in the world. His wedding band gleamed in the lights from the chandeliers and ought to have reminded him that he had a wife at home who knew full well what he was doing with his secretary.

"You *are* the most beautiful," he repeated, speaking so loudly that the whole room would have heard if it hadn't been for the band.

Agnes would have almost been tempted to agree if the compliment had come from another man, in another time and another world. She was well aware that she looked good in the new black dress that he'd obtained from Paris via one of his contacts, presumably a close associate on German *Reichskommissar* Josef Terboven's staff. But she had another reason for wanting to look her best, and it was one that Schreiner must never know. As she fidgeted with the diamond ring he'd bought her, she couldn't help but find the whole situation disgraceful. She was here to do a job, not to go to bed with indifferent Nazis like Schreiner, and Attorney Wilhelmsen before him. Wilhelmsen had been even more hopeless when it came to supplying her with useful intelligence information. At least Schreiner had contacts in the higher circles. But Agnes was nonetheless beginning to suspect that all her attempts to accomplish anything in Oslo had been futile. Both Number 1 and the Pilgrim were apparently satisfied with her work, but she couldn't see how the information she'd obtained from this Nazi attorney would be of any use to the Allied forces. Schreiner did socialize with the county administrator in Oslo and a few high-ranking German officers, but most of what she had been able to glean was common gossip that anybody could pick up by agreeing to sex. If she was very unlucky, she might end up pregnant. And who would come to her rescue then? Would the service take responsibility after using her as a prostitute? Agnes was beginning to doubt that she could rely on them. As it was, she felt completely out of touch with the service and occasionally wondered whether it even existed anymore, except as a very thin thread between Oslo and London. Archibald Lafton and all the others had been forced to flee for their lives two years ago. Those who remained had probably been thrown out after the disastrous campaign in Gudbrandsdalen. Only an ignoramus like Christopher Bratchard and his colleagues would try to launch a campaign down a narrow valley. Even a child would have known it would fail. Chamberlain had sent over nothing more than a ragtag bunch of family men with pipes in their mouths and rifles slung over their shoulders. Was it all that surprising then to think that the whole world would soon be kowtowing to Hitler? They'd be speaking German in London any moment now. And all that Agnes had accomplished was to play errand girl, running between safe houses and empty offices, as well as serving Schreiner in every disgusting way. Sometimes she cursed both Number 1 and the Pilgrim, not to mention Bratchard. Did they think this was all a woman was capable of? Bratchard, that drunkard, had demeaned her for months, tearing her apart, making her kill Bess, her only real friend, and then he'd dumped her here in Oslo. If she ever saw him again, she planned to give him a good slap on the face.

Agnes opened the menu as she distractedly ordered a glass of champagne. "A *bottle!*" she heard Schreiner exclaim. He had that look in his eye this evening. He almost always had that look in his eye. Soon the rest of their dinner party—a bunch of naïve and gullible Norwegian Nazis—would arrive . . . God help her, she was really in a quandary now. The Pilgrim had mentioned traveling to England via Stockholm. *Maybe I could do that too,* she thought, giving Schreiner one of her phoniest and most convincing smiles as he offered her one of his Turkish cigarettes.

The band started playing a jazz number that Schreiner described as "Negro music." Yet it still seemed to have an energizing effect on him. He grabbed his glass by the stem and downed the contents, then refilled both their glasses, an unambiguous leer on his face. As she listened to the jazzy riffs, Agnes thought it was a miracle that the Germans hadn't yet shut this place down, though it might be only a matter of time before they threw out all the Norwegian patriots. *That's it!* she thought grimly. That was the sort of intelligence she could offer the Pilgrim and Number 1. The Rainbow would soon be closed. There would be only military marches and creamed cabbage at the Rainbow from now on! Tell Churchill and Trygve Lie at once. Agnes almost giggled at the thought, but she restrained herself as the rest of the guests were arriving.

Schreiner stood up abruptly and began effusively greeting his colleague, Rolf Jordal, and his dim-witted girlfriend, Bjørg, showering them with compliments. It was enough to make Agnes sick, but she had to make the best of things. She thought how similar she must appear to Bjørg as she played the role of an empty-headed young woman who gladly accepted the money and worldly ways of middle-aged Nazis.

Agnes surveyed the room, which was now nearly full. The tables were positioned on several tiers, with the band taking center stage along one wall. The crowd consisted of a mixture of Norwegian Nazis, a few decent Norwegians who had scraped together enough money to spend a Friday evening in the city's best dance club, and a small group of German officers with girls like herself in tow.

Lately she'd occasionally had to resist an intense and irrational urge to stand up and scream to the non-Nazis that she wasn't who they thought she was and she was here to help them. But of course she always managed to suppress the shame she couldn't help feeling, and it no longer really mattered anyway. The few old friends she had in Oslo no longer spoke to her, and the only family she had was her sister, who was crazy enough to admire Agnes's decision to become an ardent Nazi. Although a man who claimed to be her cousin had spat on her in this very place a year ago, she hadn't seen any other relatives since she'd arrived in town. Her father had become estranged from his family when she was a child. Although she wasn't sure why, it made her current situation somewhat easier. So many years had passed since she

Gard Sveen

lived in Oslo that only a handful of people even knew who she was. Besides, almost no true Norwegian patriots could afford to go out on the town anymore.

She was listening to the conversation at the table with only half an ear, occasionally interjecting a remark, but mostly thinking about other things. She poked listlessly at her food and finally gave up trying to look interested.

The Pilgrim, she thought. *London.* Imagine living—and loving!—in London with him. No Germans, just the two of them. For nearly two years she had managed to resist him, but it had eventually become too much. It had just been a matter of time before they fell into each other's arms. One morning last fall they'd woken up in bed together. They'd had too much to drink with Number 1 in a safe house the night before. It was one of the few times she'd seen Number 1 since April of 1940, when she'd been questioned. He had seemed depressed and neurotic, but she hadn't really been paying attention. The only thing she could think about was getting the Pilgrim into bed after Number 1 fell asleep on the sofa. And it had proved to be so easy. The Pilgrim said that he'd loved her ever since the first time they met at the Floris. Agnes was old enough to know that men often said such things, but she wanted to believe him, and he actually seemed to mean it.

What a fine mess, she thought to herself now. Two men. The damned war. And she hadn't seen the Pilgrim in two months. Two whole months without him. The first month had been almost unbearable. She'd had to sleep with Schreiner every Monday, Wednesday, and Friday. And no Pilgrim. Not a single word from him since March. And she couldn't very well ask Number 1 where he was.

Maybe it was best if he stayed away. Their relationship was sheer madness. It was suicide.

The worst part was that she'd started to get used to the idea that they might never see each other again. For all she knew, he might be dead.

"Darling, what is it?" Schreiner asked when dessert had been served. The lights had been dimmed, and the dance floor was crowded with women in evening gowns, a few men in tuxes, and the Germans in uniform.

The chocolate cake tasted strongly of some kind of ersatz butter, no doubt whale blubber, which the chef had tried to disguise under a deluge of vanilla sauce that tasted nothing like vanilla.

"It's nothing," said Agnes, pushing the cake away and reaching for Schreiner's cigarettes. He held up his lighter, feigning concern and giving her a sheepish smile. As she took her first drag, she suddenly sensed that someone was staring at her. Without changing her expression she leaned back and squeezed Schreiner's hand, which he had clearly placed on the table in the hope she would do exactly that.

Agnes discreetly surveyed the various tiers, which were arranged in a horseshoe shape around the dance floor. Their table was close to the wall, so she didn't have a very good view, but she remained convinced that someone was watching her. She was used to men staring at her, but this felt different.

"Come on," she said to Schreiner. "Aren't you going to ask me to dance?" She stood up, pulling him with her. Although much could be said for Supreme Court Advocate Schreiner, he would never be described as a great dancer. In fact, he was terrible. But Agnes didn't intend to dance with him for long. After a few bumbling rounds on the dance floor, with Schreiner's hand indecently planted on her lower back, she spotted the man who was practically staring her down.

He was sitting at a table on the other side of the room with a large group of German officers, a couple of civilians, and some young Norwegian women. His graying hair was slicked back and his tux was so new that the lapels gleamed. He sat there, motionless, watching her every move. Every time Schreiner swung her in the man's direction, she met his gaze. Even through the haze of cigarette smoke hovering over his table, she could see that he looked terribly sad. Agnes tried to step back from Schreiner a bit so she could get a better view of her admirer. He looked a little gloomy for someone sitting in the Rainbow Club, but his face seemed to brighten every time she looked at him. And the German officers at his table wore insignia proclaiming ranks that Schreiner's Teutonic acquaintances could only dream of. Something made her think that the officers were deferential to the man in the tux, and not the other way around. He might be a German himself, but that was of little importance. What mattered was that he was taking a discreet and yet obvious interest in her. This was an opportunity she ought to seize.

When the music stopped they remained on the dance floor for a few seconds until Schreiner decided he'd had enough. Agnes was facing the man's table, with her arm around Schreiner's back. The man in the tux raised his glass, and for a moment it looked as if he might smile, but then he changed his mind. Agnes gave him a quick smile before Schreiner led her from the floor.

Agnes felt disappointed at having to sit down at the table with the attorney again. *This could be my big chance,* she thought. *That man over there is not just anybody.* She lowered her eyes and evaded Schreiner's attempt to start up a lengthy conversation. A few minutes later, the band took their second break of the evening, giving her just the opening she was looking for. While some people headed back to their tables, others went up to the bar on the uppermost tier. Suddenly Agnes had a clear view from her table to where the man in the tux was sitting. He met her eyes as he raised his glass. This time he did smile. Although the German seated next to him was clearly speaking to him, he kept his gaze fixed on Agnes.

Finally, even Schreiner noticed that Agnes was exchanging glances with another man. He placed his hand on hers. She turned to look at the dim-witted Bjørg, who stared at her and frowned, as if she couldn't understand how Agnes would be interested in anyone but Helge Schreiner.

"You're here with me," said the attorney between clenched teeth. "Yet you're sitting here making eyes at another man."

"Who is he?" asked Agnes, unfazed. She leaned across the table and motioned toward the other side of the smoke-filled room, where two high-ranking German officers had gotten up from the table and were now escorting their young dates over to the bar.

Schreiner's expression turned surly, as if he could read her thoughts. All she could see were the officers' insignia and the patently attractive man in the tux. *If you only knew,* thought Agnes as she took his hand. He was twenty years her senior. If he'd looked in her purse, he would have found a cyanide capsule wrapped in toilet paper. She'd hidden it in her panties several times when she was panicked. Fortunately he was enough of a gentleman that he never put his hands between her legs until after she'd undressed.

"It's a tragic story," said Rolf Jordal. "That's Gustav Lande. Maybe you've heard of him? Lande's wife died in childbirth a few years back. Now he lives alone with his daughter and all his money in that big house in Vinderen."

Agnes tried to hide her glee, but she felt goosebumps appear on her arms. She'd heard Lande mentioned several times at the countless NS meetings she'd had to attend over the past two years. Mostly it was just a lot of sentimental gibberish, but Agnes had understood that Lande was a man whom every Norwegian Nazi admired. He didn't allow anyone to take advantage of him, not even the Germans. He'd helped the Party through difficult times several years ago when nothing was going Quisling's way, and now he was apparently on familiar terms with Terboven and everyone who came to beg for the scraps from his table.

So that was Gustav Lande smiling at her. His face had regained some of its spark. Though he wasn't exactly handsome, he was far more dapper than Helge Schreiner.

"You're here with me," said Schreiner, putting his hand on her thigh and squeezing so hard that it hurt. When she tried to move her leg away, he just squeezed even harder.

"We're going for a walk," said Rolf, pulling Bjørg out of her chair.

Agnes lifted Schreiner's hand off her thigh. Strangely enough, he offered no resistance. *This is an opportunity I can't pass up,* she thought.

"Helge," she whispered, squeezing his hand. "We can't go on like this anymore. You know that."

She didn't how he would react. Schreiner had been increasingly worried lately that his wife was getting more suspicious. *As if she doesn't know,* thought Agnes.

His eyes filled with tears. It looked like he was about to cry like a boy. *Amazing,* she thought. Maybe she should try to hold onto him a little longer. Schreiner blinked and then apologized. But it was too late. Gustav Lande was already heading over to their table. Agnes felt her heart pounding under her black dress. As he approached, she saw that he was more attractive than she'd thought.

"Would you mind if I invited your friend here to dance?" Lande asked Schreiner when he'd reached their table. Lande held out his hand to Agnes without waiting for a reply.

She felt relieved when Lande's hand grasped hers. But suddenly—as she had done so many times before—she wondered what the cyanide would taste like the day she got caught. Because surely she would get caught. No doubt it would taste awful, but it would spare her so much pain. Briskly she dismissed the idea, as if it were too dangerous to even contemplate, as if it might actually come to pass if she thought about it too long.

"Isn't he too old for you?" said Lande when they were out on the dance floor. The band was playing a waltz, probably requested, or maybe even ordered, by some German officer. He gave her a smile, well aware that he wasn't much younger than Schreiner.

They danced in silence for a while. Unlike Schreiner, Lande was a good dancer who confidently led her across the floor. Agnes stopped thinking about what would happen if he searched her purse and found the cyanide capsule. She stopped thinking about the fact that Schreiner might fire her on Monday. Instead, she closed her eyes, leaned close to him, and imagined that all this was over, that she was with the Pilgrim and not Lande, that her own mother was not her mother, that her father was still alive, and that she and the Pilgrim lived in a small house out in the country, maybe in Kent or out near Westerham Ponds.

"I haven't danced in years," Lande said in her ear as the music was coming to an end. He smelled of aftershave and cigars and alcohol, but she almost found it attractive.

"I couldn't tell," she said.

"Would you dance the next tune with me?"

Agnes nodded.

"I have a strange feeling that I've seen you before," said Lande.

God have mercy, thought Agnes.

"I don't think so," she said.

"Maybe in my dreams," said Lande. Strangely enough, she found his smile appealing, even disarming; it was as if he wanted to show her that he wasn't dangerous. That she didn't need to be afraid.

Fifteen minutes later Schreiner was gone, and Agnes told herself that she didn't need to be scared as she sat down at Lande's table and conversed with an *SS-Sturmbannführer* about the importance of deporting the Jews from Norway too, in order to cleanse the country of all internal enemies. Lande kept his hand discreetly resting on her back the whole time.

"You make me feel alive again," he whispered in her ear. A shriek came from across the table as one of the young women burst out laughing in response to something one of the other guests had said. The German officers joined in, laughing in a boisterous and vulgar way that would have been more appropriate out in a field than here at the Rainbow.

Agnes smiled and reached out to squeeze Lande's hand. He looked away for a moment, as if he were embarrassed by what he'd said. Agnes studied his profile. Though he couldn't be more than forty, his hair was already gray. His face was almost free of wrinkles, and although not exactly handsome, he was attractive and had nice eyes. *Even if he is a Nazi,* thought Agnes.

A light rain was falling from the black sky as Agnes Gerner stood on her street. The cab she'd taken from the Rainbow had driven off, and Hammerstads Gate was utterly quiet. She'd been fumbling for her keys in her purse when she'd paused at the sound of an approaching car. Had it followed her here? The headlights only came on when the car was ten or twelve yards away. Though she still couldn't find the damn key, she made it to the front door faster than she would have thought possible, considering how drunk she was.

She looked over her shoulder and saw two faint lights from under the blackout headlights. Thank God. It wasn't the Germans. They would never drive a Dodge—at least she thought it was a Dodge. But it wasn't a taxi either. She made a futile attempt to hide her face under the brim of her hat, then turned back to the door to keep searching for her key.

Through the faint sound of the rain, she could hear the car behind her slow down. Then it sped up again and disappeared.

At last she found her key.

She cautiously climbed the stairs to the third floor. By the time she reached the landing, she felt so tired she could hardly stay on her feet. For a moment she stood swaying in front of the door on which, for some reason, her mother had put up an expensive brass sign engraved with the name "Gerner." Images from the evening whirled through Agnes's mind: the glittering chandeliers, the way Lande smelled, the candid behavior of the German officers toward her, and the fear of what Schreiner might do, although that had gradually lost its hold on her. But most important of all: Gustav Lande, who had not once made a pass at her or pressured her for anything but the pleasure of her company that evening. When she said that she needed to be going, he didn't try to stop her or persuade her to join the after-party at his villa in Vinderen. All he'd done, aside from paying her cab fare, was to stroke her cheek and thank her for a most enjoyable evening. Agnes had almost forgotten that Lande was a Nazi who had practically single-handedly saved not only Quisling's career but the finances of the Party.

When she finally unlocked the door to her apartment and stepped inside, she started to cry. In a strange way she'd been on the verge of tears ever since she'd leaned close to Lande when they danced for the first time and her thoughts had turned to the Pilgrim.

Stop it, she thought. *Stop it, you sentimental bitch.* She bit the inside of her cheek, just as she'd done when that damn Christopher Bratchard made her shoot Bess. With quick, determined steps, as if she'd suddenly sobered up, she walked across the parquet floor and kicked off her high heels. Then she drew the blackout curtains in front of the two big windows in the living room. The light from the floor lamp next to the sofa hurt her eyes, as though reminding her that she mustn't forget why she'd ended up at Gustav Lande's table.

Only when she turned around did she notice that she'd left the front door open.

What was that?

A sound.

In the stairwell.

A shadow fell across the floorboards in the entryway.

She opened her mouth to scream, but stopped herself. The outline of a man filled the doorway. The light from the floor lamp didn't reach that far, so it was impossible to see his face. No lights were on in the stairwell, and the entryway was pitch dark.

My purse, she thought as the man took a step forward. *I have to get my purse!* But she was incapable of making the slightest move forward. It wasn't Schreiner, and it couldn't be Gustav Lande.

"Didn't you see me?" the man said quietly as he closed the door behind him. "I was sitting on the stairs right behind you." He took off his hat and stood there, holding it in both hands.

The familiar voice was like a punch in the stomach. He'd been gone for two full months, and now, on this very evening—this strange evening—he was standing there in her entryway.

"Where have you been?" she said, speaking so softly she could barely even hear herself. Or maybe her words were just drowned out by the blood hammering in her temples.

The Pilgrim's face seemed to have changed over the past two months, just as everything else had changed. The last time he was here, sneaking in like a thief in the night, it was still winter outside, and the world had seemed impossible. But now mild winds were sweeping through the city, leaves were appearing on the branches of the birch trees, and there was a sense that all the evil would come to an end one day.

He came over to stand in front of her.

"You're back," she said.

Suddenly he began kissing her. Then he tore off her dress.

Agnes practically bit him bloody, and she let him come as deep inside her as he could, as if she wanted only one thing, and that was to carry his child. Afterward, he lay on top of her for a long time. Their heartbeats seemed to merge into one, and she tried to hold on to him when he rolled off the sofa and went to find his coat on the living room floor. She studied his boyish, almost ungainly body as he rummaged through his pockets. When he found his cigarettes, he lit one without turning around.

When he still hadn't turned around after several minutes, Agnes got up. Only then did she notice how cold she was from lying naked on the sofa. She put her arms around him from behind.

"You smell like aftershave," he said in a low voice. "And it's not Schreiner's."

Agnes turned him around. His eyes were wet with tears. It was the first time she'd seen him cry. In fact, it was the first time she'd seen him show any emotion at all.

"Where have you been?" she asked.

"Are you seeing someone else?" he said. Agnes held his head in her hands. His face was still so handsome, so astonishingly symmetrical, almost feminine. Only the dark smudges under his eyes and a slightly distant look told her that something had happened. Something she didn't know about, something she might not want to know about.

"I spent the evening with Gustav Lande," she whispered, as if the whole building might hear them. There was a sudden thudding in the water pipes, followed by the sound of a man urinating upstairs, audible through the open bathroom door.

The Pilgrim wiped away his tears. Agnes took the cigarette out of his hand and went into the bedroom. Still naked, she got under the covers and took two final drags. As he stood in the doorway, running his hand through his hair, he looked like a child compared to Lande.

"I spent the evening with Gustav Lande," she repeated. "Do you understand what that means?"

The Pilgrim walked slowly across the room and sat down on the bed beside her. After stroking her hair for what seemed like an eternity, he lay down on top of her and clung to her body like a child, as if he wanted nothing more than to disappear into her and never come back to this world again. Agnes lit another cigarette from the pack on the nightstand, then stroked his back. The smoke rose to the ceiling in the faint light coming from the living room.

"What's your name?" she asked.

She waited for him to merely sigh in that dramatic way of his, but nothing happened. He almost seemed to be deliberately holding his breath. Finally she felt him breathe again.

"Did you forget about Gustav Lande?" he whispered. "If they catch you, and you know my name . . ."

"Tell me."

"Carl," he said. "Spelled with a *C*."

Agnes started laughing, first quietly, then louder. She couldn't help herself. Of all the names she'd imagined for him, Carl was the last one that would ever have occurred to her.

"What's so funny?" he said, pressing his face against the hollow of her throat. "It's actually Carl Oscar," he told her, getting up.

Agnes laughed so hard that she finally had to hide her head under the covers. The Pilgrim said something that she didn't catch. Suddenly he pulled the warm covers off her.

"Carl Oscar Krogh," he said, staring at her, his face expressionless. "Carl Oscar Krogh."

Agnes stopped laughing. He seemed to be trying to convince himself the name was really his.

He sat on the bed, staring at her for a long time. Finally he pulled the covers back over her naked body.

"I'm not laughing at you," she said, reaching out her hand toward him. "I love you, Carl Oscar."

Before she could touch his unshaven cheek, he turned away.

"What's the matter?" she asked, sitting up now, without covering her breasts.

The rain was coming down harder, pounding against the windowpane.

Carl Oscar Krogh lit a cigarette and went over to the window. The blackout curtain hadn't been closed, but he didn't seem to notice. He stood there with the cigarette hanging from his lips for several minutes as he stared out at the rain.

Agnes got out of bed, went over to him, and put her arms around him. His body felt cold from standing at the window.

"Don't stand here like this. Someone might see you," she whispered in his ear. He shook her off. She sighed in resignation and drew the blackout curtains. Krogh opened them again.

"Why were you gone so long?" asked Agnes, crossing her arms.

He sighed, then shook his head.

"Number 1," he said, taking a drag on his cigarette and letting the smoke out through his nose, then his mouth. "He thought I should lay low for a few weeks."

"Eight weeks," said Agnes. She was about to say his name again, but it suddenly didn't seem right. She thought of him as the Pilgrim.

"I killed a man," he said. His voice was flat, lifeless, as if he were reading a statement that he himself didn't understand. "That's why I had to . . . leave you." He opened the window and tossed out his cigarette.

Agnes didn't speak, merely pressed herself closer to his back.

"Didn't you hear what I said? I killed a man."

"I don't want to hear about it," she said, running her hand over his chest, which was bare as a child's. *We're both children,* she thought. *And now Number 1 has made this child kill another human being.* It was necessary, she knew, but she didn't want to know anything more about it. She didn't want to think about how Number 1 might destroy the Pilgrim—Carl Oscar! Her own Carl Oscar—if things continued this way.

"One of our own," he murmured to himself. "He had two children, two small children. I lured him into a trap, Agnes. Now he's lying out there in Østmarka, buried, gone forever."

"I don't want to know," she said. She knew full well that they lost people. Far too many. And that there was no mercy for traitors. But she didn't want him to tell her anything more.

"Number 1 gave me an assignment. I carried it out. I buried him myself." He was talking to himself now.

"Come here," she said, turning him around. He avoided looking at her, staring instead at the strip of light coming in the door from the living room. Moving like a sleepwalker, he went back to bed with her.

Agnes lay close to him until dawn, when a grayish light began filling the room. Neither of them had slept, nor had they said a single word all night.

"Carl Oscar," she said, propping herself up on her elbow to get her first good look at him in daylight since March. She ran her finger along his straight nose, then over his strong chin. "Will you marry me? When all this is over?"

"This war is never going to end," he whispered, keeping his eyes closed.

CHAPTER 29

Wednesday, June 11, 2003
Police Headquarters
Oslo, Norway

The large conference room in the restricted area on the seventh floor of police headquarters was filled with investigators who didn't have the faintest idea why real-estate entrepreneur and former trade minister Carl Oscar Krogh had been murdered with exactly sixty-two stab wounds. This was something the whole country now knew after the police chief had held a quickly organized press conference the night before. No doubt he'd consulted with or received orders from the police commissioner, who for his part had probably sought advice from Norway's minister of justice.

"As I'm sure you realize," said Fredrik Reuter, standing, his shoulders stooped, in front of the screen, "there is now a certain amount of pressure to solve this case." He gave them a wan smile. Tommy Bergmann would have bet big money that Reuter hadn't slept more than two or three hours. And judging by the wrinkled state of his uniform, he may have slept on a cot in his office.

"The only thing most people don't know yet is what the murder weapon looked like." Reuter stifled a yawn and pressed a button to display a close-up of the Hitler Youth knife lying in a pool of blood. "If we make this public, I fear that the tips we've gotten so far will seem moderate in comparison." That prompted a few laughs, not because it was funny but because people under tremendous pressure often laugh in the hope of drawing attention away from the fact that they're on their knees.

Bergmann tuned out when Abrahamsen began reviewing the autopsy results. The details were of no interest. Old Krogh had been murdered, and there had to be a reason why. It was as simple as that. Nothing in the house had been stolen. They'd been able to determine that much. Not a single thing had been touched. The killer hadn't been in search of secret documents, nor was he a junkie looking for money or drugs. *No*, thought Bergmann. The needle in the haystack had something to do with the three old skeletons in Nordmarka and an old man who was dying in Ullevål Hospital. He wouldn't have more than that to share when it'd be his turn to speak.

As Abrahamsen talked, Bergmann stared at the papers in front of him. Two sentences in particular jumped out: "Holt died under mysterious circumstances in Stockholm in May 1945." and "Kaj Holt was Krogh's superior in Oslo." The article listed the same source that he'd seen previously: Professor Torgeir Moberg. But it also gave another source—Finn Nyström, a name that Bergmann hadn't seen before. He drew a big circle around both names. He needed to talk to these two individuals, and the sooner the better. Maybe Moberg knew something about why Krogh had been prevented from investigating Kaj Holt's mysterious death. Then Bergmann turned the page and found himself looking at Cecilia Lande's skull. He knew that somewhere in these fifteen or twenty pages lay the answer to who had killed the three of them, and maybe also who had murdered Krogh.

As if from far away, Bergmann heard somebody saying his name. He looked up and found Reuter looking at him. Bergmann's brief report contained little more than what everyone in the room already knew.

Krogh had been a key figure in the Resistance, but he'd never talked much about the role he'd played in Oslo and Stockholm, nor about his part in the liquidations of a number of Nazis and traitors. After the war he became a prominent member of the Labour Party, even though he came from a solidly bourgeois family. He later was appointed under-secretary in the Ministry of Trade and eventually minister. For close to forty years after stepping down from government service, he ran his own business. In the late 1980s he sold the company to a Finnish conglomerate, apparently for such a large sum that Krogh still had more than enough money at the time of his death.

"What did Marius Kolstad say?" asked Reuter.

Bergmann paged through his notes.

"Not much," he replied. That was a lie, but he wanted as few people as possible chasing after his leads. He'd have a word with Reuter about it in private later.

Reuter sighed heavily.

"What interests me most is the claim that Krogh liquidated the traitor Gudbrand Svendstuen in March 1943," Bergmann said.

"So one of Svendstuen's descendants butchers Krogh with a Hitler Youth knife sixty years later?" said Reuter.

Bergmann shrugged.

"Halgeir, I want you to check it out," said Reuter. "Find out whether Svendstuen has any descendants, but for God's sake, be discreet."

Halgeir Sørvaag dutifully wrote himself a note, looking as if the expectations of an entire nation rested on his shoulders.

"What about the three skeletons found in Nordmarka? That was pretty much our last hope, wasn't it?"

It was Bergmann's turn to sigh.

"Agnes Gerner, Cecilia Lande, and Johanne Caspersen. I don't know," he said. "I just don't know. Kolstad says neither he nor Krogh knew anything about them." He decided to keep the matter of Kaj Holt to himself.

Reuter looked as if he were cursing under his breath. He rubbed his hands over his face and then gave his team a resigned look. Bergmann was again grateful he didn't have his job. Reuter had to deal with the stress of knowing that it was in jeopardy several times a year.

"What about the phone records, Halgeir?" said Reuter. "Are they equally dismal reading?"

Sørvaag leaned forward. For further emphasis, he spoke in that phony, self-important voice of his, which he did whenever he took the floor in front of more than two people.

"Krogh was clearly a man who didn't like talking on the phone. In the last seven weeks only ten calls were posted to his landline and five to his cell, two of which were from telemarketers. Not even his children saw fit to call him."

"So not much to go on," said Reuter.

Bergmann had to agree. All they had left was Kripo's preliminary profile of the killer, which stated that they might be dealing with an individual who was, in plain English, a madman. Or, as Reuter said impassively, "The murder could have been committed by a person experiencing an episode of acute psychosis."

Bergmann paged through his papers until he came to the profile that Reuter had quoted from. He reminded himself of his basic premise: it couldn't be mere coincidence that Krogh was murdered only a few weeks after they'd dug those bodies out of the ground in Nordmarka.

If an individual experiences a temporary acute psychosis, it is often the result of having suffered a psychological trauma of some kind in the previous week or two. For this reason, the illness was previously called reactive psychosis, i.e., a psychosis that is a reaction to psychological trauma. An episode of temporary psychosis is most often caused by an event that resulted in psychological trauma. For instance, the individual may have lost someone close to him, gone bankrupt, lost his job, or just gone through a stressful divorce; or he may have experienced a dangerous situation such as a fire or a serious car accident.

What was it Reuter had said yesterday? That the person who had killed those three females in Nordmarka may have murdered Krogh so that Krogh wouldn't take the matter further? But that was no real lead. Bergmann closed his eyes.

Reactive psychosis, he thought. Marius Kolstad had given him the idea that Kaj Holt's death had something to do with Krogh's murder. Did Holt kill those three females? Why had he died under so-called mysterious circumstances? That the author would put it that way could only mean that he thought Holt had been murdered.

Bergmann found a blank page in his notebook. He drew a triangle and in one corner wrote "Nordmarka." In the second corner he wrote "Krogh," and in the third, at the top, "Kaj Holt." He was reasonably certain that Krogh had been killed because of something to do with Holt or the three people buried in Nordmarka. Or maybe all four of them. But he wasn't getting anywhere with the skeletons. He needed to shift his focus. *Kaj Holt.* What was it Kolstad hadn't wanted to tell him? He'd be damned if Kolstad and Krogh had talked only about the war when they met at the nursing home on May 20.

Bergmann ran his pen over the triangle he'd sketched, retracing the line between Holt and Krogh several times. *This is what Krogh and Kolstad talked about,* he thought as he studied the thin line between Holt and Krogh and Nordmarka.

When he glanced up, he saw that Reuter was the only one left in the room. He was sitting quietly at the head of the table, looking at Bergmann.

"So?" Reuter said. He downed the last of his coffee and wiped his mouth with his hand. "What have you got for me? Because you do have something, right?"

"I need to go see Marius Kolstad again," said Bergmann.

"Okay," said Reuter. "But I thought he didn't have much to tell you."

"Have you ever heard of Kaj Holt?" he asked.

"Don't think so."

Bergmann told him what little he knew about Holt.

"So why the interest in him?" asked Reuter. "A dead man can't kill anybody." A small smile appeared on his face.

"I don't know what Holt has to do with it. But Krogh and Kolstad were prevented from investigating his death right after the war. The Swedes in particular weren't very forthcoming."

Reuter nodded.

"Let's keep this between you and me for the time being," he said. "Understood?"

Like a child, Bergmann couldn't help asking, "Why?"

"Because I suspect that the Holt case is a real wasps' nest. If a man like Krogh was stopped from looking into a colleague's death, how do you think they'll react to us investigating it? Think about the position Krogh held after the war. By comparison, you and I seem about as important as a Somali scrubbing toilets in the city jail."

"Don't you know someone at the National Police in Stockholm?" asked Bergmann.

Reuter took in a deep breath. Then he shook his head.

"Don't even think about it."

I'm not, Bergmann muttered to himself when he got back to his office. For the umpteenth time that day he took out his cell phone to look at the text message from Hadja. It had kept him awake almost until dawn. When he had gotten out of the shower, he had sent a reply: *Dinner would be great. See you tonight. Tommy.* Looking at his message, he thought he could have written something better.

Or maybe not. He didn't know. He didn't know anything anymore. *It'll just have to wait until tonight,* he thought as he looked for his car keys. Marius Kolstad might die at any moment, and Bergmann needed to try and coax a few more secrets out of the old man. Otherwise, he'd end up taking them to his grave.

CHAPTER 30

Friday, May 21, 1942
Helge K. Moen's Beauty Salon
Majorstua
Oslo, Norway

Helge Moen glanced at Agnes Gerner in the mirror and gave her a nearly imperceptible wink, as if he were her father and she were a little girl, and they were sharing a secret.

You're crazy, she thought.

Moen smiled to himself and whistled a tune between his teeth as he headed back to the counter.

Agnes leaned back in the leather chair and closed her eyes as the assistant put her hair up in curlers. Maybe she was the one who was going mad. It seemed that nobody she knew had been able to hold on to their sanity during these years of war. Her sister was not only an ardent NS member, but she'd even gone so far as to get engaged to a German sergeant and then train as a frontline nurse. At the moment she was somewhere on the endless Russian steppes. Agnes had almost thrown up when she'd heard and felt sick about it all weekend.

At least that gave her a nearly perfect alibi. Her own mother and sister were the most fanatical Nazis imaginable. Agnes had to smile at the thought that her family's lunacy could prove so useful.

When the assistant was done, Agnes opened her eyes and stared for a moment in the mirror at the steady stream of people outside the window, heading through the passageway and going either out to Majorstutorget or down to the Holmenkollen tram line. What were they thinking about on this first steamy, hot summer day, when the whole town seemed to be aflutter with foliage and life? Were they thinking the same thing as Agnes? That things had never looked so dark as they did today? Presumably it was only a question of time before the Germans took Sevastopol. And with the fiendish U-boats sinking American ships before they'd even gotten past Long Island, it looked like the thousand-year Reich would soon stretch from North Cape to the Sahara, from Brest to the Crimea. *It would never end,* thought Agnes. She forced herself to dismiss these thoughts and take a more positive view of the situation. It was summer, after all; Schreiner had allowed her to keep her job; and even though he'd disappeared into the shadows, the Pilgrim was back. And she herself was on the threshold of a breakthrough so major that she could hardly believe her good fortune.

A middle-aged NS woman was sitting in the chair next to her. As soon as Moen stepped away, she put down the magazine she was reading and turned to Agnes. Nazi women had started frequenting Moen's beauty salon back in the spring and early summer of 1940 when money in Norway began changing hands. At first Agnes was nauseated by the sight of all these Nazis, but now, two years later, she realized just how valuable they might be.

"So, a special occasion, Ms. Gerner?" The woman's voice was cold, bordering on arrogant, and her expression was patronizing at best.

"I've been invited to Gustav Lande's tonight."

The woman's face fell. Maybe she had been expecting Agnes to say that she didn't have anything special going on, even though many of the Nazi women knew that Agnes Gerner would go to bed with Helge Schreiner, if need be. But Gustav Lande? That was something else entirely.

Agnes turned to look at the woman and flashed her most enchanting little-girl smile.

The only thing that bothered her was that she'd arranged to meet the Pilgrim in Sten's Park that evening, but was going to have to miss it. Last week he'd told her that they would have to meet in parks and doorways for the time being, until he could possibly borrow an apartment from friends who were unaware of what he was doing, but those sorts of friends were few and far between. Number 1 thought that their relationship was dangerous and had apparently forbidden him to continue seeing Agnes. The Pilgrim thought he was so determined to end their relationship that he'd put both her apartment and all the safe houses under surveillance. According to Number 1, love had no place in war. It was a danger to them all.

As if anyone has to convince us of that, Agnes thought as she let the front door close quietly behind her. She took down the invitation from Gustav Lande, which she'd stuck in the frame of the mirror in the entryway, and ran her finger over the heavy card stock. Even at times like this, Gustav could apparently afford to spend money on dazzling white stationery edged with a gold border. "Dear Agnes," he'd written. "Thank you for an unforgettable evening." His signature was confident and verging on stylish. Agnes set the invitation down on the teak bureau under the mirror and cast a quick glance at her watch so she could calculate how much time she had to get ready. Then she opened her purse and took out the envelope from Helge K. Moen. She crumpled up the beauty salon receipt and placed it on the bureau. Then she took out the strip of paper tucked into the bottom of the envelope. She looked at herself in the mirror, then took off her hat and studied her hair, which was stiff with hair spray. The darkness of the entryway made her face look white, almost like a death mask. She unfolded the strip of paper and headed to the kitchen, studying the brief, cryptic message on her way. By the time she had lifted up the loose floorboard at the end of the counter with only a butter knife, then wiggled out the baseboard, she had almost memorized all the letters. Tucked away in the dark among the old junk and dust bunnies was the codebook.

Agnes sat down at the kitchen table, gripping the strip of paper as if it were the most valuable object in the world.

The fox is a wily hunter.

Number 1

She lit a match to the paper and then tossed it into the sink. During the few seconds it took to turn to ash, she managed to think about nothing at all. Then she snickered. What sort of message was that? But when she turned on the faucet to wash it away, she suddenly remembered who had said those words.

"The fox is a wily hunter." Those were the words of Archibald Lafton, the head of the Oslo service. He'd said that the Germans were like foxes, and that a fox was so smart it would play dead to lure its prey.

Everything had happened so fast. She hadn't even cleared it with Number 1 whether she should get involved with Gustav Lande. She'd merely taken the Pilgrim's blessing as the signal to go ahead.

This must be Number 1's way of warning her. As long as she'd been Schreiner's lover, the German intelligence service hadn't taken any interest in her. But now, assuming Gustav continued to shower her with affection, she needed to be extra careful. She was well aware of that, of course, but the terse message from Number 1 still put her on high alert.

And so it begins, she thought.

She knew that they'd lost people, as recently as a week ago. The Pilgrim had told her about it, even though she didn't want to know. The only thing she wanted to know was that she'd been given the green light to continue. If it eventually turned out that she was in imminent danger of the Germans closing the net around her, they would make sure to get her out of the city and then out of the country. Wouldn't they? Besides, she'd been in the Germans' sights before and managed to emerge unscathed. She'd been one of many Brits who were questioned at Nazi headquarters at Møllergata 19 in April 1940, but the Germans had let her go after less than an hour. They'd even offered her an apology. Now, two years later, with a mother and sister like hers, and after spending several months with a Nazi and faithful NS member, it didn't matter that she still held dual citizenship.

But things were undoubtedly getting more serious. She tried to imagine how the evening might go. The Germans clearly knew that Gustav Lande desired her. She wondered what the Brits would do in their place. *We'd put in a man to stay close to Gustav,* she thought.

A man who played dead.

From the moment she entered Lande's home, she would be under scrutiny. Maybe she already was.

The hot water from the shower almost scalded her skin, but it also liberated her from the chill she'd felt ever since she'd remembered Lafton's words. How naïve she'd been when she was first recruited.

She turned off the shower and leaned her head against the wall.

"The fox is a wily hunter," she whispered.

Dripping wet, she went into the bedroom. Without drawing the curtains, she let the white towel fall to the floor and then stood there, studying herself, wearing only a shower cap. Carefully she pulled it off, but her hair was so plastered with hairspray that it only took a slight touch-up to restore it to the way Moen had styled it.

She decided to wear the same black cocktail dress she'd worn at the Rainbow two weeks ago. Though it revealed that she was a bit too thin in the hips, it also showed off all her best attributes. In the entryway she cast another glance at the invitation with Lande's handwritten greeting. If drinks were served first, it wouldn't be so bad.

She opened her makeup case and began applying rouge, transforming the pale death mask into a woman who would be able to manipulate Gustav Lande until she had him exactly where she wanted him.

Gustav Lande's house was like a dream. It couldn't have been more than ten years old, built in the functionalist style, with three stories and a two-car basement garage. Glass bricks covered large portions of the façade and formed a semicircle that filled nearly an entire gable wall. The house was surrounded by an enormous garden, and Agnes even caught a glimpse in the pale evening light of a tennis court in back. She paid the cab driver, then walked up the flagstone path to the house, trembling slightly. A gentle breeze brushed her cheek, somehow calming her before she reached the steps to the front door, which stood open. Another car pulled up at the gate behind her. Agnes turned around and saw a German officer get out of the vehicle before his adjutant managed to open the door for him. The officer practically bellowed an order, waving away the adjutant, who saluted as he stood in the middle of the street. The black SS uniform was unmistakable. She couldn't see what rank the man held, but she wouldn't have had to be a member of the Oslo service to know that he was no ordinary staff officer.

Dear God, thought Agnes. She checked once more to make sure the cyanide pill was still in the little pocket of her clutch. Inside she was greeted by a strikingly ugly maid. Her birdlike face and gray, lifeless eyes were unlike anything Agnes had ever seen before. The large room was crowded with guests and filled with the buzz of voices and muted piano music. Hired waiters hurried to the kitchen, carrying silver trays with empty wine glasses. The doors leading to the dining room stood open, and she could see a group of people inside, all of whom were smiling. A man wearing a dark suit doubled over, apparently unable to stop laughing at some amusing remark. On either side of the French doors stood pedestal tables holding flower arrangements. The table to the left was adorned with an NS banner, and the other displayed a swastika.

Amid the crush of people—though perhaps not as many guests as she had initially thought—Agnes saw the maid with the strangely birdlike face emerge from the dining room. Fortunately, someone Agnes finally recognized was right behind her. Gustav Lande wore a white tux that showed off his suntanned face. He was still no match for the Pilgrim, but she found herself struck by his bold appearance—he looked like a savior who would rescue her from any fears she had of being found out in this place.

"Ms. Gerner," he said, kissing her on each cheek. He smelled strongly of aftershave lotion, and she could see from his eyes that he'd been drinking. Or crying. Or both. "You have no idea how much this means to me," he said, touching her hand.

"Please call me Agnes," she replied, giving him a look she otherwise reserved for the Pilgrim.

"Agnes," said Lande. Out of the corner of her eye, she saw that the SS officer who had arrived after her had been detained by several other Germans near the door. He cast a quick glance in her direction, and she quickly turned toward Lande and gave him a smile. He placed his hand on her bare shoulder. The feeling of his large hand on her skin immediately brought her pulse rate down to an acceptable level. She was once again able to think—if not rationally, at least coherently. The SS officer had been in the room less than a minute, but something about her seemed to have already caught his attention. His gaze was different from that of other men. He was not looking at her with desire. *It's my nerves,* she thought. *He smells my anxiety.* But she quickly pushed that thought aside. The SS officer was probably no different than any other man. She needed to be on the attack. It was the only way. Fortunately, Lande steered her away from the SS officer just then.

Agnes was introduced to more than forty guests on her tour of the house, many of whom were Norwegian. She tried to memorize their names, and even recognized one of the NS women from Moen's beauty salon. But she saw no one from Schreiner's social circle. She effusively greeted a couple of high-ranking German Wehrmacht officers, and she wouldn't have been surprised if Terboven himself—Norway's top Nazi—had been present.

She noticed that her hands were shaking when she retreated to the guest bathroom. She had excused herself before Lande had managed to introduce her to the remaining guests, including the SS officer. She tried to calm her nerves by running cold water over her forearms. Just as she was about to reenter the crowd, she instinctively stopped. She heard a sound behind her, barely audible, but one that shouldn't have been there in the quiet corridor. It was a long hallway, its walls lined with black-and-white lithographs in narrow wooden frames. It ended at a glass wall facing the garden, from which the neighboring house could be glimpsed between the trees. A door on the left seemed to have opened. *No*, thought Agnes. *I'm just imagining things.*

She turned back.

As she reached for the door handle to exit the corridor, she heard a voice behind her say, "Can I help you, miss?"

Agnes gave such a start that she almost dropped her clutch.

The maid was standing in the middle of the hall. With the light at her back, shining through the window at the end of the corridor, she appeared almost demonic. Agnes wondered how Gustav Lande could stand having such a creature in his house. Dressed in that black maid's uniform, she looked like the living dead.

"Mr. Lande was kind enough to direct me to the ladies' room," Agnes said as she opened the door. She was relieved to be able to escape this woman, this *creature*. She felt a tremor ripple through her body, and for a few seconds it was as if she were in a dream, in which she kept trying to open the door but never managed to do so, as the black-clad maid with the transparent bird-face soundlessly approached from behind.

Acknowledging the irony, she felt greatly relieved to be rejoining the other guests. But while she was away, the inevitable had occurred: she saw Lande take two glasses from a waiter's tray and hand one of them to the SS officer. The three oak leaves on his uniform revealed that he was a brigadier and major general. He and Lande were talking to a Wehrmacht officer and a middle-aged couple who were clearly Norwegian. *There's no way around it,* she thought, and made her way over to them. Lande's face lit up with a smile.

"Agnes," he said, motioning for her to come closer. "May I present Brigadier Seeholz?"

"Pleased to meet you," said Agnes, holding out her hand. *The fox is a wily hunter,* she thought, *so watch every word you say.*

He took her slender hand in his and raised it to his lips to kiss it lightly, keeping his eyes fixed on hers, probably to see whether she flinched.

"Freu' mich, Fräulein." He released her hand. Agnes forced herself not to stare at the skull-emblazoned ring that he wore on his right hand. She now saw that he was missing the little finger on his left hand. Suddenly she recalled who he was. *Seeholz.* He was the righthand man of Heinrich Fehlis, who was in charge of the Gestapo in Norway. He'd arrived last fall to head up the commerce division of the SS in Norway. *Oh yes,* she thought. *Either I will enter into heaven, or the gates of hell will open and swallow me whole.*

"Your first time here?" asked Seeholz after Agnes had been introduced to the middle-aged couple. She understood they were contributors to one of Lande's many projects, as well as Party members, of course. They may even have been among the first to join.

Agnes nodded and felt Lande's hand disappear from her back. Seeholz said something to the Norwegian couple, but she didn't catch what he said. Lande murmured his apologies and followed the maid upstairs.

Don't leave me here, she thought. *You're throwing me to the wolves!*

"So. How is your mother?" Seeholz asked after Lande was out of earshot. Agnes felt the floor give way beneath her, as if she were sliding across ice, and for a moment she felt weightless. In the brief time she'd known Lande, the Germans had clearly managed to live up to their reputation as meticulous intelligence agents. She shook her head in a charming fashion, as if she were only twenty-four and didn't understand the question.

"I hope Churchill hasn't interned her husband," said Seeholz, downing the rest of his champagne. "We're going to bomb some sense into him. Mark my words." He took two fresh glasses from a waiter's tray and handed one to Agnes. Then he raised his glass in a toast.

They clinked glasses. Apparently none of the others standing nearby dared even open their mouths.

"These are difficult times, *Herr Brigadeführer*," said Agnes. "Terribly difficult."

Seeholz didn't reply. He seemed to be clenching his jaw.

"The best-case scenario," said Agnes, "would be if he came to his senses and realized that the Führer's fight against the Bolsheviks is also of benefit to Great Britain. You must understand that it's hard for me to see the English suffer."

All other conversations seemed to come to a halt, or maybe they merely became one big blanket of background noise. *No, no,* she thought a moment later. Everything was proceeding normally. The other conversations were unaffected by the fact that she, Agnes Gerner, was about to be cross-examined by Brigadier Seeholz, a man who could have her arrested, tortured, and executed with a snap of his fingers.

Though his gaze was piercing, it wasn't unfriendly. She wasn't sure how to interpret it.

"I fully understand your view, Ms. Gerner," said Seeholz. "And believe me, your mother's new husband would have aspired to a good position in a government with Mosley as the British prime minister. I can almost guarantee that. But why did you decide to return to Norway? Why not Germany, like Ms. Mitford?"

Unity Mitford was one of Hitler's biggest admirers, and her sister Diana was married to Mosley. They were Great Britain's worst fascists—people for whom Agnes had the greatest contempt. Unfortunately, all of them belonged to the same social circle as her own mother. Seeholz seemed to have chosen to ignore the fact that Unity Mitford had tried to kill herself in Munich after Chamberlain's declaration of war.

"Well, my mother sent me to Norway," Agnes told him. She immediately regretted her remark, which sounded implausible, although it could just as well have been true.

The SS officer studied her, trying to meet her eye.

Only now did she notice how her pulse had quickened. Her veins felt as thin as threads, and her face had probably lost all color. Yet she managed to assume a confident expression and give him a little smile, the sort that no man, or at least not one like him, could resist.

"Excuse me, *Herr Brigadeführer*, but are you questioning my loyalty to Germany?" Agnes hastened to say before she could change her mind.

This time there was utter silence all around her. A tense silence that spread in ripples through the entire room. Even the pianist must have noticed because the melody he was playing faded away. A man standing next to Agnes nervously cleared his throat.

Brigadier Seeholz looked surprised, as if her response were the last thing he'd expected.

"My father's family immigrated to Norway from Germany . . . in 1645. Perhaps that was before your own family arrived in Germany, *Herr Brigadeführer*?"

Seeholz gave her a long look. Someone clinked a glass. Someone else flicked a cigarette lighter. Seeholz frowned and exhaled through his nose, like a bull preparing to charge. Yet a smile seemed to be tugging at his lips.

"My dear Ms. Gerner. I like you," said Seeholz. "You don't try to appease me, and you're not afraid of me. I can't abide people who are afraid of me." He gave her a smile that for the first time seemed genuine. Then he laughed, hinting that there was a real person inside that black uniform. Gradually sounds returned to the room, and the pianist began to play again. To Agnes, it seemed as if the whole place were relieved, as if the pianist were playing the loveliest of tunes, as if all this were no longer real.

"As a member of the NS, I was persecuted in England," she quickly added, maybe to keep him engaged. She wasn't sure. "That's something you ought to know, *Herr Brigadeführer*. In Norway, on the other hand . . . Well, if you were to offer me a good position in Germany, I'd leave tomorrow."

She smiled and placed her hand lightly on Seeholz's, noticing that it almost immediately had the desired effect on him. He couldn't resist flattery. *Men will always be men,* thought Agnes.

"Ah. Good. Very good," said Seeholz, squeezing her hand. "Please don't take offense, Ms. Gerner." He put his hand on her shoulder. His hands were not the sort belonging to a man who held a desk job. They were rough and dry and felt like sandpaper against her skin.

"I'm merely curious, by nature. England wouldn't be the right place for me either," he said. Then his face lit up with a smile. "At least, not yet," he said, laughing at his own joke. Agnes felt another flood of relief wash over her. Then she noticed a fresh gust of wind coming in through the open front door.

"What pains me most about the English, Ms. Gerner, is that they don't yet see that we should join forces against the Bolsheviks. If we don't, we might all be defeated. It's the Führer's foremost goal, you know, to get all good people to stand together against that monster in Moscow and all his followers."

The couple standing nearby gave him an approving nod. Before Agnes could come up with a reply, Seeholz shifted his attention to the stairway. Agnes and the others turned to look in the same direction.

Gustav Lande was coming down the stairs carrying a nightgown-clad child in his arms. For a moment Agnes was seized by an overwhelming sentimentality at the sight of the little girl. Lande had spent half the evening at the Rainbow telling her about his daughter.

"*Ah, das schöne Kind,*" said Seeholz, reaching out to caress the girl's cheek. Agnes stared at the skull with the SS emblem on the brigadier's ring as his hand moved up and down.

The child pressed her head against the shiny lapel of her father's tux.

"Cecilia, say hello to Agnes," said Lande. Cecilia pressed closer to him, hiding her face for a moment.

"Hi," said Agnes. "So you're Cecilia."

She nodded, her face still turned away.

"Hi, Cecilia. Can't you sleep?" said Seeholz, speaking faltering Norwegian.

Lande bounced her up and down a couple of times and then whispered something in her ear. The child was attracting the attention of everyone in the room. A sigh passed through the crowd, as if Gustav Lande were showing them a newly acquired pet.

"I had a nightgown just like yours when I was little," said Agnes. She had managed to make eye contact with Cecilia, and she saw an opportunity to reach even deeper into Lande's heart. The child gave her a shy smile.

"All these people are going to have dinner with us tonight," said Lande. "So be a good girl, Cecilia, and do as Johanne tells you."

"Oh, let the child stay up," said Seeholz, this time in German. His remark prompted laughter.

Cecilia whispered something to her father. Agnes noticed the maid standing halfway down the stairs. Her eyes rested on Agnes, making her feel uncomfortable.

Lande paused to think, then glanced at Agnes and gave her a wry smile.

"I'm afraid that won't do, Cecilia. We're just about to sit down to dinner. Johanne will put you to bed. And that's that."

Cecilia pushed her long brown hair away from her face and pointed at Agnes.

"I want that lady to read to me," she said quietly before hiding her face against her father's chest.

"Cecilia, sweetheart. We're just about to have dinner," said Lande.

Again she pointed, with that little smile on her face.

"Of course I'll read to you," said Agnes, casting a quick glance at the maid on the stairs.

Lande sighed in resignation, but something in his expression told Agnes that this was what he'd been dreaming of.

"Excuse us for a moment, Ernst," he said to Seeholz.

"My dear Gustav, we have the whole evening ahead of us," replied the brigadier.

Ernst, thought Agnes as she climbed the stairs. *Gustav Lande and Brigadier Seeholz are on a first-name basis, and here I am on my way upstairs to put his daughter to bed.* She slipped past the maid without meeting her eye. Yet she was aware of the woman's poorly concealed jealousy as she passed.

Cecilia jumped out of her father's arms as soon as they got upstairs and walked between Lande and Agnes down the bright corridor. The child limped slightly, though it was not as bad as Agnes had imagined, given what Lande had told her at the Rainbow Club. The walls were covered with modern art that was actually far too progressive for a Nazi such as Lande. She caught herself wondering what his art collection was worth, just as they passed the open door to a bedroom halfway down the corridor.

"That's Papa's room," Cecilia said as she hurried on ahead.

Lande laughed and shared a smile with Agnes.

"You mustn't read too long, Agnes," he said when they reached Cecilia's room. "Two pages should be enough."

"We'll manage," she said, giving him a gentle push toward the door.

"She's so trusting," he whispered. "I . . ."

Agnes held her finger to her lips. He took her left hand and squeezed it lightly. She sent him off with a smile that was only for him.

In Cecilia's room the setting sun shone softly over the herringbone pattern of the parquet floor, which was visible between two large Persian rugs. The bookcases held an array of teddy bears and porcelain dolls. On the wall above the little desk, which stood between the windows that faced the garden and terrace, hung a photograph of a woman, perhaps in her early thirties. She was smiling at the photographer from under a wide-brimmed summer hat. Agnes saw at once how much the woman resembled Cecilia. The lovely nose, the arched eyebrows, the round cheeks, the small mouth.

"All right. What shall we read?" she asked.

Cecilia was already sitting on the canopy bed with her head tilted back and an old, worn volume of fairy tales in her hands. She held the book up toward Agnes, who sat down on the bed and spread the comforter over her. As Agnes leafed through the book, she caught sight of a name printed in childish script on the colophon page. "Sonja Bratberg" it said in big letters in the upper-right corner.

"Is this your mother's old book?" asked Agnes.

Cecilia nodded.

"Is your mother still alive?" said Cecilia.

"Yes," replied Agnes, thinking that it would have been best if her own mother had died and Cecilia's had lived.

After Agnes had finished reading the story and the troll was dead, she stayed with Cecilia until the girl fell asleep. For several minutes she looked at the child, following her slumbering pulse until it merged with her own breathing, and then began stroking Cecilia's hair. A cacophony of voices and a boisterous surge in mood rose up from the open terrace door below. The clinking of glasses and the clattering of silverware against three dozen china plates told her that the party had started on the first course. She could hear Seeholz's coarse laughter mixed with the women's shrill chatter. Fragments of German and Norwegian filled the room. Agnes drew the heavy drapes and, uncertain what would be best, left the door to the corridor ajar.

When she entered the large dining room, she was greeted as some sort of heroine. Women she'd met only half an hour before nodded and smiled at her. The men looked at her as if she were a born spouse and mother, and Gustav Lande introduced her once again, then proposed a toast in her honor. He had seated her right across from him, with none other than Brigadier Seeholz as her dinner partner for the evening. After the toast, Seeholz stated that never had he felt such anticipation as he awaited his dinner partner, who was delayed for such a noble cause. And Seeholz proved himself to be as deliberately charming as Agnes had suspected he would be. He entertained at least ten of the forty guests at the table with amusing little anecdotes from the field and witticisms that were sophisticated enough not to be considered inappropriate. He also praised the women in Agnes's family to the skies. She put a good face on things. Several days earlier she had received the first letter from her sister, and she needed no reminder from an SS officer to know what an enormous sacrifice that entailed.

Every time she surveyed the table, her eyes met Lande's. He looked almost ten years younger than when she last saw him. She reminded herself why she was here. For God's sake she needed to be careful not to drink too much. There were limits, however, to how cautious she could be, because she didn't want to arouse Seeholz's suspicions.

When everyone had finished eating, she excused herself. Instead of heading for the bathroom, she went through the adjoining library and out the door to the terrace at the opposite end of the house. She needed to be alone to gather her thoughts and have a smoke. She sat down on one of the metal chairs.

How beautiful, she thought, looking out at the garden, which was bathed in the last rays of sun from the west. These grounds, this house. A light breeze brushed her cheek. She took a deep drag on her cigarette and closed her eyes for a moment, enjoying the relief she felt at escaping Seeholz's attempts to pin her down.

The door behind her opened.

That must be Gustav, she thought, and slowly turned around.

But it wasn't. The man came outside, carefully closing the door behind him. She vaguely recalled Lande introducing her to him over aperitifs. He was a short, thin man with thick dark hair slicked back with pomade, and she'd thought he was rather shy, although they hadn't exchanged a single word.

"A lovely evening," he said in almost perfect Norwegian. Though the slightest trace of a German accent revealed that he was not a native of Norway, he spoke Norwegian better than any other German she'd met. "We'll soon have to put up the blackout curtains," he went on without waiting for her to respond. He stared up at the sky, as if it were filled with hundreds of British planes.

If only, thought Agnes. *If only they would arrive soon to free us all, to free me and the Pilgrim, so that I can prove to him that we're not doomed, that this life belongs to us, to the two of us alone.*

The man took a silver cigarette case from the pocket of his tux. Strangely, his jacket reminded her of England. Maybe he'd had it made there sometime before the war. How she longed to go back.

But she would never leave the Pilgrim. Not even if it meant dying.

Her heart lurched. She simply had to get hold of him tonight. She had to.

"A truly lovely evening," said the man again, gesturing inquiringly at the chair beside her.

"Yes, it truly is," she replied and motioned for him to take a seat.

"I must say that Mr. Lande throws a good party. My only quibble with the presence of so many officers is that there's always too much dancing and singing as the evening wears on."

Agnes laughed quietly.

"Don't be fooled by Brigadier Seeholz. His job is to find enough prisoners of war to work in Mr. Lande's factories. He's also vulgar and shameless whenever there are no women present."

Agnes shook her head. How could he say such things?

"Remind me which company you work for? I believe Mr. Lande told me, but I forget things so easily." The young man, who couldn't have been much older than Agnes, smiled at her. She cast a discreet glance at his hands. No SS ring, no emblems on the lapels of his jacket.

"A little mystery," he said as he leaned close and flicked his silver lighter. She drew on her cigarette, and for a second their eyes met.

He looked away.

Loud laughter issued from the open door to the dining room. Several officers could be heard breaking into spontaneous song.

"I love mysteries," she said.

"All right," said the man, brushing ash from his trouser leg. "I'm the head of a company that exports something to Germany. Something that you have in great quantities here in this country. Or, to be more precise, we export something made from this something that you have so much of."

"Fish," she said.

He laughed quietly and stubbed out his cigarette.

"Well, not exactly. And don't worry, it's a civilian company, though under military control, of course." He took the silver case from his pocket, took out another cigarette, and lit it.

"You said the company is under military control?" Agnes tilted her head and feigned confusion without taking it too far. "I truly have no idea."

"Try again," said the man, giving her a smile. There was something disarming about his face, something honest and boyish. But what was hiding behind that trusting mask? *Darkness and death,* she suddenly thought, then quickly pushed that thought aside.

"I know you'll get it," said the man. He ran his hand over his hair, as if to reassure himself that it was as perfect as it had been before he left for Lande's house that evening.

"No, I really don't know," said Agnes.

"Here's a hint. We Germans are big on receiving orders, which have to be written—"

"Forests," said Agnes. "Paper. You're exporting paper!" She leaned toward him, placed her hand on his arm, and laughed.

"Right," said the man.

Agnes let her laughter fade away before she removed her hand.

"What was your name again? I'm afraid I've forgotten . . ."

"Waldhorst," he said, holding out his hand. "Peter Waldhorst."

"Paper. How interesting," she said. "How long have you been in Norway?"

"Since the fall of 1940."

"You speak excellent Norwegian," she told him.

"Language is the key to doing business in a foreign country."

"Then I think you must be a very successful businessman, Mr. Waldhorst."

He thanked her and gave her another trustworthy, boyish smile.

A group of people came out onto the terrace, talking and laughing loudly. Waldhorst turned to look at them.

Waldhorst, thought Agnes. *You're just the sort of man that Archibald Lafton warned me about.*

CHAPTER 31

Wednesday, June 11, 2003
Ullevål Hospital
Oslo, Norway

Traffic was backed up along Finnmarksgata, and Tommy Bergmann only got as far as the pedestrian overpass between the Munch Museum and Tøyen Park before coming to a standstill. He lit a cigarette and looked once again at the text from Hadja. It was a good thing he'd replied so quickly. If he had waited until this morning, he would undoubtedly have turned down her invitation. And he needed to get on with his life. He couldn't carry on this way.

The nurse at the reception desk tilted her head to one side as she introduced herself. A swiftly growing headache gripped his temples. A steady stream of people passed by on either side of him. Bergmann stood there at the desk like an exhausted tourist in his own town, surprised and dumbfounded by all the people in what yesterday had been a deserted hospital. He was especially surprised by the nurse, who was now smiling at him.

"Tommy? Don't you recognize me?" she said with a drawling Nordland accent. Her black hair was pulled back into a ponytail. She wore rimless glasses, and her dark eyes shone with warmth. He knew he'd seen her somewhere before, but was suddenly overcome with shyness. In fact, he'd crossed paths with her several times and even been over to her place for dinner a few times. She was one of Hege's friends, not a close friend, but still part of her social circle. An awkward silence ensued, primarily because he couldn't begin to remember her name. There was also the fact that he was the one who'd been left behind. And that this woman knew that he had mistreated Hege. He had once promised a child—an abused and murdered child—that he would never become the sort of man who beat up women. Yet here he stood in front of this dark-haired nurse, and they both knew that he, Tommy Bergmann, was indeed that sort of man. And it was unforgivable. Disappointment seemed to be etched into her expression. He had no doubt been on his best behavior whenever they'd met before. He'd been gentle and charming and generous. But that was all merely a mask, and a monster lay beneath it. Who could forgive a man like that?

"Oh, sure," said Bergmann. "Of course I recognize you." He managed a brief smile. Someone bumped into him from behind. He turned to see an old man coming out of the cafeteria, pushing a walker in front of him. It made Bergmann think of the walker he'd seen near the butchered body of Carl Oscar Krogh.

"Are you . . . ?" said the nurse whose name he couldn't remember.

Bergmann shook his head, even though he wasn't certain what she was hinting at.

"No. I'd like to talk to Marius Kolstad. He's in intensive care. I spoke to him yesterday."

She gave him another smile, making him feel embarrassed.

"Is this related to a case?" she asked, looking at the computer screen in front of her.

"I just need to ask him a few questions," said Bergmann.

She stopped tapping on the keyboard. *No, don't say it,* he thought.

"Marius Kolstad is dead," said the nurse. "He died last night."

Bergmann groaned.

So Kolstad had left this world, taking with him secrets that Bergmann would have given almost anything to know.

"Well, at least he's no longer suffering," he said. The nurse nodded. She opened her mouth to say something, but then seemed to decide otherwise.

"Say hello to Hege if you see her," said Bergmann.

He left without another word. But when he reached the exit, he changed his mind and went back, walking straight past the reception desk to the cafeteria. It was just his luck that Kolstad should die practically right in front of his nose. Kolstad said that he and Krogh had talked only about the same old things. *That was a damned lie,* thought Bergmann. *A damned, stinking lie.*

At the newsstand he bought a BIC lighter and a copy of *Dagbladet.* The word "SHOCKER" appeared across the front page in huge type. Inside was a photo of the police chief and Reuter at last night's press conference. Bergmann scanned the text without really reading what it said. Krogh was killed with sixty-two stab wounds. The police chief had asked people to phone in if they had any information. According to the reporter who covered police headquarters, the police were depending entirely on tips from the public, but for the sake of the ongoing investigation, she couldn't divulge any details.

He tossed the newspaper in a trash can only steps from where he'd purchased it.

After having a smoke, sitting on the same bench where he'd sat last time, Bergmann remembered what Krogh's daughter had said. There was a man who knew more about Krogh than his own children: the history professor Torgeir Moberg. And he was only a few blocks away.

Out of sheer contrariness, Bergmann switched on his vehicle's flashing blue light when the traffic backed up in the intersection between Kirkeveien and Sognsveien. As the cars moved aside to let him get through, he thought that this was the closest he'd come to a breakthrough in this damned case.

CHAPTER 32

Wednesday, June 11, 2003
Humanities Department
University of Oslo
Oslo, Norway

"Rubbish," said Torgeir Moberg. "Pure rubbish. The connection between Carl Oscar Krogh and Kaj Holt has nothing to do with this. You need to look elsewhere. Do you understand?" The poorly concealed agitation in his voice made it sound even more shrill than it already was. Bergmann shook his head. He'd seen Moberg on TV several times, and he'd always seemed gentle and reserved, showing no aggression toward people who had some cause to defend.

Moberg stood at the window, looking out at the square between the Humanities and Sociology Departments. A few students were crossing the cobblestone square three stories below. For a moment Bergmann thought about how different his life would have been if he'd studied here instead of applying to the police academy, as he had almost on a whim.

"So you're saying—" Bergmann broke in once again, not unkindly but with an air of resignation.

"I'm saying that people need to stop poking around in the past of a man who's been dead for nearly sixty years. What good can possibly come of it? When is everyone going to let poor Kaj Holt rest in peace?"

Moberg turned toward Bergmann with a slightly melancholy smile on his face. His expression was that of someone trying in vain to convince others of something important, even though they had no basis for understanding the matter. He stroked his well-groomed beard, which was completely white, as were the few remaining strands of hair on his head.

"Coffee?" he asked, once again sounding amenable and friendly.

I wonder what he's going to try next, thought Bergmann. He nodded and then cast a quick glance at his notebook. The only thing he'd written down was the word "rubbish."

"But why was Krogh stopped from investigating Holt's death?"

"Because Krogh had a tendency to get manic. Of course it's terrible when one of your best friends—someone with whom you've gone to the very limits of human experience—suddenly decides to kill himself when victory is won."

"I thought there were mysterious circumstances surrounding his death," said Bergmann.

Moberg held up his hand, his brow furrowed. One of his bushy eyebrows was a good deal lower than the other, which gave him an odd appearance.

"Where did you read that?"

"Not sure," said Bergmann. "On the Internet."

Moberg exhaled loudly through his nose.

"*Mysterious* circumstances?" he said, as if tasting the word. "That's not really the right term, is it?"

"I would probably call his death suspicious," replied Bergmann.

"So where exactly did you read this?" Moberg asked again, trying to meet Bergmann's eye. But he had turned to look at a number of framed photographs hanging on the wall, and if Bergmann wasn't mistaken, Carl Oscar Krogh appeared in several of them.

He decided to ignore Moberg's smug question.

"I figure that a man like Krogh would have had a few enemies."

"Enemies? Now listen here," said Moberg. He chuckled. "A man like Carl Oscar will always have enemies. People with opposing views, old Nazis, and God knows who else. But none who could . . . well, you know."

Bergmann looked down at his notebook. He saw no reason to add anything to the one word he'd already written. Rubbish. With that single word, Moberg had given himself away. The Holt case was anything but rubbish.

"So you're saying that Kaj Holt wasn't murdered, and that Krogh shouldn't have poked around in the case?"

"Come on now," said Moberg. "Holt was what we used to call manic-depressive, though today we would say he was suffering from bipolar disorder. He left his wife in May 1945 and ended up sleeping on benches and crashing at friends' places. He went on a drinking binge and who knows what else. I can personally show you the investigative material on Holt and refer you to his medical records from prior to the war up through 1941." Moberg threw up his hands. "The man was a genius, but he was also extremely suicidal."

"But . . ." said Bergmann. He sank back in his chair.

"But what?" said Moberg with a faint smile.

"Then why did Krogh contact Marius Kolstad after those three skeletons were found in Nordmarka?"

Moberg opened his mouth, but nothing came out.

"I suppose they were in touch about a variety of things," he said, though he sounded less confident than he intended.

"Do you know who I think they talked about?" asked Bergmann.

Moberg sighed heavily, as if Bergmann were a child who ought to be shipped off to a reform school.

"Kaj Holt," he said.

"Do you know anything about the three people who were found in Nordmarka? Agnes Gerner and the two others? Gustav Lande's daughter and his maid?"

"No," said Moberg. "Not a thing."

"Huh. So you don't either," said Bergmann.

"What does that have to do with anything?"

Bergmann hesitated before replying.

"We think that . . ." he began, but then stopped.

"That there's a link between the murder of Carl Oscar, the three skeletons in Nordmarka, and Kaj Holt's so-called mysterious death?" said Moberg so hastily that Bergmann realized he had underestimated the man. "Forget about Holt," he went on. "That's my best advice. It won't get you anywhere." He stroked his beard, which was so meticulously groomed that it suggested he was a very vain man.

"You don't like these inquiries about Holt?" said Bergmann.

"It's just . . ." said Moberg. "I'm merely trying to help you, and really . . ." He let the sentence fade.

"Have you given any thought to who might have a motive for killing Krogh?"

"No," said Moberg. He looked away as Bergmann studied him. Moberg was not the sort of person to keep things inside. That was evident from his body language. As if the seat of his chair had suddenly grown spikes, he jumped up and took a few steps around the massive desk. Then he stopped and gave Bergmann a pained look. Finally he sat down on the edge of the desk.

"I understand it was pretty bad, up there at Carl Oscar's place . . ."

"He was killed in an especially vicious manner," said Bergmann. "That much I can tell you. One of the worst scenes I've ever encountered, in fact. And I've seen almost everything. Unfortunately."

Moberg looked genuinely sad. He sat there motionless, perched on the edge of the desk, staring at a spot on the floor.

"The last time I talked to Carl Oscar was a few weeks ago," he said finally, getting up and walking over to the window. "And he was again obsessed with the Holt case."

Bergmann clutched his ballpoint pen in his right hand. He crossed out the word "rubbish" and wrote "Holt." A tiny glimmer of hope made him feel suddenly lighter.

"You talked to Krogh?" he asked.

"I *frequently* talked to Krogh," said Moberg, a bit indignant.

"Did he call you, or did you call him?"

"I called him. Carl Oscar wasn't the type to call people at all hours of the day and night. I always called him. Not the other way around."

"You said it was a few weeks ago. Can you be more precise?"

"Hmm. Maybe two weeks ago."

"Before or after the three skeletons were found in Nordmarka?"

Moberg frowned. Again he did that breathing exercise of his, holding his breath and then letting it out.

"Before or after May 16?"

"After."

Bergmann leafed back through his notebook. *So we're back to square one,* he thought, looking at the triangle he'd drawn. One corner said "Krogh," the second "Nordmarka," and the third, on top, was labeled "Kaj Holt."

"And he was once again *obsessed* with the Holt case?"

Moberg nodded. "Do you really think there could be some connection?" he said in a low voice.

"At the moment we're not speculating," said Bergmann.

Moberg looked as if he had more questions about the three people found in Nordmarka. At least Bergmann imagined so.

"So you know absolutely nothing about those three females?" Bergmann persisted. "Or who might have killed them?"

"No."

"And Krogh didn't say anything?"

Moberg shook his head. "Not a thing."

"What about Gustav Lande? What do you know about him?"

"No more than what has been published in the newspapers. And I'm probably the source of a lot of that information. Lande was a lawyer and merchant, an NS supporter with close ties to the business activities of the SS and to the German trade attaché both before and during the war. He owned the Knaben mines and many other enterprises, you know. He was very important to the Germans here in Norway. He opened a lot of doors for them, and he believed in the Greater Germanic Reich. What more could the Germans have asked for? Lande was an extremely prominent man, right up until he took his own life and disappeared from memory."

"But someone killed his fiancée, his daughter, and his maid."

Moberg nodded several times as he stroked his beard.

"Gustav Lande was so important to the Germans that his family may have been targeted by the Resistance. Am I right?" Bergmann insisted.

Moberg shifted restlessly.

"Yes."

"The National Police investigated the case as a possible terrorist killing, as they called it. A man committed suicide at Nazi HQ while the interrogations were being conducted. I mean, it seems entirely possible that the Resistance killed those three people up in Nordmarka."

Moberg didn't reply. Instead, he took off his glasses and rubbed his close-set eyes.

"Do you think that Krogh may have known who killed them?" asked Bergmann.

Moberg repeated his breathing exercise, as if he were a free diver about to plummet to an unknown depth. He held his breath for a long time. When he released it, his face was crimson, his breathing labored.

"You must realize that this is a sensitive matter. It's practically the last taboo subject in this country. Carl Oscar declined to deny the claim that I made in a book published in the seventies that he had liquidated Gudbrand Svendstuen. But aside from that indirect admission, he remained as silent as a clam. Nobody would run around boasting that they'd killed someone, Mr. Bergmann. To be honest, I can't shed much light on the matter. And very little research has been done about who killed whom in Norway. Almost nothing compared to what we know happened in Denmark. When it comes to questions of liquidation, that is."

"Everything indicates that this was a liquidation," said Bergmann. "And Krogh was murdered. That must be a sensitive matter too. Even more so, if I have to call you in for an official interview."

Moberg held up his hands.

"Okay, okay," he said. "If, and I underscore the word *if*, those three were killed by the Resistance, then it's highly likely that Carl Oscar knew who did it."

"Is it possible that Kaj Holt also knew who killed them?"

Moberg nodded. Then he sat down in front of his computer. A few seconds later a page slid out of the printer behind him.

"Look at this," he said. "This is a list of the five people in Carl Oscar's group who are still alive. But I don't think they can or will tell you anything specific."

Bergmann took the piece of paper and glanced at the names. He had a feeling that he'd forgotten something.

"Holt took a great deal of information with him to his grave. A great deal indeed," said Moberg sadly. "Any historian would give his right arm to bring him back to life. Yes, I'd say there's a hundred percent chance that Holt knew who liquidated them. I mean, if they were, in fact, liquidated."

"What did you tell Krogh about Holt? The last time you spoke on the phone."

"The same thing I always say whenever anyone gets obsessed with something," Moberg said, giving him a brief smile.

"And what's that?"

"That this mania will only prevent you from seeing things clearly."

"Oh?"

"Don't fall into the same trap that Carl Oscar did. Don't waste your time on Kaj Holt. It was tragic enough that he took his own life. Don't make it even worse."

Bergmann stared at Moberg for a moment, then back down at the list. Only five of them were still alive. All the others had a red cross printed next to their names. *Krogh's killer could be one of these five,* he thought. In his notebook he wrote himself a reminder to have someone cross-check Krogh's phone records with the visitor lists at the Oppsal nursing home. He leafed through some of the previous pages in his notebook. Something had flitted through his mind during the last half hour, something he couldn't quite pinpoint.

That's it, he thought as he came upon a printout from the Internet that was stuck in between the cover and the first page of his notebook. The article about Holt quoted a book written by Moberg, but there was also a reference to another author by the name of Finn Nystrøm.

"So," said Bergmann. "I see that Finn Nystrøm is mentioned in connection with things that have been written about Holt."

He raised his eyes to look at Moberg.

Moberg leaned his head against the back of his chair. Sunlight came in from the window to his right and lit up his face. Yet his expression had darkened, as if he were suddenly filled with rage, or maybe it was sorrow. Bergmann couldn't tell for sure, but something was seriously wrong.

"Does he still work here?" he asked.

Moberg didn't reply. He merely stared vacantly into the distance.

A long silence ensued. Not a sound was heard, either outside or from the corridor.

"No," Moberg said at last. "Finn doesn't work here . . ."

"Where—"

"He hasn't worked here since 1981." Moberg seemed to have pulled himself together, and he shifted his gaze back to Bergmann. "But he's the one you should have talked to about all this. Not me."

"Talked about what?" said Bergmann, jotting down several exclamation marks after Finn Nyström's name.

"About Kaj Holt."

Bergmann felt his pulse hammering in his left temple. He leaned forward, suddenly aware there was no time to waste.

"Where can I find—"

"Finn?" said Moberg. A melancholy smile flitted across his face and disappeared. "He wrote his doctoral dissertation on Holt, but no one was very interested in it, other than me. Captain Kaj Holt didn't fit into the generally accepted narrative about World War Two in Norway, you see. And he never will. Finn's dissertation is probably gathering dust somewhere in the university library. Provided he hasn't had it removed and shredded. And God knows it was a miracle that he managed to get a PhD dissertation out of Holt's story, considering the meager resources available. He made countless trips to Moscow, London, Stockholm, you name it."

"So where is he now?"

Moberg held up his hand. Bergmann saw that the armpit of his pale-blue short-sleeved shirt was dark with sweat.

"Finn was the most talented student I've ever had. I became a professor at a young age, but Finn . . . he was unique. I took him on as a research associate and coauthor of two books. And to be perfectly honest, he wrote most of the last one. He was juggling way too many things. He started as a research associate, then became an associate professor after he received his degree. In addition to teaching classes and writing books with me, he was working on a major research project."

"Where is he now?"

"I don't know," said Moberg. He got up, looking very tired now, more like the retiree he would be in a few weeks' time. He went back to stand by the window. "It was damned cold that summer. Do you remember?" he asked. "Back in '81?"

"No," said Bergmann.

"I thought about it in the fall. That the summer had knocked the wind out of him, his project, his life. But I have no idea where he is now. I haven't seen Finn in twenty-two years. He never came back after that summer. He'd cleaned out his office, so he must have had some sort of plan. I went over to his apartment several times. I called him. His parents were dead, and he had no siblings. Just a casual girlfriend, actually several. But Finn had disappeared. I went to the places he used to frequent. He was gone."

"Places he used to frequent? What do you mean?"

"Everyone has his weaknesses, and Finn certainly had his."

Silence. Bergmann chose not to delve into what Finn's weaknesses might be.

"So you have no idea where he is?"

"Not a clue," said Moberg without turning around. He leaned his forehead against the windowpane and stood there with his eyes closed for a moment. "I liked Finn. He was the kind of person everyone likes. I did everything for that man, and then he disappeared, taking with him everything—the documents, the research project he'd spent three years working on, everything."

Bergmann stood up. Moberg looked drained.

"I'll see if we can find him. If he's dead, I'll at least be able to confirm it."

The two men stood there, staring at each other. Bergmann thought Moberg was a damned poor liar.

"All right," said Moberg. "Finn . . . he lives up in the mountains. He's fine. I just don't think he'd want to get mixed up in this. It might make him start working again . . . and, well . . ." Judging by Moberg's expression, he seemed ashamed. Trying to divert Bergmann from the subject of Kaj Holt and Krogh's inquiries into his death in Stockholm had been little more than a feeble attempt to keep him away from Finn Nystrøm.

"In the mountains, you said?"

"Vågå or Lom, or whatever it's called up there. You'll find it."

Bergmann reached for the door handle. An old calendar from 1988 hung from a hook right in front of him.

"One last thing. What was the subject of Finn's research project? The one he was working on when he disappeared?"

Moberg took in a deep breath through his nose.

"Liquidations."

CHAPTER 33

Early Saturday Morning, May 22, 1942
Villa Lande
Tuengen Allé
Oslo, Norway

Gustav Lande gently caressed Agnes Gerner's bare arms, touching her as if they were the only two people in the world. She closed her eyes and fleetingly imagined it was the Pilgrim who stood there with her on the front porch on this warm spring night.

"Thank you for a wonderful evening," said Lande, removing his hands. His voice sounded remarkably lucid given how much he'd had to drink. "Are you sure you won't join me for a little nightcap?"

"I really must be getting home." Agnes turned and placed her hand on his. He enclosed it in both of his.

A cacophony of voices issued from one of the houses down the street, shouts pouring into the darkness. Several Germans had started in on what sounded like a drinking song. Lande shook his head, then nodded in the direction of the noise.

Agnes thought to herself that she had nothing against Gustav Lande, other than the fact that he was thirteen years older than her and a staunch Nazi.

He was still holding her hand.

"We're going out to the summer house next Friday. There will be a small party on Saturday. It would be so nice if you'd care to join us." He reached for her other hand, then let it go. "I think Cecilia would also enjoy seeing you. That is, if Schreiner has nothing against it."

Agnes uttered a sigh and then slipped her arm around his waist.

"He and I are finished, Gustav."

Lande gave her a long look. Then he leaned down and kissed her on the cheek.

"Good," he said. "That's good."

"Saturday?" said Agnes.

"You're welcome to go out there with us on Friday evening, if you like. That would make Cecilia happy. It's up to you, of course."

She leaned in close, kissing him lightly on the lips and stroking his back.

"I'd love to," she said, pulling away, about to slip past him to the cab. "So, Gustav . . ."

He was breathing hard. For a moment he seemed disinclined to let her go, but then he released her hand.

"You'll phone me?" she said, opening the cab door and then turning to look at him.

She sank onto the seat and closed her eyes. The whole evening flitted through her mind.

"Hammerstads Gate," said Lande to the driver, handing him a banknote before he tapped lightly on the roof of the cab.

Drive, thought Agnes. *For God's sake, just drive.*

The driver turned the key in the ignition, and the eight-cylinder engine started up with a roar loud enough to wake up the entire neighborhood.

Agnes felt her shoulders relax and her pulse slow as the driver put the cab in motion. *The danger's over,* she thought.

After only ten yards or so, the driver gave a resigned sigh. Agnes opened her eyes to see headlights flashing in the rearview mirror. It had been too good to be true. Her whole life flashed before her in a matter of seconds.

It's only a car, she told herself. But there was no doubt about it. The car was German, and it had been waiting specifically for her to get into the taxi. She suspected that it would have waited all night, in the event that she had decided to spend the night with Lande. And she had in fact considered doing just that when the effect of all the alcohol was at its height.

The headlights flashed a few more times in the rearview mirror. Agnes felt her heart lurch. Her hands were suddenly very cold as she fumbled in the dark for the tiny box inside her clutch. She took off the lid and placed the capsule in the palm of her hand. The driver pulled over, muttering to himself, "Permit, registration, ID." Then he turned around to look at her.

"I hope you have your papers in order, miss."

A shadow appeared on the driver's side of the cab. A German soldier leaned down to speak to the driver. Agnes stared straight ahead, trying for a weary expression, as she held the glass capsule tightly in her right hand. Somebody tried to open the passenger door.

"Öffnen Sie bitte," said the soldier.

Bitte? thought Agnes. "Please" was a strangely polite word for a soldier to use after stopping a cab in the middle of the night. The driver turned around and unlocked the door behind him.

"Danke," said a voice in the dark. Agnes recognized who it was and clutched the capsule even harder.

SS Brigadier Seeholz got into the cab. The driver turned around to hand over his papers.

"Nein, nein, weiter," said Seeholz with a wave of his hand. The driver kept his expression impassive as he faced forward and started up

the engine. The cab lurched as it set off, suggesting that the driver was much more nervous than he looked.

Agnes smiled at Seeholz.

"So, it's you, *Herr Brigadeführer*." She quickly placed her left hand on his and tilted her head to one side. "What a pleasant surprise."

He looked away, his expression impossible to read.

Out of the corner of her eye, Agnes saw that he was staring out the window. She and the driver briefly exchanged looks. Even in the darkness of the cab, she could see that he was frowning, uncomprehending. She relaxed her tight hold on the cyanide capsule.

"I'm a married man," said Seeholz. "You don't need to worry, Ms. Gerner."

Agnes had no idea what to think. But his words, and his tone of voice, suddenly eased her concern.

They rode in silence along the darkened street with its slumbering patrician mansions on the left side and the black rails of the Holmenkollen tram line on the right.

"What number is it on Hammerstads Gate?" asked the driver, slowing down. Agnes felt her hand that was holding the capsule begin to sweat. For some reason her heart was pounding again. Maybe Seeholz had gotten into the cab to find out where she lived.

"Number twenty-four," she told him.

Seeholz turned to look at her, nodding. Then he went back to staring at the deserted streets. Agnes silently counted to herself, like a child. She quickly counted to ten, then started over. And then again.

As the cab pulled to a stop in front of her building, Seeholz took hold of her left wrist. Her only thought was how to raise her other hand to her mouth so she could swallow the capsule.

"Be careful with Mr. Lande, Ms. Gerner," said Seeholz. "I would hate to see him get his heart broken. He's a very vulnerable person, so if you're playing with him . . . Well, you understand what I'm saying, don't you?"

Agnes managed a strained smile.

"That's actually all I wanted to say to you," he said, giving her a brief, cynical smile. As if the Devil himself were sitting next to her in the dark, clearly amused.

"So this is where you live, Ms. Gerner?" Seeholz leaned forward a bit to get a better view of the building. "Let me guess. On the third floor, right?"

Her heart sank.

She tried to look surprised, as though unfazed by the situation. Judging by Seeholz's expression, she had succeeded.

"I apologize. I like these sorts of guessing games, and you look like a girl who would live on the third floor." Again he smiled that barely perceptible smile of his.

In a flash Agnes realized that Seeholz intended to do what she feared most. Slowly he removed his hand from hers, which was resting on the seat, and reached for her right hand. She recalled how he had kissed her hand when he left the party earlier in the evening. He was about to do it again, and if he discovered the capsule she was holding, she was dead.

God have mercy on my soul, she thought.

Seeholz was about to touch her hand.

One last time, she thought. *I have to look at him one last time.*

"Oh, wait a moment," he said suddenly. Instead of taking her hand, he picked up his black hat from the seat, then turned to open the door on his side.

Agnes opened her clutch and dropped the capsule inside. A second later she was sitting there pretending to look for her keys. Just as she wrapped her fingers around them, Seeholz opened the door on her side. Agnes calmly snapped closed her clutch. He took her right hand. Her fingers, which only a moment ago had held the cyanide capsule, were so sweaty they almost slid out of his grasp. Seeholz paused for a fraction of a second, like a wild animal that can smell the fear of its prey. Then he raised her hand to his lips and kissed it lightly.

Two seconds away from death, Agnes thought as she walked as steadily as she could toward the front entrance, certain that he was watching her. She hadn't yet heard the car door close behind her. The street was utterly silent, as if holding its breath.

The key slipped into the lock on the first try. Agnes willed her hand not to shake, clenching her teeth almost hard enough to crack the enamel.

When she stepped inside, she almost fainted. Her high heels felt like towers under her feet, and the blood drained from her head. She stood there in the dark with her back pressed against the door, squeezing her eyes shut for a moment before attempting to climb the stairs to the third floor. Seeholz would no doubt be looking for an apartment on that floor where the blackout curtains hadn't yet been closed. A window without blackout curtains would look different even without any lights on.

With cautious, quiet steps she went upstairs. At first she wasn't quite sure what was different about her apartment. She stood in the dark entryway and looked around. Her shoes were lined up on the floor under the hat shelf. Two coats hung on hooks, as they always did. Her hats were in their usual place. And the door to the living room stood open.

But there was something about the darkness that was different. Even with the entire city cloaked in darkness, there was always still a shimmer of light on a May night. Light that would have cast a faint glow over the floor in the entryway. Were the blackout curtains closed? Agnes was positive that she hadn't touched them before she left. She stood motionless, listening for any sounds that might indicate someone was in the living room. Had Seeholz tricked her? Had he been toying with her?

Down in the street she heard a motorcycle start up abruptly, followed by the brigadier's Mercedes. After the small cortege headed off, silence descended all around her.

Without making a sound, she took off her right shoe, holding on to the wall to keep her balance, and then her left. Barefoot, she moved along the wall in the entryway, cursing the Pilgrim and his boss for not giving her a gun so she could defend herself. If she'd only had a pistol, she'd be able to get out of this situation alive.

Finally she stood in the doorway to the living room. Her heart was hammering in her chest as she peered into the dark room; she noticed that the blackout curtains had indeed been drawn. Her pulse thundered so loudly in her temples and ears that she wouldn't have been able to hear herself scream.

Who did that? she thought. *Who could have done it?* She was suddenly aware of a familiar smell in her apartment. The faint scent of aftershave.

"Why didn't you come?" said a voice from the dark living room.

She took a step back, momentarily afraid that the parquet floor would give way beneath her. Then she recognized the voice as reason took over, cutting through the roaring in her ears.

Agnes felt for the light switch. When the ceiling light came on, she surveyed the room—the piano, the sofa, the chair next to the bookcase—but no one was there. Then she turned to her left, raising her hand to shield her eyes from the glare of the light. There he stood, wearing a suit she'd never seen before, his hair newly cut, his skin smooth, his eyes looking rested. He gave her a mischievous smile.

"I'm happy to sit in the park," said the Pilgrim. "But not all alone."

"Good Lord," said Agnes. "Carl Oscar . . ." She took a few hesitant steps forward and sank onto the sofa. "Good Lord, how you scared me."

The Pilgrim remained standing.

"We had agreed to meet."

"I couldn't get hold of you. I've been trying for days," she said. "Gustav Lande called me on Wednesday."

"Lande?" The Pilgrim crossed the room and sat down on the chair.

Agnes told him everything, including the fact that Lande had invited her to his summer house for the following weekend. She'd soon have him wrapped around her little finger.

The Pilgrim got up and knelt down in front of her. He reached up to take her head in his hands and smiled.

"That's fantastic," he said. "*You're* fantastic."

And you're crazy, she thought. *And I'm crazy for loving you.*

"You can't come here ever again, Carl Oscar," she said, keeping her voice so low she could hardly hear her own words. "Do you understand? Never."

He stroked her cheek, over and over, as if she were a child in need of comforting.

"Dearest Agnes. Nothing's going to happen," he said. "I didn't mean to scare you. It's just that Number 1 was getting hysterical . . . he's . . . I'm a little worried about him. Forget what I said, okay?"

"Carl Oscar. You need to promise you won't come here." Agnes caught his hand and sat up straight. She took a cigarette from a case lying on the coffee table.

"Why?" he asked.

"Just promise me." She struck a match and stared at the flame.

He nodded.

"Say it."

"I promise," said Carl Oscar Krogh. "Trust me. I promise."

"Brigadier Ernst Seeholz knows where I live. He even knows which apartment is mine."

Agnes picked up the cigarette and ashtray and went into the bedroom. She lay down on the bed, listening to the faint sounds of the Pilgrim as he showered. She rested her hand holding the cigarette on the nightstand and covered her eyes with her left arm. *How close was I to dying?* she wondered.

By the time she awoke in the morning, the Pilgrim had already left. Only his scent lingered in the sheets. She realized that she'd once again let him come inside her. Then she turned over and went back to sleep.

She awoke much later that morning and recalled her dream of the young German on the terrace who was ostensibly the manager of a paper company. They had danced and danced, but no one else was around. She saw only a dark room with no music playing. Finally he put his hands around her neck and squeezed, harder and harder. There was something very strange about him—his elegant hands, like those of an office worker, and his oddly close-set, yet beautiful eyes.

What was his name again?

She took a piece of paper from the nightstand and found a pen in her purse.

"Peter Waldhorst," she wrote, then crumpled up the paper and tossed it onto the floor of the bedroom. *How long are you going to play dead, waiting to make your move on me?*

She looked up at the ceiling. It hadn't been painted in years. In the farthest corner of the room, she noticed a spider web. A fly had landed in the web and was trying to break free.

Doomed, thought Agnes.

You are doomed.

CHAPTER 34

Wednesday, June 11, 2003
Lofsrudhøgda
Mortensrud
Oslo, Norway

Tommy Bergmann pressed the intercom labeled "Torkildsen Hajd-Said." No response. *Okay,* he thought and then slipped inside after an older Pakistani man who had a key. Maybe she hadn't gotten home yet. He looked at his watch. It was 8:05. He paused on the third floor landing to check her message. She'd written between 8:00 and 8:30. He continued on up to the sixth floor. As he climbed the last stairs, he felt his pulse pounding harder than it ever did when he went running with Arne Drabløs.

The apartment was in the middle of the corridor. "Sara & Hadja" it said on the ceramic doorplate that Sara had probably made in school. Bergmann closed his eyes for a second before ringing the doorbell, which vibrated under his finger. He took a deep breath, and his nose suddenly filled with the unfamiliar aromas lingering in the hall from the suppers cooked by the various tenants.

He gave a start when the door opened.

Hadja stood in the doorway, dressed in a short white bathrobe. On her head was a pink towel twisted into a turban. A path of wet footprints was visible on the floor behind her, presumably leading to the bathroom. A fresh scent of soap and perfume streamed out into the corridor.

"Please forgive me," she said and then burst out laughing. Bergmann couldn't help laughing too. "I don't usually open the door like this, but my replacement was late, and I had to run to the store and take a shower, and . . . well, you know." Bergmann could see a couple of grocery bags. Two bottles of wine stuck out from a third bag.

"Could I . . . ?" Bergmann gestured toward the door.

"Oh, good Lord. Please come in," she said, taking a few steps back. "It was my invitation, after all."

For a moment they stood in the entryway, as if they were both thinking that maybe they didn't know each other well enough for this sort of thing. Then Hadja leaned forward, and they ended up giving each other a hug. She even patted him on the back.

"I'm glad you're here, Tommy."

When she let him go, her eyes gleamed in a way that almost made him regret accepting the invitation. He wasn't sure whether he was up to meeting the expectations that she seemed to have.

"I hope you don't think I'm completely nuts," said Hadja. She took off the turban with another laugh, and Tommy started to feel more relaxed.

"You're not nuts," he said. *You're fantastic,* he thought.

"Help yourself to some wine. I just need to get changed. Okay?" She picked up one of the wine bottles and handed it to him.

"Then we can get dinner going. I was so late getting home . . . But you're a good cook, aren't you?"

"An excellent cook," said Bergmann, staring at the door to Sara's room, which was covered with posters of teen idols. He barely recognized any of them.

Bergmann gripped the wine bottle firmly and went into the living room. It was a one-bedroom apartment with a big, bright living room and a spacious balcony with scenic views. Above the gray-upholstered sofa hung a big expressionist lithograph in black and white. He stood there, studying it. Only then did he notice the music playing. On the corner bookcase he saw what looked like a newer model of record player. From the old JBL speakers came the low tones of Radka Toneff's version of "My Funny Valentine." The *Fairytales* LP cover had been tossed on the floor. He shook his head.

"What?" said Hadja behind him. She was barefoot, wearing a light summer dress, her head tilted to one side.

"Nothing," said Bergmann. "This just reminds me of something."

"What does?"

"The bookcase, the music, the record player . . . I grew up with all this." The music reminded him of his childhood in a similar apartment, with lung mash and blood pudding for supper, the feminist magazine *Sirene* on the bookshelf, and the smell of cigarette smoke lingering in the air. Along with the music of Radka Toneff and Joni Mitchell and expensive prints on the walls, which had taken several years of savings to buy. And a mother whose hair was almost as dark as Hadja's. Bergmann had to smile.

"Sorry. My mother used to listen to that record. I could put on something else. It's kind of depressing, isn't it?"

"No," said Bergmann, touching her arm. "Keep it on. I like her." *My dear Hadja,* he thought, stealing a glance at her as she went back to the bathroom. *Will our mothers be the connection that brings us together?* Then his eyes fell on a photograph next to one of the speakers. A dark-haired woman standing on a dock, probably Sørlandet, and holding a three- or four-year-old Hadja in her arms. She was smiling at the photographer, wearing the pastel colors typical of the seventies.

Before the food was ready—lamb chops that she'd soaked in a chermoula marinade the night before—they'd each finished off a couple of glasses of wine. Bergmann was feeling pleasantly muddled as he went to the bathroom to splash cold water on his face. They were not alike at all at first glance, yet he already felt as if they were quite similar deep down. Or maybe it was just that there was something about her that made him feel relaxed and happy. The way Hadja spoke to him—the calm and confident air she exuded—made him almost feel like a different person. As he dried his hands on the towel, he happened to catch sight of two packets of sleeping pills on the shelf under the mirror. *That's not so unusual,* he told himself. When he'd done shift work, he'd sometimes taken one of Hege's pills to be able to sleep during the day. And Hadja was a nursing assistant. That was explanation enough.

They ate their dinner out on the balcony, and Hadja talked openly about her life, as if they'd known each other for years. He occasionally asked a question or told her a few things about himself, but she did most of the talking. The trust she showed by confiding in him made her seem even more beautiful, but it also made him a bit nervous. He was relieved, however, that he didn't have to say much about himself.

"Mama committed suicide when I was fifteen, so after that it was just Papa and me. And when I came back home from the States, pregnant with a black man's child, he washed his hands of me. He's such a hypocrite. Down in Morocco he's a Muslim when it suits him. He goes to the mosque when he pleases, then has a drink when he comes home. You see?"

Bergmann lit a cigarette for her.

"I shouldn't be bothering you with all this, Tommy."

He shook his head and emptied his glass. Although it was already 11:30, it was still warm enough to sit outside. A few kids were playing six stories below. He was feeling giddy from the wine, from the fragrance of all the jasmine and lavender plants she had on the balcony, from the sight of her, and from the fact that she'd placed her bare feet in his lap. He ran his hand lightly up and down her calves. Not once did it occur to him that this was going much too fast.

"My father was a liberal Muslim while Mama was alive. Ours was an artist's home. He ran a restaurant and looked the other way regarding Mama's love affairs. She painted, and the apartment was always full of people. But after she died, he changed. It was as if he was scared that I'd turn out like her. So he suddenly insisted that I start acting like an obedient Muslim girl. I moved in with my aunt and started at the local Catholic high school . . ." She paused and stared into the distance. She didn't speak for several minutes as her cigarette burned down.

"How long were you married?" she asked at last.

"We were never married."

"Was she the one who broke it off?"

Bergmann hesitated before answering.

"Yes."

"What a fool she was," said Hadja.

She took his hand.

He couldn't remember how long it had been since he'd kissed anyone. Hege had left the previous August. *A year,* he thought to himself.

"The first time I saw you," she said quietly. She was now sitting astride him and didn't say anything more. She simply leaned forward and put her arms around him, breathing hard.

Bergmann stopped thinking altogether.

Not even when he lay down on the sofa in the living room did he allow himself to think. All he did was stare at the petite woman walking around the room half-naked, turning off the lights, one by one, until finally the only light left came from the summer night outside.

CHAPTER 35

Friday, May 28, 1942
Kristian Augusts Gate
Oslo, Norway

From the window Agnes Gerner could see a National Police patrol walking up the street toward the Royal Palace. A black-clad police officer led the way with determined strides. The young militia boys followed like a flock of ducklings, eager to put into action the orders issued by the man in front of them. A small German military column passed, heading in the opposite direction. The three trucks drove in single file, one of them filled with Wehrmacht soldiers who were waving to several girls on the sidewalk. The police officer raised his arm in greeting. A little farther down the street, he badgered two young men who had stopped to have a smoke.

Agnes pressed her head against the windowpane, offering up a silent prayer that those two men had the proper identification papers. The National Police had standing orders to open fire on anyone who tried to flee from having their ID examined, and this particular officer looked like he wouldn't mind enforcing such orders. Agnes murmured a curse. She would have loved to end the life of one of these Norwegian Nazis instead of going to bed with them. So many times she had asked both the Pilgrim and Number 1—on the rare occasion when they spoke—whether this was all she could do. Wasn't there more they needed from her? She gave a start when the phone rang on the executive secretary's desk beyond the potted plants. The door to Helge Schreiner's office stood open, and he hadn't gone out for lunch. So she was going to have to take the call.

It rang four times before Schreiner appeared in the doorway. His expression was businesslike, though he'd had a hard time hiding the fact that their breakup had been haunting him nearly every hour of the day and night.

"Could you answer the phone, please?" he said, leaning against the doorframe.

Agnes nodded and walked over to the other side of the reception area.

"Schreiner and Willum Attorneys at Law," she said. She cast another glance out the window, mostly to avoid the pleading look in Schreiner's eyes. He stood there like a beseeching dog, eager to sit at her feet and obey her slightest command. The police must have taken the two young men with them, since she couldn't see them down on the street anymore.

Then she heard a voice on the phone say, "You're the best thing that ever happened to me."

"Gustav," she said without thinking.

Schreiner's face fell. He stared at her blankly for a few seconds, then backed away in an attempt to make a dignified retreat.

"I'll send a driver to pick you up," said Gustav Lande. "If that's all right with you."

Agnes hesitated before saying, "What . . . what should I bring with me?"

"Pack enough for the weekend," said Lande. "I want you to feel comfortable. I want you to feel at home, Agnes."

"I've been thinking about you," she said.

Lande didn't seem to know what to say.

"I've been thinking about you too," he finally said.

In some other time, she thought. *And some other place.*

She agreed to be ready at three thirty. Absurdly, Agnes actually felt so elated that she walked right into Schreiner's office and told him that unfortunately she would have to leave an hour early. Schreiner merely nodded with that hangdog look on his face.

"Gustav Lande, right?" he said.

Just before three thirty there was a knock on the door, startling Agnes. What if it was the Gestapo and not the driver? *Nonsense,* she told herself. She finished putting on her lipstick and studied herself one last time in the mirror. There was another knock.

When she opened the door, she saw a young man with a pale complexion. A glance at his collar insignia told her that he was a corporal, and his uniform indicated that he belonged to a regular Wehrmacht division. Thank God he wasn't part of the SS.

"Fräulein Gerner," he said, clicking his heels together. "I have orders to take you to Herr Gustav Lande's summer estate."

"Yes," said Agnes. "Good."

"Allow me," said the corporal, picking up her suitcase.

If only Christopher Bratchard could see me now, she thought when they stopped at the checkpoint in Skøyen. The corporal nonchalantly handed his papers to the soldier, who had stuck his head in the window, just to make sure that the black BMW really belonged to the Germans. Agnes gave him a weary, uninterested look as she held out her papers too.

They drove down to Rødtangen in silence. The corporal didn't say a single word to her, and not once did he glance in the rearview mirror. Nothing could have suited Agnes better. She closed her eyes and dozed, not waking until the car turned onto a bumpy road. The road headed down a steep slope, and there, nestled amid the dense woods, she caught a glimpse of a white chalet-style house and the mast of a sailboat gently rocking in the water.

Agnes was speechless as she stood, a short while later, at the end of the dock, with Gustav Lande's hand on her shoulder and Cecilia's little hand in hers. The whole setting seemed surreal. She turned back to cast her gaze over the big white house, the two bathing huts, and the reddish expanse of rocks between the dock and the garden, where a variety of fruit trees grew. She imagined what it would be like if all this belonged to her and the Pilgrim; what it would be like if the little girl holding her hand were theirs.

"Over there," said Lande. "That's Holmestrand, between Langøya and Bleikøya." He stroked her shoulder and then took his pipe from his mouth to point. "And beyond Bleikøya is—"

"Goose Rump Island," said Cecilia, letting go of Agnes's hand so she could hide her mouth as she giggled.

"Is that true?" said Agnes. "Is that the real name of the island?"

"Yes," said Cecilia.

"Are you sure you're not the one who named it Goose Rump?"

Cecilia laughed even harder, and then all three of them were laughing. Agnes almost felt guilty when she saw how Gustav's eyes sparkled. He actually believed in this whole charade. It was clear that he was envisioning a future in which he often found himself laughing out there on the dock. The sea breeze blew in from the open waters of the fjord, the slate roof on the white house gleamed in the bright sunshine, and the Norwegian flag fluttered gently in the warm wind. And the young woman standing here at his side would be his forever.

Thank God, thought Agnes an hour later as the first guests began to arrive. Not because she hadn't played her role perfectly. Or because her heart leaped every time Cecilia looked in her direction or openly showed her affection. What was unbearable was the thought that none of it was genuine.

She and Cecilia had just finished taking a swim at the small beach nearby when Brigadier Seeholz came walking around the side of the house wearing a light summer suit and a very unbecoming straw hat. Agnes waved to him and his companion, a woman who looked far too young to be his wife. Then she slipped on a bathrobe that had belonged to Cecilia's mother and began drying the child's thick hair. She wrapped a towel around the girl and pulled her close. She breathed in the smell of salt water in Cecilia's hair as she rubbed her cold little feet.

"A swim fit for a Viking, Ms. Gerner," said Seeholz, doffing his hat once he reached the dock. He introduced the woman who had come with him. She was about Agnes's age, a German secretary who was apparently of no significance, like Agnes herself. Seeholz moved off to inspect the big sailboat bobbing in the water where it was moored at the end of the long dock. The young woman went with him, squealing with delight when Seeholz lifted her down into the boat so they could take a closer look.

Gustav Lande came strolling across the lawn with a few others in tow. Agnes picked up Cecilia and carried her over the rocks up to the bathing hut. The man who trailed the small group was someone Agnes had hoped never to see again, though she knew that would have been too good to be true. Lande looked happier than he'd probably been in the past eight years as he accompanied his guests out to the dock. But the handsome figure in the blue blazer and light slacks walking a few paces behind the others made it impossible for Agnes to even try to delude herself into pretending any of this was genuine. The man hesitated before setting foot on the dock. Then he turned and left the group to head straight for the bathing hut where Agnes was draping towels over the white-painted fence.

The reflection in Peter Waldhorst's sunglasses competed with the shiny pomade in his black hair. He took off his shades as he approached and stuck them in his breast pocket. Agnes had rarely felt so exposed, and no doubt that was his intention as he came over to her. Here she stood, dripping wet, wearing a bathrobe that belonged to Gustav Lande's late wife, with his daughter clinging to her leg.

"So, Ms. Gerner, we meet again," said Waldhorst, shaking her hand. "And you must be Cecilia. Am I right?"

"Say hello to Mr. Waldhorst, Cecilia," said Agnes.

"Call me Peter," he said, squatting down to look at the girl. Strangely, he looked happy, almost lighthearted, as if he'd had a few drinks before coming out here. Agnes felt a little calmer. She cast a glance at the dock where the other guests had now boarded the sailboat, a J-class yacht that Lande had bought in the United States before the war. Waldhorst stuck his hand in the pocket of his blue blazer.

"Look here," he said to Cecilia. She took a step back and clung even harder to Agnes's leg.

"What's that in your ear, Cecilia?" Waldhorst asked, putting his hand up to her ear. Then he held out his hand. A fifty-øre piece lay on his palm. The little girl uttered a cry of joy and let go of Agnes's leg.

"Didn't you know that money grows in your ear?" said Waldhorst. Cecilia shook her head, making her damp curls swing from side to side.

"Well," said Waldhorst, "you'll have to keep this. It's from your ear, after all." He pressed the coin into her hand and closed her fingers around it. "Do you think there's something growing in your other ear?"

"No," said Cecilia. Then she glanced up at Agnes, who once again felt a pang in her heart at the sight of the girl's lively expression. It was a feeling she didn't want to acknowledge.

Agnes reached out to stroke her hair.

"We should go now," she said.

"No, wait a minute," said Waldhorst, conjuring forth another fifty-øre coin. "Can you believe it?"

Then he stood up and lit a cigarette, with the same movements that Agnes recalled seeing on the terrace at Lande's house. *What a fine paper-company director you are, Peter Waldhorst,* she thought.

"I suppose this isn't what you're planning to wear to dinner," he said, giving Agnes a wink. Then he pinched Cecilia's nose, which made her squeal with delight.

"Did he do the same thing to you?" asked Cecilia as they got undressed in the bathing hut and looked out the windows toward the sailboat. Waldhorst was now examining the foredeck of the beautiful vessel along with the rest of the guests.

"No," said Agnes. *He's got other tricks in mind for me,* she thought.

She put on her dress and then helped Cecilia with hers. As they walked barefoot through the grass up to the house, she thought the little girl was the best protection she could possibly have. *You wouldn't dare take me away as long as I have her,* Agnes thought as she poured a glass of juice for Cecilia on the terrace and watched the guests coming back to the house. Only Waldhorst remained on the dock, looking toward the bathing hut. It took him a few seconds to spot them on the terrace. Agnes turned on her heel and disappeared inside the house.

When she was putting Cecilia to bed that evening—once again under the disapproving eye of the maid—the child asked the question she was hoping never to hear: "Can't you stay here forever?"

She was lying next to Cecilia, the curtains fluttering by the open window. The horizon was turning pink, and the steady hum of voices on the terrace below merged with the sound of a fishing vessel returning to Holmsbu for the night. A flock of seagulls flew behind it, shrieking like a flock of fledgling cuckoos waiting for their mother. The moment Agnes cautiously pulled her arm away, the little girl opened her eyes.

"Go to sleep, sweetheart," whispered Agnes.

"I wish you could stay here forever," Cecilia said quietly.

Agnes felt her throat close up. All she could manage was a nod. Finally she said, "We'll have to see . . . maybe."

All I want is to get out, she thought as she stroked Cecilia's forehead. *With another man, not your father.* Then she realized that there was probably no plan for getting her out. How many Resistance cells were there? If what she was now getting involved in turned out to be too dangerous, would they be able to get her across the border to Sweden or to the west coast and from there by boat to England? Agnes walked across the old pine floorboards to draw the curtains. Down below on the terrace she saw Peter Waldhorst conversing with another German in civvies she had not yet met.

When she went down the winding staircase, she saw that Lande and Brigadier Seeholz must have come inside from the terrace while she was putting Cecilia to bed. She paused on one of the last steps to listen. She could hear their voices coming from the kitchen or maybe from Gustav's office in an adjoining room. When she continued down to the entryway, she saw that Seeholz's young female companion was sitting on Waldhorst's lap out on the terrace. Seeholz evidently didn't care. In the entryway she could hear his rough voice, occasionally interrupted by Lande's softer one. She made sure no one on the terrace had noticed her before she turned and briskly headed for the kitchen.

"Yes. Good. We need to post another squadron down there. You see that, don't you, Gustav?" Seeholz's voice could be clearly heard through the open door of the office.

One of them seemed to be leafing through some papers. A faint glow from the office fell like a fan across the darkened kitchen.

"Look at this," said Seeholz. "We need to have antiaircraft positions . . . here and here." Agnes heard the scratch of a pen on paper and wondered if he was drawing buildings surrounded by flak cannons. "It's urgent."

"It'll be expensive," said Lande.

"That's not your concern," said Seeholz. "And I also need an underground laundry. It's much too exposed down there. The English could easily bomb the whole place to hell and back. It's just a question of time. And what will we do then? It'll set us back years."

Gustav Lande didn't reply.

Agnes held her breath. Her pulse was pounding so hard in her temples that she was afraid the men would hear it from inside the office. She couldn't simply stand here. *Get out!* she thought. *Do something!*

"It's the biggest molybdenum mine operating in all of Europe, Gustav. Do you realize that?"

"I hope that one day I'll be able to accommodate your needs," said Lande. "As you say, it's the biggest mine in Europe right now, but the ore is of low grade. However, I may soon have some very good news for you, Ernst." He had lowered his voice, clearly not wanting anyone to hear. Least of all her. But she'd already heard enough. If she could pull it off, this was an infinitely greater coup than anything she'd gleaned over the course of two years with Helge Schreiner.

As Agnes cautiously took a step back, she heard a sound on the threshold.

For a moment she stood frozen in place, staring out the window at the gleaming black cars parked in the yard. Although the two men in the office were now practically whispering, Agnes was still able to catch fragments of what they said. Something about a director of research.

The person behind her took a step forward into the kitchen, making the floorboards creak. *What shall I say to him?* she thought. Waldhorst. He'd caught her now. And her purse was upstairs in her room. How could she be so . . .

But no, it was a woman she heard clearing her throat. Agnes hoped against hope to turn and find one of the hired maids or serving girls from Holmsbu. Instead, she found herself gazing right into the birdlike face of Lande's maid.

The two men continued talking in the office.

Neither Agnes nor the maid said a word. Looking annoyed, Johanne walked past her to the window to draw the blackout curtains. Then she began taking the plates out of the sink where they'd been left to soak.

Agnes hurried out to the terrace before Lande stuck his head out the office door. *How am I going to get out of this?* she thought.

She put her hand on the railing and tried to focus on the beautiful view instead of dwelling on the fact that the maid must have realized she was deliberately eavesdropping on Lande's conversation with Seeholz. Surely she saw what was going on? Agnes had taken a chance and been caught in the act. Now she wondered how dearly this would cost her. If Johanne was a fool, nothing would happen. Unfortunately, that didn't seem to be the case.

After Agnes had been standing on the terrace for a while, someone came up beside her. She heard the blackout curtains being drawn behind her. That was enough to subdue the mood out on the terrace, and the voices of the others became more muted, more serious in tone.

"What a lovely evening," said Waldhorst quietly, setting a whisky glass on the railing. His face was like a black-and-white photograph in the growing darkness. "No one could blame you for turning your affections to Mr. Lande, since he owns such a beautiful summer place." He tried to meet her eye, but she didn't dare look at him. Instead she stared at the flowering lilac bushes next to the terrace.

"Lilacs," said Waldhorst when he saw what she was looking at. "How can God make something so alluring and then allow the flowers to live only a few weeks?"

Late that night, she did the only safe thing. While the other guests snored softly a few doors away, she stepped out of her panties, unbuttoned her nightgown, and left her room, closing the door quietly behind her. Then she tiptoed along the corridor. Through a window at the end of the hall she could see that the sun was already appearing on the horizon. She pulled her nightgown over her head, opened the door to Gustav Lande's bedroom, and sank down onto the bed next to his naked body.

CHAPTER 36

Thursday, June 12, 2003
Steinbu Lodge
Vågå, Norway

It had been a long time since Tommy Bergmann had driven over two hundred miles in one stretch. On his way up the slope where Highway 51 diverged from the 15 at Vågåvatnet, he had trouble staying awake. The long drive wasn't helping the feeling that this was a complete waste of time. He'd spent all day trying to locate the five people in Krogh's circle who were still alive. So far he'd found three of them, though his efforts had produced nothing more than a cup of coffee and a few cookies from an old man in the shipping business who lived in Ullernåsen.

He slowed down to maneuver the tight curves that were taking him higher up the mountain. It seemed as if the road wouldn't stop until it reached the stars above. At last he came upon the exit to Steinbu Lodge and started bumping down the narrow gravel road.

Bergmann parked next to one of the smaller buildings. When he got out of the car, he was greeted by a gust of cold mountain air. It was 11:30 p.m., and the temperature had to be close to freezing. Goosebumps appeared on his skin. He paused to look at the glow from the moon on the shiny, dark surface of the lake at the foot of a slope right in front of the main building. There was not a sound to be heard. A half dozen cars were parked out front, but people who paid to come up here for "good food and relaxation"—as it said on the lodge's website—apparently went to bed early. No lights were on in any of the windows. Aside from the two porch lights and the illuminated sign welcoming guests to Steinbu Lodge, it was as dark as it ever got at Midsummer in Norway. The vast vault of the sky overhead suddenly made him feel sentimental.

Bergmann turned when he heard a sound near the main building. A large figure was leaning against one of the rough-hewn timbers that formed columns on either side of the front entrance.

"A city guy, I see," said the man as he approached. Two English setters trotted over to Bergmann to say hello. Finn Nystrøm was of stocky build and half a head taller than Bergmann, and his handshake was strong and firm. In the dim light he looked much younger than sixty, though Moberg had said that was how old he was. Maybe it was just his long, thick hair pulled back into a ponytail that made him look younger.

"Long drive?" asked Nystrøm.

Bergmann nodded.

"You'd better write your name and phone number in the registration book, even though you're the law here at the moment."

"Actually, I was planning to drive back tonight," said Bergmann.

"Then we'd better go inside, though I was thinking of turning in pretty soon. So we can't stay up talking all night."

Bergmann moved like a sleepwalker as he followed Nystrøm, keeping his eyes fixed on the back of the man's Icelandic sweater so as not to get lost. The two dogs padded behind him.

They entered the main building, which looked to be well maintained judging by the tasteful, discreet prints on the log walls and the fact that half the room keys behind the reception desk had been handed out to guests. Bergmann stood there, swaying like a drunk.

"Here," said Nystrøm, going behind the desk. He placed a key on its surface, which was made from a massive birch plank. "You look tired. I'll put you in room 204. It's in the small cabin near where you parked."

Bergmann was beyond tired. He could hardly even hold on to the key properly. Yet he was still alert enough to sense that there was something oddly familiar about Finn Nystrøm. He turned around at the door.

"Is there anything else I can help you with?" Nystrøm asked without looking up from his paperwork. In the subdued lighting Bergmann felt sure that he'd seen him somewhere before.

He shook his head. Nystrøm looked up and gave him a brief but friendly smile, treating him like a fool, just as Moberg had done at first.

"You'll sleep well in the mountain air," he said, looking back down at his papers. "Leave your window open a crack and you'll drop off like a reindeer in molting season and wake up a new man in the morning."

"Have you ever been on TV?" asked Bergmann. "I mean, sometime in the past few years?"

Nystrøm laughed.

"On TV?" he said. "That TV channel doesn't exist, Bergmann. But now that you mention it . . . maybe once in the late seventies, but that's so long ago I hardly even remember it."

Bergmann shook his head, but said nothing more.

As he pulled the covers over him in the cold room, he realized how little sleep he'd had recently. He couldn't even recall the last time he'd slept the whole night through. He placed one arm over his mouth and nose and breathed in what he imagined was the cool perfume from the hollow of Hadja's throat.

He awoke to the sound of dogs barking out in the yard, and the sun was already shining on his face through a slit in the curtains. It was a plain room, verging on spartan. The walls were paper thin, and from the next room he could clearly hear a woman singing in the shower, accompanied by a man's steady snoring. After lying in bed a little longer, he heard heavy footsteps on the gravel outside. The outer door of the cabin opened and the sound of boots grew louder, followed by two loud knocks on the room door.

Then Finn Nystrøm walked right in.

"Rise and shine," he said. "It's almost nine o'clock."

"Give me a few minutes," said Bergmann, looking at the man's furrowed and weather-beaten face. He didn't look as young as he had the night before. Bergmann suddenly recalled that he'd asked Nystrøm if he'd ever been on TV, and he blushed with embarrassment. In the light of day it was obvious that he'd never seen this man before, much less ever heard his name until he'd started investigating the murder of Carl Oscar Krogh. Nystrøm was wearing the same sweater and pants that he'd had on the night before, with a heavy Sami knife stuck in his belt and a pair of new hiking boots on his feet. He looked like a slightly vain outdoorsman with traces of gypsy blood. Not someone that Bergmann had remembered seeing on TV or in the newspapers.

"Do you like to fish?" asked Nystrøm, rubbing his newly shaven chin. The faint scent of shaving cream filled the room, reminding Bergmann of the times he'd spent the night at Erlend Dybdahl's place as a boy and watched his friend's father shave. He would dab his face with a brush that he'd dipped in foam from a red-and-white Gillette canister. Bergmann had always wondered what it would be like to have a father and smell that scent every day. "Okay," said Nystrøm. "Breakfast is over at ten, but I'll fix you something if you don't get there in time."

"Kaj Holt," said Bergmann as he sat up, fumbling for the pack of cigarettes in his jacket, which lay on the ice-cold linoleum floor. "Tell me about Kaj Holt." The brisk mountain air coming in through the open window made him shiver.

"Not before breakfast," said Nystrøm. "You can borrow a fishing pole from me. I'll loan you my best one."

Bergmann muttered, "All right," and turned to face the window, where sunlight was playing over the curtains.

"You can't wear these," Nystrøm said, picking up his old sneakers in the big claw of his right hand. "What size do you wear?" he asked, dropping the shoes on the floor.

"Forty-three," said Bergmann.

"Forty-three?" said Nystrøm, sounding resigned as he rolled his eyes. As if that were the shoe size of music-school applicants and not a big-city policeman. "Get dressed and grab some breakfast. We leave in half an hour," he said.

Bergmann watched the broad back of his Icelandic sweater disappear as the door slammed shut. *What sort of man is this Nystrøm?* he wondered as he climbed out of bed. Associate professor of history, Torgeir Moberg's protégé, who abruptly abandoned his career to marry a gourmet chef and take over this mountain lodge in the middle of nowhere.

He leaned out the window and studied the property. It looked to be a decent place. Nystrøm stopped before the sod-covered eaves, stuck his fingers in his mouth, and whistled. The two English setters came running around the corner of the cabin where Bergmann was staying, and he suddenly pictured himself on the terrace of Krogh's villa, looking down at the man's dead setter.

Only after they'd been walking for fifteen or twenty minutes did it occur to Bergmann that he really didn't have time for this. Finn Nystrøm apparently planned to be out all day, but Bergmann knew that he represented Fredrik Reuter's best hope of finding the person who had virtually decapitated Krogh and gouged out his eyes. With every day that passed, it was less likely that a murder would be solved. That was an irrefutable fact. On the other hand, he couldn't risk dropping Nyström. Besides, Bergmann found he actually liked the guy. It was just the opposite of the way he'd felt about Moberg, who had initially made a favorable impression, which had subsequently diminished considerably.

"Great, huh?" said Nyström as they reached the top of a hill that Bergmann had thought would never end. They had turned off the gravel road a ways back and begun climbing up through the interminable heath. Far below he could see the lodge and the small lake nearby. "Rondane," he said, using his snuff tin to point to the left.

It took all Bergmann's effort to catch his breath. Luckily Nyström had found a pair of well-used hiking boots for him to wear. They were size 44 and belonged to his wife's son, but they would do.

"What a country," said Nyström, squinting at Bergmann. "There's good fishing down there." The two setters were already way down the slope, heading for the famed fishing spot.

Bergmann straightened up to survey the landscape for the first time. Even though there was a brisk wind and the sun had disappeared behind several ominous-looking clouds, he had to admit the view was incredibly beautiful. For a moment he was seized with a touch of melancholy at the sight of the green mountain pastures, the open sky, and the seemingly endless ridges all around.

"Are you coming?" shouted Nyström as he began to head down the slope.

"What do you know about Kaj Holt?" Bergmann called after him. They couldn't keep on making small talk as they had been.

But Nyström didn't turn around, so Bergmann had to jog through the heath. "Kaj Holt!" he shouted again. Nyström stopped twenty-five or so yards away. Bergmann slowed down. The knapsack that Nyström had loaned him was only filled with a few logs, but it still felt as though the straps were about to slice right through his skin.

"Why are you so damned obsessed with Kaj Holt?" Nystrøm asked when Bergmann had caught up with him. He took off his knapsack and dropped it to the ground. Then he shook his head, grinned, and took out a pack of tobacco from a side pocket of his green touring pants.

"Because it was the last thing Marius Kolstad asked me to do," said Bergmann as Nystrøm finished rolling himself a cigarette. "He asked me to find out what happened to Holt. And because Carl Oscar Krogh phoned Torgeir Moberg right after the three skeletons were found in Nordmarka, wanting to talk about Kaj Holt. And because Moberg only reluctantly told me that you were researching the people who were liquidated by the Resistance when you suddenly decided to disappear in 1981. That's why I'm so obsessed with Kaj Holt."

"I don't blame you," said Nystrøm, clicking his Zippo lighter to light his smoke.

"So, tell me about Kaj Holt."

"Have you done much fishing?" said Nystrøm, weighing the two red fishing poles in his hands. He seemed completely uninterested in anything to do with Kaj Holt as he looked out across the water.

"No," said Bergmann, dropping his knapsack on the ground. He was starting to be annoyed by Nystrøm's tendency to change the subject.

"Give me a soda," said Nystrøm, pointing at his bag. "And help yourself to a beer. It's probably been a long time since you were this far away from your boss while on duty."

Bergmann didn't move. It didn't take a genius to understand what Moberg had meant when he'd mentioned that Nystrøm had had a certain weakness. He opened the green Bergen knapsack Nystrøm had been carrying. Inside he found three half-liter soda bottles as well as a thermos of coffee, three cans of beer, a bottle of water, two cups, and a bottle of Rød Aalborg aquavit. As if that weren't enough, he'd also brought along an old frying pan, a spatula, and a container of butter.

"We're not going to drink the red schnapps, if that's what you're wondering," said Nystrøm, holding out his hand.

"I haven't gone fishing since I was ten or twelve," said Bergmann. That was when his mother had sent him to summer camp, which had been one long nightmare. But there was no need to tell Nystrøm about that.

"All right. You talk, and I'll fish," said Nystrøm, opening his soda. "Since you're a policeman," he went on, making a poor attempt to hold back a belch, "you can tell me whether this sounds plausible or not, since you're so damned interested in what happened to Kaj Holt."

Nystrøm took a container of bait out of his knapsack. "The official cause of Holt's death was suicide," he said, cutting the end of his line with the Sami knife. "But as far as I know, there was never any autopsy, and his file folder is missing from the archives of the Swedish Security Service, otherwise known as Säpo. I went there countless times ages ago. Säpo has files on hundreds of Norwegians, but they'd never heard of Kaj Holt. To top it all off, I was denied access to the regular police report from 1945, which probably still exists. So tell me whether you think this stinks or not: Holt's file was missing from the Säpo archives, I wasn't allowed to see the report filed by the regular Stockholm police, and, even more suspicious . . ."

"What's even more suspicious?" said Bergmann. He was paying close attention, but was momentarily distracted by Nystrøm's intonation. Was that the trace of an accent, a hint of some other language?

"The police officer who investigated Holt's death was shot in the middle of the street in Stockholm only a few days after Holt's body was found."

"So you think he was murdered?"

"I don't think anything," said Nystrøm, raising his fishing pole and reeling in the line. "But it does seem rather unusual that an ordinary suicide should stir up so much turmoil."

"What did Krogh think? According to Kolstad, he and Krogh were the ones who attempted to find out what had happened to Holt."

"That's probably true," said Nystrøm. He pulled a char out of the water, unhooked it, cut off its head, and then put the fish in a plastic bag. It didn't look as if he intended to answer the question.

"Did you ever meet Krogh?"

"A few times." Nystrøm wiped his slimy and bloody hands on his pants. "A couple of times with Torgeir and once in connection with my last project. I don't know how much Torgeir told you about that." He shrugged.

"Moberg told me about the project you were working on when you disappeared back in '81."

Nystrøm lowered his fishing line back into the water.

"Disappeared? Did he say that?" A smile spread across his face, and Bergmann caught a glimpse of the boy he used to be.

"Are you saying that you didn't disappear?"

Nystrøm shook his head.

"Torgeir has always had a talent for drama," he said. "I called him a few days later, told him I didn't want to continue."

Bergmann nodded.

"So Torgeir didn't tell you anything else?"

"Not really."

Nystrøm smiled and again shook his head.

"I suppose you started out like everyone else, driving a patrol car, right?" he said.

"You have to start somewhere."

"If I say Storgata 38, entrance on Hausmanns Gate, what would you say?"

Bergmann didn't reply. He couldn't even count the number of times he'd dropped off drunks for rehab at the Blue Cross back in the day.

"Torgeir got me admitted there countless times, from my student days onward, until I finally stopped drinking. I've been sober since May 1980," said Nystrøm. "Every morning when I arrived for work, Torgeir would force me to take those fucking Antabus pills. But I thought I worked better when I drank, I taught better and wrote better . . ."

"He said you were the best student he'd ever met, then graduate student, associate professor and . . ."

"I suppose he was right." Nystrøm finished his soda and gave Bergmann a wry smile. "But I was also a really great alcoholic. When Torgeir wasn't there every morning with that shitty white pill bottle . . . things didn't go so well."

Bergmann felt guilty holding the half-empty can of Hansa beer in his hand. He felt a little tipsy as he looked out at the mountain ridges, and the sun stung his eyes.

Silently he cursed himself.

All this talk of alcoholism reminded him of his mother, and he didn't want to think about her. She'd always been so neurotic about making sure he didn't drink, not because alcohol was intrinsically bad, but because she insisted that it was easier to get hooked on booze than on any other kind of drug. She was a nurse and claimed to have a good understanding of such things. He hadn't wanted to disappoint her, or maybe he simply didn't dare defy her wishes, so he drank very little up until those last years before she died. Only after he graduated from the police academy did he begin to understand that something in her past must have shaped her attitude toward alcohol. Presumably she had fled from an alcoholic, fled so far away that he couldn't ever find her again. She was originally from somewhere up north, but they had never once gone up there. In fact, they hardly ever went anywhere. It was as if she had been afraid that that man might find them if they left the impenetrable network of people and streets and buildings in the big city. When Bergmann had directed his own fury at Hege, a rage he'd previously only unleashed upon inanimate objects, he realized that his mother must have fled from a man who drank and nearly killed her. Where else could all the rage inside him have come from? Bergmann had decided that he was a pathological abuser, that it was part of his

DNA. But he couldn't blame how he'd been brought up. The simple and cruel truth was that he was someone who didn't know where he came from, and deep in his heart, that tormented him more and more as the years passed. One day he would have to deal with it, find out why his mother had come south and what she'd left behind up north, what had made her look over her shoulder for the rest of her life. The key to his own soul lay in what she had abandoned, and he needed to summon the courage to find out what it was, or he would never be able to move on with his own life.

Bergmann set down the beer can on the heath-covered ground. It instantly fell over, and he sat and stared at the foaming contents slowly spill out. Nystrøm said something that yanked him out of his own thoughts, though he didn't grasp the exact words.

"So you fell apart that summer? In 1981?" he said instead as he smashed the beer can in his right hand.

"Yes," said Nystrøm quietly. "I was in Stockholm and had just been denied access to the Säpo files yet again, and well . . . That may have been the last straw. It was too much work. I spent a whole week drinking, squandered all the money I'd saved up, every last krone. When I came to in Karolinska Hospital, my first thought was that I was never going back to the University of Oslo, and I was never going to finish that damned research project."

"About the liquidations?" said Bergmann.

Nystrøm didn't reply. He just stared vacantly at the lake.

"Now I've got that fucking Antabus implanted." He held up his left arm, as if that were proof of anything.

"So you did meet Krogh a few times?" said Bergmann, wanting to change the subject.

Nystrøm nodded.

"Did he warn you to drop the project?"

"Krogh wasn't like that," Nystrøm said after a moment. "He didn't say much."

"I thought he threatened you."

"Aren't you going to ask me where I was on Whitsunday?" said Nystrøm, casting his fishing line again. "Krogh could be a cold and cynical bastard, but at heart he was an all-right guy. He just didn't want anyone poking around in those liquidations. It was a closed chapter, as he said. But he never threatened me."

"Did you throw out your research materials? All the documents?"

"What do you think?" said Nystrøm, pulling in a trout and slicing off its head with his knife. "I may be an old alcoholic, but I've never been a fool."

Bergmann studied the man standing before him, noting the calm way he was gutting the fish. The two setters whimpered quietly, and Nystrøm tossed the guts over to them.

"All right then. What do you make of the skeletons that were found in Nordmarka?" asked Bergmann. He patted one of the dogs as it sniffed skeptically at the fish guts and then turned away. "Is there anything about those three individuals in your research materials?"

"No, but I didn't finish the project, you know," said Nystrøm. "It seems clear that we're talking about a liquidation, don't you think? The Resistance buried a woman and her child alive in Østmarka in 1944. So why not a family a couple of years earlier in Nordmarka?"

"It's not a family. Agnes Gerner was engaged to Gustav Lande. She didn't live long enough to become his wife."

"Maybe she had a lover," said Nystrøm. "The most basic of motives: morbid jealousy. And maybe the child and the maid just happened to be on the scene. But you're the cop, not me." He grinned. The cigarette butt hanging from his lips had gone out, but he had his hands full landing another fish.

"And now everyone in Krogh's circle is dead," said Bergmann. "Except for five people whose names are on a list that Moberg gave me." He didn't mention that he'd already been in contact with most of them as he got out the list and handed it to Nystrøm. He'd already wasted an entire day on these people.

"You're not going to find out much from any of them, I can tell you that. So what's your theory?" said Nystrøm. "About Krogh, I mean."

"I think there's a connection between Krogh, Holt, and the three who were killed in Nordmarka."

"Liquidated, you mean."

"Liquidated," Bergmann agreed.

"What sort of connection?"

Bergmann didn't reply. He stroked the back of the setter lying beside him and gazed out at the water, following the ripples on the surface. The sky overhead was a pale blue, almost white.

"What sort of connection?" Nystrøm again asked.

"Both Krogh and Holt knew who liquidated those three women. I mean the two women and . . . the little girl," said Bergmann.

"Possibly," murmured Nystrøm as he cast his line into the water. He then looked at his dog, who had clearly taken a liking to Bergmann and didn't seem to want to budge. "It's strange," he said, "how different two dogs from the same litter can be. His brother couldn't stand strangers and ended up biting the poor mailman who had just taken over the route up to Steinbu. I had to shoot the dog myself."

He got another bite on his line.

"There's one more person left," he said. "If he hasn't drunk himself to death, that is."

"What do you mean?"

"One more person in that so-called circle may still be alive. He wouldn't talk to me, but that was more than thirty years ago. A guy named Iver Faalund. He used to live in Uddevalla, of all places."

"Iver Faalund?" said Bergmann.

"But you'll be lucky if he's still alive. I don't think you could find a worse drunk than him."

Bergmann got his notebook out of his windbreaker, an old, worn-out Norheim jacket that Nyström had found for him, and wrote down the name. *Iver Faalund,* he thought. The name meant nothing to him.

"What exactly did Kaj Holt do during the war?" he asked.

"There're two things you need to know," said Nyström. "Holt was the key person in the Norwegian Resistance during the war. No one above him, no one equal to him. That's why his cover name, or at least one of them, was Number 1."

"So Holt was called Number 1?"

"He was Number 1," said Nyström, nodding as he set about making a fire. "But he was also very reserved, someone who held his cards close to his chest. There's no photograph of him, not a single picture. And he seemed to have a guardian angel looking out for him. The Germans arrested him in the fall of 1943, suspecting him of being Raymond 'Hvitosten' Gudbjørnsen. But they released him a week later at Victoria Terrasse, because Hvitosten had just been killed with a limpet mine that exploded by mistake. Kaj Holt had five different identities. All with watertight backstories. And he'd created them all himself."

"Then why did he end up dead in Stockholm? Moberg thinks he suffered from depression," Bergmann said. But then he suddenly remembered that Moberg had lied to him in an attempt to keep him away from Finn Nyström.

Nyström waved his hand dismissively and then scraped some remaining pieces of fish out of the frying pan, which now rested on the embers of the fire he'd made.

"Torgeir had a strong maternal instinct. He's afraid I'll fall apart because you've found your way up here." Nyström smiled to himself. "Does he really think I'd give up everything I have here just because a policeman wants to talk to me?" He laughed briefly, then turned serious again. "But Torgeir may have a point when it comes to Holt, even though I was the one who wrote the dissertation. The problem is that no one knows for sure what Holt was mixed up in. After several Milorg cells and the British network in Oslo collapsed in the fall of '42, Holt was the only one left who had contacts in all directions—with the Brits, with Osvald and the Russians, with the Swedish intelligence service. In principle, any of them could have killed him in Stockholm. The Swedes, Russians, Germans, Americans. You name it."

"And the last thing we know is that he was found dead in Stockholm on May 30, 1945."

"The last thing we know," said Nystrøm, licking his thumb, "and this is something that Torgeir knows too, is that Holt was a couple of hours north of Oslo in Lillehammer on Monday, May 28, 1945. But no one knows what exactly he was doing there. Two days later he was found dead in Stockholm. Then later that week, the detective in charge of the case was killed in broad daylight on a street in Stockholm."

Bergmann poked at the food on his plastic plate. Nystrøm seemed to read his thoughts.

"But if you ask me," he went on, "Holt wasn't killed because he found out something in Lillehammer. I think there was some other reason."

Bergmann nodded, then said, "Those three people in Nordmarka. Holt found out who had liquidated them when he was in Lillehammer."

"No," said Nystrøm. "Why would he find that out in Lillehammer? There were only German and Russian prisoners of war up there at the time. I don't think any of them would have known who killed those three. Unless the Germans did it themselves. But why would they?"

"You're probably right," said Bergmann.

"So what do you think happened in Nordmarka?" said Nystrøm, fixing his eyes on Bergmann.

I have *seen you somewhere before,* Bergmann thought. *There's something about your cheekbones or your eyes.* Maybe it was just the beer that was making him feel muddle-headed.

"Who do you think was capable of killing two women and a child?" Nystrøm stood up and threw a stick up the slope for the dogs, who raced off as if the Devil himself were at their heels.

Bergmann looked at Nystrøm, whose expression had turned serious, as if he'd been pondering this question for years.

"Let me ask you a question," Nystrøm said. "How much of what happened during the war in Norway is actually known?"

"Hmm. Maybe eighty percent," said Bergmann. He considered mentioning that Krogh had been killed with a Hitler Youth knife, but then decided not to. God only knew what that might have triggered in Nystrøm.

"Let's say seventy percent," said Nystrøm. "But how much death and destruction do you think was in the other thirty percent?"

"A lot," said Bergmann.

"Those three people who were killed in Nordmarka belong to the unknown percent, and that means their killer belongs there too. But I think you already know who did it. You just don't dare entertain such a thought," said Nystrøm.

"And?" said Bergmann.

"Carl Oscar Krogh shot one of his best friends in 1943. One shot to the head and two shots to the chest in a stairwell in Bolteløkka. I'm convinced that he had a dozen lives on his conscience by the time the war was over. He was capable of doing absolutely anything to win the war. When he found out that one of his best friends was a high-ranking deserter, he volunteered to go across the border to Sweden to shoot him. And if the Pilgrim—that was his cover name—were given orders to kill the fiancée of a prominent Nazi, he would do it. And if a little girl and a maid happened to get in his way or were named in his orders, he would kill them too. He would have done whatever it took to drive the Germans out of Norway. Absolutely anything."

"That can't be true," said Bergmann.

"Why not? When were they killed?" said Nystrøm. "When did Krogh flee to Sweden? The same day, or the next day. Originally I thought that he fled because of the crackdown on Milorg, but he had at least one damned good reason to leave. The Germans were working round the clock to find out what happened to Agnes Gerner and Lande's daughter, Cecilia."

"Do you really think that—" Bergmann began.

"It was nice of you to visit," said Nystrøm, taking the stick out of the panting setter's mouth. "But I don't know why you came all this way when it's so obvious who killed them."

"So you're saying that it was Krogh who did it?" said Bergmann, speaking more to himself than to Nystrøm. "He killed Agnes Gerner, Cecilia, and the maid?"

CHAPTER 37

Friday, June 13, 2003
Skogslyckan
Uddevalla, Sweden

Uddevalla probably wasn't on the list of potential UN world heritage sites, but the town was nicer than Tommy Bergmann had expected. He stopped in a bus pullout near a cemetery and looked at the map he'd picked up at the Hotel Gyldenlöwe. This should be the place. According to the hotel desk clerk, the street that Iver Faalund was last known to have lived on, Östanvindsvägen, was lined with a series of apartment buildings that had been built north of town to house dock workers at the wharf, which had since been shut down.

As he put the car into gear, fragments of his conversation with Hadja the night before popped into his mind. He had called her, overcome with longing, after spending an hour alone in his hotel room. A longing to talk to Hadja, not Hege. She had told him quite candidly that she couldn't stop thinking about him. That was all he needed to hear in order to get a good night's sleep. But now he found himself wondering whether it had been such a wise idea to suggest they get together as soon as he got back to Oslo. There was little doubt that she was good for him. But whether he was good for her was another question.

Unlike what he was used to in Norway, the entrance door was not locked. In the stairwell he found a list of the tenants who lived on each floor. There were no buzzers to press, just a list of names in white plastic letters. The elevator on his right chimed, and an old lady got out and swept past him to the door without so much as a word of greeting.

He ran his finger down the list until he found the tenant he was looking for. Iver Faalund. *So you're still alive,* thought Bergmann. On the seventh floor the walls of the corridor were painted pale yellow, with a decorative border of blue-and-white sailboats, heeling into an imaginary wind. Bergmann could hear the sounds of a TV coming from the apartment on his left. As he took the last few steps toward the door, he noticed a slight tingling in his fingertips and the soles of his feet. He was breathing faster than usual.

Iver Faalund's apartment was in the middle of the corridor. Posted on the door was his last name, formed from the same type of plastic letters as downstairs in the vestibule. The whole place reminded Bergmann of an old-fashioned dentist's office. Only the clinical smell was missing. The sound of the doorbell ringing inside the apartment pierced through the door panels and out into the corridor.

The TV was still blaring from the apartment at the end of the hall, but not a sound came from Faalund's place. Bergmann pressed the doorbell again. Still no response. He crouched down and looked through the mail slot in the middle of the door. He could see another door inside. *If only it had been left open,* thought Bergmann. Just as he stood up the elevator door slid open behind him. He turned around and met the eye of an elderly man wearing a blue poplin jacket, a newly pressed white shirt, sharply creased beige slacks, and a white sailor's cap with a black brim. His face was covered with an intricate network of burst blood vessels, and his nose was more blue than red. He was carrying two bags from the state liquor store.

"Who are you looking for?" said the man in Swedish as he came over to Bergmann.

"You," said Bergmann. "If you're Iver Faalund, that is."

The man paused and stared. He blinked once, then twice. Bergmann would have given anything to know what was going through the man's head at that moment. It was as if his expression clearly said, "Carl Oscar Krogh."

"Well, yes, that's me," said Faalund.

"You knew Carl Oscar Krogh well," said Bergmann. "At least that's what I've been told." He took out his police ID, but Faalund didn't even glance at it. He merely shifted the bags from his left hand to his right and moved past Bergmann. Without a word he put his key in the lock. His hands were not shaking, and his movements were as confident and practiced as only an inveterate alcoholic could manage. His eyes left little doubt about how he spent his days. They glistened as if he were about to burst into tears.

Bergmann caught a glimpse of the kitchen as Faalund opened the inner door and went inside his apartment. Three empty Stolichnaya bottles stood on the kitchen counter.

"I don't want to talk to you," said Faalund, taking off his cap and hanging it on a hook on the wall. He ran his hand over the few strands of white hair that were plastered to his pink skull. Sunlight slipped through the blinds, casting thin stripes across the old parquet floorboards. The apartment seemed well maintained, just like the rest of the housing cooperative, but the place was filled with the unmistakable and impenetrable smell of stale cigarette smoke and years of drinking. Even Bergmann, who smoked more than he should, knew from the smell what the focus of this man's life must be: drinking and smoking himself to death.

Iver Faalund took off his jacket. The back of his white shirt was soaked with sweat. He picked up the bags and went into the kitchen. Bergmann heard him put the newly purchased bottles away. Then he saw him take out a shot glass from the blue-painted cupboard and twist the cork off the cold bottle he took from the fridge. He filled the glass to the brim and downed it in one gulp. Then he poured himself another.

"I have nothing to say," said Faalund from the kitchen. "Not to you or to whoever it was you talked to."

"Then I'll have to ask you to accompany me to police headquarters to answer questions regarding the Krogh case. You're the last person left alive who hasn't told his story. Marius Kolstad died two days ago. Did you know that?"

"I'm a Swedish citizen," said Faalund. He came over and reached for the handle of the inner door, about to close it in Bergmann's face. "You can't ask me to get involved in a Norwegian criminal case."

Bergmann was caught off guard for a few seconds. He hadn't thought that far ahead. Of course the man had become a Swedish citizen.

"We need your help," said Bergmann, putting his hand on the door that was about to close.

"Nobody has needed my help since 1951," said Faalund. "Then it was thanks and good-bye from the army, and I've never looked back. Now, if you'll excuse me . . ." He looked Bergmann in the eye. His irises were a strange blend of green and brown, and the whites were almost yellow with blood vessels squiggling in all directions.

"But you knew Krogh well," said Bergmann, his voice sounding more desperate than he'd intended. He couldn't let this man slip through his fingers. "And Kolstad said they were looking for sensitive information about—"

"And now they're both dead," said Faalund, slamming the door shut.

Someone opened the trash chute on the floor above. Bergmann closed his eyes as he listened to a bag of garbage sliding down to the cellar.

He raised his hand to knock on the door, but changed his mind when he heard Faalund turning the deadbolt.

◆　◆　◆

Bergmann banged his hand on the steering wheel. It was Friday afternoon, the sun was shining, and here he sat in a parking lot in downtown Uddevalla, for God's sake, not even capable of getting an old drunk to talk. When he climbed out of the car, the temperature made him feel like he was closer to the tropics than the North Pole. He cut across the parking lot and headed back to his hotel.

First he phoned Arne Drabløs and asked him to supervise handball practice. He could have driven home in two hours and made it to the gym in time, then spent the evening—or even the whole night—with Hadja. But he couldn't bear the thought of that, not right now. He could hardly even stand his own company. He sent her a text to say that unfortunately he had to spend the weekend in Sweden. She replied at once that he must have an exciting job, and she looked forward to seeing him when he got back, followed by a smiley face.

Bergmann was lying on his bed in the hotel room, staring up at the ceiling for almost an hour, when his cell rang on the nightstand. He looked at his watch, then picked up his phone. The call was—unsurprisingly—from Fredrik Reuter. Not a person he wanted to talk to at the moment. It had been difficult enough to get Reuter's okay for this little trip to Sweden, and now he planned to stay the weekend, at taxpayers' expense. Reuter had been moderately interested in Finn Nyström's theory that Krogh was the one who had killed Agnes Gerner, Cecilia, and the maid. He'd shown the same degree of enthusiasm for Iver Faalund's possible candidacy as the key witness.

But Reuter needed to establish a credible motive for Krogh's murder. It turned out that Gudbrand Svendstuen, whom Krogh had liquidated in 1943, had no descendants. So Krogh's involvement in the deaths of the three victims in Nordmarka seemed to be the only hope of establishing some kind of motive. In addition, Bergmann was trying to solve the mystery of Kaj Holt's death.

"I'll wait here until you can get approval," said Bergmann.

"It's three o'clock on a Friday," said Reuter.

"I'm staying here until Monday."

"In Uddevalla? Are you out of your mind?"

"Phone Stockholm," said Bergmann. "Call your friend there. He'll find out what he can about Holt and send us the information on Monday. How hard can that be?" Right now he didn't dare share with Reuter his own theory about why Holt was important to the Krogh case. He hadn't even managed to get Faalund to talk, so this was hardly the time to try out a theory on Reuter that would completely destroy Krogh's image.

Reuter sounded like he was about to say something, then changed his mind.

"Call him," said Bergmann. "Didn't you say that you might lose your job over this case?"

Reuter sighed in resignation.

"I need you here, not in Sweden. You're chasing ghosts, Tommy. We have a crime scene, a murder weapon with an almost perfect fingerprint—albeit one that doesn't match a single print in the registry—and a footprint from a size forty-one or forty-two shoe. All we need is the killer."

"You won't find him without me," said Bergmann.

"I won't find him unless you're back in the office."

"The answer isn't in Oslo. I need a few days away," said Bergmann.

"And so you choose Uddevalla of all places?" said Reuter. "Fine."

"I'm going to get Iver Faalund to talk before I leave here."

"At least that's a start," said Reuter. "Is he holding back about something?"

"I think so."

"Okay. But this theory that Krogh killed the three females in Nordmarka? Keep that to yourself, for God's sake. Unless this Faalund guy happens to bring it up himself."

Bergmann didn't reply. *The fact that Krogh killed them is just the beginning*, he thought.

"By the way . . . your friend Halgeir Sørvaag found something odd at Krogh's house this morning."

Bergmann wasn't surprised. A lot could be said about Sørvaag, but he was a demon when it came to tearing apart a crime scene. Only his own sick imagination limited what he might find.

"Something *odd*?"

"There was a piece of paper inside one of the curtain rods in Krogh's office on the third floor."

"He unscrewed the curtain rod?" said Bergmann.

"He unscrewed all the curtain rods and opened all three toilet tanks. You know Halgeir . . ."

"So?" said Bergmann. "What was so odd?"

"There were some numbers written on the paper. Sixteen numbers, to be exact."

"Sixteen numbers?"

"And inside the curtain rod in the kitchen, he found another piece of paper with sixteen other numbers."

"A code?" said Bergmann, sitting up in bed. This was a step forward. The question was, in which direction.

"Sixteen numbers suggests a bank account number," said Reuter.

Bergmann lay back down as a wave of disappointment washed over him. For a moment there, he had thought it might be a breakthrough—the numbers might be an encrypted message—but a bank account? What could that have to do with Krogh's murder?

"In Switzerland or Liechtenstein or the Cayman Islands—" Reuter began, but Bergmann interrupted him.

"You should check to see if the head of the tax authority has an alibi for Whitsunday."

Reuter gave a strained laugh that sounded much like the shrieks of the gulls outside the hotel window.

After Bergmann hung up, he went down to the lobby and paid for Internet access. Then he started reading through all the same articles about Krogh and Holt that he'd already read countless times before. Who hated Krogh enough to stab the man beyond recognition with a Hitler Youth knife? Did Kaj Holt have any descendants?

He took his cell phone out of his pocket to tap in Reuter's number, but then changed his mind. What would he say? That he'd come up with the idea that Krogh himself might have killed Holt to prevent him from talking about the liquidations in Nordmarka? *No,* thought Bergmann. Even he hardly believed that.

He studied the text about Holt on the screen of the hotel's old computer once more. *There's something here,* Bergmann thought, scanning the article word by word. *There's something so fundamental here—right before my eyes—that I just can't see it.* "It's so damned close," he murmured, "so uncomplicated, so fucking simple that it's blinding me."

When his Internet time was up, the screen switched back to tourist information for Uddevalla. *The beach,* thought Bergmann. *I need to cool off and forget about all this for a few hours.* He asked the woman at the front desk to point him to the closest beach and headed off, picking up some sunglasses and two light beers on his way out. It was on a bay southwest of town, surrounded by old oak trees. Quite picturesque, and not too crowded. With a cigarette in hand, he could hardly have been happier. Unfortunately, this idyllic scenario didn't last long. After finishing off one beer, he caught sight of a beautiful and very pregnant blonde wading in the water, holding the hand of a naked little boy. Bergmann couldn't take his eyes off her. She reminded him so much of Hege that he had to leave. Back in town, he sat down on the outdoor terrace of a restaurant across the street from his hotel. Though he was sitting in the shade, he kept his sunglasses on.

Am I any less alone than old Iver Faalund up in that apartment building? Bergmann wondered.

He lay awake half the night. He knew that he couldn't live with Hege, or anyone else, for that matter. Including Hadja.

He didn't fall asleep until daybreak.

For what seemed like an eternity, he dreamed about sixteen numbers hovering over his head, spinning around as though part of a game or a riddle.

At noon he woke up with a pounding headache. Outside he could hear the sounds of an amusement park. *Sixteen numbers,* thought Bergmann as he studied the sunlight seeping into his hotel room, falling softly over the desk, the chair, and the clothes he'd tossed on the floor. Carl Oscar Krogh had hidden small pieces of paper with two sixteen-digit numbers on it. Reuter had said the numbers were most likely bank accounts. The kind of account that only the owner himself and maybe one or two bank employees would have access to. And no ordinary banks operated like that. It had to be a bank in Switzerland or Liechtenstein. Or somewhere even farther away.

Carl Oscar Krogh must have hidden money away.

CHAPTER 38

Saturday, June 14, 2003
Skogslyckan
Uddevalla, Sweden

Several retirees sitting at a plastic patio table nodded at Tommy Bergmann as he walked past.

He headed inside. This time he leaned on the doorbell. He could again hear the TV blaring from the apartment down the hall.

He pressed his ear to the door.

Not a sound came from inside. And there was no peephole in the door panel.

"What happened to Kaj Holt?" Bergmann said loudly from where he stood in the corridor. His words echoed between the walls. "Holt," he heard. "Kaj Holt."

Bergmann heard the approach of shuffling footsteps, then the sound of the inner door opening.

"I don't want to talk to you," said Faalund through the door. "Get out of here before I call the police."

"I'm going to sit out here in the hall," said Bergmann. "Go ahead and call. I'm not going anywhere."

He squatted down in front of the old door. He glanced at his watch and decided to wait five minutes.

He heard a lock turn and the door to his left opened. An elderly woman stuck her head out and stared at Bergmann with a fearful expression.

"Hello," he said. There was nothing more to say. She closed her door without a word.

Five minutes later he peered through the mail slot in the door. The old drunk hadn't closed the inside door this time, so he could see right into the sparsely furnished apartment. There were no knickknacks or souvenirs, as he normally saw in homes belonging to people over eighty. Faalund was nowhere in sight. He must have gone out to sit on the balcony.

"Who *murdered* Kaj Holt?" shouted Bergmann through the mail slot.

He held his breath for several seconds. The draft coming through the narrow slot suggested that the balcony door stood open. Faalund had to have heard what he'd said.

Then he heard the balcony door closing. The sound of glasses being set on the kitchen counter. A faucet was turned on, then off. Then he saw Faalund's trouser legs approaching from the kitchen. He had on the same trousers as the day before. Then Faalund closed the inside door and Bergmann saw only darkness through the mail slot.

Damn, he thought. *He's not going to give in.*

He had just sat back down on the floor when the door behind him opened. He jumped up too fast, stumbling a bit from the head rush. For a moment he thought he might actually faint, but he pulled himself together and leaned on the doorjamb. Faalund gave him a skeptical look.

"Thank you," said Bergmann. "Thank you for agreeing to talk to me."

"I haven't said I'd talk, but you can't sit out here shouting all day."

Faalund left the door open as he turned on his heel and went back inside his apartment.

"I never thought it would happen," he said.

"You never thought what would happen?" asked Bergmann, closing the door after him.

"That a Norwegian policeman would ask me what happened to Kaj. Not a single person in authority has ever asked that question before."

They stood in the middle of the living room, staring at each other. Faalund tilted his head to one side, as though to get a good look at Bergmann.

"Why are you asking about Kaj Holt?" he asked at last.

Bergmann studied the man standing before him. He looked surprisingly lucid, even though he'd probably already had more to drink that day than Bergmann could have handled at Christmas lunch.

"We think there might be a connection to the three bodies we found buried in Nordmarka. You've heard about that, right?"

Faalund nodded.

"I can still read," he said.

Bergmann took a piece of paper from his jacket pocket and read the names aloud: "Agnes Gerner, Cecilia Lande, and Johanne Caspersen."

Faalund's expression didn't change. He walked over to the old easy chair next to the window. The blinds were still closed. He turned on the floor lamp and sank down into the chair with a small sigh. Bergmann followed, sitting down on a worn love seat next to the coffee table.

"So why are you asking about Holt?" said Faalund in a low voice.

"Could Krogh have killed them? Those three in Nordmarka?" Bergmann ventured.

An almost shy smile appeared on Faalund's face. He ran his hand over his sparse hair, then rubbed his chin. A faint rasping sound was audible.

"Why would Carl Oscar have killed them?" said Faalund, downing what looked like vodka from a glass on the side table. He stared into his empty glass. Music could be heard playing from the apartment above. Several kids laughed on the front lawn below. Bergmann kept his eyes fixed on the old man, who was tilting his empty glass back and forth. Finally he raised his eyes and looked at Bergmann.

There's something there, thought Bergmann. Something hiding behind Iver Faalund's shiny, clear eyes. He was seldom mistaken about such things, but the old man had been an intelligence officer before the booze took hold of him, so he was presumably more skilled at disguising his weaknesses than Bergmann.

"Because Agnes Gerner was engaged to a big-time Nazi," Bergmann said.

Another small smile appeared on Faalund's face. He set his glass down on the side table, then picked up the vodka bottle and filled the glass to the brim with a steady hand. *His hands probably shake when he's not drinking,* thought Bergmann. He watched the old man grip the small glass in his big hand. Again he knocked back the drink in one gulp and then repeated the ritual. Finally he picked up a pack of Egberts from the table, took out a paper, and rolled himself a perfect cigarette. Bergmann thought he might as well smoke too. He tore the cellophane off a newly purchased pack of Prince cigarettes, but that was as far as he got before Faalund spoke.

"Agnes Gerner was not a Nazi," he said. Then he calmly lit his cigarette as if he hadn't said a word.

Bergmann crushed the cellophane in his hand.

"What do you mean?"

"Just what I said. Agnes Gerner was not a Nazi."

Bergmann shook his head as he took a cigarette out of the pack. He felt more confused than ever.

"I don't know what she was involved in, but something wasn't right. She wasn't a Nazi. Kaj mentioned her name once after the war, but he said he didn't know much about her."

Bergmann didn't say anything.

"But that was probably a lie," said Faalund.

Agnes Gerner wasn't a Nazi, thought Bergmann. *But she was a member of the NS.* There weren't many reasons for joining the NS if you weren't a Nazi. He began to think more clearly after taking a few drags on his cigarette. If what Faalund had just said was true, that changed everything. What was it he'd heard about Agnes and the Germans earlier in the case? He couldn't remember.

"Why haven't you ever told anyone about this before?" he asked.

"Why should I have said anything?"

"But . . ."

"Because nobody ever asked me. And because no one would have believed a man who was virtually kicked out of the army's intelligence service fifty years ago," said Faalund. He refilled his shot glass with vodka. "It would have been my word against the authorities'. And how do you think that would have turned out?" He raised his glass, as if drinking a toast.

"Krogh is dead. Murdered," said Bergmann.

"And besides," said Faalund, "I wanted to be left in peace. Ever since I moved here in 1951, all I've ever wanted is to be left in peace. I got an office job down on the wharf and worked there until I retired, but I never made any friends there."

"Why not?"

"As you may have realized," said Faalund, "I don't care much for other people." He got up and walked past Bergmann.

And yet you let me in, thought Bergmann. *You let me in when I asked you who killed Kaj Holt. That must mean that you're willing to make an exception for Holt and, by extension, for me.*

Marius Kolstad! The thought occurred to him just as he heard Faalund taking a piss in the bathroom. He put out his cigarette in the crystal ashtray. Could Finn Nystrøm be wrong? Maybe Nystrøm had some reason to be so angry at Krogh that he was willing to lie, laying the blame for the Nordmarka victims at Krogh's feet.

Bergmann got up and went over to the window, opening the blinds enough to look out. Another identical apartment building was on his left. Several lower buildings stood across the road, and to his right was a big forest of old-growth oaks.

Faalund was taking his time in the bathroom, but Bergmann didn't give it much thought as he walked over to look at the bookshelf in the living room. It was filled with reference works, old novels, and Gerhardsen's memoirs. There were also a few framed photographs. One showed Faalund with a woman, presumably his wife, taken many years ago. Another photo, much newer, was of a bridal couple. Bergmann assumed the groom must be a grandson, judging by his resemblance. Under the shelves were several drawers. Bergmann was just about to pull one of them out when he heard the toilet flush. Faalund came shuffling toward him. His footsteps sounded heavier, as if something were tormenting him. There was an air of melancholy about him that hadn't been evident a few minutes earlier.

"If she wasn't a Nazi, what was she?" asked Bergmann when Faalund came over to stand beside him.

"Who knows?" he said as he sat back down in the armchair. "Why did you really ask me about Kaj?"

"Because I thought you could help with the investigation."

"I can't," said Faalund.

"Yet you opened the door."

Faalund looked away.

Only now did Bergmann realize that the shiny gleam in the old man's eyes was not from vodka alone.

"Tell me about Kaj Holt," said Bergmann quietly. "What do you know about him?"

"Kaj is dead," said Faalund. "And there's nothing to be done about it."

"Holt survived for five years as Norway's most wanted man. Then only three weeks after the war ended, he was killed in Stockholm. And I think you know why."

"No, I don't," said Faalund.

"Then tell me what you do know about him."

Faalund turned to look at Bergmann. He seemed to have regained control of his emotions.

"Well, Kaj was Carl Oscar's boss. That's really all I know. He trained him. They had set up cells with as few as four people in each one, in order to reduce the risk if someone was tortured. The fewer names anyone knew, the better."

Bergmann nodded.

"What else? You know more about Holt. You haven't sat here since 1951 without knowing a lot more. I'm sure of that."

Faalund made no move to answer.

"Why did you open the door when I asked you who *murdered* Kaj Holt?" said Bergmann. "Because he was murdered, wasn't he?"

He didn't know how long the two of them sat there staring at each other. Sunlight fell in streaks over Faalund, who was gripping the arms of his chair so hard that his knuckles turned white.

"It's strange," said Faalund at last. "You're the first person who has dared to say it out loud."

"Say what?"

"That Carl Oscar . . . that Krogh killed those two women and the little girl up in the woods."

Bergmann felt the hairs rise on the back of his neck. Two men had said the same thing in the last two days.

"But I asked you a question," he said.

"And I'm telling you the answer," said Faalund. "It was him. It was Krogh. If anyone could have killed them, it was Carl Oscar Krogh."

"I thought you doubted he could have killed Agnes Gerner, since she wasn't a Nazi."

"No. It's just that I'm positive Agnes was working for Kaj."

Bergmann put his pen down on the side table. He shook his head. He no longer understood a thing.

"And Holt knew that Krogh had killed them?"

"I think so," said Faalund in a low voice.

Bergmann waited in silence.

"I think I was . . ." Faalund spoke so quietly that Bergmann could barely hear him.

"Yes?"

"I was probably the last person to talk to Kaj. He'd been in Lillehammer that day and was leaving for Stockholm in the evening. I happened to run into him in the office. I knew him well enough to see that something was very wrong."

For a moment neither of them spoke. Finally Bergmann gestured toward Faalund, to encourage him to go on.

"He'd unofficially interrogated a German in Lillehammer. A man by the name of Peter Waldhorst. That's all he would tell me. I promised not to tell anyone about the interrogation, but a few years later, I made my own inquiries to find out what happened to that German."

Faalund explained that he'd found out that Waldhorst had been in the Gestapo in Kirkenes, but all traces of him had disappeared after that. Bergmann took notes automatically, letting Faalund talk. It sounded as though he'd spent several years trying to track him down.

"What do you think this Waldhorst told Holt?"

"That Krogh had killed the woman and the girl," said Faalund, though it sounded more like a question than a statement.

"But why? I don't understand . . . You say that Agnes Gerner wasn't a Nazi, that she most likely worked for Kaj Holt."

Faalund cleared his throat, but not a word came out. He filled his glass again, but this time his hand was visibly shaking.

They sat in silence for a long time until Faalund suddenly exclaimed, "That's the only answer that makes any sense! Don't you understand?" He stared at Bergmann, clutching his glass in his big hand. Then he closed his eyes as he raised the glass to his lips.

"Don't I understand what?" asked Bergmann quietly.

Faalund seemed to be gathering his strength. He still had his eyes closed as he took a deep breath.

"I'm going to tell you what I really think, Bergmann. I never thought I'd ever tell this to a living soul. I think that Kaj doubted it was Gudbrand Svendstuen who betrayed the Resistance in the fall of 1942. Gudbrand didn't know enough to do any real damage. But we needed a scapegoat, and London needed one too. Liquidating Gudbrand would be enough to frighten off anyone from turning traitor for a long time. Or so we thought. It was wrong, but people were panicking. There was no time to think clearly. And that's why I think Kaj—either toward the end of the war or right after it was over—made a list of people who actually did possess enough information to have done such major damage."

Faalund opened his eyes and looked at Bergmann, who was frowning.

"Which was why he interrogated Waldhorst. To find out who the real traitor had been."

"What are you trying to tell me?" asked Bergmann.

"What do you think I'm trying to tell you?"

"So it wasn't Krogh who liquidated Svendstuen?"

"A twist of fate," said Faalund. "The gun was meant to be found in Gudbrand's hand."

"So you're saying that . . ."

"Why was there no file on Krogh in Lillehammer?" asked Faalund. "He was the only Resistance member, absolutely the only one, who had no file. Did you know that?"

"You mean that . . ." said Bergmann, shaking his head. He couldn't bring himself to say anything more.

Neither of them spoke for several minutes.

Bergmann was about to break the silence, but Faalund beat him to it.

"I think that Carl Oscar Krogh was the double agent Kaj was looking for." He slapped his big hand on the armrest of his chair. "There. I said it. But I'm just an old drunk, right?"

"No."

Faalund snorted.

"Go ahead and tell me I'm not just an old drunk." He drained his glass. His expression had closed and he had a remote look in his eyes, as if to suggest that this conversation was now over for good.

CHAPTER 39

Saturday, August 22, 1942
Villa Lande
Tuengen Allé
Oslo, Norway

Gustav Lande had just tapped his fork against his crystal glass and was now standing at the table with a small piece of paper in his hand. Agnes could see how nervous he was and tried to calm him with a gentle smile, but the page nonetheless slipped out of his fingers, carried away by the warm, fresh breeze blowing in from the open terrace doors. The paper eventually settled on the floor at Lande's feet.

The two dozen guests burst out laughing, and finally Lande had to smile too, if a bit uncertainly at first. Then he seemed to give up and joined in, laughing as merrily as he could. But he left the piece of paper on the floor.

Agnes surveyed the guests as she held Cecilia's hand. At Brigadier Seeholz's request, the little girl had been allowed to come downstairs. No one should need to sleep on such a beautiful summer evening, he'd said. And Agnes had to admit that he was right. She looked down at the little hand in her own. Both were suntanned after spending the summer at Rødtangen. Cecilia's hair was blonder, and Agnes thought it still smelled of sunshine and hope. If a Nazi could produce such a wonderful child, there must be hope for everyone in this world, maybe even herself. Cecilia's hip even seemed to be doing better after the summer; all the swimming that she'd done with Agnes had worked miracles for the little girl.

Lande again tapped on his glass. Agnes knew what was coming. Her blood vessels constricted and she felt a pounding against her skin. Her pulse had quickened so suddenly that she hadn't had time to register it. Gustav gave her a smile, and she smiled back, but then lowered her eyes. Seeholz's chair creaked as he sat beside her. She glanced at him, but then regretted looking in that direction as she met the eye of Peter Waldhorst, seated across from her. He smiled briefly and silently raised his glass to her. Then he downed his drink and began looking around the room. He signaled to the waiter, who moved soundlessly around the table to pull out the bottle of white wine that was sitting in a cooler in front of Waldhorst. Waldhorst leaned toward the woman seated next to him and whispered something in her ear as all other conversation faded.

"My dear friends," said Lande. A slight break in his voice indicated he was still not in complete control of the situation. "We . . . How should I say this? We have gathered here so often, though in my opinion not often enough, but today . . . Well, I have invited all of you here to officially salute General von Manstein and the Führer for the fall of Sevastopol this summer."

The group broke into spontaneous cheering, thanking both the Führer and every soldier who had given his life in the fight against the Bolsheviks. Agnes found herself thinking about her own sister—something she did only rarely—who was somewhere between the Führer's Wolf's Lair in East Prussia and either Moscow or Sevastopol.

"But there's more. There's more!" Lande picked up his Bohemian-crystal wine glass. "There are two other very special reasons I've invited you here to my . . . modernist home." Lande raised his glass to Seeholz, who had claimed earlier that evening—only half jokingly—that the house could be said to be too much in the Bauhaus style. "First of all," he said. "Business."

"Business," said Seeholz, giving Agnes a poke. "Always business, right?"

Seeholz's remark caused a quiet murmuring around the table, if for no other reason than to give him the attention he craved. Cecilia clutched Agnes's hand and looked up at her, her green eyes shining. Agnes pulled her close, setting her on her lap.

"Second, love," said Lande.

"Finally," said Seeholz. This time there was loud laughter.

"So first, let's talk about molybdenum," said Lande.

"That's *our* love," replied Waldhorst from the end of the table as he drained his glass. Laughter resounded through the dining room. The fresh breeze again swept through the room, fluttering the linen drapes at the French doors. The drapes billowed into the room for a moment, then fell back into place. Agnes looked at the other guests before turning her gaze to Waldhorst. He was staring at her, as though gazing right through her, deep into her soul. She dismissed the idea and bent over Cecilia, stroking the child's cheek, breathing in the scent of her newly washed hair, noting her quick pulse, thinking that she and the Pilgrim should have had a child like this. *If only you were mine,* Agnes thought, taking the soft little hand in her own.

"As you all know," said Lande, taking a step back, "thanks to my friend Ernst Seeholz, I am the fortunate investor in the Knaben mines."

"Now, now," said Seeholz.

"Knaben is a valuable asset to our cause but, as we all must acknowledge, it's not enough," said Lande. "The Führer needs more of this wonderful metal to break the Bolsheviks and bury Stalin and his cohorts forever. I'm pleased to tell you now that I had a meeting yesterday with Research Director Rolborg of Knaben Mines. And it was a breakthrough meeting. As I've said before, I've put this man—who can only be called a geological genius—in charge of mapping the occurrence of molybdenum all over Norway. And he has discovered a deposit of historic proportions in Hurdal, of all places. Rolborg thinks it can produce six times as much as Knaben. Rolborg is the only person who knows the exact details for now. I don't know where the site is, or how much ore there is, but he's the most honest man I know, and I have no reason to doubt his claims."

Lande paused and reached for his glass. No one said a word.

"Rolborg says there's enough molybdenum in the ore up there to armor two thousand combat vehicles this year, which would significantly reduce our losses resulting from the Russians' tungsten. A divine blessing for all of us. And upon closer consideration, I'm willing to discuss the possibility of inviting my dear friend, Ernst Seeholz, to join the business."

A mischievous smile appeared on Lande's face, the smile that made Agnes able to tolerate him and this assignment of hers. The smile that revealed the sort of man he might once have been.

Stop it, she thought. *Just stop it.* She knew what he was about to say. And to top it all off, there was this news about the molybdenum. Two thousand vehicles to be armored with one of the earth's rarest metals. Strong enough to help the German forces penetrate the Russian anti-tank defenses. The Russians would lose the Eastern Front.

Agnes took no part in the conversation that arose around the table. Most people seemed to be discussing this magic metal and its endless potential for the cause, but she couldn't really comprehend their words. Nothing was making any sense to her until she once again heard tapping on a crystal glass.

"After Sonja died—your mother, Cecilia," Lande began, his voice quavering. He looked at his little girl with those sad eyes of his, and Cecilia clutched Agnes's hand even harder. Agnes pressed her face against the child's curls, breathing in her scent and feeling a pang of guilt for wishing that Cecilia were her own child, that she had given birth to her, given her life, created her from her own self.

"I never thought that life would smile upon me again."

Gustav Lande cleared his throat. Out of the corner of her eye, Agnes saw Seeholz's Norwegian girlfriend wiping tears from her eyes with a linen napkin.

"Until one evening when, out of the blue, I met this woman, this divine beauty, who will soon be my wife."

Lande walked over to Agnes. She wasn't the sort to blush, but she couldn't help it when he placed his hands on her shoulders.

You don't know who I am, she thought. *You have no idea.*

The applause went on for a long time. As she stood up and kissed him, she thought, *I love the Pilgrim. I'm going to run away with this child, run away with both of them.*

Agnes put her arms around Gustav. He pulled her close and whispered in her ear, "I love you."

Only now did she notice Johanne Caspersen standing in the doorway. That horrid creature who would remain forever unmarried. She was giving Agnes a look that could have killed. When Agnes sat back down, she studied the heavy gold engagement ring on her finger. Then she looked across the table at Peter Waldhorst, determined to show him that she was not afraid of him. But his expression surprised her. He looked as though he might die on the spot. His face looked pained, as if he were undergoing the worst kind of torture. A second later he whispered his apologies to the woman seated next to him and hurried out of the room.

CHAPTER 40

Saturday, June 14, 2003
Hotel Gyldenlöwe
Uddevalla, Sweden

"Peter Waldhorst?" said Finn Nystrøm on the phone. Tommy Bergmann was standing at the window on the fourth floor of his hotel, looking down at the pedestrian street that led toward downtown. With his free hand he opened a can of strong Norrlands Guld beer that he'd bought at the state liquor store ten minutes before. His visit with Iver Faalund had made him thirsty and confused, and also a great deal wiser. Or at least he thought so.

"*Hauptsturmführer* of the Gestapo and *Kriminalinspektor* Peter Waldhorst," said Bergmann. The beer was warm, but he didn't care. Before he knew it, he'd finished off half the can. That was the last thing Faalund had told him: Waldhorst's double title.

But that wasn't the most important thing the old man had said.

The idea that Carl Oscar Krogh had been harboring a big secret—a secret that would have destroyed all opportunities for him after the war—kept whirling through Bergmann's mind. Why was there no file on Krogh in Lillehammer? Faalund was the only person who had mentioned that fact, but Bergmann couldn't help thinking he was right. It all made sense if Faalund was right.

"How do you happen to know his title?" Nystrøm asked. He was clearly trying to keep the agitation out of his voice, but he wasn't doing a very good job of it. For a moment Bergmann regretted his decision to call Nystrøm. He could have called Torgeir Moberg instead, but he had a bad feeling about that man. Moberg wasn't exactly eager to turn over every stone in this case. And there were clearly plenty of stones.

"Faalund was apparently the last person to speak to Kaj Holt," said Bergmann.

He let this remark hover in the air.

"Yes, well . . ."

"And Holt said that he had unofficially interrogated a certain Peter Waldhorst."

"Anything else?" asked Nystrøm.

"That's all Holt said. He asked Faalund to requisition a car to take him to Stockholm at once, and that was the last Faalund saw of him."

"I see," said Nyström. "So Holt interrogated Waldhorst on Monday, May 28, 1945. And two days later he was dead."

"It appears so," said Bergmann.

"Did Faalund tell Krogh about this?" Nyström asked in a low voice. "Did Krogh know about Waldhorst being questioned?"

"No, apparently not. I don't think Faalund and Krogh were exactly best friends."

"The hell . . ." said Nyström. Bergmann pictured him up there in the mountains in his Icelandic sweater, with his dogs and his fishing pole, the blazing sunset over the blue ridges. "So what did Holt find out? Faalund must know something more," he said.

"Due to the ongoing investigation—"

"You can't tell me," said Nystrøm. Then he laughed. Bergmann took another swig of his beer and stifled a belch, thinking that he had nothing more to tell Nystrøm.

"You have to help me," he said. "You need to dig up some information on Waldhorst for me."

"I thought *you* were the policeman here," said Nystrøm, laughing at his own joke. Bergmann ignored his delight and once again regretted that he hadn't called Moberg instead.

"So this drunkard kept his mouth shut for almost sixty years?" said Nystrøm, now sounding resigned.

"This is between you and me," replied Bergmann. *And you haven't even heard everything,* he thought.

"Waldhorst," said Nystrøm, as if chewing on the name.

"Faalund tried to track him down, but here's the difficult part . . ." Bergmann paused.

"Yes?" said Nystrøm.

"Peter Waldhorst doesn't exist," said Bergmann.

"So he's dead," said Nystrøm.

"Maybe. The only thing Faalund could find out was that Waldhorst was in the Gestapo in Kirkenes beginning in early 1943. After the German withdrawal from northern Norway, he was the second-in-command of the Gestapo office in Lillehammer."

"So? As a Gestapo man, he must be listed in the war settlement. And then he should have been repatriated, because he wasn't executed. I would know if he were."

"There's no record of Holt's interrogation of Waldhorst. But there must have been others. Faalund dated the last known trace of Waldhorst on Norwegian soil to May 28, 1945, and all the Gestapo documents about him seem to have disappeared."

Bergmann heard Nystrøm whistle, then murmur to himself, "Operation Paperclip."

"Operation what?" said Bergmann.

"Paperclip. An American operation that started before the war ended. They wanted to get hold of the best Nazis before the Russians did. Keep in mind that it was the Germans who enabled the Americans to get to the moon. In Norway the Swedes managed to seize a bunch of former Abwehr and Gestapo prisoners after the war. Not the ones with the most blood on their hands, but relatively discreet officers and communications experts with deep knowledge of the Russians, counterespionage, and interrogation techniques. The Swedes sold them to the Americans behind the backs of the Brits."

Bergmann didn't comment.

"I'll find out for you whether he's still alive," said Nyström.

Bergmann still said nothing. He was thinking that Kaj Holt must have stepped right into the middle of a wasp's nest. And it had cost him his life.

"There's something else," said Nyström. "Something you're not telling me. And by the way, I'm sure you're right. I believe you're right."

"What do you mean?" said Bergmann at last.

"That there's a connection between the three skeletons found in Nordmarka and the murder of Kaj Holt."

"What sort of connection?" asked Bergmann.

"Let's assume that Krogh killed the two women and the child," said Nyström. "Holt finds out about it, but he's a mental wreck after the war and can't manage to keep this information to himself. Krogh, for his part, has to make sure that it never gets out that he committed one of the most appalling liquidations in Norway during the war. He's in line to play a major role in the rebuilding of the country. He also has such a good network in Sweden that the Swedes might be able to shut Holt up. Remember that Krogh was the Swedes' man in Norway after the war. They couldn't risk having him lose his position in the decision-making apparatus here at home."

Bergmann considered what Nystrøm just said. It seemed a reasonable argument, but he didn't know what Bergmann knew. So he decided to tell Nystrøm before he changed his mind.

"There's just one complicating factor. And it's much, much worse."

"What's that?"

"Apparently Agnes Gerner was not a Nazi. And Faalund thinks the liquidation was not a mistake."

"What are you saying?"

"Faalund claims that Agnes Gerner wasn't a Nazi even though she was engaged to Gustav Lande. And Holt knew that. Faalund said that Agnes worked for Holt."

Nystrøm didn't reply right away.

Then he said, "So Krogh killed one of his own? Is that what you're saying?"

Bergmann closed his eyes. He had no choice. He would have to trust Nystrøm. Who else could help him find Waldhorst? Maybe Moberg, but after their recent conversation he didn't really trust the man.

"What I'm going to tell you," said Bergmann, then stopped. "What I'm going to tell you has to remain between you and me. Or rather, *everything* we're discussing has to be considered confidential."

"Confidential," said Nystrøm. "Of course."

"We found two sixteen-digit numbers in Krogh's home. Most likely numbered bank accounts. You know, anonymous accounts like the ones they use in Switzerland and Liechtenstein."

Nystrøm said nothing at first.

"Well, that's not an unknown phenomenon for people who live in that part of town," he said. "Though it would surprise me if he'd stashed away money in that manner."

"I have a feeling that the money came from another source. Not from his company. And that the account was set up many years ago," said Bergmann.

"What do you mean?"

"Faalund thinks . . . and I think he's right. It's too damned outrageous, but . . ."

"But what?" said Nystrøm. "What does Faalund think?"

"He thinks Agnes saw what Krogh was really up to."

"What he was up to?" murmured Nystrøm.

"What do you think Holt found out from Waldhorst in Lillehammer?" said Bergmann. "Faalund told me that there's no file on Krogh in Lillehammer. The Germans apparently had no file on him. What does that tell you?"

At first Nystrøm didn't reply. Then he almost whispered, "I knew the file on him was gone, but good Lord . . . That can't be right."

"But what if it *is* right?" said Bergmann. "The worst thing about it is that it would make everything else fall into place. The liquidation of Agnes Gerner, the numbered bank accounts . . . Didn't the Germans often set up accounts in Switzerland and Liechtenstein for their agents? I think I read about that somewhere."

"Good God," said Nystrøm. "There's only one . . . No, good God. I can't believe that." He gave a strange laugh.

"So you don't have any theory that would support Faalund's claim?"

"Theory?" said Nystrøm in a low voice.

"Something in Krogh's background that would make it plausible that he was a double agent during the war? Money problems, hidden Nazi sympathies? Could he have been caught working for the Resistance? Anything like that?"

Nystrøm paused to consider this. "No," he said. "I would have known about it. He came from a well-to-do family, so no . . ."

"We need to find Waldhorst," said Bergmann. "If he's still alive, that is."

"I have good contacts in Germany."

"Find Waldhorst for me," said Bergmann. "Just find him."

After hanging up, he lay down on the bed and felt the blood rush to his head.

He wrote two words on the hotel notepad.

Double agent.

If that were true, who else besides Iver Faalund knew about it?

CHAPTER 41

Thursday, August 27, 1942
Hammerstads Gate
Oslo, Norway

When she heard someone knocking on the door, Agnes Gerner's first thought was that it didn't sound like Gustav Lande's personal driver. The knocking was lighter and more cautious. And besides, it was too early. It was only two o'clock, and they'd agreed that the driver would pick her up at three thirty.

The feeling that she'd made some sort of mistake washed over her as she got out of bed. She'd been half-asleep, enjoying the smell that she and the Pilgrim had left in the sheets. Her intuition told her that they hadn't gotten away with it this time. But it would be good to have a child with the Pilgrim, wouldn't it? *In any other situation but this one,* she told herself a second later. But what could she do? The Pilgrim had been waiting in her apartment again, and of course it was madness, but surely it meant something too? She looked at the engagement ring Lande had given her and acknowledged to herself once more that whoever was knocking on the door couldn't be his driver. If Lande found out about her relationship with the Pilgrim, she'd be dead before winter. But every time the Pilgrim, her own Carl Oscar, came inside her, she prayed he would give her a child like Cecilia.

I must be going crazy, she thought as she walked through the living room. *Maybe I've always been crazy.* As she reached for the door handle, she felt untouchable, as though nothing could ever possibly go wrong. The sight of the German SS noncom quickly banished that thought.

"Fräulein Gerner?" asked the sergeant. His voice was friendly enough that Agnes thought he must be making fun of her. Yet her pulse slowed instinctively. "Herr Waldhorst wishes to have a meeting with you."

He's got me now, she thought.

"A meeting?" she said. "We haven't made an appointment, and I'm on my way to visit my fiancé at his country estate. You'll have to ask him to phone me."

A surge of ill-disguised panic spread through her when the SS officer stopped her from shutting the door.

"I'm on my way to Rødtangen. I . . ."

"Bitte. If you will come with me, please."

"What is this about?"

"Would you come with me, *Fräulein*?" The sergeant held out his hand and motioned toward the stairs.

"One moment. I need to use the bathroom."

Agnes grabbed her purse, which was lying on the mahogany dresser. She looked at herself in the mirror, then set the purse down again.

The sergeant stepped inside the apartment.

"I need to change my clothes," she said. He nodded but followed her into the living room. As she changed in the bedroom, she could think only of how she had to appear calm. She'd almost lost her head and headed into the bathroom with her purse containing the cyanide pill.

On her way downstairs she dismissed the idea of putting the capsule in her mouth as they drove. She would wait for a later opportunity. All she had to do was stick her hand inside her purse. The thought of how it would taste worried her as she leaned back against the leather seat. The car crossed the Majorstua intersection, driving between block-ades and sandbags.

She wasn't even particularly nervous when the sergeant stopped, got out of the car, and rang the doorbell of a white building that looked like a fancy layer cake. A brass plate with the name "Berkowitz" engraved in big letters had been newly polished. Her reflection gri-maced back at her.

After climbing the stairs all the way to the top floor, her legs still managed to hold her up. *That's good, at least,* she thought. The sergeant slowly pressed down on the handle of the massive door. A moment later, she was inhaling the strong scent of cleaning agents mixed with the perfume coming from a vase of fresh flowers on a side table next to the door. She could taste blood in her mouth.

The sergeant clicked his heels.

"Herr Kriminalinspektor Hauptsturmführer, Fräulein Gerner."

For a moment Agnes felt incapable of absorbing the shock. Had she simply suppressed all thought of how dangerous this man could be? Had she believed that her impending marriage to Gustav Lande would make her invulnerable? Had he really managed to trick her? Quickly she pondered whether she'd made any mistakes, any obvious blunders. Captain Waldhorst. Detective Inspector. He was too young to hold such a title. But no. She knew full well he wasn't. But he wasn't Gestapo. She would have known if he was. Number 1 would have mentioned him. *Of course he would have,* she thought.

She'd seen this coming the very first time she spoke to Waldhorst. If only she hadn't met the Pilgrim. Then she'd have nothing to lose.

Dear God. Have mercy on me.

"My dear Ms. Gerner," said Peter Waldhorst as he closed the door behind them. Agnes found herself standing in a large hall with dark herringbone-patterned parquet flooring and burgundy wallpaper. Large oil paintings, a mix of portraits and landscapes, lined the walls. As far as she could tell, they'd been painted by Christian Krohg, Nikolai Astrup, and Lars Hertervig. Agnes peered into the living room through the open French doors. The family who had lived here must have been precipitously thrown out. They'd left behind a fortune in art and furnishings. No doubt cash and stocks as well, and who knows what else.

From somewhere inside the large apartment, she could hear music playing on a gramophone.

"Don't look so scared, my dear." Waldhorst was now standing beside her. He smelled of aftershave and toothpaste, yet Agnes also noticed a trace of alcohol on his breath—had he had a few drinks before she arrived? The thought made her pulse slow to a manageable rate. He actually seemed more nervous than she was. She loosened her grip on her purse and stopped thinking about the cyanide capsule inside.

Waldhorst placed his hand on her back and ushered her through the living room, filled with Louis XVI furniture and heavy double-lined drapes that were partially drawn in front of the windows. They continued on through the open doors to the library, just as the last notes of music died away. The walls were lined with bookcases, separated by still more paintings. Next to one of the windows stood a mahogany desk. An extinguished cigar lay in the ashtray, papers were strewn across the surface of the desk, and there was a single framed photograph of a young man.

Agnes realized only now what Waldhorst had been playing on the gramophone in the corner. The Comedian Harmonists. But that music was banned. The Comedian Harmonists hadn't performed in Germany since the early '30s, and as far as she knew, most of the musicians had fled Germany shortly thereafter. Either Waldhorst had brought the record with him, or it had been left behind by the Berkowitz family. But the mere fact that he'd played a record by a group with several Jewish musicians put her immediately on her guard.

Waldhorst went over to the gramophone and set the needle back on the record. *"Mein kleiner grüner Kaktus"* started playing from the speaker, prompting an involuntary smile from Agnes. But maybe it was simply a reflection of the smile on Waldhorst's face as he whistled softly, moving about the room in search of some unknown object. Or maybe it was sheer panic as she realized that Waldhorst would never have played music by the Comedian Harmonists without some specific purpose in mind. No doubt he was trying to provoke a reaction from her. A few record covers were scattered on the floor. She tried to see what they were, but she recognized only Zarah Leander's face.

"Do you live here all alone?" asked Agnes.

Waldhorst smiled briefly and motioned toward the two Chesterfield sofas, separated by an antique coffee table.

"All alone," said Waldhorst. "Would you like a drink?"

"No, thank you."

"No?" said Waldhorst. "Just a small one? It's after the lunch hour. A sherry, perhaps?"

Agnes felt chilled by the cold upholstery as she sat down on the sofa. She set her purse on her lap and nodded. Waldhorst's face was pale; he'd probably been sitting in this room all day. The only daylight came in through the window near the desk. The rest of the room was dimly lit, as if right before or just after dawn.

Agnes accepted the crystal glass from Waldhorst, whose hand shook slightly, like the leaves on the chestnut trees outside when a light breeze blew through them. Waldhorst poured himself a generous amount of whisky, then set the carafe back inside the bar, which was an open globe—the sort that Agnes remembered from her childhood.

"Skål," said Waldhorst, sitting down on the sofa across from her. For several minutes he sat there motionless, staring out the window, holding his glass in both hands.

Agnes opened her mouth to say something, but before she could speak, Waldhorst said, "Cigarette?" He took a cigarette case from the inside pocket of his suit jacket.

After lighting her cigarette—made of strong Turkish tobacco that burned her throat—he went back to the gramophone, took off the Comedian Harmonists record, and dropped it on the floor.

The next record he put on was Zarah Leander. After a few scratchy sounds, Agnes heard the tune *Bei mir bist du schön* begin to play. Also banned. Although Zarah Leander was a Nazi, the song was denounced as Yiddish. A paradox that confused Agnes as well as a great many other people.

"I suppose you're aware that you are playing banned music, Mr. Waldhorst?"

He merely snorted and shook his head.

"Or should I say *Detective Inspector* Waldhorst? Why didn't you tell me you were a detective? I assume you told Gustav the truth. He doesn't enjoy being treated like a fool."

Waldhorst studied her, his expression impassive, as if he simply didn't understand what she'd said. Then he lit a cigarette for himself and drained his glass. He went over to stand by the window.

"We're going to lose this war," he said.

Without thinking, Agnes cleared her throat twice. She tapped the ash from her cigarette into the ashtray. Then she raised the cigarette to her lips again, managing to keep her hand from shaking.

"Somebody ought to kill that man," said Waldhorst to himself. "That little Austrian corporal."

Agnes felt the hair on her arms rise.

This was exactly what they'd warned her about. All of them had been warned about this. After the Venlo Incident three years earlier—when two British agents in the Netherlands were caught by Gestapo officers pretending to be against the Nazis—the British intelligence service had sent out a directive to display extreme caution if any German officers claimed to be anti-Nazi. The Pilgrim had told her a few months ago that not all operatives in the field had taken the warning seriously, and it had been the downfall of several of them. Nothing was more dangerous, he'd said, than to believe a German who said he was tired of the Führer and wanted to conspire to aid in the fall of the Reich.

"You should be careful what you say," Agnes said. "What does your friend *Brigadeführer* Seeholz think about you saying such things? You're not only listening to banned music, you're also demeaning the Führer."

Waldhorst turned to face her. His face had an unhealthy pallor, as if he were seriously ill. Only his thick black hair and dark eyebrows indicated there was still life in him.

"Don't worry about Seeholz. He's a boor who couldn't find a kernel of corn if you stuck it in his mouth. As for the Führer, that Austrian needs only one thing to pull off his wizardry. He needs an audience that truly wishes to believe. The Führer is the only one who has understood that. Don't you agree, Ms. Gerner?"

"Agnes," she said. "Please call me Agnes."

Waldhorst shook his head. He rubbed his face, then ran his hands through his hair, which was shiny with pomade.

"Why did you ask me to come here?" she asked.

His shoes squeaked as he crossed the floor. An unbearable silence ensued. Waldhorst was once against standing before the gramophone. The record turned a few more times, almost soundlessly, before the needle rose and clicked back to its starting position. The apartment was once again utterly quiet. Only the old grandfather clock in the parlor issued a steady ticking sound.

"Do you like it?" he asked, holding the record up to show Agnes.

"It's a Jewish song," she said.

"All right. Then we'll break it." Waldhorst snapped it in half and dropped the pieces on the floor. "It was something they left here. Berkowitz . . . Berkowitz!" He said the name as if spitting it out.

Agnes clutched the sherry glass as she raised it to her lips. For a second she thought she might drop it, but she managed to take a sip without spilling.

"Why have you taken up with Gustav Lande?" asked Waldhorst in a low voice. He was now sitting on the armrest of the Chesterfield sofa across from her.

"I must go," said Agnes. She leaned forward and set her glass on the coffee table.

"Answer me. Is it for money?"

Agnes stood up, but she felt like she couldn't move her feet. Her head felt drained of blood. She took a few steps, staggering a bit. *The bathroom,* she thought. *I need to throw up. Or put the capsule in my mouth. I don't know . . . I . . .*

"Please forgive me," said Waldhorst behind her. "I didn't mean to upset you."

"But you did," said Agnes, pausing in the doorway to the living room.

"You're so beautiful," said Waldhorst. "Gustav Lande is a man with money—and power."

Agnes regained her footing.

"Why did you bring me here?" she said, turning to look at him. He was now sitting on the edge of his desk, an almost ashamed expression on his face.

"My brother . . ." said Waldhorst, nodding at the framed photograph on his desk.

Agnes took a few steps back inside the library. She could see the resemblance to Waldhorst, though the picture had to be several years old. It looked like a school photo. The boy in it couldn't have been more than thirteen or fourteen, but he had the same crooked smile and the same stern eyes, though with a certain softness to his expression.

Waldhorst picked up one of the papers from the desk, holding it between two fingers. Agnes read a few words upside down. Died for the Führer. She looked back at the photograph.

"I just needed to see you," he said, his voice so low Agnes could barely hear him. "I'm a married man, but I find myself thinking about you whenever life gets difficult."

Agnes took off her hat and set it on the sofa. Waldhorst merely stared at the floor. She took his hand, then lifted his chin. They stared into each other's eyes for a moment before he leaned close.

She let him kiss her.

"I shouldn't have said that. You're an engaged woman."

She stroked his cheek, practically bubbling inside. Could it really be this easy?

"You need to leave now," said Waldhorst.

Only when she was back out on the street, waiting for his driver to come back, did she think that nothing in the world was as easy as it appeared at first glance. When she put her key in the lock at Hammerstads Gate, she again had that overwhelming feeling that she'd made a mistake, but she didn't know what it was. Without knowing why, she sank to the floor in the entryway, buried her face in her hands, and wept.

CHAPTER 42

Sunday, June 15, 2003
Uddevalla, Sweden

Heavy, cottony gray clouds hovered low over the canal that passed through town, sending one downpour after another over Tommy Bergmann and the few others who had ventured out. He didn't really know why he hadn't driven straight to Stockholm after breakfast instead of wandering around under a borrowed umbrella in this godforsaken place.

He smoked two cigarettes as he watched a pair of ducks bobbing around in the black water of the canal being pummeled with rain. Then he walked up to the square to have an early lunch and maybe allow himself a beer or two. Just as he was sitting down in the Rådhus restaurant, his cell phone rang.

"I talked to a German colleague," said Finn Nystrøm.

"Yes?" said Bergmann as he pointed to an item on the menu to indicate to the waitress what he'd like to order. "On a Sunday? Not bad."

"We apostates have to stick together," Nystrøm said, then laughed.

"So he's out of the game too?"

"No, but he's not exactly popular either," said Nystrøm. "A historian by the name of Rudolf Braun. Maybe you've heard of him?"

"Possibly."

"Regardless, he's positive that Waldhorst is living in Berlin under another name, most likely something that sounds British," said Nystrøm. "He's going to contact another colleague tomorrow."

"Tell him for God's sake to keep quiet about all this," said Bergmann. "I don't want any of this showing up in the newspapers. And not a word about what Faalund said about Krogh. Not even to your dogs."

"Don't worry, Tommy. Regardless, the missing Peter Waldhorst was the personal secretary to the German trade attaché in Oslo during the fall of 1939."

"Trade attaché?"

Bergmann paused, then added, "But . . ."

"Abwehr," said Nystrøm. "The relationship between the Abwehr and the Gestapo wasn't great, but in Norway the boundaries were somewhat fluid. That might explain why Waldhorst showed up in the Gestapo in 1943. Before that, nobody knows how long he worked as personal secretary and what exactly that job entailed. And most of the Abwehr archives and information about their activities went missing after the attempted coup against Hitler in 1944. Some things are known, of course, but the Security Service, the *Sicherheitsdienst*, took over most of the files and destroyed whatever didn't suit them. Rumor has it that Waldhorst isn't on any list of individuals convicted after the war. I'm guessing that he was in Finland for a while or on the Kola Peninsula on the Arctic Ocean front. Otherwise he wouldn't have been able to escape with Operation Paperclip."

"What does your colleague think?"

"More or less what I just told you. As I said yesterday, the Swedes got hold of a bunch of Abwehr and Gestapo after the war. Waldhorst most likely ended up in the United States, either via Sweden or directly."

The waitress set a pint and his lunch on the table in front of Bergmann. He didn't reply, so Nystrøm repeated what he'd just said.

Bergmann was looking at an elderly couple who sat in silence at a table next to the window.

"And you know what? I did a little poking around yesterday in my own archives. I knew that I'd heard that name somewhere. Peter Waldhorst, I mean."

"*Your* archives?"

"All serious historians have their own archives. Sometimes people donate things to us for free, or they're willing to sell things for a small sum. I haven't thrown out anything from the old days, and I've even acquired a few more things over the years. And I'll be damned if I didn't find a photograph from a dinner party given at Gustav Lande's home."

"Gustav Lande?" said Bergmann.

"I received a private archive from an old Nazi who died twenty years ago, an attorney from somewhere out in Asker. He'd written in his will that I, of all people, should be given his effects. Apparently I'd made a good impression on him back in the late seventies."

"Why would I be interested in a photo of Gustav Lande?"

"You don't think Lande is the only one in that picture, do you?" said Nystrøm in a low voice.

Bergmann said nothing.

"Visible at the very edge of the picture, which was taken at dinner on Midsummer Eve 1942, is Peter Waldhorst."

"Do you know if he ever belonged to the Hitler Youth?"

For a moment the only sound on the phone line was a faint rustling. The restaurant door opened, and someone could be heard shouting out in the square. Bergmann looked at the last rays of sun disappearing behind the roof of the building across the street.

"Why do you ask?"

"Can you answer the question?"

"I don't know if he did or not."

"It doesn't matter," said Bergmann.

"You're a terrible liar," said Nystrøm. "But guess who's sitting at the other end of the table, near Lande?"

"I have no idea," said Bergmann.

"Waldhorst is looking at her as if he's about to die."

Bergmann grabbed his beer glass. Before taking a sip, he said, "Agnes Gerner."

"Bingo," said Nystrøm.

"You need to find Waldhorst for me," said Bergmann. "And scan the photograph and e-mail it to me."

Now we're onto something, he thought. *We're really onto something.*

"This is unbelievable," Nystrøm murmured. "This whole thing with Krogh . . . If that turns out to be true, it's unbelievable."

If it's true, thought Bergmann as he hung up, *then it's truly beyond belief.*

He was about to pay the bill when Fredrik Reuter called him.

This could go either way, he thought when he picked up. Reuter had said very little when Bergmann had recounted his conversation with Iver Faalund the day before. He had seemed to need some time to allow everything to sink in.

"Get yourself over to Stockholm," said Reuter before Bergmann even had a chance to say hello. "Ask for Claes Tossmann at the National Police. Ten o'clock tomorrow morning."

One to zero in my favor, thought Bergmann. He paid the bill and tried to walk off the effects of the beer by making a few rounds of the center of town.

After a half hour on the road, he phoned Drabløs to tell him that he couldn't make it to handball practice the next day. Drabløs was as easygoing as always and took the news in stride. For a moment Bergmann wished he was more like Drabløs, who kept up an uncomplicated and positive outlook, even when faced with occasional setbacks.

Talking about handball made him think of Hadja. He pulled over at a gas station and called her. She sounded relieved.

"I've been thinking about you," she said. He thought he heard her turn over in bed. She'd probably worked the night shift.

"I've been thinking about you too," he said before he could stop himself. He told himself he was too old to play games, too old to be coy. As if that was the problem. He pushed those other thoughts aside.

They agreed to get together as soon as he got back to Oslo.

CHAPTER 43

Sunday, September 6, 1942
Vigeland Park
Oslo, Norway

A group of children were running in and out of the granite gate to Vigeland Park. One of them stumbled and dropped his cap on the gravel. Agnes Gerner bent down and picked it up. The boy was on his knees, staring at the palms of his hands, but he had nothing but a scrape on the left one.

"Here's your cap," said Agnes, holding it out to the boy, who was maybe nine or ten. Though his eyes glistened with tears, he gritted his teeth. He reached for his cap, murmuring his thanks.

An elderly man said hello as he slipped out the gate ahead of Agnes. She had to restrain herself from looking over her shoulder. The feeling that she was being followed had never been stronger. It was as if the entire boulevard were one long line of black Mercedes and the face of Peter Waldhorst were staring out of hundreds of car windows. He could have easily laid a trap for her the previous Thursday. What if he was just waiting until she made some irrevocable mistake to sink his claws into her? She had talked to the Pilgrim about it in Sten's Park the following day. She asked him to take it up with Number 1, but he had seemed distracted. He didn't seem to grasp how serious it was that Waldhorst had summoned her. Of course she hadn't told him what actually happened, but surely he must have understood. Agnes would have preferred to speak to Kaj herself, but she didn't know how to get hold of him. Her only means of contacting him was through Helge K. Moen. Otherwise everything went through the Pilgrim. *Carl Oscar,* she thought, feeling the warmth radiating from her heart into her whole body. But then it was gone and she once again felt only coldness inside. She remembered throwing up earlier in the day, but she didn't feel sick now. A little weak, perhaps, but not sick.

She had gone only a few steps into the park when she saw the boy again. He was standing there with his head bowed, clutching the cap in his hands. The other children had moved away.

"Is something wrong?" asked Agnes, putting her hand gently on his shoulder. Almost reluctantly the boy turned around.

"Papa is going to kill me," he said as tears spilled down his face. Only then did Agnes notice the holes in his pant legs. "He says he doesn't have any money."

She opened her purse and took out five one-krone coins. She wanted to give him more, but that would draw too much attention. Quickly she took his hand without the scrape and pressed the coins into his palm.

"Go now," she said. "The others are over there." She nodded toward the children, who were making their way toward the bridge, which was crowded with people even though parts of the park were still under construction.

"Thank you, ma'am," said the boy. Then he turned and ran to join the others. A German soldier with a Norwegian girl on his arm turned to look at the boy and then laughed, whispering something in the girl's ear. Agnes avoided looking at him. Instead, she headed for the bridge, where she had already noticed the Pilgrim leaning on the railing, staring at the pond below.

On her way there, she saw the boy run across the bridge, limping a bit, with his right hand still tightly clutching the coins. *One day,* she thought, *one day this will all be over.*

Even as she went to stand next to the Pilgrim, she knew what was coming. He seemed distant and hesitant, as if he were mustering his courage so that he could place a big burden—perhaps too big—on her shoulders.

"A lot of people here today," she said quietly. "Far too many."

"It's perfect," said the Pilgrim without looking at her. He was merely staring into space.

Agnes looked down at the sluice where the northern part of Frogner Pond ran down into the southern part. Though a couple stood not far from them, the shouts of the children from the other side of the bridge made it impossible for anyone else to hear what they said.

"Have you met him?" asked the Pilgrim.

Agnes turned and walked toward the fountain, which was under construction. When she reached it, she pretended to study the scaffolding set up around the huge bowl that formed the top of the fountain.

"Who?" she asked, as if she didn't know.

"Rolborg," said the Pilgrim between clenched teeth.

"Carl Oscar . . . How many times are you going to ask me that?" she whispered. All of a sudden she knew what she'd done, what her irrevocable mistake was. She should never have mentioned Research Director Rolborg of Knaben Mines and his shocking discovery of molybdenum in Hurdal.

The Pilgrim came over to stand beside her.

"London has made a decision."

Agnes said nothing.

"We need to get to him," said the Pilgrim. "And quickly."

"I miss you," she said. She couldn't help herself.

The Pilgrim didn't answer; he merely straightened the wide brim of his hat and pulled it farther down his forehead.

"Pull yourself together," he said at last. Their eyes met for a moment, then he looked away and took a step to the side. He touched his hat to greet an elderly couple who had come over to the scaffolding.

"Waldhorst," she whispered. "He scares me. Have you talked to Number 1?"

The Pilgrim shook his head.

"But . . ."

"Lots of them do that. Say derogatory things about the Führer."

"What about the Venlo Incident?" she asked.

"You haven't blown your cover, have you?" said the Pilgrim tensely. She shook her head.

"Then what's the problem?"

Agnes didn't reply. The nausea refused to go away. It was because she'd thrown up earlier in the day. This was all too much for her. If Waldhorst wanted to take her, she would be sacrificed. The Pilgrim clearly wasn't going to believe her. For several seconds she was sure she was about to pass out. The Pilgrim was saying something about the fountain to the elderly couple next to them. Agnes wasn't listening. Instead, she opened her purse to make sure the cyanide pill was still there. She reached in and touched it. Then she removed her hand and instead touched the letter from her sister.

Finally the elderly couple left.

"He's trying to draw you out," said the Pilgrim. "He's testing you. If he really thought you were red, he would have grabbed you immediately."

"Maybe you're right."

"You know what I think?" said the Pilgrim. "This is a simple world we live in. Waldhorst is in love with you. Plain and simple. A damned simple world." He tore off a match and lit a cigarette. His expression was blank and remote, and he looked as though he really didn't know her. As though he couldn't care less about Agnes Gerner.

How can he know that? she wondered.

"Number 1 wants to see you," he said.

"Why?" she asked.

"I think you know why."

Agnes didn't reply. For a moment the whole park seemed to whirl around her.

"I'll be in touch."

Her heart sank. "I'll be in touch?" Why would he say such a thing?

Agnes walked around a bit by herself, then circled back to stand a few steps away from him. He fleetingly touched her hand, then moved past, his head turned away. But then he paused for a moment. She merely nodded, staring at his hand, wanting him to stroke her cheek, right there in public. She wanted to run away with him and take Cecilia with them. Run away from all this.

Agnes stayed where she was, staring vacantly at the scaffolding around the fountain. The noisy group of children suddenly came running up behind her and ran rings around her. She caught the eye of the boy she had given money to. He was still clutching the coins in his hand, but the smile was back on his face. She caught him looking at her several more times. *All right,* she thought. *This is what I have to do. For your sake, and for your friends.*

CHAPTER 44

Tuesday, June 17, 2003
Headquarters of the Swedish National Police
Polhemsgatan
Stockholm, Sweden

Tommy Bergmann paused to look across the waters of Riddarfjärden before heading up the street. He'd often heard that Stockholm was a beautiful city, and the view certainly was just that. But for some reason panoramas like this always made him feel lonely and melancholy, and that was not the sort of mood he wanted to succumb to just then. It was a good thing he traveled as little as he did. Yesterday morning he'd received a phone call from Claes Tossmann's secretary, who told him that unfortunately the meeting had to be postponed a day. So he'd had more than enough time to look around. God built Stockholm, the king built Copenhagen, and City Hall built Oslo. Wasn't that how the saying went?

The police headquarters was not as easy to find as the map suggested, and he lost his way several times before finally reaching the labyrinthine building. It looked like an impregnable fortress with its shiny, rust-red exterior. Bergmann felt as if he'd been turned away even before the door under the glass canopy opened.

Detective Inspector Claes Tossmann's office was nothing to brag about. It was a narrow, cramped room whose only window faced an atrium between the two wings of the building.

"I suppose Persson died decades ago," said Bergmann.

"Yes, that's probably true," said the Swede, turning to look out the window, as though hoping there might be something worth seeing. He couldn't stop scratching a bare spot on top of his head.

Bergmann leafed through the documents that Tossmann had somewhat reluctantly slid across his bare desk. He was eager to read the yellowed file of statements from witnesses. Several brief sentences had been typed on the top page. In one place the typewriter had punched right through the paper. The report had four attachments, and Bergmann had little hope that they'd be any more interesting than the report itself. The first was a so-called technical preliminary examination, which concluded in the very first line that Kaj Holt had chosen to fade into history by taking his own life. The powder burns on his head, the fingerprints on the gun, and the angle of the entry wound were all consistent with suicide. Next was a statement from a witness, Ms. Barbro Wilén, who'd apparently been quite involved with Holt. On the night before he was found dead, she was awakened when Holt rang her doorbell. Ms. Wilén had asked him to come back the following day because he sounded very drunk and always got so despondent when he was drinking.

Bergmann turned to the third attachment, which was a statement given by another witness, Ms. Karen Eline Fredriksen, who was the secretary at the Norwegian legation in Stockholm, Military Office IV. Ms. Fredriksen confirmed that the apartment had been leased by the Norwegian legation. Bergmann stopped short when he read the last line. "Ms. Fredriksen knew the deceased well, and she confirms that he was periodically suicidal." He placed that statement aside and looked for the fourth attachment, but apparently he'd come to the end. There were no other attachments in the folder. He looked up, but Tossmann's chair was empty. He turned and saw the inspector standing next to the conference table with his back to him. He was pinching some withered leaves off a potted plant as he continued to scratch his head. A second later he returned to his desk and gave Bergmann an inquiring look of feigned friendliness. Bergmann went back to the report that had been compiled by Detective Inspector Gösta Persson. He considered asking Tossmann whether he knew that Persson had been killed, but decided against it. No doubt Tossmann would simply evade the issue.

Where is the fourth attachment? Bergmann wondered. According to the list of numbered attachments, there should have been a piece of paper with the words "I'm sorry. Kaj." But the note was missing. He picked up Holt's ID, which had been fastened to the back of the report with a paper clip. For a moment he held the dry, yellowed document and studied Holt's photograph. There was a sad look to his face, as if he harbored a great sorrow. Hadn't Nyström told him that there wasn't a single photo of Holt? Bergmann might have been one of the very few people to ever see this file.

"Where's the note?" he asked, looking up at Tossmann, who was now seated behind his desk again.

The phone on the desk rang.

"Excuse me," said Tossmann.

Bergmann got up and went over to the window. The sun was baking the glass roof of the atrium. It was all one big gleaming surface.

"Yes. I see," said Tossmann to whoever was on the phone. His side of the conversation was monosyllabic, interspersed by murmured grunts.

"Give me five minutes," Tossmann finally said before putting down the phone.

Bergmann turned around to face him.

"So, how is Fredrik?" asked Tossmann.

"He's fine," said Bergmann.

The clock on the wall behind Tossmann ticked toward three o'clock.

"Do you know what happened to the note?" asked Bergmann. "The one from Holt?"

Bergmann held up the report for Tossmann to see.

The inspector sighed heavily. Then he spent several seconds rubbing his eyes. When he opened them again, they looked bloodshot, as if he'd been on a long drinking binge, trying to forget something he didn't wish to recall.

"According to rumors here at headquarters, the note was sent to Norway. But nobody knows that for sure."

"To Norway?" said Bergmann.

Tossmann nodded.

"Do you know where in Norway?"

He shook his head. "I'm afraid not."

"To the police?"

Tossmann threw up his hands. He got up from his chair again with some effort. "Bergmann, I'm sorry, but I have a meeting now."

Bergmann nodded and quickly jotted down a few key words about the report. Without knowing why, he also wrote down the name of the secretary at the Norwegian legation. Karen Eline Fredriksen. Underneath he wrote, "I'm sorry. Kaj."

"Peter Waldhorst," said Bergmann. "Does that name mean anything to you?"

"I'm afraid not."

"Are you sure?" he insisted.

"My dear Bergmann," said Tossmann. "Everything I know about this matter is in the papers you're holding."

Bergmann nodded.

"Do you think there's anything in the Säpo archives?"

"About this . . . Waldhorst? Was that his name?"

Bergmann nodded.

"Maybe, if he was in Sweden during the war." Tossmann shrugged. "I really need to leave now," he said, glancing at his watch.

"We appreciate your help," said Bergmann.

"It was nothing. Though I don't know what use this will be to Fredrik." Tossmann picked up the document folder and then dropped it in a drawer of the file cabinet under his desk.

No, you wouldn't understand, thought Bergmann.

The drive home took longer than he'd anticipated. But it gave him plenty of time to think. Perhaps too much time.

As he walked out of the Statoil gas station in Karlskoga, he stopped abruptly, his hand still grasping the door handle. He was staring at the front page of *Aftonbladet* in the newspaper box outside.

Why would someone send the note to Norway? He'd been pondering this question for the past two and a half hours. There seemed to be only one possibility. And where would that person have sent it?

Just before crossing the border into Norway, he phoned Halgeir Sørvaag.

"Find out whether Kaj Holt had any children," he said.

"What the hell are you talking about?" said Sørvaag.

"Find out—"

"Do you know what time it is? Do you really think I'm still at work? I'm not as hard up as you are, Tommy."

Bergmann could hear a TV in the background and was about to respond, but Sørvaag had already hung up.

He looked at the time displayed on the car's dashboard. Six thirty. How had it gotten so late? He moved into the left lane to pass a truck. Only when he reached a hundred miles per hour did he move back over to the right—just in time too, or he might have ended his days by colliding with an oncoming van.

Right before he reached Ørje, a thought surfaced in his mind. Bergmann veered over to the exit and parked next to a red-painted café near the entrance to the locks. He got out and walked over to the small beach by the lake. Several kids were yelling as they shoved each other off a raft out on the lake. Bergmann watched them, feeling a hint of their joy deep inside him. Sun rays struck the surface of the water at almost ninety degrees. The only disruption was a motorboat cutting through the water at low speed over near the opposite shore.

It all suddenly made sense.

He leafed through his notebook. Page by page, watching the whole case like a film in slow motion, but in reverse. He'd written the name Marius Kolstad at the top of one page and scanned the four or five lines of notes he'd taken beneath it. Key words that he alone would understand: *Krogh fell apart after his wife's death. Karen.*

Then he skipped ahead until he came to the last page and the scribbled notes from his meeting with Tossmann: *Witness from the Norwegian legation. Karen Eline Fredriksen.* Hadn't he read somewhere that Krogh's wife had worked in the Norwegian legation in Stockholm during the war?

He had to go back to his car to think this through. He set the notebook on the passenger seat and got back on the E18. He suddenly had a sense of urgency. After only a couple of minutes he came to a small rest stop and pulled off the highway. He had to stop to think clearly.

Was that really what happened? Did Carl Oscar Krogh kill Kaj Holt in Stockholm and then send his future wife to his apartment to reassure the Stockholm police that Holt was suicidal? Bergmann paged through his notebook until he found what he'd written down about his interview with Bente Bull-Krogh. He'd jotted down her cell number in the margin on one of the pages. Bergmann stuck a cigarette in his mouth, got out of the car, and sat down on a bench in the rest area. A few raindrops landed on his forehead. He lit the cigarette and tapped in the phone number, tipping his head back to see where the raindrops were coming from. Above him the sky was as blue as it had been all day.

The only thing that didn't fit was why Krogh should have played such a big role in the investigation of Holt's death. Had he really been such a coldhearted bastard?

Wait a minute, he thought as he watched a lumber truck rush past and disappear. For a long time there were no other vehicles on the road.

He put his cell back in his pocket.

Better not give Bente Krogh any leads. He wasn't sure what to do next. But before he did anything else, he needed to find out whether Karen Eline Fredriksen was indeed the same person as Karen Krogh.

Bergmann looked at his watch. He also needed to know whether Holt had had any children. He cursed Sørvaag, but couldn't really blame him for not wanting to search for people who might not even exist, especially after work hours. He could phone Nyström, of course, and find out the answer at once, but he was reluctant to do that. He'd already told Nyström too much. He knew what direction Bergmann was going in and could easily put two and two together. But Torgeir Moberg wouldn't get the connection, at least not right away. Bergmann got out Moberg's business card, which he'd paper-clipped to one of the pages in his notebook. First he called his office number. Moberg seemed like the type who might still be working at this hour, even on a nice summer evening.

Just as he was about to give up, someone answered.

"Moberg?" said Bergmann.

"I'd be more curious to know who *you* are," said the voice on the line. Bergmann knew it was him.

"This is Bergmann, from the police—"

Moberg interrupted him with a sigh.

"I thought we were done, Bergmann. But all right, fire away . . ."

"Just one question," he said. "About Kaj . . ."

"Holt," said Moberg, finishing his sentence for him.

"One simple question. I'm just trying to complete the picture of Holt." He could hear from his own voice that he wasn't the best liar, but it would have to do.

"Yes?" Moberg sounded as if he wanted to underscore that he thought this was all a waste of time.

"Did Holt have any children? And do you know whether his wife is still alive?"

Moberg snorted.

"Yes to the first question. One child, as far as I know. No to the second. But listen here, Bergmann, don't tell me that you're spending any more time on this."

"A son or daughter?"

"Surely that doesn't make any difference. The child couldn't have been more than a toddler when Holt died."

"I'd really appreciate it if you'd answer the question," said Bergmann.

"A daughter," said Moberg.

"Do you have any idea—"

"Have I ever met her? Talked to her? No," said Moberg.

For a moment neither of them spoke.

"Thank you very much," Bergmann said.

He could just picture Moberg sitting in his office, thinking he was some total incompetent off on some wild goose chase. So be it.

"I suppose you'd like to know her name too?" said Moberg.

"That would be great."

"Vera," said Moberg. "Whether she's still using Holt as her last name, you'll have to find out for yourself."

Bergmann thanked him again, then paused before hanging up. He wanted to give Moberg the opportunity to ask why he was suddenly so interested in whether Holt had any children. But Moberg merely grunted and wished him good evening before hanging up.

Vera Holt, thought Bergmann. He needed to find Vera Holt.

How long would it take him to drive to Oslo? Another hour at most. He could have called the officer on duty and asked him to do a computer search, but he decided it could wait.

His key card to get into the police garage wasn't working. Bergmann reluctantly pressed the buzzer, feeling this was requiring unnecessary effort on his part.

He sat dozing in his car for a full five minutes before he was abruptly awakened by a patrol car turning on its siren as it drove out of the garage. He felt momentarily disoriented, unsure why he was sitting outside the garage in an unmarked police car. When he finally got to the seventh floor, he found it nearly deserted. Only a couple of fools were still sitting at their desks, thinking they could save the city from perdition. Bergmann looked at his watch and noted that he was one of them. He consoled himself with the thought that it was only 9:15—and he had a better view from his office than Claes Tossmann did from his in Stockholm.

His first search in the National Registry was simple enough. Karen Krogh had died about a year ago. And her maiden name had indeed been Karen Eline Fredriksen, born November 24, 1917. She was still married to Krogh when she died on February 25, 2002. No matter how much he wanted to deny it, Bergmann had to accept that it was no coincidence that Krogh's future wife was the person who had turned up from the Norwegian legation when Holt was found dead. He told himself to pay close attention. Was he in the process of building a house of cards based on flimsy suppositions he'd simply made up? He needed to find out whether Karen Krogh had ever said anything about Holt, anything that would give him reason to believe that things were not as they appeared regarding his death. And the daughter, Bente Bull-Krogh, must have been closest to her, at least among those who were still alive.

Bergmann took out Bente's number, but again changed his mind about calling her. He decided instead to show up at her place unannounced in the morning. If he wasn't mistaken, Bente was keeping something from him, so it would be better not to give her any warning. But the first thing he had to do was clear his mind. He couldn't understand why Krogh would be involved in Holt's death, only to make a lot of noise about it in the following years. Very few people would be coldhearted enough to put on such a performance. Bergmann got out a Post-It notepad and wrote himself a reminder to call the psychologist Rune Flatanger, who worked for Kripo's profiling group.

He thought his second search in the National Registry would be more complicated. But there was only one person in Norway named Vera Holt, and she lived just a few blocks from police headquarters. He read through the information on the screen slowly, to confirm that it was a match. Vera Holt was born on January 6, 1945, in Stockholm, Sweden. Father: Kaj Holt, captain. Mother: Signe Holt, housewife. Marital status: Single. Address: Kolstadgata 7, 0652 Oslo. He did a quick search on Holt's wife, Signe, but she died in 1997. So Vera Holt was most likely the one who had in her possession the piece of evidence from the Stockholm police—if Kaj Holt's supposed suicide note still existed at all.

Bergmann closed his eyes for a couple of seconds and noticed how tired he was. Maybe this was all his imagination, nothing but the wishful thinking of a police detective. He turned the desk lamp away from the screen and perched on the edge of his chair.

"Vera Holt," he said out loud. "You've been here all along, right before my eyes."

But Kolstadgata 7? Kaj Holt's daughter must not be doing very well if that was her address. There wasn't a worse place to live in this whole crazy city. The communal housing project just a stone's throw from police headquarters was no better than a slum.

He looked her up by her birthday, using the search engine that linked all information the government had on everyone who'd had contact with any official agencies for one reason or another.

What's this? thought Bergmann, studying the screen.

There were no remarks pertaining to Vera Holt. She had never filed a complaint, been a witness, or received any sort of court judgment. However, there was an asterisk in the comments field to the right of her name. Bergmann knew that the search engine contained only links to court files and investigations from the last ten years or so. So there was apparently some older case involving Vera Holt that must have been filed and taken out of the system long ago. Either someone had forgotten to remove the asterisk, or it was a serious matter. *A very serious matter,* Bergmann thought.

His cell rang, interrupting his thoughts.

"Are you back?" he heard Hadja say.

Bergmann suddenly felt wide awake.

"Yes," he said, printing out the screenshot. It would take him only five minutes to go over to Vera Holt's place on Kolstadgata. But it was too late for that, and his reason for paying her a visit was flimsy at best. Besides, he was more interested in seeing Hadja than Vera Holt.

"Where are you?"

"At the office."

"Oh." She sounded a little disappointed. "Martine is spending the night with Sara. I have the evening free, if you have some time."

"Couldn't you come over here?"

"To police headquarters?"

He had to laugh. Hadja laughed too.

"Take a cab," he said, switching off his computer. "I miss you." It wasn't like him to say that, but he meant it.

As he walked over to Café Oliven on Nordbygata, he could hardly wait to see her again. He couldn't help it if this wasn't the most sensible thing he'd ever done.

Half an hour later they were sitting across from each other. After a few minutes of empty chatter during which they both seemed a little nervous, they settled back to where they'd been less than a week ago. Bergmann once again had the feeling that she could really be the right woman for him. He held her hand for a moment, just to show her how glad he was to be with her. The smile she gave him before exchanging a few words in Arabic with the waiter made him deeply happy, as if a ray of light had pierced the darkness he sometimes felt that he carried inside. He studied her profile. She was wearing more makeup than usual, and he noticed that other men in the café were openly staring at her. Strangely enough, it didn't bother him that other men found her attractive. Instead, he was proud to be the one sitting there with her. Much better than being filled with a rage whose source he couldn't identify, much less control.

"You're a lucky man to have such a beautiful girlfriend," the waiter told Bergmann. "She says she's not Palestinian, but I think she is. Only Palestinian girls are so beautiful, my friend." He laughed as he took the menus from them. They looked at each other, both of them smiling shyly, a bit embarrassed.

"Tell me about your trip to Sweden," she said.

He told her what little he could, and then she gave him an update on handball practice, most of which she'd heard from Sara. He laughed several times as Hadja mimicked Drabløs's gestures and drawling Sunnmøre dialect.

"You have a talent for that," he said.

She frowned.

"Tell that to the theater school. After applying twice, I gave up trying to get in. Maybe I'm good enough for community theater. Some sort of romantic comedy, with the nurses and patients. What do you think?"

They shared a large selection of meze and a bottle of red wine.

"This has been the longest week of my life," she said quietly, stroking his arm.

He couldn't remember how long it had been since he'd made out with someone in a taxi, but it made him feel years younger. The Pakistani cabbie drove slowly, turning up the bhangra music, as though wanting to give them as much time as possible. Bergmann would have preferred it if the guy had driven like the wind.

Within minutes, they had shed their clothes and tumbled into bed.

When he came and she whispered "I love you" in his ear, he thought of repeating those same words back to her. She had him locked between her legs, arching up toward him, almost through him.

Afterward they lay in bed and fantasized about things they could do together, starting with a trip to Stockholm and continuing south through Europe, to Spain, and from there across the Strait of Gibraltar to Tangier.

"Morocco," said Hadja. "Someday I want to show you Morocco."

Then neither of them spoke for a while. She lay on top of him until they were breathing as one.

After she'd left, two hours later—when the thudding of the taxi's diesel engine had been swallowed up by the roar of traffic on the E6 and he was leaning against the windowsill, looking at a spot on the street corner where the red taillights had disappeared—he thought to himself that this wasn't going to work. He went back to bed, breathing in the smell of her, her perfume and sweat, red wine and spices. Hadja's voice filled his head as he closed his eyes, but he was determined to try to sleep away the guilt he felt over having hidden his true self from her.

He got up and stretched out on the living room sofa instead, chain-smoking until dawn rose over the neighborhood.

CHAPTER 45

Wednesday, June 18, 2003
Police Headquarters
Oslo, Norway

It was only a little past eight, but Tommy Bergmann had already given the secretary two tasks before seeing Fredrik Reuter at the morning meeting. The first was to find Vera Holt's file in the archives and find out what the asterisk in the agency records meant; the second was to book him a plane ticket to Berlin and a room at a medium-priced hotel. He was sitting with his phone in his hand, about to call Information.

He carefully wrote down the twelve digits of the phone number in Berlin. Then he opened the window and lit a cigarette. He reread the e-mail that Finn Nyström had sent at 1:30 that morning.

Tommy,

Here's the photo as promised. BTW, this might interest you: Peter Waldhorst lives in Berlin as an American citizen under the name Peter Ward. Address: Gustav Freytag Strasse 5. According to

Gard Sveen

my colleague it's the Waldhorst family's
old house, and it's an open secret that
Waldhorst moved back to Berlin about ten
or fifteen years ago. Iver Faalund doesn't
seem to have done much besides drink in
recent decades, unfortunately. I'm a bit
suspicious of all this guesswork on his
part. (By the way, the Waldhorst/Ward
house in Berlin is not exactly in the
city's worst neighborhood . . . Take
your tennis racket if you have one.)

Best, Finn

PS Keep me posted . . .

Keep me posted, Bergmann thought. I'll keep you posted all right.
He had to admit that he might be leaning toward Nyström's skepticism
about Faalund. The e-mail attachment was the photo from Midsummer
Eve 1942. The first file showed the back of the photo, on which someone had written the initials of Peter Waldhorst, Gustav Lande, Agnes
Gerner, and the others in the shot. Bergmann then opened the scan of
the photo. Lande wore a tux and stood with his face turned away from
the camera. Waldhorst—dark-haired, with eyes set too close together
to call him handsome—was staring at Agnes. She made Bergmann feel
an odd pang of jealousy, even though she was long dead and buried
in Nordmarka. Maybe that was precisely what had happened. Maybe
Agnes was a woman that men would kill for, and the other two—
Johanne Caspersen and little Cecilia—had just gotten in the way.
Maybe it was no more complicated than that. Maybe Krogh was obses-
sively jealous, and Kaj Holt had nothing at all to do with the case.
Because this was what Bergmann couldn't make add up: If Faalund

was right that Krogh had killed them and later got rid of Holt, then why would he go on to make such a fuss about Holt's death? It would have been pure foolishness. Although it could have made him appear innocent, he could just as easily have ended up a suspect.

Bergmann waved off the secretary when she came in the door. He already had the phone to his ear and was dialing the number for Rune Flatanger in Kripo's profiling group. The secretary ignored the signal and plopped a stack of papers in front of him. He skimmed through them while he waited for Flatanger to answer. A hotel reservation and an itinerary with a late afternoon flight to Berlin via Copenhagen.

Flatanger picked up the phone just as Bergmann was about to give up. Though he'd been helpful on several occasions when the Oslo police district lacked the necessary expertise, Bergmann almost never felt like talking to him. He was nice enough, but he always made Bergmann feel naked and inadequate, as if he could peel away all the lies he was carrying around and see right through him. Maybe he simply didn't like talking to psychologists in general. He should be going to a therapist himself. In a flash he could feel Hadja's skin against his own. He swore to himself. Things couldn't go on like this.

"Long time no see," said Flatanger on the other end.

"Must be good news then," said Bergmann.

He brought his colleague quickly up to speed on the case.

"Our leading theory," Bergmann said, realizing that he was laying it on a bit thick, "is that Krogh liquidated the three females, but that it may have been a mistake. Or he didn't have a clear conscience about what he'd done."

"Oh yeah?" Flatanger said in his accent-free manner of speaking. It was hard to tell what part of the country he was from.

Only a faint hum could be heard from the traffic on the street below. Bergmann thought he knew the answer, but he wanted to have it confirmed by someone who wasn't up to his neck in the case. Maybe he'd be shocked or say that it was going to cause a scandal. Instead the man merely said "Yes?" the way psychologists do, placing the entire question back in Bergmann's hands.

"And Kaj Holt interrogated a German Gestapo officer in Lillehammer two days before Holt was found dead." Bergmann hesitated a moment, suddenly confused by his own interpretation. What was he actually after?

"So he learned something in Lillehammer that turned out to be disastrous, is that what you mean?" Flatanger said.

Bergmann cleared his throat, then jumped right in.

"This has to remain between the two of us for now . . . but I think Krogh had Holt murdered in Stockholm. Probably because Holt had begun talking about the fact that Krogh killed the two women and the little girl we discovered in Nordmarka. Or even worse, that Krogh was working for the Germans. I don't know when Holt found out that Krogh had done the killing. Normally Holt would have known about it when it happened, even bringing the orders with him from London. But I suspect Holt may have found out about it in Lillehammer, and that it upset him so much that he started talking about it. Krogh had close friends in Säpo."

The psychologist on the other end of the line said nothing.

"What I just don't understand is why Krogh took the lead in the Norwegian attempts to find out what happened to Holt—if indeed he was the one who had Holt killed, or killed him himself," said Bergmann.

Flatanger cleared his throat.

"Who's the most helpful person at the scene of an arson?" Flatanger asked.

"The pyromaniac," Bergmann muttered.

Neither of them spoke for a long moment.

Finally Flatanger broke the silence.

"If your theory about Holt's death is correct, then someone connected to Holt would have a relatively obvious motive, don't you think?"

Bergmann didn't even want to consider that possibility.

Yet his eyes fell on two words on his computer screen.

```
Vera Holt.
```

Bergmann hastily left the large meeting room. It was five past ten. The morning meeting hadn't gone well. He'd been pressured by the police advocate to explain what the Kaj Holt case had to do with the murder of Carl Oscar Krogh, and had barely managed to present a reasonable argument. Iver Faalund's assertions were serious, but pretty much nothing but guesses, and Bergmann knew it. And the whole affair with Hadja was making him depressed. He should be happy, of course, but despite wanting to see her again as soon as possible, it was never going to work. Not now. Back in his office he picked up his cell phone and dialed her number.

No, he had to see her face-to-face. But that would have to wait until after Berlin. He stared down at his notebook where he'd written Peter Ward's phone number on Gustav Freytag Strasse. There was really no reason to put it off any longer.

A woman picked up the phone just as he was about to give up. He remembered enough German from his school days to understand what the woman said, and to realize that she wasn't German, but an immigrant, most likely Turkish.

"I'd like to speak with Peter Ward," he said in English.

The woman made a sound, then fell silent, as if she were holding her hand over the mouthpiece.

"With whom am I speaking?" a man's voice said in perfect English.

"Peter Ward?"

"Who is this?" he said in a friendly tone, but now in almost perfect Norwegian. Only the slight hint of a German accent revealed that the man wasn't Norwegian.

Bergmann took a couple of seconds to ponder this.

How come Waldhorst spoke such good Norwegian after all these years? No doubt he had a phone that displayed the caller's number and the country code for Norway, 47, but Bergmann felt a bit bewildered for a moment.

"Tommy Bergmann from the Oslo police."

The man on the other end remained silent. Bergmann didn't know what to make of that.

"Am I speaking with Peter Waldhorst?"

"You're speaking with Peter Ward," he said, but in a tone that sounded like an admission.

"I know that you're Peter Waldhorst."

"And how do you know that?"

"I'm investigating a homicide, and I've had help from a Norwegian researcher in locating you, I—"

"Researcher?" said the man. "I don't know any researcher in Norway."

"He's a former associate professor at the University of Oslo and has colleagues in Berlin."

There was a long pause. Only a slight hiss on the line indicated that the man was still there.

"I would like to be allowed to—" Bergmann began.

"You would like to ask me a few questions. Why else would you call?"

Bergmann didn't answer. Instead he tried to think. The man's reaction was surprisingly calm; in fact, it conveyed not even the smallest trace of surprise.

"A few questions about what?" Waldhorst continued.

"I think you know what this is about. Or don't you read the Norwegian papers anymore?"

"Believe me, I haven't read a Norwegian paper since the summer of '45, Mr. Bergmann."

"It's about—"

"On the other hand, I do read the German papers. And even they have published a few articles about Carl Oscar Krogh." Waldhorst waited.

"What did you tell Kaj Holt? In Lillehammer."

Waldhorst exhaled heavily through his nose. For the first time he sounded like an old man.

"Have you ever been to Berlin?" he asked. "I prefer to see the people I'm talking to."

"I'll be in Berlin tomorrow."

Waldhorst paused. "Good," he said at last.

"What did you tell Kaj Holt in Lillehammer?" Bergmann asked again. He knew he shouldn't have pressed the matter just then, but he couldn't help himself. He picked up the photograph from Midsummer Eve 1942 that he'd printed and studied the face of the young Peter Waldhorst, whose eyes were fixed on Agnes Gerner. *She must have been a real knockout,* he thought.

Waldhorst said nothing.

"I know that you were stationed in Norway during the war, that you were probably in the Abwehr before you served in the Gestapo, and I hope you might be able to help me with my investigation. We have to evaluate whether Krogh's murder might have something to do with his activities during the war."

Only silence from Berlin.

After what seemed like a small eternity, Waldhorst said in a low voice, "Let's speak more about this tomorrow, Mr. Bergmann. You know where to find me."

Bergmann didn't hang up until the dial tone began irritating his ear. The certainty that he'd made a big mistake filled him from head to toe. He shouldn't have called Waldhorst first; he should have just shown up at his front door and rung the bell. He'd given the man twenty-four hours to think. That was surely more than he needed.

He placed a brief phone call to Arne Drabløs and said that he'd have to miss handball practice again this week, because he didn't know how long he'd be in Berlin. The prospect of the cup matches in Göteborg ending with some serious losses couldn't be avoided, but there was nothing he could do about it.

After he hung up he opened his notebook and looked at what he'd written. Karen Eline Fredriksen was Karen Eline Krogh. He picked up the phone to call Bente Bull-Krogh.

As he waited for her to pick up, he checked the clock, then double-checked his flight's departure time to Berlin.

Bente Bull-Krogh didn't seem overjoyed to hear his voice, but she had no choice but to invite him out to Bygdøy when he said he had some questions he preferred to ask face-to-face.

At the end of their brief phone conversation, he said, "Does the name—" but stopped. *Does Vera Holt mean anything to you?* he silently finished the question.

"What name?" Bente asked absentmindedly.

"Let's talk about it when I see you in person," he said.

Down in the garage he sat in the car without being able to make up his mind. Kolstadgata was only a few blocks away. Vera Holt. He had to get hold of her. But he didn't like changing his plans; now that he'd gotten in touch with Bente, she'd have to come first. As he turned the key in the ignition, he had a vague feeling that he'd overlooked something quite obvious, almost banal. *What am I not seeing?* He turned off the radio, then switched on the police radio and turned right down Hollendergata. Patrols had been called to a kiosk robbery in Sagene. F-34 responded at once, a young voice, tense but clear. For a moment he missed the life of a uniformed officer—the camaraderie, the pride. After only a few seconds he turned off the police radio.

Fifteen minutes later he stood on the slate steps in front of Bente's enormous house. The Filipino maid opened the door and nodded silently at him. Two big Samsonite suitcases stood in the hall next to the stairs.

Bente was sitting in the larger of the two living rooms, staring out at the rain. Bergmann saw the gray waters of the fjord being pummeled by the rain pouring down from the sky. Even the pine trees seemed to be hanging their heads out in the yard. Leading up from the private beach was a floating dock, bobbing lightly in the water.

"Have you made any progress?" asked Bente without turning around to look at him.

The question threw him off balance for a moment. What should he say? That he was rethinking some aspects of the case? That an old alcoholic in Uddevalla had claimed that her father was a double agent during the war?

"Could be," Bergmann said. It was a poor answer, but the best he had.

Bente looked indifferent.

"This question may sound odd, but . . . could your father have had a bank account in another country, in Switzerland or Liechtenstein or somewhere like that?"

Finally something seemed to register in Bente's face. A worried, or perhaps insulted, furrow formed between her eyebrows. But her voice revealed that she wasn't insulted. She just didn't understand the relevance of his question.

"No, or I don't know. You'll have to ask his lawyer, but . . ."

"But what?" said Bergmann.

She shook her head. "Nothing."

"What was his relationship to money? In general."

Bente stared at him, appearing not to understand, though there was no longer any doubt. This question offended her, and Bergmann couldn't blame her.

"Why in the world are you asking me about such things?"

Bergmann took a deep breath. He couldn't very well tell her the truth.

"We're trying to get an overall picture of your father."

"An overall picture," she said. She shook her head.

"Okay, you don't have to answer. It's not that important."

She opened her mouth to say something but apparently changed her mind.

"Is that all?" she then asked.

"I just have some questions about your mother."

She didn't reply, didn't even have the presence of mind to ask what her mother had to do with her father's murder. She just sat there, looking out at the rain.

"Her maiden name was Fredriksen, wasn't it?"

Bente gave a slight nod.

"And she worked at the legation in Stockholm during the war?"

"Yes, she met Papa in Stockholm after he had to escape from Oslo," she said, so softly that Bergmann could scarcely distinguish her voice from the sound of the rain hammering on the terrace flagstones outside the French doors.

"Does the name Kaj Holt mean anything to you?"

Bente raised her eyes and looked at him properly for the first time since he'd come in. Her face was pale and without makeup, and Bergmann could now see that she was pushing sixty; the past twenty-four hours had made her look ten years older.

After a while she shook her head faintly.

"Try to remember," Bergmann said. "In late May 1945 a Milorg captain who also worked for the Brits was found dead in the Norwegian legation's apartment in Stockholm. His name was Kaj Holt. Your mother was interviewed as a witness in the case. She identified him on the day his body was found. And the Swedish police placed great weight on her testimony that Holt was suicidal."

"I see," said Bente. "But the name still doesn't ring a bell."

"Are you sure that your mother never mentioned him? They worked together for a year and a half at the Norwegian legation in Stockholm. She must have known him well, don't you think? Holt was also your father's immediate superior in Oslo during the war. Your father made a great effort to find out what really happened to him. So she never said a word about Holt?"

"Sorry."

"And your father?"

An old grandfather clock struck the half hour in another room.

"No, not that I can recall. Is it important?"

Bergmann checked his watch. He still had to stop and see Vera Holt before he took off for Berlin.

Twice he opened his mouth to ask the same question, but he stopped both times. Bente accompanied him to the hall.

He stopped at the front door and nodded at the suitcases.

"My brother," said Bente. "He arrived early this morning."

"Is he here?" Bergmann asked.

Bente shook her head. "He's meeting with the funeral director."

Bergmann nodded. "I'd like to speak with him again."

Bente closed her eyes for a moment and leaned her head against the doorjamb.

"Could you ask him to call me?"

"Of course."

"Thanks for taking the time to see me," said Bergmann, turning up the collar of his jacket before setting out into the rain.

He paused for a few seconds on the stairs after the door closed behind him. He'd forgotten to ask her one important thing. Just as he pressed the doorbell, the massive teak door opened. Bente was staring at him.

"I wasn't being completely honest," she said with downcast eyes.

"What do you mean?" Bergmann hunched his shoulders and looked at her.

"My mother . . . Once many years ago there was something on a TV program. We were home alone . . ." Bente passed her hand nervously over her hair.

"What was it about?"

"About an officer who'd been found dead, I don't remember in what town . . ."

Stockholm, Bergmann said to himself.

"It was so many years ago, I think I was twenty-five or six, home visiting one summer, and Father wasn't home. I came into the living room and found her in tears. I've never seen her cry like that. I sat in the chair beside her until the program was over."

"And then?"

"I remembered it just now, as you walked out the door. Mother said something odd, something I didn't understand at the time."

"What did she say?" Bergmann asked, fixing his gaze on her brother's luggage just to avoid looking at her.

"Is it wrong to do anything for the one you love?"

"What do you mean?"

"That was what Mother said: 'Is it wrong to do anything for the one you love?'"

Bente looked at Bergmann as though asking him to interpret that for her. She almost had the innocent look of a child who didn't understand something an adult had said. A child who, out of naïveté and love, couldn't grasp the innate wickedness of the world, and worse still, the sins of her own parents.

"Vera Holt," said Bergmann. "Have you ever met anyone by that name?"

Bente furrowed her eyebrows once more. She stared blankly at him and shook her head.

"What do you think Mother could have meant?" she whispered.

"I don't know," he said. "I really have no idea."

In the car he sat and smoked two cigarettes in quick succession as the rain poured down the windshield.

So, maybe it was true.

Maybe Carl Oscar Krogh really did have Kaj Holt murdered.

Maybe he even did it himself.

Bergmann felt calmer as everything fell back into place inside his head. *That's how it must have happened.* The confusion, the sudden surges of doubt, were gone. For some reason Agnes, the girl, and the maid had been liquidated by Carl Oscar Krogh. After the war Kaj Holt must have started talking about it, and Krogh had had him silenced. Now someone had slaughtered him in retribution. Either because he killed Agnes and the other two, or because he had gotten rid of Holt. Or maybe both.

He closed his eyes and listened to the sound of the rain on the car roof. Iver Faalund must be right. What else would have thrown Holt into such a state of turmoil? What else could Waldhorst have told him other than that Krogh was a double agent?

Bergmann looked at the clock in the police car. He still had time to stop by Kolstadgata.

He had to find Vera Holt.

CHAPTER 46

Wednesday, June 18, 2003
Kolstadgata 7
Oslo, Norway

Kolstadgata 7 was the closest one could come to rock bottom in one of the world's richest countries. Bergmann had been there countless times before, when he patrolled the area by car many years ago, but he couldn't recall it ever looking worse than it did today. Outside the main entrance some Somali kids were playing with a couple of garbage bags. There was garbage everywhere, and he could hear kids fighting in the playground on the other side of the building.

The elevator wasn't working. Bergmann suspected that it hadn't worked since the last time he had been there. He slowly climbed up to the sixth floor, studying the tagging on the walls. On the third floor the smell of piss was even stronger than he recalled from the old days.

He pounded hard on a door that had a strip of duct tape stuck to it. The name Holt had been scratched on the tape with a ballpoint pen that had no ink.

The stairwell door slammed, and a Somali woman came down the hallway with three kids in tow. She gave Bergmann a quick once-over before averting her gaze back to the hall. The biggest of the kids gave him a look that said he could tell from a mile away that he was a cop. The smallest boy turned his head and stared at him. The mother pulled him along and said something unintelligible in a high voice.

He banged on the door again.

"Vera Holt?" he said loudly, leaning close to the doorjamb, which was splintered from what looked like several attempted break-ins.

He waited a moment, then looked at his watch. *Damn,* he thought. *I have to get to the airport soon.* He turned around and looked down the row of doors on the other side of the hall. Finally he took a step toward the door across from Vera Holt's apartment.

The peephole in the door was black. Somebody in there must have been watching him the whole time.

As he took another step toward the door, it opened hesitantly until the safety chain wouldn't go any farther.

"Whaddaya want?"

Bergmann held up his police ID, which hung from a cord around his neck.

"I'd like to talk to Vera Holt."

The door closed. He could hear someone fiddling with the chain.

The woman's face revealed she'd had a hard life. Bergmann could see the marks of alcoholism in her numerous wrinkles. She pulled her robe tighter. A roll-your-own cigarette hung from her lips. Her toes were sticking out of a pair of old orthopedic sandals.

She picked at her tongue and studied her fingers. The TV was blaring. An excitable American woman was touting the excellence of some ab-training device.

"She's been locked up again; they came and got her on Sunday. Lay there screaming all day, so finally I called the medics."

"Where'd they take her?" Bergmann asked.

"I don't know where they take people like that. It's unbelievable that they let her live here, really. Everybody's afraid of her. I know this place is a dump, but I don't want a neighbor sticking a knife in my back."

"What do you mean?" Bergmann said and thought, *Knife in my back*.

"When she moved in about ten years ago, a friend of mine said she'd killed her stepfather with a knife years ago."

Bergmann felt a chill.

Everything came crashing down inside his head in a second. The asterisk in the agency records. The profile of the perp. Acute psychosis.

Vera Holt had apparently killed before, and, if his theory was correct, she had a motive for killing Krogh. Had Vera killed Krogh to avenge her father? Because she'd found out that Krogh had murdered him? But how could she know that Krogh had ordered her father killed?

Bergmann ran down the stairs and out into the fresh air. As soon as he got in his car, he called Fredrik Reuter.

"I found Vera Holt."

"Vera Holt?"

"Kaj Holt's daughter is still alive. She's in some hospital psych ward."

Silence on the other end of the line.

"Are you sure?" Reuter asked. "Do you really think she might be involved? Damn, that would be weird. I was thinking about it earlier today. We may have been on the wrong track. The shoe print we've got is an ECCO size forty-one. Most likely a man—"

"But it could just as well be a woman," Bergmann said, finishing his sentence for him.

"Are you sure?" Reuter asked. "Do you think it's her?"

"She has a motive, at least. If my theory is right." He grabbed his notebook and feverishly leafed through it backward. Where had he gotten sidetracked? Bente Bull-Krogh might have delivered the killer right into his arms days ago.

"What is it?" said Reuter.

"A woman. Krogh's wife thought it was a woman." He found the page from his first interview with Bente, when they had sat out on the terrace in Bygdøy and he'd asked her if her father'd had an affair with another woman.

Bergmann studied his own handwriting for a few seconds. *Wife thought a woman had phoned Krogh. An affair? His mistress's husband? Began in 1963, lasted for a few years. Father stopped going hunting.*

"What the hell are you talking about?" said Reuter.

"One time, years ago, somebody phoned and didn't say a word. Krogh's wife thought it was a woman. It was in the fall. During hunting season."

"Hunting for what?"

"Grouse."

"September, then," said Reuter.

"It was September when Agnes, Cecilia, and the maid were killed."

"That was . . . what year was that?"

"1963," Bergmann said. "It went on for a few years. Then Krogh stopped going grouse hunting."

"How old was Vera Holt in 1963?"

"Eighteen," said Bergmann.

"My God. Do you really think it could be Vera Holt?"

"You'll have to get her prints. And find her record."

"Record?"

"According to her neighbor, Vera murdered her stepfather with a knife when she was young. Kaj Holt's wife must have remarried, and then Vera eventually killed the man. There's an asterisk in the agency records, which means there's a file on her in the stored archives. It must be the old murder case."

Bergmann could imagine Reuter's chin dropping to his shirt collar.

"Do you realize what you're saying?" said Reuter. "Krogh was murdered with a knife."

"Find her."

"You're going to have to skip Berlin," Reuter said. "Vera Holt may have killed Krogh. You understand what I'm telling you?"

"I'm not sure."

"You're not going to Berlin. Do you hear me, Tommy? You have to come down here right away."

Bergmann turned on the blue light on the car's roof and moved into the left lane. He was going almost a hundred miles an hour.

"No," he said. "I can't skip Berlin."

"You can't? Why not?"

"If Vera Holt was admitted to the acute psych ward, she won't get out for at least a week," Bergmann said.

He heard Reuter sigh in resignation.

Bergmann flicked on the siren to warn a hapless driver who hadn't noticed he was coming up fast, much too fast. He could almost feel the heat from the disc brakes as he reluctantly slowed down. At last the car in front pulled over and let him pass.

"There's just one thing that I haven't figured out," Bergmann said. "How would Vera Holt know who ordered her father killed?"

"How about Peter Waldhorst?" Reuter suggested.

CHAPTER 47

Thursday, June 19, 2003
Hotel InterContinental
Budapester Strasse
Berlin, Germany

An intense whistling sound slowly roused Tommy Bergmann from sleep.

He recognized the sound of a truck backing down the street. He pulled up the covers and turned over to escape the strip of light coming through the curtains. When the truck stopped backing up and the soothing hum of Budapester Strasse had returned, his cell phone started ringing on the nightstand. Bergmann swore and reached for the clock. Already ten. He must have slept through his alarm. Or he'd never set it. Images from the night before flickered through his mind. He'd taken a walk along Kurfürstendamm, seen the famous ruined church, and bought some beer at a kiosk. He hadn't wanted to see anyone, and had fallen asleep with his clothes on.

Bergmann studied the display on his cell phone closely. Hadja had called him the night before, but he hadn't picked up. He didn't know what to say to her. She might be just what he needed, but he was afraid of hurting her, of pulling her down with him, the way he'd almost done with Hege. He let the phone ring and go to voice mail, and waited for Fredrik Reuter to call again. It only took a few seconds. All of a sudden Bergmann remembered his dream from last night, a terrifying, inhuman dream that haunted him several times a year.

"And how are we doing today?" Reuter asked.

Bergmann didn't feel like replying.

"Have you found Vera Holt?" he said, his head still half under the big pillow.

"Ullevål. The acute psychiatric ward is quite nice. Not that I'd want to end up there, but . . ."

"And?"

"And she's not in any condition to be interviewed. According to the doctor she's working her way out of a psychosis."

"And the search?"

"We'll have a warrant by tomorrow morning. Maybe even this afternoon, if we're lucky."

"What day of the week did Our Lord create lawyers?" Bergmann asked.

"Democracy is never perfect, isn't that how the saying goes?" Reuter said.

Oh, shut up, Bergmann thought. The hotel room was full of the sort of ambient background noise that only a city the size of Berlin could produce. His gaze wandered around the room and ended up on the rotating TV, which was folded into the wall by the bathtub, making it possible to watch TV from the tub behind Plexiglas.

"Don't go into the apartment without me," Bergmann said. "Wait till I get there."

"Okay. But we might have her, Tommy. I've got her file in front of me right now."

Bergmann felt his pulse quicken.

"She was fourteen when she killed her stepfather."

Bergmann didn't say a word, but flipped open the top of a twenty-pack of Prince cigarettes from the duty-free store. He hardly recognized himself in the mirror. His hair was greasy and unwashed, and his eyes had dark smudges underneath.

"On the night of Advent Sunday, November 29, 1959, Vera Holt murdered her stepfather with nine stab wounds in an apartment on Normannsgate. A patrol apprehended her on the steps of Kampen Church. Vera was sitting there with a bloody kitchen knife in her hand, wearing only her nightgown."

Bergmann lit a cigarette and took a deep drag. He thought about Vera Holt, a mere girl, in her nightgown, barefoot, with a kitchen knife in her hand. *What god had created that life?* he wondered.

"She was judged to be temporarily insane at the time of the murder and not criminally responsible, though she easily could have landed in Bredtveit women's prison at the age of fourteen."

"So what happened?"

"She was at Dikemark psychiatric hospital for a few years."

"A few years?"

"Good behavior, was declared cured, or so they said."

"When?"

"1963."

"1963," Bergmann repeated, stubbing out his cigarette before heading into the bathroom.

"This could be our woman, Tommy."

"Wasn't she given a clean bill of health?"

"If a person is psychotic . . . you know this, Tommy. Think how many of them you've brought in—driven to the emergency room yourself—and then run into them again in the same condition a few months later."

"Don't touch the apartment," Bergmann said.

The shower felt like a small cleansing. As soon as he got out, the sound of the TV—a German news program—reminded him what awaited him.

The Turkish cab driver drove slowly up Kurfürstendamm. Bergmann sat with his arm halfway out the window, enjoying a gentle breeze on his bare skin. He'd never been to Berlin before, but he liked it—the old apartment buildings with their central courtyards, the endless green-edged boulevards. Though he had no real basis for his opinion, it seemed as if the city had shaken off the indignities of the war. In all the pictures he'd seen of Berlin over the years, it had looked dilapidated and half in ruins. Now something new and unprecedented seemed to be rising from the ashes. He felt a pang of fear at the thought that the Germans might one day rise again.

Forget it, he thought as the cab stopped at a traffic light by the department store KaDeWe. He glanced at the clothes he had on and thought that maybe he ought to look a bit more presentable when he met with Waldhorst. A former German officer probably wouldn't have much respect for a long-haired Norwegian policeman dressed in worn jeans and a pair of deck shoes that had seen better days. He touched the new light-blue shirt he'd purchased at Oslo Airport the day before and decided it was businesslike enough. He shook his head in resignation—he usually didn't think like this. He was nervous about what Peter Waldhorst would have to say. He leaned back in his seat, noting the smell of new leather coming from the neck rest. An old German cabaret song issued softly from the loudspeaker in the door. Bergmann squinted at the sunshine and the dappled light coming through the trees.

Peter Waldhorst's house looked more like a small palace than a residence. Bergmann kept an eye on the pale brown villa as he paid the driver with a twenty-euro bill and asked for a receipt and five euros back. The gable wall faced the street behind a high wrought-iron fence covered in ivy. As the cab drove off he stood on the sidewalk and watched it vanish toward the city center. As he looked around, he realized that Waldhorst's house was less ostentatious than the others in the neighborhood.

He tried the handle of the gate. Locked. It occurred to him that Vera Holt might have stood there too. How else could she have found out that Krogh was responsible for her father's death?

Bergmann found the doorbell next to the wrought-iron gate. After quite a long time a woman's voice answered.

"Bergmann here. I have an—" He was interrupted by a buzzing sound from the lock in the gate.

On the stairs he turned to look around. *What a place,* he thought. Hard to believe that it wasn't bombed during the war, but it must be true. The neighborhood was filled with the grandest patrician villas he'd ever seen, tucked away behind old gardens and shielded by trees so tall that it seemed they wouldn't stop until they reached the sky.

A young girl appeared in the doorway. Bergmann assumed that she was Turkish.

"He isn't home. But he is expecting you."

She showed him into the huge dark hall.

"When will he be back?"

"Soon," she said.

Bergmann was led across the ground floor out to the terrace, where the maid suggested he could wait. He'd expected the interior to be furnished in an old, heavy style, but with the exception of the dark parquet flooring, the rooms were bright.

The Turkish girl brought him coffee on a silver tray. When she saw that he had lit a cigarette, she came hurrying back with a crystal ashtray. Something was tugging at Bergmann's mind as he sat gazing at the shining lake below the garden.

The sun was scorching, even under the big umbrella, but he didn't let it bother him. He looked at his watch and then went to open the door leading into the house. For a moment he simply took pleasure in the cool air inside. Then he examined the room more closely. There was a dining table with space for twelve at one end, a sitting area at the other, a couple of sideboards, some modern bar furniture, and a couple of modernist oil paintings on the walls.

There's something not quite right here, he thought, *something in these rooms.* He walked over to the other end of the room and opened the double doors. He found a dimly lit room dominated by heavy leather furniture. Bookcases with glass doors lined one wall, separated by a liquor cabinet.

There, Bergmann thought when he saw the photographs on the liquor cabinet. A glimmer of light hovered over the room, and thousands of dust motes danced in the dim rays entering the room from outside.

One by one Bergmann picked up the almost identical silver frames that stood on the polished mahogany cabinet. He recognized people who had similar features to Waldhorst in the photos, most of which were black and white, but none of the pictures showed Waldhorst himself. Of the twenty frames he figured that three of the faces were his children, the rest grandchildren. Most of the old color photos looked like they dated back to the sixties and seventies. A small silver frame held a photo of a German soldier. Bergmann guessed that he was a brother. A mere boy in a black uniform, with stern eyes but a soft expression. Bergmann set it down in the very back, where he'd found it.

He took a step back and reexamined the only photograph that really interested him. It was a black-and-white photo of a young man and a very pregnant woman sitting on a flat rock, somewhere in northern Europe, perhaps even Norway. They were both smiling at the camera. The man, whom Bergmann had a vague sense of having seen somewhere before, had his arm around the woman, who held a cigarette in her hand. He didn't recognize her—but wasn't there something familiar about the shape of her mouth?

No, this man . . . it was on the tip of his tongue.

"Herr Bergmann," said a voice to his left.

A rather short, stocky man stood in the doorway to the hall, dressed all in white: tennis shirt, shorts, tennis shoes. His gray hair was combed straight back, and there were a couple of streaks of dried sweat on his face. Though he was older now, with a slightly stooped posture, Bergmann had no trouble recognizing him. He had the same bushy eyebrows, with eyes set a little too deep and close together for him to be called handsome. Unlike Carl Oscar Krogh.

"Herr Waldhorst," said Bergmann, moving toward him.

He felt his cheeks flush when he discovered that he was still holding the photograph in his hand. Without releasing the man's gaze he put it back.

The man in the doorway smiled, as if to suggest that Bergmann was welcome to snoop around as much as he liked.

Although his hand was sinewy—almost bony and full of liver spots—his handshake was the firmest Bergmann had experienced in a long time. Waldhorst looked him straight in the eye and said in his remarkably clear Norwegian, "Yes, Herr Bergmann, I am Peter Waldhorst."

Something doesn't seem right here, Bergmann thought. *What is it?*

CHAPTER 48

Monday, September 14, 1942
Villa Lande
Tuengen Allé
Oslo, Norway

Agnes Gerner sat down in the window seat in Cecilia's room. The little girl was sitting at her desk reading a book. She liked having Agnes nearby. Once in a while she would look up at the photo of her mother and murmur a few words. Agnes was momentarily seized with guilt at fooling the child into believing there was a future for them. She turned away from Cecilia and rested her forehead against the cold window-pane. A glimpse of early autumn sunshine penetrated the heavy cloud cover. A strip of light passed over the terrace before the clouds moved in once again. It seemed like another lifetime, that evening only a few months ago when she had sat on the terrace with Peter Waldhorst. Could it really be as simple as the Pilgrim had claimed, that Waldhorst was merely in love with her? Both Number 1 and the Pilgrim seemed to have settled on that idea, but she couldn't make herself believe it. Maybe he was just trying to trick her into making some fatal mistake. But if they were right, someone else in Gustav Lande's circle must be keeping an eye on her. Someone must be that notorious and cursed fox that Archibald Lafton had warned her about, the apparently dead beast that was waiting and waiting until she was positive it was dead before rising up and ripping out her throat. If it wasn't Waldhorst—if he was simply in love with her as they claimed—who else did she need to watch out for? She'd considered every individual she'd met through Gustav, and she didn't suspect any of them—except those wearing German uniforms, of course.

But what if Number 1 and the Pilgrim were right? What if Detective Inspector *Hauptsturmführer* Waldhorst was nothing more than an ordinary man—with flaws and weaknesses—who had fallen in love with her? On the one hand, that might be good news, but it didn't make things any easier for her. She was now in so deep that she hardly dared think about how she was going to get out alive. And the nausea was still plaguing her. She put her hand on her stomach. There was nothing left inside to throw up.

She had no words for how awful the weekend had been. Only in the last few days had she fully grasped the situation. She must be pregnant, and the Pilgrim must be the father. Gustav always used protection. It was a small miracle that she'd managed to make it through the weekend at all. On Saturday she'd done little more than lean over the toilet bowl. Luckily Gustav had been in Berlin all week and hadn't returned until just this afternoon. She didn't know how she was going to continue hiding her nausea from him. It would be all right for a few days, but if she continued to vomit every morning, he would soon understand that something was wrong. And the maid, Johanne Caspersen, always seemed to be following her around. There was something odd about her. Johanne practically cross-examined her every time Agnes was about to leave the house. On the surface, she merely seemed to be showing a normal amount of interest, but beneath her polite façade, it was clear that she harbored a great distrust of Agnes, who could hardly even go back to her own apartment anymore without first coming up with some lie.

She glanced at her watch. She was already late. She'd had her hair done at Moen's salon on Wednesday, and Number 1 had left her a message asking her to come to an apartment on Kirkeveien today. She reminded herself of the tenant's name and the password—"Looks like rain this evening"—for the umpteenth time.

This awful nausea, she thought, giving Cecilia a hug before hurrying along the corridor and down the stairs.

"May I ask where you're going?"

The voice behind her echoed in the empty hallway. Agnes had initially loved the modern architecture—it gave Gustav Lande a conciliatory trait, almost bordering on anti-Nazism, and the house's pure lines and bright, open spaces were like a soothing balm during this terrible war—but now the white, transparent surfaces seemed cold and lifeless. These days, she felt as though she were trapped inside a white coffin with a glass lid.

Agnes let go of the door handle. The cab was waiting at the gate, where the branches of the birch tree hung low. Above the tree was a wall of dark clouds, which at any moment would drown them all—Norwegians and Germans, Nazis and patriots alike—in what looked to be an epic rainstorm.

"Do you ask Herr Lande why he is going into town?" said Agnes, turning to look at the maid, who stood in the kitchen doorway.

The maid didn't flinch. That ugly, birdlike face of hers hurt Agnes's eyes. She was not a good person, and Agnes wanted to wipe that smile off her face once and for all.

"I'll be back tonight," Agnes said quietly.

"There is only one Mrs. Lande in this family, and unfortunately she is dead."

Agnes didn't reply. She put her red hat back on the shelf and took the black one instead. A red hat was more likely to draw attention.

"So who is he? The other man." The maid took a few steps closer as she dusted the bureau that stood to her right.

Agnes looked at herself in the mirror. Johanne was now standing right behind her. Agnes turned around and met her eye. Swiftly she raised her right arm. The sound of her palm striking the maid's cheek rang through the large room, like the lash of a whip. Johanne hardly knew what had hit her as she doubled over, holding her cheek. Agnes's hand stung. With a pounding heart she glanced over at the stairs. But Cecilia wasn't there. She hadn't seen what just happened.

Johanne straightened up slowly, still holding her cheek. Her eyes were brimming with tears.

"You're finished in this house," said Agnes in a low voice. "Do you understand? As soon as Gustav and I are married, you're fired!"

With trembling fingers she reached for the door handle. The cold metal soothed the stinging sensation, but only for a moment.

"Poor you," said Agnes as she stepped out the door. "Condemned to live the life of an old maid." She felt as though every step she took might be her last. By the time she finally reached the gate and the driver got out of the cab, her legs were barely supporting her.

On the way to Fagerborg Church, she had to bite the inside of her cheek to keep from crying. As if that weren't bad enough, she experienced another wave of nausea. Instinctively she pressed her hand to her stomach. In a flash she came to a realization. *Maybe this isn't the worst possible thing,* she thought as she made the long walk back to Kirkeveien. She'd been given orders to take all sorts of detours to make sure she wasn't being followed. *Maybe it's not so bad to be sent on a suicide mission.* Especially now that she'd brought this misfortune upon herself.

By the time she entered the vestibule—which wasn't as well maintained as her own building on Hammerstads Gate—she'd been wandering one street after another for nearly half an hour. In her view, that had been enough to ascertain that no one was following her. Least of all Peter Waldhorst. When she reached the fourth floor, it occurred to her for the first time that Carl Oscar might not have mentioned Waldhorst to Number 1 at all. How could he—who was precaution personified—take such a chance?

No, she thought. *No.* She knocked twice, paused, then swiftly knocked twice again. She heard the slow, shuffling footsteps of an old person inside the apartment. An elderly man with big bags under his eyes opened the door. Impeccably attired in suit and tie, he looked as if he'd just gotten home from work. His expression was neutral as he waited for the password.

Agnes felt exhausted as she whispered, "Looks like rain this evening." She was also hungry. The man nodded silently. Agnes stepped inside, closed the door, and then leaned her back against it. The smell of stale cigar smoke coming from the living room made her press her hand to her mouth.

"Is something wrong?" asked the man with a touch of warmth in his voice.

Agnes shook her head and lowered her hand. She took off her gloves. Even the smell of the leather made what little was left in her stomach rise to her throat.

"The bathroom?" she said. "I just need to . . ."

Agnes walked through the living room without even greeting the man's wife, who was sitting in an armchair knitting, apparently unfazed by the appearance of a visitor. She hardly noticed Kaj Holt, who was standing in the kitchen doorway, wearing only an undershirt and trousers, his face white. He was holding a Sten gun.

In the bathroom she turned on the cold water and knelt down with her cheek resting on the toilet seat, surrendering to the dry heaves. She just managed to take off her hat before it would have fallen into the toilet bowl.

Holt was waiting for her in the kitchen. His eyes looked empty, as if the war had already been lost, as if they were all dead.

"Are you sick?" he asked, stubbing out his cigarette in an overflowing ashtray. The blackout curtain had been drawn over the window facing the back courtyard, and only a single candle lit up his face. The Pilgrim appeared in the doorway to the maid's room. Agnes tried to suppress the feeling, but she couldn't help the girlish joy that filled her when she saw him. He gave her a brief smile, and she saw that old glint in his eyes, the look he'd had before the war came to Norway. A moment later, his face shut down and his expression turned hard. But it was enough for Agnes. She didn't need anything more. It was enough to keep her alive for another week.

"I think it's just something I ate," she said.

Holt got up and nodded toward the maid's room. The Pilgrim stepped aside to let them pass. Agnes had almost forgotten what he smelled like. It had been over a week since they'd last met. And they might never see each other again.

Holt closed the door and motioned her toward the desk chair. He set the Sten gun on the bed. The room was so small that the Pilgrim had to sit on the bed to make room for all three of them. At the foot of the bed was another door, which probably led down a back stairway to the courtyard. *So that's why Holt chose this particular maid's room,* thought Agnes.

"I like the maid they've hired," she said, sitting down.

Holt laughed quietly, pressing his finger to his lips. He perched on the edge of the desk next to Agnes. Even a child would have realized he was a hunted man. His face lacked all color in the dim light coming from the ceiling lamp, and the dark smudges under his eyes suggested he hadn't slept in a while. He ran his hand over the blackout curtain and then looked at the dust on his fingers.

"You don't look well yourself," whispered Agnes.

"We're losing too many," he said, his voice as dry as sandpaper. "And I take that personally."

"It's not your fault," said the Pilgrim, sitting on the bed.

Holt buried his face in his hands and kept them there for several minutes. His shoulders shook, indicating a sudden fit of sobbing.

"Kaj . . ." said the Pilgrim softly.

Holt wiped his hands on his undershirt. Then he got up and put on a shirt that was draped over a chair. Finally he seemed to regain his composure.

Agnes stared at the Pilgrim, who was semireclining on the bed, looking more handsome than ever. *How I've loved you,* she thought. *How I still love you. But you'd kill me if you knew what I know. How I've betrayed you. And Kaj, and all the others. How could I get pregnant? And I can't tell a soul. Not now. Maybe later. Maybe never.*

"All right," said Holt, almost whispering. "Agnes, London has chosen you. They say you have what it takes. And I trust London and your handler, who was once mine." He stared at her with newly regained strength, as if he'd drawn energy from a source deep inside. A little smile tugged at his lips. She could see the boy he once had been, a devil-may-care lad, but above all, honest.

Agnes nodded, cursing Christopher Bratchard. *May you burn in hell,* she thought.

"London says that Research Director Torfinn Rolborg has to go. And there's nobody else who can do that except you, Agnes."

"But how . . ."

Holt placed his hand on her shoulder.

"I'll explain."

She nodded.

"Now that you've been here, and you've met with me personally, there's no going back. Understand?"

He motioned toward the Pilgrim, who was kneeling on the floor, bending down to pull up two floorboards under the bed. He carefully removed two paper packages and handed them to Holt. Agnes shook her head when the Pilgrim offered her an English cigarette. Their eyes met. *In my belly,* she thought. *I have you inside my belly.*

Holt set the packages on the desk and opened them. In the first was the strangest thing Agnes had ever seen. A completely black steel rod, maybe thirty centimeters long, with a short shaft and a trigger mechanism at the base. It looked like a big silencer, but she knew it had to be some sort of gun.

"Show me how it works," said Holt, handing the steel rod to Agnes.

"What is it?" she asked as she took it. It felt oddly light, as if made of air.

"They call it a Welrod," said Holt close to her ear. "It's the first and only one we have. So . . ." He squatted down next to her. "It has to work."

Agnes didn't respond as she studied the gun for a whole minute, maybe more, pulling out the circular bolt in the end and pressing her finger on the heavy trigger.

"Okay," said Holt. "As you may realize, there's no time to test-fire it. You'll need to shoot Rolborg in the chest from a distance of two feet. Reload, then shoot him in the head. Reload, another shot to the head. Don't get any blood on yourself. The only way out is through the main entrance. If there's blood on you, you're finished. There'll be one round in the chamber. You'll have to reload for each shot."

"Stop," she said. "Stop . . ."

Holt smiled faintly to himself and shook his head. Then he started over from the beginning, more calmly this time.

"What about the noise?" asked Agnes.

"I could have shot you right now, and the Pilgrim wouldn't have heard a thing if he were sitting in the kitchen. We'll get the gun inside the building. Security is tight down there. But don't worry about that. We have a man on the inside. He'll leave the Welrod in the toilet tank in the ladies' room. First, you'll be searched by the guard. Then you'll need to ask to go to the bathroom before your interview. And put on a good act, for God's sake. You must know that I'm placing a huge responsibility on your shoulders."

"But how . . . how will I get to Knaben?" She shook her head, totally confused. Was she going to Knaben's headquarters? She had no idea what Holt was trying to tell her. What interview?

"It's just the opportunity we needed," said Holt. He pulled out the desk drawer and showed her a newspaper clipping from *Aftenposten*. It was a short job announcement from Knaben Molybdenum Mines, Inc., Oslo Division: "The Research Department seeks a new assistant secretary. Bring your papers with you." Then a few key words about qualifications and the like. The interview times were listed as Thursday or Friday of the following week.

"Rolborg will be conducting the interviews personally, even though it doesn't say that here. Our man says that the secretary will be working for him."

"Our man?" said Agnes. "Couldn't he . . ."

"Our man isn't capable of killing anyone," whispered Holt. "Even if I could convince him that Rolborg isn't a human being—just a monstrous Nazi whose discoveries will take the lives of thousands of good men—even then he wouldn't be able to do it. But London says that you, Agnes, have what it takes to remove this monster for good." He placed his hand on her shoulder and squeezed hard. "And haven't you said yourself that you wanted to make a difference in this war?"

"You need to think this through. Improvise," said the Pilgrim. "My suggestion is to have . . ." He stopped.

An image of Johanne Caspersen inexplicably appeared in Agnes's mind. *How could I?* she thought, and then cursed herself for having such thoughts.

"But this is a suicide mission," she said. "I might run into Gustav or the administrative director or . . ."

None of them spoke for a long time.

"You've never met Rolborg, have you?" Holt then asked.

She shook her head.

"And Gustav Lande is seldom at the office on Rosenkrantz Gate. He spends most of his time in his office in Majorstua, and when he's not there, he's traveling around the country. Isn't that so? He has a large number of other business interests, some of which are even bigger than Knaben. So what's the chance that you'd run into him there on that particular day?"

She nodded.

"And besides, you'll be unrecognizable, Agnes. I promise you that. You won't look anything like yourself. You'll be blonde, with blue eyes . . ." He stopped himself, but smiled like a boy. As if this whole operation were a trivial affair.

"I see," said Agnes.

Holt placed a stack of papers on her lap. Identification documents that lacked a photograph. *That's what the camera on the bookcase is for,* she thought. She paged through the fictional life that had been created for her.

"You'll try out the disguise, we'll take your picture, and voilà . . ." He pointed to the identification papers.

So, that's it, she thought. Everything seemed to have been decided. She needed to do this. She had to do it. She had no choice. She glanced at the Pilgrim, only two feet away. *For your sake,* she thought. *This is for us, for our freedom, for our . . .*

She felt a sudden stabbing sensation in her chest. This was real, wasn't it? Suddenly everything Kaj Holt had said seemed disconnected, randomly and hastily put together; it appeared that he wanted to have Rolborg removed, no matter what the cost.

"With these papers, they'll have to give you the job. You'll change here, try out everything here first. Stay here all night if you have to, but get yourself completely ready here before the operation. We have the entire night ahead of us now, and by the time we're done, you'll be able to do it in your sleep. Do you understand?" Holt took out a blonde wig that had to have been made from real hair, along with two cans. She couldn't see what they contained.

"What about someone from England? Couldn't they . . ." Agnes began, but then stopped herself.

"It's a matter of time," said Holt, now sounding a bit annoyed. Then he regained his composure and spoke more gently. "He's already done too much damage. He's been given a lot of leeway by Lande, who in turn has been granted the same by Seeholz. He enjoys the full trust of the Germans. You know that. And very few others in Norway—maybe nobody except Rolborg—know the exact location of the molybdenum deposit. They might have to spend years searching for it up there in Hurdal."

"They'll figure it out," said Agnes, stroking the Welrod. "Not many people know about him . . . about Rolborg . . . and I . . ."

Holt touched her shoulder.

"You're the only one who can get to him without us losing everybody involved. Do you understand? He's guarded at all times, except beyond the reception area in Knaben's offices. And you're a woman. No one is going to suspect a woman of shooting someone, Agnes."

"All right," she said, hardly hearing her own words. Those seemed to be the only words she had left, an automatic reply: all right.

Holt took her face in his hands, which smelled of tobacco and sweat and nervousness.

"I'm counting on you. I know you were meant to do this, Agnes."

She nodded, then closed her eyes. Again she pictured the hideous face of the maid. The sound of her hand slapping her cheek rang in her head.

CHAPTER 49

Peter Waldhorst laid his knife and fork down on his plate to signal he was done eating. He took the sheet of paper that Tommy Bergmann was holding out to him. It was a scanned copy of the photograph that Finn Nystrøm had e-mailed to him. The photo from Midsummer Eve 1942. Waldhorst took his reading glasses out of the breast pocket of his short-sleeved shirt. Bergmann was seated across from the old man, who was now staring at the old photo.

"You knew the woman sitting on the right. Agnes Gerner," said Bergmann.

Waldhorst didn't say a word as he shifted the paper in his hand, gripping it so hard that his fingertips turned white.

"Was I ever really that young?" he said finally.

Bergmann didn't reply. Waldhorst had been avoiding the topic for so long that he was starting to have doubts that this trip had been worth the effort.

"Judging by your expression in the photo, it seemed that you must have known her quite well. Am I right?"

"What do you mean?" said Waldhorst without looking up.

"You look like a man in love," said Bergmann.

Waldhorst glanced up then, a little smile on his face. Looking into his eyes, Bergmann could see the innocent boy he had once been.

"You're certainly making a lot of assumptions, Mr. Bergmann."

"But you do remember the case, don't you? The two women and a child who were reported missing?"

"I don't remember much about it," said Waldhorst. "I was in the Abwehr back then, you know. This was a police matter. And keep in mind how much is going on during a war. Three missing people are quickly forgotten, Mr. Bergmann. Statistics. Nothing more."

"Why did you transfer to the Gestapo only three months after they were killed?"

Waldhorst took off his glasses and held them up to blow on the lenses. Then he carefully polished them on his shirttail. He showed no sign that he would answer the question. Instead, he looked out at the lake, as if the sight of it might give him inspiration or provide the answers to Bergmann's questions. From the highway on the other side of the lake came a faint roar that seemed to hover like a blanket over the veranda. The only other sound was the chirping of birds in the trees down by the water.

"This may sound crazy, but the Gestapo was a good place for me at the time. The Abwehr was already hanging on by a thread in 1942. Perhaps you know the story. Canaris . . . and, well, you know."

"Yes," said Bergmann.

"I wanted to stay alive."

Bergmann didn't say a word.

"War is a matter of survival," said Waldhorst. "Once it starts, the only thing that matters is the struggle to survive."

"Agnes Gerner didn't survive. Nor did Cecilia Lande or Johanne Caspersen."

"No, they didn't," said Waldhorst.

"Who killed them?" asked Bergmann.

"Didn't you tell me that Carl Oscar Krogh killed them?" said Waldhorst, with a wave of his hand.

Bergmann wondered whether Waldhorst had ever killed anyone, whether that hand of his had killed. *Undoubtedly,* he thought. Waldhorst had killed people and sent even more to their deaths.

"You think Krogh did it, right?"

"Yes," said Bergmann. "But there's something that doesn't make sense. It turns out Agnes wasn't a Nazi. So that means she was liquidated by mistake."

Waldhorst nodded. Bergmann had decided to wait to tell him the rest. It was unlikely that Waldhorst would confirm Faalund's claim that Krogh was a double agent.

"It could have been a mistake, as you say," replied the old man. "And Krogh could still have done the killing. So you're on the right track."

Neither of them spoke for a moment.

Waldhorst studied the photograph again. He seemed to be murmuring to himself the names of all the people seated at the table in the picture. His lips were moving, but no sound came out.

"What did you tell Kaj Holt in Lillehammer?"

"What do you think I told him?" said Waldhorst without looking up. It was clear that he was having a hard time remembering the name of one of the guests in the photo. He took off his reading glasses and folded them up. He left the photograph lying on his lap.

"Why don't you just tell me?" said Bergmann. "It had to be something that got Holt killed in Stockholm the very next day."

Waldhorst's hand shook as he filled Bergmann's coffee cup. Then he filled his own cup, without looking at his guest. For a moment he seemed unaware of Bergmann's presence at all. He sat motionless, staring at a spot to his left.

"Whatever it was that Holt and I talked about, it's something I'm going to take to my grave," Waldhorst said at last. "And believe me, it's not the worst thing that I'll be taking with me."

"You told Holt that Krogh was the one who murdered the two women and the child," Bergmann insisted.

Waldhorst laughed, not in a derogatory way, but as if Bergmann were a child who had asked an obvious question even though he already knew the answer.

"I won't lie to you, Mr. Bergmann. A lie, big or small, will always be found out sooner or later. A lie catches up with a person and slowly strangles him—even a man of my age. It was not an insignificant matter that we discussed, Holt and I. But there's one thing I can assure you. It had nothing to do with those three who were killed in Nordmarka. Absolutely nothing."

"And you're not lying about that?" said Bergmann.

Waldhorst's expression changed, but Bergmann couldn't tell if he was smiling or giving him a scornful frown.

"I'm not lying, Mr. Bergmann." He stirred a spoonful of sugar into his coffee. "Holt committed suicide, didn't he?"

"I think he was murdered," replied Bergmann. "And the police investigator thought the same thing at the time. He was also murdered . . ."

"Well, believe whatever you like, but I know nothing about that," said Waldhorst. "On the night that Holt died, I was taken from my cell in Lillehammer. Or it may have been the night before. I don't really remember anymore . . ." Waldhorst smiled faintly. "A week later I was working in the Office of Strategic Services in Frankfurt. I figure they burned all my papers."

"And where were you before that?"

"I was transferred to Stockholm," said Waldhorst. "Then to Frankfurt for a year before I was moved to Langley."

"Stockholm?"

"Yes."

"So you were in Stockholm on May 30, 1945?"

Again Waldhorst smiled briefly. His gold teeth glittered in the sunlight.

"Don't go getting any ideas, Bergmann. Would I tell you I was in Stockholm the night Holt was killed if I was the one who murdered him? And how could I possibly have done it? I was a prisoner. Do you understand? A prisoner with no papers, without a past, maybe without a future as well. I couldn't even go to the bathroom without guards accompanying me."

"How do you know he died at night? Or that he was murdered?"

Waldhorst stared at him.

"Newspapers, Bergmann. Newspapers. And didn't you yourself just say that he was murdered?"

Bergmann didn't reply. He felt more confused every time Waldhorst opened his mouth.

A long pause ensued. Both of them watched a Lufthansa plane descending almost soundlessly toward Tegel Airport on the other side of the lake.

"Did you know that Kaj Holt had a daughter?" asked Bergmann at last.

Waldhorst nodded. Then he abruptly got up and took a few steps toward the edge of the veranda.

"He told me in Lillehammer," said Waldhorst, speaking more to himself than to Bergmann. "'Don't we all have a little daughter?'" he said. At the railing he stopped, looking suddenly older. His body, close to ninety years old now, leaned over the flowers, his hands moving slowly, like claws about to stiffen for good. Without a word he carefully plucked several withered leaves from the flowers planted in wrought-iron boxes.

"Have you ever met her?"

"Why are you asking me this?"

"I think she's the one who killed Krogh."

For a moment Waldhorst stood motionless next to the flower boxes. He seemed to be pondering this statement. Then he continued his gardening efforts, his fingers working their way arduously over the three big boxes, all of which were filled with blue flowers that Bergmann didn't recognize.

"No," he said then. "I've never met her."

Bergmann didn't say a word. Vera Holt could have found out what happened back then some other way. He considered confronting Waldhorst with what Faalund had said—that Krogh had been working for the Germans—but this didn't seem like the right time. And the old intelligence officer probably wouldn't have given him an answer anywhere close to the truth.

"Those three . . . Agnes, the child, and the maid," said Waldhorst. "How were their bodies found?"

"It was just by chance," said Bergmann.

"Hmm," said Waldhorst. "If there's one thing I've learned after all these years, it's that chance is nothing but fate, and fate is nothing but chance."

The door opened behind Bergmann. He turned partway around and caught sight of the Turkish maid wearing a blue-checked apron. She apologized for interrupting and said something in German to Waldhorst. "A taxi is waiting," she repeated for Bergmann's benefit in English.

Waldhorst nodded and waved her away.

"I forgot to mention it yesterday," he said. "But if you'll excuse me, I'd like to visit my wife before visiting hours are over. At our age, it's hard to know how much time we have left together."

"Your wife is ill?" said Bergmann.

"Yes. But you're welcome to wait here. I'll be back in an hour, maybe an hour and a half. Stay to dinner, if you like." He threw out his hands and gave Bergmann such a big smile that he thought it might almost be genuine.

"Thank you, but no. I have a plane to catch."

"All right. But we can share a cab. My wife is at the German Red Cross Clinic, which is on the way to Tegel Airport. Or does your plane leave from that awful Schönefeld?"

"Tegel," said Bergmann, though that was a lie.

"Let's go, then."

Bergmann followed the old man through the house, moving through the same white-painted rooms as when he'd arrived. *Nothing but paintings on the walls,* he thought. The only photographs were of children and grandchildren. But something told him these were not the offspring of his present wife.

He stopped in the middle of the massive entryway, whose marble floor was covered with a huge Persian carpet. A tall mirror hung on the wall between the two doors leading into separate living rooms. Bergmann stood there, studying his reflection from a distance of several feet. Behind him he noticed Waldhorst looking at his back from the front doorway. Bergmann turned to look up the grand staircase to the second floor.

"Is something wrong?" asked Waldhorst. In one hand he was holding a rose swathed in cellophane, in the other a small gift-wrapped package.

Yes, thought Bergmann. But he couldn't put his finger on what it might be.

"Do you have children?" he asked. "Grandchildren?"

"The children are from my first marriage," said Waldhorst.

Bergmann nodded and stepped out the front door. The heat was almost unbearable on this side of the house.

"It was too late for us to have children. Gretchen and I," said Waldhorst pensively as they got in the cab.

Bergmann sank back against the seat, not giving any more thought to what the man sitting next to him had said.

CHAPTER 50

Friday, September 25, 1942
Kirkeveien
Oslo, Norway

Agnes Gerner drew her beige coat even tighter around her and looked to the left, then to the right, and again to the left before crossing Middelthuns Gate and heading for Kirkeveien. She wasn't sure why she'd bothered, as there was hardly any traffic in the city anymore. But if she was going to die today, it wasn't going to be from getting struck by some Nazi-owned BMW or ending up under the wheels of a German truck loaded with soldiers.

The same old man opened the door to her on Kirkeveien. Without a word he ushered her through the apartment, shuffling along in his worn-out slippers. In the kitchen he motioned toward the maid's room, which was now clean and deserted. There was not a trace of Number 1 or the Pilgrim. Only the unmistakable smell of stale cigarette smoke gave any indication that someone had been there. Agnes switched on the ceiling light. The blackout curtains made it almost impossible to see anything otherwise, even on this sunny morning, which was brighter than any she'd seen in a long time. She found what she needed in the wardrobe and quickly changed into the blue suit. Then she took out a little metal box from the brown plastic bag, opened the lid, and stared down at the two nearly invisible contact lenses. Only when she was about to insert the second one—as hard and uncomfortable as the first—did her nerves fail her. Staring into the mirror, she raised her finger to her eye. But her finger refused to go any closer. She started shaking all over. She tried once more, but she was shaking so hard she couldn't do it. A new wave of nausea rose up in her throat.

For several minutes she sat there, simply staring at herself, with one brown eye and one blue. Finally she heard a shuffling sound out in the kitchen. "Pull yourself together," she murmured. "You need to pull yourself together!"

The shuffling came to a halt right behind her. Agnes didn't turn around. The old man took a few steps into the room. He smelled the way men of his age often did, of alcohol and pipe tobacco. Most likely he'd slept upright in an easy chair all night. He placed his hand on her shoulder.

"All of us will thank you," he said in a low voice, "when this is over." Then he removed his hand.

Someone flushed a toilet. His wife must be awake. Agnes closed her eyes for a moment and nodded.

The old man turned on his heel and shuffled out of the room. Her hand was no longer shaking and she was able to insert the contact lens in her right eye. *There,* she thought. Two blue eyes. How paradoxical, the Pilgrim had told her, that contact lenses were a German invention, used by the movie industry in America when they switched from black-and-white to color films. Now the Germans were going to get a taste of their own medicine. Five minutes later she had rubbed Vaseline on her hair, smoothed it down, and fastened it with bobby pins. The man came back in to help her put on the blonde wig. He handled it so expertly that she suspected that Helge K. Moen, the hairdresser, had been the one to put him in touch with Number 1.

"Don't worry, it won't fall off. Not even in thirty years," he told her and then went back to the kitchen. He returned with a bottle of hair spray, which he applied to the wig.

Agnes ran her hand over the wavy blonde hair, which fell to her shoulders. There was no doubt it had been made from the finest human hair. She shivered at her reflection in the mirror, unable to recognize the person staring back at her. She put on the horn-rimmed glasses she'd been given and studied herself from the left and then the right.

It's not me, she thought as she opened her purse and took out the little box containing the cyanide pill. She held it up to the ceiling light and studied the shimmering blue contents. Didn't people say that you saw a light as your life ebbed away?

In the bathroom she wrapped the capsule in a stiff piece of toilet paper made from newsprint on which the headlines were still visible. Then she stuck it inside her panties. The stiff paper scratched at her abdomen, and that was all it took to bring on another attack of nausea. She just managed to push the hair of her wig out of the way before she threw up into the toilet.

The old man is right, she thought, rinsing her mouth. *This wig is never going to fall off.* She scrubbed her fingers with a nailbrush, being careful not to soil her new blue suit. She studied the stranger in the mirror one last time. She smiled, but that only frightened her even more. Her right hand suddenly started hurting, but Agnes assumed it was just a phantom pain, and not from the time she slapped the maid.

The thought of Johanne continued to whirl through her mind. Those eyes of hers and the way they stared at her every day, every hour she was with Gustav. Agnes studied the palm of her hand. She could still feel the stinging sensation. And soon this same hand was going to kill a man.

And yet her hand was calm. Completely calm. *Everything's in order,* thought Agnes as she washed her hands and then dried them. For a second she felt a sense of peace that she'd never before experienced; it was as though it wasn't her at all standing in the cramped bathroom on Kirkeveien. In a way, she had already died many years ago, maybe when her father died, maybe even before. There were only two people in the whole world she wanted to think about if she was going to die today: the Pilgrim and Cecilia. No one else. Not even the baby that was making her throw up every morning and every afternoon. There was no future for that child. Only Carl Oscar and Cecilia. But even those two she could do without. Forget them. Erase them. If only she could avoid being tortured, everything would end well.

She silently exchanged her identification papers for those the old man handed her. He studied her for a moment, then nodded. Agnes was about to say, "Take good care of them." But she didn't. Maybe it was best this way. She draped the blue coat over her arm and watched as he disappeared into the living room.

On her way down the back stairs, she went through everything in her mind one more time. Go to the bathroom as quickly as possible. The first stall on the left. Stand on the toilet seat. What if someone came in? No. She'd simply leave. *Quickly, quickly,* she thought. The Welrod was tightly wrapped in plastic. What if it failed to fire? Then she'd have to beat him to death. Or find some other weapon. Fast, before he had time to think, before he had time to scream. She decided to look for a letter opener in Rolborg's office.

The sunlight was dazzling, and a cold wind was playing with the few leaves left in the gutter. Somewhere behind her a group of children were shouting with joy. Worst of all was that she knew she would kill him, no matter what it took. Suddenly she found herself standing at the Majorstua intersection, looking right at the stairs where she'd met Kaj Holt for the first time.

As she looked for a tram that would take her into town, she repeated to herself, *I'm going to kill you, no matter what it takes.*

CHAPTER 51

Thursday, June 19, 2003
German Red Cross Clinic
Westend
Berlin, Germany

"You speak good Norwegian," Tommy Bergmann said as he looked at the mansions in the neighborhood. The cab driver turned at the intersection. *Much too good,* he thought. Peter Waldhorst spoke Norwegian as if he'd hardly done anything else since the war.

"Thank you," he said.

"I have to say . . . I mean, that's quite an accomplishment, considering how long ago you were stationed in Norway."

Waldhorst looked at his watch.

"I speak seven languages, Mr. Bergmann. Norwegian is easy. It's a Germanic language, like my own."

"So your wife isn't Norwegian?"

Waldhorst shook his head.

"Swedish. My Gretchen is Swedish, Mr. Bergmann. I also speak Swedish, in case you were wondering." Waldhorst laughed quietly, as if amused by all this talk about his fluency in Norwegian.

"I see." Something fell into place in Bergmann's mind—like puzzle pieces fitting together. If Waldhorst spoke Swedish with his wife, that could explain why he spoke such good Norwegian, since the two languages were so similar. For a moment he was filled with relief. He'd been about to list Waldhorst as a suspect, but the fact that he had a Swedish wife reassured him. His thoughts returned to another woman, Vera Holt, who found herself in an alternate universe, in the psych ward in Ullevål.

"It sounds as if you wished you'd had children," said Bergmann. "With your second wife."

Waldhorst gripped the armrest in the cab and turned to look at him.

"Sometimes you really jump to conclusions, Mr. Bergmann."

Bergmann merely nodded. Waldhorst had a point.

"And who said I don't have children? My children and my first wife live in the United States. Or rather, my first wife *lived* in the States, may she rest in peace. It still saddens me to think of her buried over there, in Virginia of all places—the first colony of the English, if you can believe such a thing—and not here in her hometown."

Waldhorst motioned toward the windshield, as if that might clarify things for Bergmann.

For several minutes they rode along in silence. Eventually they emerged from Grunewald and entered an area that looked more like the center of town. Filled with block after block of white-painted buildings, it had to be one of the city's better neighborhoods.

"My own children turned their backs on me," said Waldhorst suddenly. "We became naturalized citizens in the States, my first wife and I. Years after we were divorced, right before I retired, I told my son and daughter the truth, in confidence. That I hadn't come to the US as a German refugee in 1938. That I'd been a German officer during the war. And a Gestapo officer at that. They washed their hands of me. I was dead to them. Just dead."

Bergmann sat up straight. The feeling of relief vanished as quickly as it had appeared. Instead he was beginning to realize that he'd been misled, just as Waldhorst's own children had been. Or maybe not. He could no longer make any sense of this case.

"Were you in the Hitler Youth?" he asked.

Waldhorst exchanged a few words with the cab driver, something about the route the driver had chosen. Bergmann was about to repeat his question but apparently Waldhorst had heard him the first time.

"Why are you asking me that?"

"It's just a question," replied Bergmann.

Waldhorst seemed to be pondering what to say.

"You don't have to answer, of course."

"No," Waldhorst then said. "I was never in the Hitler Youth. My father was not a fanatic Nazi, so he dissuaded me from joining. This was before it became obligatory. He must have turned over in his grave—God be with him—when I joined the Gestapo."

"I have to confess something," said Bergmann as he looked out the window at this city that he knew he would never understand. Any preconceptions that he'd had about Berlin only a few hours earlier were now gone. It felt as if a great sorrow hovered over it, a sorrow that would never go away. "I'm starting to doubt that Krogh actually killed those three people."

"Really?"

"And if I don't know who killed Agnes, Cecilia, and the maid, then I don't know who killed Krogh either. And then it can't be Vera Holt."

Waldhorst nodded.

"Why have you been so convinced about the connection?"

"Because Krogh was killed shortly after the three skeletons were found in Nordmarka, and because he was in the Resistance cell that is thought to have liquidated the most people during the German occupation of Norway. I think the discovery of the three bodies unleashed something in the killer. Rage directed at Krogh. And Vera Holt? Well, she has killed before."

"Rage," Waldhorst murmured to himself. He turned to look at Bergmann, his lips parted. They were bluish, moist, and dry and cracked all at the same time. His eyes looked sad, as though covered with a veil of tears that might spill over as soon as Bergmann was out of sight. Then he seemed to regain his composure. He turned away to look out at the street. Bergmann was surprised to see which of his words struck Waldhorst the most. Rage.

He decided to mention what he'd been thinking ever since he went to the National Library—the key to the doubts he had.

"Was it Agnes Gerner who killed the research director at the molybdenum plant?"

"What are you talking about?" said Waldhorst.

Bergmann sighed with resignation.

"Mr. Waldhorst . . . You are a former security and intelligence officer," he said. "You were so brilliant that the Americans even got you out of Norway after the war. Officers like yourself never forget such matters. In the fall of 1942 Research Director Torfinn Rolborg was murdered in his office on Rosenkrantz Gate. An assassination, according to the Swedish National Police. And from what I understand, it resulted in an intense hunt for the killer."

"Hmm," said Waldhorst.

"A man like you would know immediately what I'm talking about."

Bergmann took out the file folder from the bag he'd set on the floor of the cab and leafed through the pages until he came to the *Aftenposten* printouts from the fall of 1942. The hunt for a blonde woman.

Waldhorst didn't even glance at the papers. He merely shook his head.

"Agnes Gerner wasn't blonde."

"So you do remember the incident?"

"Believe me, that woman, Ms. Gerner, was a Nazi. I would have known if she wasn't. Believe me."

"How would you have known?"

Waldhorst uttered an annoyed sound. He looked worn out, as if it was foolhardy for a man of his age to play tennis the way he had that morning.

"Because it was my job to clear her."

Bergmann settled back in his seat.

"My superiors sent me to Gustav Lande when our intelligence discovered he was falling in love with a woman—and someone who was half British. My job was simply to clear her."

"And?" said Bergmann.

"She was genuine."

"I see," said Bergmann. He had nothing more to say. He had only Iver Faalund's theory that Agnes Gerner was not a Nazi to hold up against Waldhorst's claim.

The driver signaled for a right turn and pulled up in front of a large old red-brick building covered with ivy. Bergmann thought it must be a private clinic for wealthy patients. The cars in the parking lot were not exactly economy models. It was true that he was in Berlin, where almost every vehicle surpassed most of the cars in any Oslo lot, but even so, he'd rarely seen so many luxury-class Mercedes or BMWs.

"For a while I thought you'd found out something about Agnes and killed her," he said.

Waldhorst shook his head as he took some euros out of his wallet and handed them to the driver. Yet Bergmann thought he noticed a slight shift in the old man's body language—as if he froze for a second—before he regained his composure.

"I'm afraid I have to disappoint you, Mr. Bergmann. If we'd thought she was an assassin, she would have been arrested and not killed in the woods. Don't you agree?"

Waldhorst climbed out of the taxi with some effort, the driver having gotten out too late to offer him any help. Bergmann got out to say good-bye to the man, who stood there stretching his back after the short cab ride. He took a comb out of the pocket of his poplin jacket, which he wore in spite of the heat, and smoothed back his gray hair. Then he stared up at the building behind Bergmann, who turned to look up at the clinic windows. The reflection in the glass made it impossible to see if anyone was standing there watching them.

"Is she seriously ill?" asked Bergmann.

"At our age, most things are serious. That's why I like to bring her something special when I can." He nodded at the gift and rose he was holding.

"When did you first meet?"

"Why do you ask?"

Bergmann shrugged. He really didn't know.

"When Kennedy came to Berlin and said he was a Berliner, I was here, a real Berliner, as an American in my own town. It was awful."

"So you met here? In Berlin?" asked Bergmann.

"We met in the departures hall at Tempelhof Airport, of all places."

Waldhorst looked at Bergmann and frowned, as if to say, yes, that was a long time ago. Then he shook his head.

"Well," he said, turning to the cab driver and saying something about taking Bergmann on to Tegel. They were so close to the airport that they could see the planes on the runway.

The old man stepped forward until he was standing right in front of Bergmann.

"I have to confess," said Bergmann, "that I feel like I've overlooked something."

"That's how things go in your line of work," said Waldhorst. "It was the same for me. There's always something you've overlooked. Something simple, something totally banal."

"I've overlooked something banal?" said Bergmann.

"Start at the beginning and ask yourself one question," said Waldhorst, pausing for effect. "Who was Carl Oscar Krogh?"

"Who was Carl Oscar Krogh?" Bergmann repeated.

Waldhorst nodded.

"I'm sure the answer lies in that question. In the question itself."

"He had bank accounts in Switzerland or Liechtenstein," said Bergmann.

Waldhorst shook his head dismissively.

Bergmann didn't bother to ask to what extent Krogh had worked for the Germans. Waldhorst would simply have brushed aside such a notion.

"Well, he must have put some money away from his business, don't you think?" said Waldhorst. "Don't make too much of it. The world is much simpler than that." He glanced at his watch. "It's getting late, Mr. Bergmann. I don't have any more time to waste." He shook hands with Bergmann, who was leaning against the open car door. Their eyes met. Waldhorst's eyes now looked guarded, as if he'd found his way back to the man he'd once been in Norway during the war. Bergmann didn't want to think about the things he had done.

"Good luck," said Waldhorst. "I'm sorry I couldn't have been of more help."

"You've actually been a great help," said Bergmann. *Though I'm just not exactly sure how yet,* he thought.

"You were right about one thing," said Waldhorst.

"Oh yes?"

"Agnes," said Waldhorst.

Bergmann looked at him, his expression neutral.

"I loved her. I don't think I've ever loved anyone else that much . . . No, I haven't."

Bergmann opened his mouth to speak, but he didn't know what to say.

"From the very first time I saw her," Peter Waldhorst said quietly. Then he grimaced—or maybe it was a smile—turned on his heel, and headed up the pathway. He was stooped over now. Nothing remained of the man who had come in from the tennis court only a few hours earlier.

Bergmann watched Waldhorst as he slowly made his way to the entrance of the German Red Cross Clinic. He thought that if the old man turned around, there must be something more, something he hadn't said.

But Waldhorst didn't turn around, and the sliding door closed behind him.

Bergmann tilted his head back and raised his hand to shield his eyes. He looked at one window after another in the big hospital building.

"*Mein Herr?* Shall we go?" said the cab driver behind him.

I loved her, Bergmann whispered to himself.

CHAPTER 52

Friday, September 25, 1942
Knaben Molybdenum Mines, Inc.
Rosenkrantz Gate
Oslo, Norway

After she got off the tram, Agnes Gerner stopped for a moment to glance down the street, then up. No National Police patrols or checkpoints were set up. A man coming toward her was flirting with her rather obviously. She avoided his gaze and pulled her hat down to hide her eyes. The blue contact lenses felt hard and dried her eyes out, making them sting.

She turned the corner. There was no turning back now. Her heart was beating so hard that as she stood outside the main entrance to Knaben's offices, she thought everyone could see it hammering against her coat, pounding beneath the thin blue fabric of her blouse.

At the provisional checkpoint beyond the entrance stood a Wehrmacht corporal armed with a handgun and a private holding a Schmeisser across his chest. The bored corporal waved her forward and asked for her papers. He studied them briefly, then took her purse and rummaged through it. He barely looked at her when he ordered the private to pat her down.

"Your business?" he asked. By this time, Agnes had managed to conceal her nervousness. It was as though Agnes Gerner no longer existed, had never existed.

The echo of her heels across the marble floor resounded under the high arched ceiling and meshed with the sound of quiet conversations and ringing telephones. As she stood at the reception desk of Knaben's Oslo offices, she *was* Ms. Irene Bjørnsen from Hamar and no one else.

Without looking around the large reception area, she stated her name and her purpose for being there.

The middle-aged receptionist regarded Agnes for a few seconds with a skeptical expression, as if she wanted to let her know that it wouldn't help to dress like a whore to get a job at this firm. Research Director Rolborg wasn't that sort. He wasn't like other men.

"Did you bring your papers and references?"

Agnes smiled her most trustworthy smile and pulled the folder out of her purse.

"Identification papers?"

Agnes smiled again as she shoved the papers across the counter.

"Miss," said a voice beside her. A man was looking her straight in the eye. For a moment, she feared he could see the false pupils of glass behind the lenses of her spectacles.

"I'm sorry, miss . . ." he began, still gazing straight into her eyes. Agnes smiled at him. He blushed.

"Standing orders, miss, I assure you that . . ." He let the sentence die out and reached for her purse.

Only now did Agnes realize that the man beside her was a plain-clothes security officer. For a moment she felt as though she were going to collapse onto the marble floor, but all he did was take a look inside her purse, not even bothering to rummage through it. The stiff toilet paper rubbed against her abdomen whenever she moved, but now it didn't make her feel sick. She was glad when she got her purse back for the second time that day. The security man nodded to her, but seemed a little too interested in her eyes.

"There's someone ahead of you," said the receptionist, "and one person already waiting, up the stairs to the left. The name is on the door. Please have a seat. You'll be called in by his private secretary."

"I see," Agnes said quietly, her body stiffening. "So the private secretary will also be present?"

"Yes," said the receptionist in a tone that revealed her surprise that anyone would ask such a question. "Of course."

Agnes was not prepared for this. She just hadn't thought that far ahead. None of them had. Her perfectly crafted plan fell apart when the receptionist said, "Of course."

Agnes hadn't even had a chance to test-fire the pistol, and each round had to be loaded individually. And now she was supposed to kill two people. *How?* she wondered. Which one first? And a woman at that. Maybe a mother. *No . . . a Nazi,* she thought. Like her mother's husband. Like the research director himself.

The receptionist gave her another skeptical look with her head cocked, as if Agnes were something the cat had dragged in.

"Excuse me?" Agnes said, straightening her glasses and smiling as best she could. "Where is the bathroom?"

The woman pointed to the right and then went back to reading Agnes's papers, shaking her head as she did so. Agnes nodded to the security man, who sat in one of the visitors' chairs to the left of the entrance. She now realized that he had simply stared at her with the same look she got from most men. She walked with assured steps toward the door of the ladies' room, which was marked with a brass nameplate. She felt the security man's eyes watching her back—and imagined his gaze probably moving farther down. She grasped the door handle without trembling, and once inside she rapidly scanned the tiled room. There were no feet visible in the stalls, and no other women were at the mirrors. Agnes caught sight of herself, a blue shadow, in the mirrors as she took the two steps toward the first stall by the door. When she had closed the door behind her, she stood with her back leaning against it. She again felt how hard her heart was pounding in her chest.

Just as her heartbeat began to calm down, the bathroom door opened. Automatically she held her breath. She waited as though frozen in place for the person to step inside.

The security man, she thought.

The door closed and the sounds from outside vanished. Everything was quiet.

A woman, Agnes thought. *Yes, it's a woman.*

Thin stiletto heels crossed the floor. Agnes pressed herself against the blue wall of the stall, which extended almost all the way up to the ceiling, and breathed through her nose. The footsteps in the restroom stopped.

It was impossible to hear anything clearly, to distinguish one sound from another. The throbbing in her head was intolerable. For a second she thought there was more than just the one woman outside the stall. Maybe it was the sound of a handbag being opened, but maybe it was something else. Maybe it was the snap of a holster—maybe the corporal outside had simply lured her into a trap, or Kaj Holt's contact on the inside was a traitor.

A minute later the footsteps moved away slowly and disappeared out the door.

The pistol was exactly where it was supposed to be. Agnes didn't waste any time. She replaced the lid on the large toilet tank, making so little noise she barely heard it herself. She hurried to tear the plastic off the Welrod, which suddenly felt like it was several feet long. Then she threw the plastic in the trash can and covered it with some toilet paper. She wadded up some paper towels and scattered them on top.

She studied the strange steel barrel for a few seconds. She quietly prayed to God that it still worked and that there was a round in the chamber. She opened her purse. It fit perfectly, just as Kaj Holt had said it would.

She crossed herself and left the restroom.

CHAPTER 53

Thursday, June 19, 2003
Schönefeld Airport
Berlin, Germany

Schönefeld Airport, located just outside the former East Berlin, was small and dilapidated, but Tommy Bergmann didn't care. His mind was on other things as he flicked his cigarette butt into an overflowing ashtray outside the departures hall.

Peter Waldhorst's last words were still ringing in his ears: "I loved her." Why had he said that?

Bergmann stopped and set down his suitcase a few steps inside the airport terminal, right between a horde of hungover Englishmen and a young couple weeping and clutching at each other in a tight embrace.

He turned around. First once. Then again. Then he studied the screens displaying the upcoming departing flights in yellow lettering. Two police officers came strolling through the hall. Bergmann fixed his gaze on one of the cops' holsters, then on the German shepherd who was staring with sorrowful eyes past the muzzle fastened over its snout.

He had an inexplicable feeling that Peter Waldhorst had pulled a veil over his eyes, a kind of smoke screen that made it impossible for him to see clearly.

I loved her, Bergmann repeated to himself. *I loved her?*

If Krogh had really killed Agnes Gerner, and Waldhorst . . .

He heard a voice over the PA system call out Oslo and his name. *It's time,* he thought, glancing at his watch. How long had he actually sat at that sidewalk restaurant? Hadja had called him on his cell, but he hadn't answered. Suddenly he could feel pressure on his bladder from the three or four beers that he'd imbibed in an attempt to think about something else. At the gate he was met with a disapproving look. The woman behind the counter glanced demonstratively at the clock.

"I'm sorry," said Bergmann and headed for the restroom on his left.

"*Mr.* Bergmann," she said loudly behind him.

Bergmann kept going. It wouldn't be the worst thing if he missed his flight. Maybe it was meant to be. *I loved her,* he thought as the urinal filled up with Berlin beer.

He was studying his face in the mirror when his cell phone rang. The bags under his eyes had shrunk a little, and his skin almost seemed to have a healthy glow. Once again—probably for the last time—he heard his name over the PA system.

"What is it?" said Bergmann into the phone, heading straight past the angry flight attendant toward the gate, where the Norwegian Air flight was still waiting for him.

"We've gotten the search warrant for Vera Holt's residence."

"Not bad," said Bergmann, standing in the aircraft door. There was no backing out now.

"We'll do it tomorrow morning," said Reuter.

Bergmann walked down the center aisle, momentarily enjoying being the object of every idiot's envious interest.

"No, we'll do it tonight," he said. "As soon as I've landed."

Reuter said nothing.

"I thought you were in such a hurry?" said Bergmann. He found his seat, dropping his carry-on in the middle of the aisle to leave the problem of stowing it to the already irritated flight attendant.

"Boarding completed," the loudspeaker above him announced in English.

"Okay. Call me when you land," said Reuter.

"And bring Halgeir with you," said Bergmann.

There was a grunt from Oslo. None of them liked Halgeir Sørvaag, but he was unbeatable when it came to getting through locked doors and hitting the jackpot during searches.

"So, did you meet this Waldhorst?" Reuter asked.

The plane had already backed out of the gate and was approaching the runway. The flight attendant came marching down the aisle and gave Bergmann a withering look to indicate he had to turn off his phone.

"We'll talk about it when I get there. I've gotta go."

"Okay, but . . ." Reuter said.

"What is it?" Bergmann said with a sigh.

"Something really strange has come up. It might not be important, but . . ."

"Is there anything that isn't strange about this case?" Bergmann said.

"We got the final report from Forensics today."

"On Krogh?"

"No, on the three skeletons from Nordmarka."

Bergmann sat up in his seat. "Yes?" he said softly.

"It wasn't the maid who was buried up there in the woods."

Goosebumps appeared on Bergmann's bare arms.

"Not the maid? Not Johanne Caspersen?"

"For all I know," said Reuter, "she may still be alive."

There was a pause. Neither of them knew what to say.

Bergmann turned off his phone and put it in his pocket. Exhausted, he leaned back on the headrest as the plane taxied out to the runway. An image began to form in his mind's eye. A girl, a woman, and a man had been found in Nordmarka, Reuter had said. The maid must have gotten away, but how? Then on an impulse he dug out the photo in his inside pocket. The picture of Waldhorst and Agnes Gerner facing each other at the table on Midsummer Eve in 1942. Next to Agnes was a dark-haired man, ten years older. Gustav Lande.

Gustav Lande! It struck him like lightning.

Lande was the man in the photo back at Waldhorst's apartment. The man standing on the rocks. The woman beside him must have been his first wife. Obviously pregnant with the little girl who was later killed.

But why? Bergmann wondered as the plane took off. *Why does Peter Waldhorst have a photo of Gustav Lande and his pregnant first wife?*

CHAPTER 54

Friday, September 25, 1942
Knaben Molybdenum Mines, Inc.
Rosenkrantz Gate
Oslo, Norway

Her eyes were focused on the back of the two picture frames on the desk. What else would a man with an office like this have, other than photos of his wife and children?

Agnes Gerner cursed herself for allowing such a thought to enter her mind. She cautiously shifted her position on the chair, which was set at an angle in front of the desk. The stiff toilet paper felt like metal inside her panties. She grimaced, then tried to hide it behind a smile.

Seated next to her on an identical chair was Rolborg's private secretary. Agnes took her eyes off the photographs and, clutching her purse on her lap, shifted her gaze to the woman on her right.

"So, it looks like we'll be working together. I will be your immediate supervisor," said the private secretary, sounding a bit nervous. She let her words die out as she turned to face Research Director Rolborg. He was reading through Agnes's papers and didn't look up. As he read, he grunted something to himself. His pale skin was tight across his cheekbones, like a death mask.

Agnes could tell that her own face was pale—and cold, as if she knew that this would be the death of her too. How could she have been so naïve as to think that she'd get out of this alive? There was only one way out, and that was back the way she'd come in.

For a moment she was sure she would faint. Her eyes rolled back as she thought about the director having children, three or maybe four.

"My dear, there's nothing to be nervous about," said the secretary, whose name Agnes couldn't for the life of her remember, even though they'd been introduced only a few minutes before. The secretary got up to put her hand on Agnes's shoulder. "Are you sure you wouldn't like me to take your coat? It's terribly warm in here, don't you think?"

Agnes's whole body seemed to stop functioning for a moment. Feeling as though her heart had stopped pumping blood, she sank farther and farther into a bog, a swamp.

"Would you like a glass of water?" asked the secretary, who was not at all as Agnes had imagined her. She had kind eyes and a gentle voice with a trace of a southern Norwegian dialect. She was probably married and had children.

Agnes nodded silently toward the secretary. She was no longer thinking rationally. She was about to be overwhelmed by a surge of sentimentality, and her goal was becoming less and less clear. The job she was supposed to do now seemed impossible to carry out. She heard the secretary fill a glass with water in the bathroom that adjoined the office. She glanced over at Research Director Rolborg, whose nose was now buried in the papers of the previous candidate he'd interviewed.

A steady stream of noise like an electrical current now filled her head, drowning out the sounds coming through the open window and the words coming out of the mouth of the secretary, who was speaking to her from the bathroom.

One round in the chamber, she thought as the secretary took the first step out of the bathroom. The sound of her heels striking the parquet floor sliced through the blanket of static in Agnes's head.

She quickly opened her purse, not even considering what would happen if the Welrod failed to fire. Rolborg was still sitting in front of her, muttering to himself as he studied the papers.

A sharp sound came from the street. A tram clattering along Stortingsgata, as if sent by God Himself. The sound would mute the secretary's fall, dampening the blow as her lithe body hit the floor.

She was less than six feet away now.

As the secretary realized what Agnes was pointing at her, she opened her mouth in a soundless scream.

The sound of the glass striking the floor was drowned out by the rattling of the tram below the windows. Agnes stood with her feet apart, both hands holding the gun. She would never forget the look in the woman's eyes. Never.

Slowly, as if she had all the time in the world, Agnes then turned toward Research Director Torfinn Rolborg. The backlighting from the window formed almost a halo around him, and Agnes couldn't see his face clearly. She glanced at the windows in the buildings across the street, but the gray film that covered half the pane made it impossible to see inside the office. No one was going to see what was happening. Shock was making it difficult for Rolborg to open his mouth properly. He sat in his high desk chair as though nailed to it, while a strangled sound—almost like the whimper of an injured animal—came out of his mouth. Agnes drew back the bolt of the Welrod and took four quick steps toward Rolborg, who was now trying to get up from his chair. Before any audible sound issued from his lips, she was only two feet away. He seemed to be simply incapable of understanding what was happening.

The only sound was a muffled pop that merged with the last rumbles of the tram. Rolborg fell backward in his chair with a stifled cry.

He stared down at the hole in his jacket, then pressed his hand over the blood that swiftly soaked his pinstriped suit. He stared up at her one last time as Agnes pulled back the bolt to reload.

"Sven," he said. "Sven, help me."

Agnes took aim at his chest again and pulled the trigger. She couldn't bring herself to shoot at his head, but it didn't matter. The life had already started to ebb out of him. Two shots to the left side of his chest were enough. Agnes went over to the window to examine her coat. There was no blood. When she stuffed the Welrod into the left sleeve of her coat, she started shaking all over. Rolborg's lifeless body lay slumped over only a few steps away, his head threatening to collapse onto the desk. Agnes turned her head very slowly to the right. Blood was pooling soundlessly on the floor around the dead secretary.

Agnes picked up the phony identification papers from the desk, now stained with blood. She bent down to pick up two of the empty shell casings that lay at her feet. The third one was next to the chair where she'd been sitting only moments ago.

She walked slowly over to the chair and sat down, as if nothing had happened. She opened her purse, wrapped the papers around the three casings, and then stuffed them in the bottom. She sat there motionless for a full five minutes, unable to go back downstairs yet. She'd only been in the office a few minutes. Or was it longer than that? She needed to leave. Why hadn't anyone told her what to do afterward? This was madness, sheer madness!

From time to time she heard footsteps outside. The whole floor around the secretary had now turned a dark red. Agnes tried to convince herself that the woman was merely sleeping. She told herself that if she hadn't done this, someone else would have.

She had to get out of there.

Miraculously, Agnes didn't run into anyone in the corridor. The only sound was a woman's laughter coming from an open door behind her. When she reached the stairs leading down to the ground floor, the steps looked like a steep cliff. She barely managed to stay on her feet. The receptionist frowned when she caught sight of Agnes in the middle of the lobby.

"Are you done already?"

Agnes nodded and took a few steps toward the receptionist's desk. She knew that her face was ghostly pale, but there was nothing she could do about that.

"Yes," she said in a low voice.

The receptionist motioned to a young woman Agnes's age. She was evidently the next candidate waiting to be interviewed.

"Mr. Rolborg asked me to say that he didn't want to be disturbed for a few minutes," said Agnes. "His private secretary will call you when he's ready."

The receptionist nodded sullenly.

"Good-bye," said Agnes before the receptionist could say anything. The phone under the desk began ringing. The receptionist seemed to hesitate, as if wondering whether to ask Agnes another question or answer the phone instead.

Agnes forced herself to turn away. Looking straight ahead, she started for the door. Out of the corner of her eye, she noticed the security guard who had stared at her come in from the left. He headed for the door, past the security gate where the two Germans stood, and opened it for her. Agnes attempted a smile. He said a few words, but she was beyond comprehending what they were. Then she silently brushed past the corporal and the soldier.

A light drizzle was falling on the pavement outside. Agnes walked as slowly as she could along Rosenkrantz Gate, which was nearly deserted. She fixed her gaze on the bakery on the corner, which was only forty or fifty yards away, and focused all her energy on placing one foot in front of the other. A man came toward her, but he dissolved right before her eyes. Behind her they were invisibly chasing after her, and soon her feet would stop moving. In only a few seconds the corporal and soldier would come running out the front door of the Knaben offices. The soldier would open fire with his Schmeisser, and she would be lying on the ground, riddled with bullets, only a few steps from the black cab that was parked in front of the bakery.

"Only thirty more steps," she whispered to herself. A figure that looked like the Pilgrim—*my dear Pilgrim,* she thought—came out of the bakery wearing an ill-fitting cab driver's uniform. Without looking at her, he walked over to the taxi. As she crossed the street, she pictured in her mind's eye the receptionist knocking on the door of Rolborg's office and a second later screaming so loud that it could be heard all the way out here. She almost ran right into somebody at the thought and had to resist the urge to turn around. *Don't!* she told herself. *Don't! Don't!* Why was she wearing this blue suit? They could see her from fifty yards away. *Start up the engine,* she thought. *Start it up, goddamn it! Start the fucking car!* The engine started up with a roar, and she jogged the last two or three yards. She knew she shouldn't, but she couldn't help it. She got in and slammed the door closed, and they were off.

Agnes turned around in the backseat to get one last look at Rosenkrantz Gate. Nothing was going on. All she saw was an amorphous crowd of people. The street looked like it was now full of people. And a car. No, two. But no soldiers running down the street, no National Police patrol with officers running after it.

"Your coat," said the Pilgrim from the driver's seat. "Take it off." He cast a quick glance at her in the rearview mirror, but his eyes were hard, devoid of life. Beneath that cold veneer, though, Agnes thought that she could see raw fear smoldering deep inside his soul. *That's the last thing I need,* she thought as she tore off the blue coat. From a paper bag under the passenger seat, she pulled out a beige coat. As she stuffed the blue coat under the seat, she felt the shaft of the Welrod against her fingers.

The private secretary's face flitted across her retinas for several seconds. That gentle woman who had treated her so kindly, the shocked silence as she stood there holding the glass of water in her hand, the dark-red blood all around her.

"Mission accomplished?" said the Pilgrim in a remarkably calm voice. He shifted gears and the cab raced down Rådhusgata.

Agnes mumbled "yes" without meeting his eyes in the rearview mirror. She took off her glasses and put them in her purse. Then she stuck the blue hat under the backseat and leaned forward to pull off the wig. She pulled a light-brown hat with a wide brim out from under the driver's seat and put it on. Then she straightened up. She just managed to hold back her tears as she removed the contact lenses, which were practically burning her eyes.

After a few more blocks, the Pilgrim drove the cab through a narrow doorway, which was promptly closed behind them. He brought the taxi to an abrupt halt. Agnes looked around in confusion. They were in some sort of mechanic's workshop. She heard a rumbling from out on the street. A tram was approaching, the sound cutting through the steel door, just as it had sliced through the windowpanes in Rolborg's office. *Who's Sven?* she thought. *His son. It must be his son.*

The Pilgrim opened the back door. The cab was suddenly filled with the smell of motor oil and something else. Maybe paint. The nausea returned. Without a word, he removed the things from under the seats. The Welrod brushed against her calf.

"The papers," he said. "And the casings, if you managed to collect them . . ."

She opened her purse and handed him the casings wrapped in the papers. Rolborg's blood had turned to dark splotches that had soaked into the paper.

The Pilgrim took the rounds out of the Welrod and handed them to a man wearing dirty coveralls. Then he seemed to change his mind and took back the bullets and gun.

"Oh dear God," said Agnes. "Oh dear God." She buried her face in her hands. She couldn't hold back any longer.

The Pilgrim got in the cab to sit beside her.

"Hold me," she said.

He looked out the window, though it wasn't as if there was anything worth seeing in that small workshop with the green walls.

"You know I can't do that," he told her quietly. "You have to take this. We can't leave it here."

He held out the Welrod and the bullets to her.

"Me? I can't take them with me."

"This is the best way." The Pilgrim opened the stock and carefully put the bullets back in the magazine.

"What if they search my apartment? Or what if I'm stopped on the way home?"

"They'll be looking for a blonde. Not for you. Hide it at Gustav Lande's place. Who would look there? And if anyone does find it, they'll link it to him, not to you," he said calmly. He slipped the gun into the sleeve of her coat. "In the office you'll find a beige skirt, a white blouse, and a new pair of shoes." He motioned to a spot behind her.

Agnes turned around. They seemed to be cut off from the rest of the world here inside the workshop. The man in the coveralls was standing in the middle of the filthy floor, staring down at the paper bags the Pilgrim had given him.

"So. Are you all right?" said the Pilgrim without looking at her. He seemed distant, as if she could be anybody, as if they were talking about some ordinary topic.

"All right?" she repeated.

The Pilgrim opened his mouth to say something but then changed his mind.

Agnes got out of the car and slammed the door. The sound echoed metallically under the high ceiling. Her head was now filled with the nauseating stench of motor oil.

"Where's the bathroom?" she said to the man in the coveralls. He had moved over toward a door at the other end of the room. He looked at her, then silently pointed at the mezzanine on the right. Agnes tilted her head back, blinded for a moment by the light coming in through the second-floor windows. She gripped the metal railing as she staggered up the metal stairs. The Pilgrim followed.

"Leave me alone," she whispered.

The bathroom, located in the back of the office, was cramped and filthy. She didn't even make it all the way inside, instead throwing up on the threshold. Standing there, her feet set wide apart, she stared down at her own vomit.

The Pilgrim stopped behind her, inside the office.

"You need to get the Vaseline out of your hair," he said. Agnes squatted down and picked up her hat from the floor. Her face contorted, and she couldn't stop sobbing. She pressed the palms of her hands against her eyes.

"It'll be fine," said the Pilgrim behind her. Then he put his arms around her. Finally he was holding her. "It'll be fine."

"I throw up every morning," she said quietly. "Do you know what that means?"

He didn't say a word. His only response was to take his arms away.

"Do you love me?" she whispered as she stood up.

The Pilgrim looked past her, into the dark and filthy bathroom. He blinked.

"Carl Oscar? Tell me that you love me." She held his face in her hands. He had grown old in the last few weeks. Fine lines had appeared around his eyes, and a deep furrow had settled between his eyebrows.

He removed her hands, turned on his heel, and left the office. Then she heard the pounding of his feet on the metal stairs.

Agnes rinsed her mouth several times. She didn't bother to clean up the vomit.

From the office doorway she could see down into a small back courtyard. The man in coveralls was standing over an oil drum with flames shooting up around the rim. He tossed in the bag holding her clothes, the wig, and the papers. The Pilgrim was leaning over the hood of the cab in the workshop.

Agnes could have been mistaken, but it looked as if he was crying.

CHAPTER 55

Thursday, June 19, 2003
Oslo Airport
Gardermoen
Oslo, Norway

The sliding doors slowly opened. Tommy Bergmann found himself staring at a group of people who looked disappointed that he was the one to appear in the arrivals hall. Then they looked away from him and threw themselves at the people coming through the doors behind him.

All the laughter and joyous greetings made him sink even lower. Hadja was probably waiting for him, but he had to put an end to that before it went any further. He'd checked his phone while he waited for his luggage. *Could you call me? Miss you. Hadja.* He needed to tell her, no later than tonight.

He caught sight of Reuter waving at him. The past few days seemed to have taken a heavy toll on him. He was unshaven, and his hair, which was usually as perfectly combed as a boy scout's, fell limp and unwashed over his forehead.

"Sorry I didn't have time to buy you flowers," said Reuter, handing him a bunch of papers he'd been holding behind his back. Bergmann ignored the attempt at a joke. "No duty-free shopping?" he said without a trace of sarcasm in his voice.

Bergmann wasn't paying attention.

He began walking slowly, almost reluctantly, toward the exit as he read the report from the Institute of Forensic Medicine.

"Amended evaluation: one child, assumed to be eight or nine years old; a woman of about twenty or twenty-five; and a man of about twenty or twenty-five."

"This is damned strange," said Bergmann as they got into the car.

Reuter pulled into the left lane. A plane appeared overhead. Bergmann studied the landing lights, the darkening blue of the sky, and the veil of crimson that had settled over the evergreen-covered slopes to the west.

"The maid," said Reuter. "She must have gotten away somehow."

Bergmann said nothing.

"I mean, she was reported missing. There must have been some reason why she didn't come forward. She's been missing since 1942."

"Maybe she couldn't come forward," said Bergmann. "Maybe she was killed too."

Reuter shook his head and frowned.

"Maybe she was killed *somewhere else*," said Bergmann.

This time Reuter gave a slight nod.

"But who the hell is this man who was buried along with Agnes and the girl?"

"I have no idea," said Bergmann. "Krogh could easily have killed the maid someplace else."

"So you still think Krogh killed them?"

Bergmann nodded and gave an affirmative grunt.

Then something occurred to him. A wild idea. He took his notebook from the inside pocket of his jacket and opened it to the last page.

Reuter switched on the ceiling light for him.

"Gretchen," murmured Bergmann.

"Gretchen?" Reuter repeated.

Bergmann raised his head and fixed his gaze on the taillights of the vehicle up ahead.

"What was the maid's name again?" he said.

"Johanne Caspersen," replied Reuter.

"No middle name?"

"No," said Reuter. "Why are you—"

"Just a guess," Bergmann said as he sank back in his seat. He set the notebook on his lap and closed his eyes for a moment. He couldn't get rid of the feeling that Peter Waldhorst had tricked him. *I loved her,* he thought. *And I've overlooked something banal.*

"Vera Holt is the kind of suspect that appeals to me," Reuter said. "She's a real loony, she has a clear motive, and she's already locked up."

"Couldn't be better," said Bergmann. "But there's something not quite right with Peter Waldhorst."

Reuter sighed as he drove. Bergmann was pressed back in his seat as the speedometer exceeded 85 miles per hour.

"Of course there's something wrong with the old man. He was a Gestapo officer, and before that he was with the Abwehr. The guy's an egomaniac, Tommy. But you knew that before you went to see him, didn't you?"

"That's not it," said Bergmann. "He's up to something."

"What's rule number one for any investigator?" said Reuter as he passed a BMW on the right, cursing the driver.

"Don't make a case more difficult than it needs to be," replied Bergmann.

"So don't involve Waldhorst."

"There's something he isn't telling me."

"Forget it," said Reuter. "Waldhorst probably knows more about all the evil the world is capable of than you or I will ever want to hear, Tommy."

"We need to check the passenger lists to and from Berlin. Rental cars, train tickets, ferries, everything. His name is Peter Ward now, but since he worked for the CIA he might have used several different passports. He might even have traveled under his old name. That actually wouldn't surprise me."

Reuter refrained from saying something that was clearly on the tip of his tongue.

"Why?" he finally asked.

"He said that he loved her."

"What?" Reuter slowed down and pulled into a Shell station by the Skedsmo interchange. "Loved who?"

"Agnes Gerner," said Bergmann. "Right before I left, Waldhorst said that he had loved Agnes from the first moment he saw her."

"He wasn't the one who killed her, was he?" said Reuter.

Bergmann shook his head.

"I don't think so."

"You don't think so? Just say no."

"No," said Bergmann. "But something happened . . ."

"That's for fucking sure," said Reuter.

"Something happened so that Waldhorst found out who killed Agnes."

"So you're saying that Waldhorst might have murdered Krogh?"

Bergmann nodded.

"It's not impossible. He practically confessed as much. If he knew that Krogh killed Agnes, we could put him on the short list of suspects."

"What do you mean by 'practically confessed'?"

"He did. When he said that chance is fate and fate is chance."

Reuter cursed under his breath.

"I'm not following any of this, Tommy. I'll give you till end of day tomorrow. After that, I don't want to hear another word about Waldhorst or God knows who else. If we find Vera Holt's fingerprints on the knife tomorrow morning, you can take the rest of the year off—for my sake. Okay? We've already got enough wild goose chases going on at headquarters."

Reuter opened the door, got out, and looked around for Halgeir Sørvaag.

"He's quite a small man," said Bergmann.

Reuter shook his head. "What does that mean?"

"He could easily wear a size forty-one shoe."

But I forgot to check, Bergmann thought.

CHAPTER 56

Thursday, June 19, 2003
Kolstadgata
Oslo, Norway

"So you'd like to have the airline passenger lists between Oslo and Berlin checked?" said Fredrik Reuter. He seemed to have changed his mind during the short drive from the gas station to Vera's apartment and come to the conclusion that maybe they should take a closer look at Peter Waldhorst after all.

Reuter drove the car up onto the sidewalk on Kolstadgata and set the hand brake.

"We also need to check all the hotels for any rooms reserved to Peter Waldhorst or Peter Ward." Tommy Bergmann paused, considering how Waldhorst had mysteriously turned what little he'd managed to ascertain about this case upside down. *I loved her.* What had Waldhorst meant by that?

"What if there's no connection?" said Halgeir Sørvaag from the backseat. He leaned forward and an unmistakable stink of bad breath wafted into Bergmann's face. He pressed the button to roll down the window. "Or what if the opposite turns out to be true? What if Kaj Holt told Waldhorst who liquidated those three people? That would seem more likely," said Sørvaag. "Then you'd have a case, Tommy."

"Stop," said Reuter. "You're confusing me, Halgeir. Let's not let our imaginations run wild. Okay? This is where our lady lives."

A commercial on the radio ended, and the news came back on.

"No problem," Sørvaag murmured to himself, deferentially folding his hands. Then he splayed his fingers and cracked every knuckle, as only he could. "I'm sure we'll find *someone* who hacked old Krogh to pieces. *Right or wrong.*" On his lap he held an old briefcase containing keys, lock picks, and other tools that could open most doors in Norway without leaving a trace. It was rarely necessary to call in a locksmith when Sørvaag was on the scene. Bergmann turned to look at Reuter, who was listening intently to the news on the radio. He swore quietly when the news anchor emphasized that it had been ten days since Carl Oscar Krogh was found murdered, and the police still had no leads in the case.

"Those idiots," said Reuter. "We'll give them Vera Holt. That's what we'll do. We'll get a couple of fingerprints and a pair of size forty-one shoes, and God knows they'd better match that bloodstained hell up on Holmenkollen." He turned to give Bergmann an expectant smile.

"Amen," said Sørvaag as he opened the car door.

Bergmann stayed where he was, with his arm resting on the opened window of the parked car. Maybe it would turn out that Vera Holt did kill Krogh, but the thought didn't give him any pleasure. Not that he'd ever felt genuine pleasure when arresting a murderer. On the contrary, it had always given him an empty feeling, a sense that the world would never make sense. But in this case . . . Krogh had had Kaj Holt murdered, and then, decades later, he was killed in turn by Holt's daughter.

Maybe I simply don't want *Vera Holt to be the murderer,* Bergmann thought as Reuter tapped on the roof of the car. That was probably it. He pictured Vera the way she must have looked, wearing only her nightgown as she sat on the steps of Kampen Church back in the winter of 1959, no doubt abused and ruined for life. Krogh may have only had her father killed as a precautionary measure. What a difference there was between Krogh's daughter—living like a queen out in Bygdøy—and this wreck of a woman who had ended up in the projects. Yet the two women were bound by a shared fate. The same fate that had determined that Krogh should live while Holt died.

Bergmann shook his head and climbed out of the car. A bunch of kids had already gathered around Reuter and Sørvaag. Bergmann glanced at his watch, thinking the kids should have been in bed long ago, but then had to admit that he knew nothing about children.

When they reached the front entrance, Bergmann saw the same garbage bags lying there as when he'd last visited. Sørvaag somehow managed to shoo away the kids, who took off running in all directions. With a rather stern expression he explained that he couldn't imagine anything worse than having a bunch of little kids looking over his shoulder while he picked a lock. Bergmann couldn't help but wonder how often that actually happened.

In the stairwell Reuter stepped over the worst of the trash. Sørvaag didn't seem to be paying attention to either of his colleagues as he dashed up the stairs ahead of them.

When he reached the sixth floor, Reuter took a key ring out of his briefcase and held it up to the flickering fluorescent light on the ceiling.

"Okay," he then said, selecting a key.

The door across the hall opened.

"You're back?" said the neighbor when she caught sight of Bergmann.

Reuter turned to face her, holding up the search warrant.

"It's not my concern," she said.

"Do you know whether she was home on Whitsunday?" asked Reuter. "Vera Holt, I mean."

The woman gave him a look that Bergmann preferred not to interpret.

Reuter opened his mouth to say something more but changed his mind at the last second. The neighbor slammed her door right in his face. He raised his hand to knock but stopped when Sørvaag announced that he'd unlocked the door to Vera Holt's apartment.

The rank ammonia smell of urine washed over the three men as they stepped inside. After a few seconds it became clear that piss was not the only thing they were smelling. A rotten stench was coming from the countless bags of garbage piled up in the living room. Clothes were scattered everywhere. The coffee table—typical of those found at every flea market—was covered with dirty glasses and plates of congealed food. Advertising flyers were strewn across the floor. An old wool blanket lying on the worn leather sofa looked as if it might disintegrate at any moment. On the kitchen counter were more than two dozen opened cans of Landlord-brand cat food.

"Chicken," said Reuter, holding up one of the cans with two fingers. "A little moldy, but otherwise okay."

"I think that's what she's been eating," said Bergmann.

He opened one of the kitchen drawers. All the cutlery was made of different colored plastic and looked as if it were meant for children.

"Well, at least she's eating," said Reuter, taking another step inside the kitchen. "That's something anyway."

Bergmann felt numbed by the stench in the kitchen. Thinking he might throw up, he followed Reuter back into the living room. The thin curtains were closed. Bergmann fumbled for the light switch on the wall. Then he crossed the room, opened the curtains, and tried to open a window. He finally managed it, though he feared for a second that the window might fall out altogether and land in the playground below. He looked at the city spread out before him. The colors of the sunset spread across the horizon of Holmenkollen ridge. The siren from a patrol car rose up from the Grønland district, and bhangra music thudded against the windowpane from one of the apartments below.

"Forget fucking Waldhorst," said Sørvaag. He was standing in the front hall with a smile on his face. "Vera Holt wears size forty-one shoes." He held up a running shoe toward the ceiling light.

"Well, I'll be damned," said Reuter. "I think we might actually have her."

Bergmann merely nodded. He leaned out the window and looked up toward the crest of Holmenkollen. *She can almost see the house from here,* he thought to himself.

"Did you hear me, Tommy?" said Reuter. "I think we've got the perp. Motive, insanity, and a matching shoe size."

"I think we'll need a little more than a pair of shoes. They're not even the right kind."

"Are you trying to spoil the party?" said Reuter, walking over to a door and opening it. "Oh fuck," he said. "Anybody need some dirty clothes?" He went into the bedroom, holding his arm over his mouth.

Bergmann ignored him and went over to the IVAR bookcase from IKEA by the bedroom door. An indescribable stench emanated from the bedroom. It smelled as if she'd taken a shit in there. Or maybe it was the cat. Or both of them. *How can they keep sending her back to this place?* Bergmann thought as he studied the spines of the books. An old encyclopedia, a few leather-bound classics, and several books about World War II. Plastic bags had been stuffed between several books along with an old plastic container of milk with green spots floating inside.

Reuter came out of the bedroom holding a kitten in his hands. Although the only thing to eat in the whole apartment was cat food, it looked like it was starving. It made no attempt to scratch Reuter as it stared vacantly at Bergmann, then raced off to the kitchen as soon as Reuter set it down.

He looked as if he wanted to say something but just stood there dumbfounded as Bergmann began pulling everything off the top shelf of the bookcase. But there was nothing but dust behind it all.

The same with the next shelf.

"Stop," said Reuter. "At least riffle through the pages."

When he got to the third shelf, Bergmann muttered, "Bingo." After removing all the books—most of which looked like worn psychology books—and a bag of handwritten pages, he found an old shoebox at the back of the shelf.

"Mephisto brand," said Reuter, studying the lid of the black box. The absence of any dust indicated the box was often in use.

Bergmann opened it very carefully.

"You've got to be fucking kidding me," said Reuter as Bergmann opened the folded newspaper pages on top. "We don't need to look any further," he said quietly. "We've got her now."

Bergmann was holding four pages from *Dagbladet*. All the articles were about the murder of Carl Oscar Krogh.

He scanned the pages, then gave a start when he saw what had prompted the exclamation from Reuter.

Sørvaag came over to join them.

On one of the pages was a picture of Krogh from the war days. The chiseled face was unmistakable. He was smiling, and his hair was thick and blond.

But somebody had jabbed out the eyes in the picture, leaving only a ragged gash between his nose and hairline.

"She gouged out the man's eyes," said Sørvaag.

A flood of relief washed over Bergmann. *Vera Holt,* he thought. *So it really was you.*

CHAPTER 57

Friday, September 25, 1942
Hammerstads Gate
Oslo, Norway

Agnes Gerner lay on the sofa in her dimly lit living room. Her bathrobe was open, and she was slowly caressing her stomach. The sunlight coming through the windows brushed her calves. Faintly, as if from a great distance, came the clamor of children playing down in the nearby courtyards.

Her eyes were wide open. Through the dirty windowpanes she could see that the sky was a cloudless blue. *How can the sky possibly be blue today?* she thought. She wondered how long she'd been lying here, staring up at that meaningless blue. She wasn't sure. The only thing she knew was that she mustn't close her eyes as she'd done in the shower. Just as she'd shut her eyes and raised her hand to wash her hair with a bar of soap, she felt the secretary's hand on her back, heard the woman's gentle voice in her ear. Followed by the soundless scream, the glass of water falling to the floor, and that rigid, lifeless look in her eyes.

Agnes sat up abruptly at a familiar, yet surprising sound. It began in the middle of a tone, as if the siren had merely paused since the last time it went off. *The air-raid siren,* she thought. Could it really be the air-raid siren? Yes, without a doubt. Suddenly the whole town filled with the blaring sirens, echoing after another. But it had to be a test. It was still daylight outside. It wouldn't be dark for hours.

Agnes decided that if this was the real thing, she would simply stay where she was, lying on the sofa, and wait to be taken up to heaven or down to hell. If the building collapsed on top of her, it would come as a relief.

Then the strangest thing happened. It felt like a dream. She was still staring up at the blue sky when the sound of the sirens changed. She could hear planes somewhere above the city. Agnes got up on her knees and pressed her face against the windowpane.

Far below she could hear sharp bangs. Then more, ten or twelve times. Then came the piercing sound of antiaircraft guns. It had to be coming from Victoria Terrasse. She looked at her watch. Four fifteen. That couldn't be right.

This was why Number 1 had insisted on pushing forward the assassination. He must have known.

Up to the left Agnes saw what looked like three Mosquito fighter-bombers chased by a swarm of German aircraft. Then she noticed a black stripe in the sky right above Frogner Park. A Mosquito had been hit in the tail and was slowly losing altitude. As she watched its descent she unconsciously folded her hands in prayer. A second later she began to weep. A German plane followed close behind, pumping a hail of bullets into the English plane. Agnes imagined that the pilot had already been hit, but he could still be alive, since the plane was no longer losing altitude. Finally the English plane veered to the right and disappeared behind the rooftops. A few minutes later a black column of smoke rose up in the distance. The whole city was now a strident cacophony of ambulances, police cars, and air-raid sirens.

After half an hour the sounds suddenly ceased.

Agnes lay back down on the sofa, feeling as though she might never leave it. After another half hour it was as though the bombing raid had never happened. The only thing that was real was what she herself had done.

She lay there until darkness fell.

A few times she raised her hand to her shoulder, touching the place where the Pilgrim had last put his hand. Each time she touched that spot, she felt her skin burning, as if they were once again together.

She didn't want to remember anything else. Not how he had looked away, nor how he had left her and then stood leaning against the car, weeping.

When she had gone downstairs to join him on the floor of the workshop, he had merely handed her a bottle of dry shampoo and then hurried off toward the steel gate. Without a word he had gone out the door of the gate. Agnes had a strange feeling that it would be the last time she ever saw him.

Now she lay on the sofa, simply listening to her own breathing. Finally she fell asleep and sank deep into a dream in which the secretary's face became Bess's face, which refused to stop bleeding. Then she was standing in the workshop bathroom, and she was the one bleeding and bleeding . . .

Abruptly she opened her eyes.

Like a folkloric *vardøger*—a sort of premonition preceding the actual sounds—a faint, almost inaudible ringing started up in Agnes's ears. Then the sound of car tires on the asphalt outside mixed with the distant shouts of the children in the apartment upstairs.

The only thing she could think of was that she needed to get her purse. She'd put the Welrod and the codebook behind the baseboard in the kitchen. It would take a long time to find them.

She leapt up and dashed across the room. First she searched the living room, growing bewildered when she realized she hadn't left it there. Then she desperately scanned the table and countertop in the kitchen. She went out to the front hall, but it wasn't there either. *Where did I put it?* she wondered frantically. Her legs felt unsteady as she went into the bedroom. Although she was barefoot, she felt like she had on high heels and had drunk too much champagne, as she had on that evening in London when the attaché had followed her home . . . That chance little incident—nothing more than a momentary infatuation—had led her to this moment, standing on the pinewood floor, trying to find a capsule in her purse that would allow her to end her own life. Before it had really even begun.

A moment later she heard a car door slam on the street. How late it was. After curfew.

She heard footsteps approaching the entrance to her building. She remembered that the door wasn't locked. There had been something wrong with the lock when she came home.

Where is my purse? she thought in a panic. *Where is it?* she silently screamed. On her way back to the bedroom, she saw it out of the corner of her eye. It was lying on the floor, partially hidden under the sheets. She must have set it on the bed and then torn off the covers, though she remembered nothing. She remembered only the face of the secretary and the black hole in Rolborg's pinstriped suit, and how the kind woman had fallen asleep with her eyes open while her head rested in a pool of black blood.

The door to the stairwell opened. The footsteps were almost inaudible, balancing on the very edge of each step. Agnes tore open her purse. In the bottom she saw several streaks of Rolberg's blood that must have rubbed off her identification papers. Her fingers were shaking as she took out the stiff wad of toilet paper. Thank God, there was the glass capsule. The blue-black poison gleamed, as if it were the Redeemer Himself.

She placed the capsule in her mouth. It was cold and strange, tasting of nothing, yet it still almost made her throw up. Only a thin membrane of glass, one millimeter thick, separated her from death. She grabbed her purse and went toward the front hall, listening to the footsteps outside as they came up the last steps.

One person, she thought. *There's only one.*

But the Gestapo never came alone.

CHAPTER 58

Thursday, June 19, 2003
Kolstadgata 7
Oslo, Norway

"Who knows that Krogh's eyes were hacked out?" said Halgeir Sørvaag.

"Nobody," said Tommy Bergmann, handing the newspaper to Sørvaag. An image of himself standing in Krogh's living room flashed through his mind. The old man had looked so hideous, like an animal in a slaughterhouse, the left side of his chest completely gone.

Just plain gone.

"Good Lord," said Fredrik Reuter. "I need to call the chief and tell her to get out the champagne."

What an idiot, thought Bergmann.

"Do you see a computer anywhere?" said Sørvaag. "She must have bought the knife on the Internet."

"There's one in the bedroom," said Reuter.

Bergmann watched the two men disappear into the bedroom. Again Reuter cursed the stench in the room. After a brief pause, Sørvag shouted—as if he'd won the lottery—that the computer was hooked up to a modem.

Was it really you, Vera Holt? Bergmann wondered as he riffled through the shoebox. He sat down on the filthy sofa to look through the ten or fifteen newspaper clippings of old interviews with Krogh and articles about him.

Krogh's eyes had been scratched out with a ballpoint pen or a knife in every photo. He looked through the rest of the shoebox. Held together with a big old paper clip were nearly fifty small pieces of paper from various notepads. Scribblings, doodles. A few of them were dated, others were not. In the middle of the stack was a piece of paper that looked different. A heavy piece of stationery that had been folded twice.

Bergmann carefully pulled it out from the others and spread it open on the coffee table. He was no longer aware of the smell of congealed food that Vera had left on the table.

Inside the heavy, plain piece of paper was another sheet of paper of different quality.

Bergmann read the words written on it.

"I'm sorry. Kaj."

Bergmann studied Kaj Holt's missing suicide note. He was no handwriting expert, but the writing on the note was clearly not the same as on the other notes in the shoebox. It had been written quickly, with confidence, in a nearly perfect cursive. The notes and doodles on the loose pages had been written by a hounded person, nervously and with no structure—a person who seemed subject to an unceasing torrent of thoughts.

Bergmann studied the plain piece of paper that had contained the note. What he saw made him take several deep breaths. The murdered police detective. So the rumors that had circulated at police headquarters in Stockholm were true.

Stockholm

May 31, 1945

Dear Mrs. Holt,

Please accept my condolences. This whole thing is very painful.

Yours truly,

G. Persson

Kaj Holt's wife must have realized that the suicide note was not written in her husband's handwriting. Bergmann looked at it again. Suddenly it all became clear to him. It was so obvious. Inspector Persson had sent the presumed suicide note to Holt's wife so that she would see it wasn't his handwriting. But had she done anything with this information? Had she shown it to Krogh? Was that why Krogh had put pressure on the Swedes? Or had she shown it to Krogh, who had then ordered Persson killed? Bergmann put the two pieces of paper down on the coffee table, glancing at the green mold forming on the remains of what must have been stew.

What if that was what happened? Holt's wife went to Krogh, told him it wasn't her husband's handwriting. Krogh thanked her, and the next day Inspector Persson was shot in broad daylight on a street in Stockholm. That way, no one would ever find out that Carl Oscar Krogh had liquidated three people in Nordmarka.

Nobody would have believed such a story, thought Bergmann. That was why Krogh could get away with it. No one would ever have believed the truth.

He turned to look at the shoebox on the sofa next to him. He took out the pile of loose pages, removed the paper clip, and leafed through it. Some were drawings of demonic faces, the same faces on many of the pages. The papers had been tossed together in no logical sequence.

In addition to the drawings, there were random sentences, place names, and a few fragments of what looked like attempts at poetry. "On such a day you would never believe summer will come again," he read. "January 1941. I will reach for heaven even though God has given up." He studied the almost frenzied handwriting, which he believed belonged to Kaj Holt. He kept going, scanning countless names—what he assumed to be cover names—and combination numbers. Some of the names had a cross next to them, and a teardrop had been drawn on one of the pages. But the names of Agnes, Krogh, and the Pilgrim were nowhere to be seen. In the margin of one of the pages was a note that said, "Vera. Her name will be Vera."

Bergmann had just made it to the last page when he heard cursing coming from the bedroom. Sørvaag yelled that he'd hit his head on the desk. Bergmann smiled to himself as he took the last piece of paper out of the shoebox. It seemed to be from the same notepad as many of the other pages, but this one had been crumpled up at some point. He read the few words on the wrinkled page: "We have a rotten apple in the basket."

"In the basket?" he murmured.

Next to this sentence someone seemed to have written something in pencil but then erased it until the paper had almost torn. Bergmann got up and held the paper up to the single rice-paper lamp hanging from the ceiling. The pencil had been pressed into the paper so hard that it was still possible to make out the letters in reverse on the back. Someone with different handwriting than Holt—in almost childlike script—had written a name in big letters.

KROGH.

Bergmann practically collapsed on the sofa.

So Iver Faalund was right. Krogh was the rotten apple. But who had written his name on this old piece of paper and then erased it? Vera Holt? Bergmann sighed. If that were the case, then the only two people claiming that Krogh was a traitor were an old alcoholic in Uddevalla and a psychotic woman who had previously been convicted of murder. Not exactly ideal, but Bergmann had no choice but to believe this was the case.

"We've got her," said Reuter as he stood in front of Bergmann. Sørvaag held the computer hard drive up, as if it were the spoils of war from another era.

These few scribbles change everything, thought Bergmann.

And yet they changed nothing.

Peter Waldhorst must have known all along, of course. Because what else could he have told Kaj Holt in Lillehammer except that Krogh was the man who had stabbed the Resistance in the back in the fall of 1942?

And Vera had figured that out.

And Bergmann really *had* overlooked something completely banal: the fact that a drunkard in godforsaken Uddevalla and a crazy woman on Kolstadgata might know the truth. And that only served to strengthen his belief that Krogh had ordered Holt's death.

"All right. We've got her," said Bergmann. "But I think you might want to wait to call the boss."

He held out the loose page to Reuter.

Reuter frowned, trying to catch Bergmann's eye. But Bergmann merely nodded and stood up. Then he practically stuffed the piece of paper into Reuter's hand.

They stood there staring at each other for a long moment. Then Reuter smoothed out the page and took his reading glasses out of his breast pocket.

"Kaj Holt must have written this," said Bergmann. "He mentions the name Vera somewhere in the other papers."

"'We have a rotten apple in the basket,'" Reuter read almost in a whisper. He repeated the words to himself. Then he took a step back.

"Look at what was written next to it, but then erased," said Bergmann.

Reuter held the page up to the ceiling light, then turned it around twice.

"Are you saying . . . ?"

"I think Vera Holt knows something that no one else in Norway does," he said.

"The knife," said Reuter.

Bergmann nodded.

"Of course," said Reuter. "That's why she killed him with the knife. The Hitler Youth knife."

"And that's why Krogh had to kill Agnes Gerner," said Bergmann.

"So the liquidation was not a mistake," Reuter murmured to himself. "Maybe he's right after all, that guy of yours in Uddevalla."

"Maybe Kaj Holt learned two things in Lillehammer," said Bergmann. "When Waldhorst told him who the traitor really was, he found out who killed Agnes Gerner and the two others, and he also found out who betrayed the Milorg and the British network in Oslo in the fall of 1942. The same man was responsible in both cases: Carl Oscar Krogh."

Reuter stared at Bergmann, a sad look in his eyes.

"That was why Krogh fled to Sweden," said Bergmann. "He must have duped more than just his own comrades. Or maybe he was whisked out of Norway by the Germans, and then returned to the right side. In March 1943 he placed the blame on someone else: Gudbrand Svendstuen. And he personally crossed the border to liquidate him. Then he quietly waited in Stockholm for the war to be over."

"This is unbelievable," said Reuter.

CHAPTER 59

Friday, September 25, 1942
Hammerstads Gate
Oslo, Norway

Agnes Gerner pressed her face against the door of her apartment as she listened to the footsteps coming up the stairs. *Dear God,* she prayed, *have mercy on me.*

The scent of Christopher Bratchard's aftershave from King's Cross station in London suddenly filled her nostrils. She remembered his words. As if he knew that this would happen. That a responsibility too heavy for her to bear would be placed on her shoulders. And that it would be the death of her.

"May God have mercy on your soul," she whispered.

But the footsteps didn't stop.

Nine steps left. She had counted every one of them. There could only be nine more to go.

Nine steps left in her life.

The glass capsule was pressing against her gums. *Now,* she thought. *I'll do it now.*

Eight steps, seven, six, five, four. But there was only one person. That was what she couldn't understand.

Silently she counted down. As the number of steps diminished, her pulse quickened until she could no longer distinguish her heartbeats. They had become one huge roar inside her body.

How could it all end like this?

"How?" she whispered as the doorbell rang.

She sank down on the doormat and clasped her hands. Then she bowed her face to her hands and said a prayer. The same prayer she'd always said as a child. When her father was alive, when they lived here, in this very city.

"Agnes?" said a voice through the door.

She felt as if someone had struck her in the head.

Her hands were wet with tears.

The glass capsule was still intact. She stuck two fingers in her mouth and moved the capsule so that it was positioned between her teeth.

Just before her jaws crushed the glass, she heard the voice again.

"Agnes?"

Finally she recognized who it was. She looked down at her left hand.

Yours forever, she thought.

She spat the capsule into her purse and closed it. Then she stood up and opened the door.

Gustav Lande was standing on the threshold. His face seemed to merge with the beige of his coat. His tie was loose, his hat was askew, and his hair hung limply over his forehead. The smell of booze was unmistakable.

He didn't even seem to notice that Agnes had been crying.

"Have you heard?" he said.

For a long moment he merely stood there, staring at her as though he were a child who had just lost a parent. Like his own daughter.

Agnes drew him inside.

"Yes," she whispered. And then she thanked God.

"I never want to lose you," he said. "Promise me that I'll never lose you."

For several minutes they stood there in the open doorway.

"I promise," said Agnes.

CHAPTER 60

Early Friday Morning, June 20, 2003
Police Headquarters
Oslo, Norway

After they'd searched Vera Holt's apartment and taken the items they'd confiscated over to police headquarters, Tommy Bergmann retired to his office. He turned off the light and sat idly in his chair with his feet propped up on his desk, watching the blinds fluttering in the draft coming through the open window. The warm breeze on that summer night should have put him in a good mood, creating the seductive illusion that summer may last forever this time. But the unexpectedly warm temperature only left him feeling more dejected.

He could no longer put it off.

After a few more minutes he got out his cell phone and opened the message from Hadja.

"I miss you too," he whispered.

He sighed with resignation. For a long time he tried to think of how to reply to her message, but finally ended up typing: *Are you home?* Then he sent it off. He glanced at his watch. It was almost one in the morning, but there was nothing to be done about that.

He had just sat down on the window seat after lighting a cigarette when his cell phone rang. A gust of wind stroked his arm gently, almost like Hadja's voice.

"I didn't mean to wake you," he said.

"I'm working the night shift. So I have to be awake." She sounded happy, clearly relieved that he'd gotten in touch with her.

He didn't reply, unsure what to say.

"Have you been traveling again?" she asked.

"Berlin."

"That's what I thought. You have such an exciting job."

He laughed.

"Maybe."

"I've been thinking a lot about you," she said.

"Yes," said Bergmann, as if that was any kind of answer.

For a moment neither of them spoke.

"Is something wrong?" asked Hadja.

"No," he said. "Or rather . . . I'd like to come over and see you, if that's okay."

She paused.

"Oh . . . sure, all right." He could hear the uncertainty in her voice.

He got a lift from a patrol car up to Hadja's place. The two officers were young and carefree, just like he used to be, and they provided a few minutes of pleasant distraction. The conversation flowed easily. One of them knew his name because a story had made the rounds among the uniformed officers about an arrest he and Bent had once made. Bergmann did his best to keep the myth alive and contributed yet another anecdote from the old days.

He got out at Maridalsveien and watched the patrol car's red tail-lights disappear, standing just as he'd done in his bedroom that night when Hadja had been with him. But this time he wasn't feeling nearly as euphoric.

A great despondency washed over him when he saw her standing in the doorway. She gave him a wave but stayed where she was, in the glaring light of the lobby. He took a deep breath and headed toward the entrance. Dressed in her white uniform, she reminded him of Hege. And yet they were so different.

For a moment they just stood there looking at each other without saying anything.

"Do you think I'm moving too fast? That's not my intention, Tommy. I'm just not very good at hiding my feelings. I throw myself into things."

He frowned and fumbled for his pack of cigarettes.

"That's a weakness of mine," she said, raising her hand to touch his cheek.

He stood there, rocking back and forth. He could have told her that he wanted it to continue, that he would do anything in the world for her. But it wouldn't end well. Not now.

He lit a cigarette and offered her one. She shook her head, trying to look him in the eye. He took a deep breath before he spoke.

"It's just that . . ." he began.

"You're not finished with her," she said in a low voice.

He didn't know what to say to that.

"Hadja . . ." he said, his voice barely audible.

"It's Hege."

"It's just that there are still a lot of things I need to work out, Hadja."

She nodded and blinked, her eyes filling with tears. She blinked again and tears spilled down both cheeks.

"I'm sorry," he said, slowly raising his hand to her cheek.

"Go," she said, her eyes closed. "Please, just go."

CHAPTER 61

Tommy Bergmann, Fredrik Reuter, and Georg Abrahamsen walked slowly toward the entrance of Building 32 at Ullevål Hospital.

The old brick buildings that housed the psychiatric patients had always depressed Bergmann. They reminded him of something from his past that he hadn't been able to place. Maybe it was a memory that he'd repressed, or from so long ago that he wasn't able to summon it forth. Some days he woke up with the remnants of a dream in his head, flickering fragments of himself in early childhood, running across a bottle-green linoleum floor in the hallway of a building like this one.

It did nothing to improve his mood that he'd lain awake until four in the morning; it may even have been closer to five. He hadn't dared to take things further with Hadja, hadn't dared to take things further with himself. And that had made for a long, sleepless night.

Vera Holt was sitting in the visitor's room on the third floor in a hospital gown. Two nurses and a man in a suit were with her. Her eyes were blank and glassy looking, and the wary smile tugging at her lips looked as if it might dissolve into a scream at any moment. *Maybe that's just my imagination,* Bergmann thought as he took her hand, which felt cold and clammy.

"Vera Holt," she said in a whisper, giving him a nod. Her skin was so pale that he thought it might be possible to see right through her if a lamp was placed behind her. Though her hair had been newly washed and smelled of shampoo, it still looked limp and lifeless, the cat food likely not providing her with sufficient nutrition. He noticed that her fingernails had been cut way down—maybe to ensure that she wouldn't harm herself—and her hands were crisscrossed with thin scars.

The balding young man in the suit got up to stand next to her. He introduced himself as Junior Attorney Erik Birkemoe. He told them that he was Vera Holt's defense attorney. He and Reuter exchanged a few words about the search of her apartment and her status as a suspect in the case.

"Have you seen Baltus?" said Vera, looking down at the table.

"Baltus?" said Reuter with a frown.

Vera didn't reply. She stared vacantly into space.

"The cat," whispered Bergmann.

"Oh, yes," said Reuter. "We gave him some food, and . . ." He left it at that. Vera gave him a distracted smile that made her seem simultaneously present and far away.

"So we've carried out a search of Vera Holt's apartment," said Reuter after everyone had taken a seat. His tone seemed excessively formal; Bergmann thought that he perhaps wanted to compensate for the fact that Vera had started off the interrogation by asking about her cat.

He looked at her hands. She was twiddling her thumbs, not quickly and nervously but slowly and sedately. Bergmann could see beneath the cuffs of her sleeves that her wrists were bandaged. He didn't know why—and he didn't want to know either.

Reuter set his briefcase on his lap and took out a medium-sized plastic bag with a slider closure. A felt pen had been used to write the case number and item number on the white space in the middle. Bergmann saw that it contained one of the newspaper clippings about Krogh that they'd found in Vera's apartment. Seeing how the eyes had been cut out reminded him once more of what Krogh's dead body had looked like in reality.

"Are you the one who did this?" asked Reuter, turning to look at Vera.

She kept on twiddling her thumbs as she opened her mouth and whispered something. It might have been a song or a jingle. Bergmann tried to hear what she was saying, but her words disappeared in the faint hissing from the ventilation system. Reuter glanced at Bergmann, then at the male nurse sitting on Vera's left.

The nurse picked up the plastic bag with the newspaper clipping from Reuter's lap. Reuter made a move as if to stop him, but then changed his mind and sat back. A thudding sound was heard through the closed door behind Bergmann, and someone shrieked. Then it was quiet again. Only the hissing of the ventilation system was audible.

"Did you hear what he said?" the nurse said to Vera.

Again, no reaction. Vera stared at her hands as she twiddled her thumbs.

"Did you show any of these to anyone else?" said Reuter.

"No one," she said instantly, though without looking up. After a moment she raised her head and smiled. Then she began to laugh. The sound made the hair on Bergmann's arms stand on end.

Just as abruptly she stopped laughing. The junior attorney shifted uneasily on his chair. He looked as if he were seriously starting to regret taking this case.

"Are you afraid of me?" asked Vera, looking right at Reuter for the first time.

"No," said Reuter. "Why should I be?"

"Everybody's afraid of me," she said. "Isn't that strange?" Her voice was thin and meek, almost like a child's.

"I'm not afraid of you," said Reuter calmly.

"Mama's new husband . . . The first time I was only four years old. Finally I killed him, you know. Killed," she said, her voice so faint the words almost disappeared.

No one seated at the table made any move to speak. Vera resumed twiddling the thumbs of her scarred hands.

Reuter picked up the plastic bag with the picture of Krogh.

"Did someone else give this to you?" he asked.

Vera shook her head.

Reuter put down the bag. Then he took another one out of his briefcase. Inside was one of the pages they'd found in her apartment. A page torn from a notepad.

Reuter handed it to Birkemoe, who held it up to the light.

"'We have a rotten apple in the basket,'" he read out loud.

"Notice what it says next to that," said Reuter. He turned to look at Bergmann. It was clear that he thought the case was closed, so to speak.

You haven't considered the consequences, thought Bergmann. How was this case going to turn out if Holt's daughter killed Krogh because Krogh had killed her father—or gave someone the orders to do it—in Stockholm?

"Did your father write this?" asked Reuter.

Vera nodded.

"I got everything from her before she died."

"From who?"

"Mama."

"I'd like to confer with my client," Birkemoe said, handing the plastic bag back to Reuter. He took off his glasses and massaged the bridge of his nose. He was young, maybe eight or ten years younger than Bergmann. He'd obviously been sent over by one of the partners in the law firm that would take over Vera Holt's defense if it turned out that the case would get media attention.

Reuter nodded.

"I'd just like to confirm one thing," he said. "Is it true that your client has no alibi for Whitsunday?"

Birkemoe put his glasses back on and nodded.

"As you know, we found a number of newspaper articles about the death of the three females in Nordmarka at Ms. Holt's home," Reuter went on. Birkemoe merely grunted, making it clear he thought Reuter was repeating himself unnecessarily.

"Were you at the home of Carl Oscar Krogh on Sunday, June 8?"

Vera didn't seem to hear the question. She clenched her jaw, chanting that barely audible jingle of hers and staring at her hands, which were still steadily moving in the same manner.

"Well, she's under arrest," Reuter told Birkemoe. "And if we could just get her fingerprints . . ."

Bergmann leaned across the table.

"Have you ever spoken to a German named Peter?" he asked quietly.

Vera paused for a moment, not lifting her gaze from the table.

"Peter Waldhorst. Or Peter Ward?"

Only silence. Then Vera once again began clenching her jaw and twiddling her thumbs.

Birkemoe took off his glasses and massaged the bridge of his nose a second time. For a moment he sat there with his eyes closed. Finally he put his glasses back on and motioned toward the door.

Reuter sighed in resignation and then slapped Bergmann on the back.

"Not exactly a dream client," he said quietly as they went out into the corridor. Abrahamsen was sitting on a chair a few feet away, reading a newspaper. He glanced up at them.

"So?" he said.

Bergmann had an intense urge to get out into the fresh air. He looked down at the newly scrubbed linoleum floor, following it with his gaze until it ended at the far wall with a rectangular window with bars several feet away. He headed down the stairs, taking them two at a time.

Outside he stood under the awning at the front entrance. A fierce rainstorm had moved in, soaking the ground in a matter of minutes. The road, parking lot, and lawn all looked as though they'd been inundated by a hundred-year flood.

A few minutes later the door opened behind him. Reuter looked past Bergmann at the torrential rain. Bergmann glanced down at his shoes, suddenly noticing that they were nearly soaked through.

"So that's done," said Abrahamsen behind Reuter. A barely discernible smile appeared on his gaunt face. "Two complete sets of fingerprints, Tommy. What do you think? That young lawyer is probably hoping for a lenient sentence because he cooperated, right?"

"Coffee's on me," said Reuter, giving Bergmann a slap on the back.

I can't believe it, thought Bergmann.

They stood there watching Abrahamsen trot across the parking lot with his flight case in his arms, as though it were his newborn child.

"This is going to be hell," said Bergmann, tossing his smoldering cigarette butt into the stream of water gushing out of the downspout by his feet.

"Let's not get ahead of ourselves," Reuter said, turning up the collar of his new Polo jacket, which his wife had undoubtedly bought for him to improve his appearance. "Today we're going to savor this victory, Tommy. We'll let the chief handle the bad stuff."

They ran toward the closest building, but were nonetheless soaked through within seconds. Reuter laughed like a boy as they went inside.

Bergmann had a strange feeling as he looked at Reuter. A feeling that Reuter would stop laughing before this day was over. In a lucid moment, Vera Holt may have understood, or been told, that Krogh was the rotten apple in the basket, but where had she gotten that knife? And how had she been able to get away from Krogh's villa without anyone noticing her? Someone who hardly seemed aware of what was going on inside her own head and who was barely able to take care of herself?

CHAPTER 62

Sunday, September 27, 1942
Villa Lande
Tuengen Allé
Oslo, Norway

She came to a door. Behind her stretched a nearly dark corridor. The light from the wall sconces was so faint that they might as well have been switched off. She'd been running and running along this corridor for hours, maybe even days, in some sort of *pension* or hotel. She turned around one last time and saw the outline of two faceless men who had emerged from the shadows. They were saying something incomprehensible to her. One of them leaned toward her, his breath as rotten as a dead man's. The words that spilled out of his mouth were backward. She screamed but no sound came out. She turned toward a wooden door with a leaded glass window. A glaring light shone on the other side. She felt one of the men put his heavy hand on her shoulder. She reached for the door handle and tore open the door. She was momentarily blinded by an inexplicably bright light, but then she saw in the distance, beyond the light, a woman her own age walking toward her, holding out her hands. She felt a thick, viscous fluid rise over her ankles. *That light,* she thought. *That light.*

Agnes Gerner jolted up in bed.

For several seconds she thought it was only a dream. Then everything collapsed around her.

It was true. It was *all* true.

The blackout curtains were only partly drawn, fluttering at the open bedroom window. She felt the back of her neck, damp with sweat, turn cold. She shivered in the wind gusting through the window. She pulled the quilt around her and quickly crossed the room to fasten the hasps on the window. The trees in the yard below looked like they'd drop their leaves at any moment. The referee's seat at the tennis court was drooping. Though it was still radiantly sunny, there was no longer any doubt that winter was at the door.

Death is at the door, she thought.

What day was it? Sunday. How long had she been at Lande's villa? Since that day. Since Friday evening.

How could she . . .

Yesterday the house had been filled with Germans. Nothing but Sipo officers all day long, and she had been forced to sit among them, with their newspapers and documents spread out all over the tables. "So awful," she'd said to *Brigadeführer* Seeholz, "so unbelievably awful." He had assured her that they would find this monstrous female assassin. A dozen people had already been brought in to Gestapo HQ. Agnes had escaped to the guest bathroom in the hall. She had found a package of razor blades in the medicine cabinet and surrendered to a sudden impulse to hold one of blades to her wrist. For some reason, it seemed like a much better way to die than swallowing a cyanide capsule. She had gotten as far as filling the sink with warm water before she persuaded herself that there had to be a way out of all this.

She hadn't gone to bed until one thirty in the morning. So as not to draw attention to herself, she had kept Seeholz company while he, his adjutant, and a Sipo man continued drinking even after Lande had retired for the night.

She was suddenly aware of sounds coming from the yard.

No one, she thought as she fixed her eyes on Cecilia running across the lawn after the maid, for some reason dressed in oilskins and boots in spite of the weather, limping and limping, *no one understands what has happened. Except maybe you.* Agnes looked at the maid.

There was definitely something wrong with Johanne. The maid, who certainly didn't look very intelligent, was probably much sharper than she appeared. *How ironic,* thought Agnes. Last night Seeholz, drunk out of his mind, had kissed her on both cheeks, clicked his heels together, and proclaimed, *"Heil Hitler."* She had, of course, reciprocated. Only one floor of the house separated the SS officer from the Welrod she had used to kill the research director and his secretary. And only a few centimeters separated him from the woman he was so desperately seeking.

Agnes had done as the Pilgrim had said and hidden the gun in Gustav Lande's own house. It was now hidden in Cecilia's room, on the top shelf of a wardrobe that was never used, wrapped in an old towel. She didn't know whether it was a brilliant idea or sheer madness to hide it here in this house. Nor could she understand why she had had to keep it. Yesterday she'd considered moving it back to her apartment, but she hadn't dared to leave the house. If Waldhorst followed her, that would be the end of everything. She didn't dare go back to her place on Hammerstads Gate at all right now. She needed to stay put, hide right here in plain sight, so close to the hunters that no one would ever even think she was their prey.

A sound interrupted her thoughts.

The shower in the bathroom had just been turned off. Was that what had startled her?

The bathroom door was closed, but judging by the sounds coming from under the door, it sounded as if Lande had started shaving.

When was his plane leaving for Berlin? Agnes didn't remember. She went back to bed and pulled up the covers. Oddly enough she suddenly felt calmer and safer. Here in the eye of the storm, no one could touch her. Absolutely no one. At least not today, when both Lande and Seeholz were going to Berlin. That would give her a full twenty-four hours to think things through.

She rolled onto Lande's side of the bed and stared at the small framed photograph of his first wife. *I'll take care of Cecilia for you,* she thought. *I don't know how I'm going to manage it, but I will. I promise.*

A few minutes later Gustav Lande came out of the bathroom, his bathrobe open. The scent of his aftershave overwhelmed her for a moment as he bent down and kissed her. Agnes closed her eyes. The private secretary was staring at her again, screaming soundlessly, dark blood pooling on the oak parquet floor. The glass dropping to the floor, her lifeless eyes.

"Come on," he said, squeezing her hand. "Come and have breakfast with me before I have to leave."

This will be the last time I ever see you, she thought.

The very last time.

CHAPTER 63

Friday, June 20, 2003
Ullevål Hospital
Oslo, Norway

Tommy Bergmann didn't like the fact that they were so visible sitting there in the cafeteria. Reuter had insisted that they sit at one of the tables right next to the reception area, and Bergmann could do nothing but acquiesce. He would have preferred a more secluded table because he didn't want to run into Hege, though he didn't know whether she was still working or had left on maternity leave. All he knew was that he didn't want to see her right now.

He tried to read a few articles in the copy of *Dagbladet* that someone had left on the table, but soon gave up.

Reuter tore the wrapper off the ice cream cone he'd bought and tried to find the sports pages in the newspaper. Bergmann couldn't understand how Reuter could even think of eating ice cream when he was still soaking wet. Bergmann wriggled his toes inside his shoes, feeling the water squelching under his feet. Reuter took a cautious bite of ice cream as he pulled his reading glasses out of his jacket pocket. Bergmann studied his colleague sitting across from him. Considering his paunch, ice cream was the last thing Reuter needed, but that wasn't what was bothering Bergmann. It was knowing that in a moment Reuter would start licking the ice cream. He would turn the cone around and around, sticking out his tongue to lick the ice cream like an old lady.

"What are you staring at?" said Reuter without looking up.

"Nothing. Inside we're all the same," said Bergmann, trying to find a cigarette that was dry enough that he'd have a reasonable chance of lighting it.

Reuter laughed and kept leafing through the newspaper.

As Bergmann got up with the unlit cigarette dangling from his lips, Reuter's cell phone began vibrating on the table.

That was quick, thought Bergmann, taking a deep breath. Had Abrahamsen really managed to check the fingerprints already?

Reuter took the call, looking pensive.

"I'll call you later," he said into the phone.

"Nothing?" said Bergmann.

Reuter shook his head without replying.

"It's going to be hell if it turns out that Vera Holt did it," said Bergmann.

"With a conviction based on a confession and a good dose of insanity, it's sure to be viewed as a real tragedy," said Reuter, continuing to lick his ice cream cone.

Bergmann left to have a smoke, standing just outside the front entrance. An old man with almost yellow skin was leaning on a walker a few feet away, trying to stick a hand-rolled cigarette in his mouth.

He tore his eyes away from the old man and thought that maybe Reuter was right. Maybe it would be a blessing if Vera Holt was the perpetrator.

"Has Georg called?"

Reuter shook his head. He jumped when his phone began vibrating on the table a moment later.

"Speak of the devil," he said. He glanced at Bergmann, his expression that of a five-year-old on Christmas Eve.

"So, what have you got for me?"

Abrahamsen's voice was loud enough that Bergmann could hear the results of the fingerprint test, but the expression on Reuter's face said it all. *There's no point in checking her DNA*, he thought. Those were not her fingerprints on the Hitler Youth knife.

"Not a match?" said Reuter. "Are you sure?"

Bergmann stuck his cigarette pack in his breast pocket, then turned on his heel and headed for the door without saying a word. He jogged along the side of the building to the parking lot of the psychiatric ward.

The earlier downpour had given way to a light drizzle, but Bergmann nonetheless felt like he was freezing. Maybe it was his confusion that was making him feel cold. Complete and utter confusion that only Peter Waldhorst could clear up.

If he were willing to do so.

"Where are you going?" shouted Reuter behind him.

A woman walking by cast an alarmed look at Bergmann and the man chasing after him.

"Where do you think?" said Bergmann, stopping. Reuter was only a few steps away now, his face red, his eyes wild.

Reuter didn't know what to say. He just stood there, then finally stated the obvious.

"It's not her, Tommy. It's not Vera Holt."

"Get Linda to book me a hotel room," said Bergmann as he started heading for the car again. "You'll have to take a cab back." He held out his hand to Reuter. "Toss me the keys."

"The keys?" said Reuter.

"The car keys." Bergmann patted his pockets. Then he pulled his passport out of his inside pocket. It was still there from his trip to Berlin.

At last Reuter seemed to understand that Bergmann was going back, and that he had no time to waste.

"But Waldhorst isn't on any of the airline passenger lists!" shouted Reuter, catching up. "And he didn't check into any hotels either . . ."

Bergmann ignored him.

"No Peter Waldhorst. No Peter Ward," said Reuter as they reached the car. Bergmann tilted his head back and looked up at the brick facade of the psych ward. He no longer felt guilty about suspecting Vera Holt of a murder that she might have had every right to commit, at least according to the Book of Exodus. She might never get out of this hospital, but that might be for the best—both for her and everyone else.

Bergmann took the car keys from Reuter, who merely shook his head without saying a word.

"When was Kennedy in Berlin?" Bergmann asked as he pressed the remote. The silvery Ford Mondeo beeped and the car doors unlocked.

Reuter cocked his head to one side, looking as if he thought Bergmann might also need to spend some time in the nearby building.

"*Ich bin ein Berliner,*" said Bergmann. "When did he say that?"

Reuter still didn't reply, but it was easy to tell from his expression that he was seriously considering the question.

"When did Kennedy say that?"

"Just a minute," said Reuter. "Let me think."

Bergmann stuck a damp cigarette in his mouth and managed to light it.

"1963," said Reuter, staring at Bergmann. "June 1963."

Bergmann opened his notebook. Half the pages were wet from the rain, but the ink hadn't smeared too badly, and he could still read what he'd written. He turned back a few pages, running his finger over the words.

"1963," he murmured to himself. That was the summer that Bente Bull-Krogh was in her senior year. A few months before Krogh's wife thought a woman had called them, though the other person hadn't said anything on the phone.

Bergmann looked at Reuter, who frowned.

"What is it?" Reuter asked.

Bergmann didn't reply.

"Tommy?"

No response.

"Why are you asking about that? *'Ich bin ein Berliner?'*"

"It's just something that Waldhorst said."

"1963," said Reuter.

"1963," Bergmann repeated, getting in the car.

"What does that have to do with your going to Berlin?"

Bergmann leaned forward and started up the engine. He closed his eyes for a moment, and images of himself with Peter Waldhorst flitted through his mind. The two of them standing next to the taxi outside the hospital.

Chance is nothing but fate, and fate is nothing but chance.

Bergmann started backing up. For a second he was afraid he'd driven over Reuter's feet as he stood there, throwing out his hands in a plea for him to wait and explain. Bergmann rolled down the window, exhaled a cloud of smoke, and pressed the button for the siren in the center of the dashboard.

Half an hour later he was standing at the SAS ticket counter at Oslo Airport. Afterward, two pints of beer at the bar lowered his pulse to an acceptable level. He laughed at the message he got from Arne Drabløs, who was wondering if he'd abdicated his position as head coach altogether. It occurred to him that maybe he ought to quit coaching after the tournament in Göteborg because of the whole thing with Hadja. He pushed aside any thoughts of her, stowing them away at the very back of his mind.

On the bar napkin he'd written three little words.

I loved her.

Quickly he folded up the napkin.

For several minutes he stared out the bar at the line of people about to board a Norwegian Air flight. He sat there smiling to himself without knowing exactly why.

He needed to start over, connect the dots in this investigation in a different way.

In the fall of 1963 Krogh gets a mysterious phone call.

Waldhorst meets his current wife at Tempelhof in June of the same year.

The maid was not killed after all.

Waldhorst loved Agnes Gerner.

And Carl Oscar Krogh was presumably working for the Germans during the war.

Finally: Agnes Gerner realized what he was up to and was killed.

He stared into his empty beer glass, as though hoping to find the answer at the bottom. He rubbed his hands over his face several times. It seemed hopeless. He could hardly make heads or tails of anything anymore. Had Waldhorst met someone at Tempelhof in 1963 who reminded him of Agnes? Someone who reminded him that Krogh had killed her in 1942?

A wild thought occurred to him as he waited in line to board.

Could Johanne Caspersen be his wife? The woman he'd called Gretchen?

CHAPTER 64

Sunday, September 27, 1942
Villa Lande
Tuengen Allé
Oslo, Norway

As soon as Agnes Gerner entered the kitchen, everything became clear to her. Johanne Caspersen stood with her back turned, placing a couple of logs on the embers in the fireplace. Yet she seemed to have eyes in the back of her head, because she froze as Agnes came into the room. And Agnes knew, she *knew*, that she had been careless, so damned careless that an ugly maid had seen right through her. She just couldn't figure out what it was she'd done. What little mistake had she made that had put the maid on her trail?

She heard a phone ringing through the closed door to the living room.

It's all over now, thought Agnes. *They're calling Gustav to tell him who I really am.*

A moment later she regained her composure. At least for the time being.

"I'll get it," Lande said. Something in his voice calmed her.

Cecilia was sitting at the table, lost in her own world. A sketch pad had captured all her attention, and she was moving a colored pencil over the paper. Agnes studied her. The child still hadn't noticed her presence.

Paper, she thought suddenly.

Peter Waldhorst.

Paper.

Waldhorst.

Nausea rose in her throat. For a moment she was overwhelmed by the thought that he'd backed her into a corner. She knew she ought to be glad that she hadn't heard from him in a while. But it was precisely that—his silence—that was so ominous. This certainty that at any moment he'd be standing behind her, tearing off his mask of feigned friendliness to reveal the monster he undoubtedly was.

"What would madam like for breakfast?"

Agnes stared straight into the birdlike face, those strange birdlike eyes. There was something in the maid's expression that instantly banished her sense of calm and control. Johanne was looking at her as if she herself were now the mistress of the house. As if Agnes were already dead.

"I'm sorry," Agnes whispered so that Cecilia wouldn't hear. "I shouldn't have . . ." She stopped herself. What was she actually trying to say? Was she apologizing for slapping her?

The maid had already walked over to the stove where she slammed a cast-iron skillet onto the biggest burner. The door to the living room opened. Gustav Lande came in and stood motionless in the middle of the room. He had on one of his best suits, one he wore only to meetings with the most important people. His tie hung loosely around his neck. Agnes didn't know who would be traveling with him to Berlin other than Seeholz. Maybe Norway's *Reichskommissar* Christian Terboven himself. But she had no intention of asking. Never again would she try to find out that sort of information. Right now she had only two options. She could either escape to Sweden—and God only knew how she'd manage that—or keep as low a profile as possible, hiding out here until she could think of a better idea, until someone realized that they needed to get her out of Norway.

Cecilia ran over to her father, and Lande leaned down to hug her. Then he shooed her back to the table. He kept his eyes fixed on Agnes the whole time, a sad look on his face, as if everything he'd ever worked for was suddenly gone.

"I need to talk to you," he said.

Agnes had to close her eyes for a moment. Something flashed through her mind. A memory from her childhood, on a carousel, somewhere in England, she wasn't sure where. Her mother and father were standing next to each other, waving to her.

"I don't want to lose you," Lande whispered in her ear. The pounding of her heart slowed. *Thank you, dear God,* she thought, savoring the scent of his aftershave.

Lande put his arm around her shoulders and led her into the living room, closing the door behind them. The room was cold, much too cold, and she shivered as Lande motioned for her to sit down on the sofa. A cold gust of wind made her cross her arms. Lande draped a wool blanket around her shoulders. She looked around the room, at the chairs around the dining table, at the dark oak parquet floor, at the gloomy oil paintings that seemed so out of place there, at the cold white walls. *How am I going to get through this?* she wondered just before Lande spoke.

"That was Ernst Seeholz on the phone," he said, offering her a cigarette. Agnes shook her head. Then he lit one for himself. She was staring at the rain coming down on the terrace outside, picturing herself sitting there in the summer with that stocky little German. Waldhorst.

"He told me that a dozen Resistance fighters were arrested last night."

Agnes closed her eyes for a moment.

"And you know what?" said Lande. "That hairdresser you go to?"

The Pilgrim. They've got the Pilgrim. That was all Agnes could think of.

"Helge K. Moen," she said quietly.

"He was one of the people arrested. A damned patriot." Lande sounded more resigned than angry.

She hoped that he wouldn't notice the goosebumps on her arms.

"Ernst said that those partisans will be hanged before the week is over. It's just a question of time before they track down that female assassin and her cohorts." Lande stared into space, unaware of the burning cigarette he was holding.

Agnes nodded, then leaned forward to take the cigarette out of his hand.

He seemed to wake up.

"It's so awful," she said, avoiding his eye.

Cecilia came into the room and sat down on Agnes's lap. She stroked the child's hair while Cecilia took her other hand and opened the book she'd brought with her. An old, worn picture book.

"By the way . . . Could you close up Rødtangen today?" said Lande, fixing his eyes on her again. "We should have done it last weekend, but . . . Well, it's a big job. Take Johanne with you, of course. She knows the routine even better than I do."

Agnes didn't reply. She was looking at her own reflection in the windowpane. Cecilia leafing through the book. Her warm little body, the beating of the child's pulse were suddenly too much for her.

"Did he have any children?" she asked. "Research Director Rolborg?"

Lande turned around. He stopped knotting his tie and nodded.

"A son."

Then he turned back toward the terrace and continued with his tie.

A tear ran down Agnes's face.

"Who had children?" asked Cecilia.

"Nobody," said Agnes.

"We were just talking about Rødtangen," Lande said. "You're going out there today."

"Rødtangen!" Cecilia cried. "We're going to Rødtangen!"

"Yes," whispered Agnes, stroking her hair. "We're going to Rødtangen today."

CHAPTER 65

Friday, June 20, 2003
Hotel Berlin
Lützowplatz
Berlin, Germany

An oppressive heat struck Tommy Bergmann as the doors to the arrivals hall at Tegel Airport slid open. The humid air made his long-sleeved shirt stick to his body. He tossed the bag holding his newly purchased underwear and socks into the taxi and sank back in the seat.

"Hotel Berlin," he told the driver. The name was so ordinary that he had his doubts about whether the hotel even existed.

"Lützowplatz," said the cabbie, his tone suggesting he'd be up for chatting. To shut out any such possibility, Bergmann closed his eyes and leaned his head against the windowpane.

The hotel had been newly remodeled and was much too modern for Bergmann's taste, but the view of the Tiergarten was almost worth the whole trip. He gazed out at the dark green leaves of the trees bathed in the afternoon sun and the gilded Victory Column. He opened the window facing the street, allowing the sound of the traffic to wash over him for a while.

His cell phone rang from the desk.

"Don't do anything down there until we've contacted the German police. Do you hear me? Do not question Waldhorst until you have Derrick or one of his colleagues with you." Reuter's voice left no doubt that he would be unwilling to even consider any objections Bergmann might propose.

Bergmann looked at his watch, thinking that this was going to be a long weekend. There was little chance that anyone in Oslo would send over a formal request to the police in Berlin late on a Friday afternoon. And if, against all expectations, they actually did follow through, he'd heard enough about German bureaucracy to give up hope of anything happening today.

He began looking for the minibar in his futuristic hotel room. After a few minutes he had to conclude there wasn't one, so he went down to the hotel bar and ordered a pint of beer and a double whisky.

It was already nine o'clock when Bergmann decided to go out to Peter Waldhorst's place anyway. After all, there was nothing illegal about taking a drive through town. He recognized the streets as they got closer and the fashionable homes gave way to mansions and parks.

By the time the cab turned onto Waldhorst's street, his back was soaked with sweat from leaning against the leather seat. A blessedly cool breeze blew over the sidewalk as he got out of the cab. For a moment he just stood there, gazing at the red taillights of the big Mercedes as it headed back to town.

Bergmann turned to face the villa. In the twilight it looked abandoned. Not a single light shone in any of the windows. The outdoor lights weren't on either, even though they were probably controlled by photocells.

That's strange, he thought as he took his cell phone out of his pocket and looked for Waldhorst's number.

He studied the house as the phone began ringing.

The windows remained dark. No sign of life anywhere inside. Finally it jumped to voice mail, but there was no recorded message. All

Bergmann heard was a rushing sound, followed by the unmistakable beep that indicated the caller could leave a message.

Bergmann hung up.

He had a feeling that Waldhorst had left the house for good. And that now it was too late.

CHAPTER 66

Sunday, September 27, 1942
Villa Lande
Tuengen Allé
Oslo, Norway

After Gustav Lande had been picked up by a cortège from the Wehrmacht, Agnes Gerner climbed the stairs to the third floor and locked herself in the bathroom. Unable to form a single clear thought, she lay down on the floor. For several minutes she lay staring at the light-brown tiles. If she closed her eyes, the nightmare continued. If she kept them open, she stared straight up at the white ceiling, as white as it would surely look, flickering before her eyes when Waldhorst decided to arrest her and hang her from the ceiling in the cellar at Victoria Terrasse. She chose to shut her eyes. Bess, with her head cocked, turned into the private secretary; then the research director's blood struck her mouth and entered her stomach, which Waldhorst sliced open with a knife, from her pelvis to her breastbone.

She slowly realized that someone was knocking on the bedroom door. The maid's voice almost didn't penetrate the two closed doors.

Agnes wriggled over to the bathroom door.

"Yes?" she said weakly.

"There's a German soldier at the door," said the maid.

CHAPTER 67

Monday, June 23, 2003
Tiergarten
Berlin, Germany

Tommy Bergmann leaned over the railing of the black bear enclosure at the zoo. He really should have gone home on Saturday, but instead he'd rambled all over Berlin, walking more than he'd done in the past ten years. He'd bought some new jogging shoes and a map, and practiced several phrases he remembered from his high school German classes. He'd also eaten more than was good for him. It had rained pretty much all weekend, which had put him in a remarkably good mood.

He was so fascinated by the roughhousing between two bear cubs that he almost dropped his ice cream over the edge when his phone vibrated in his pants pocket.

"Someone will meet you at your hotel in two hours," Fredrik Reuter said on the other end of the line. "What the heck is going on there anyway? Are you at the circus?"

Bergmann kept his gaze fixed on the bear cub that had just taken a tumble. The other cub came over to see if everything was all right.

"The zoo," he said.

"You must feel right at home."

"You ought to be a comedian."

"Okay, okay. Anyway, someone will be at your door in two hours."

"I'm impressed," said Bergmann.

"It's not my doing. I put in a request on Friday as soon as you left. Germany is quite an orderly country, you know. They have cops too."

"You don't say," said Bergmann.

"His name is Udo Fritz," said Reuter.

"You're kidding, right? That's quite a name . . ." said Bergmann. He dropped his ice cream cone down into the bear pit, where it smashed silently on the ground. Even amid all the hubbub, the two bear cubs noticed that something had fallen down to them. Bergmann was secretly rooting for the cub that had lost the fight. But naturally the other one triumphed this time too. The loser slunk away from the cone with his head hanging.

"I wish I were," said Reuter.

Udo Fritz, Bergmann said to himself.

After grabbing dinner at the hotel, he sat down in the lobby and waited for the infamous Udo Fritz.

For a while he pondered what he was going to say to Peter Waldhorst. Something surprising, something that would knock him off his guard. Like, he knew that Carl Oscar Krogh had been a German agent. But it would hardly be news to Waldhorst that Bergmann knew that. Waldhorst was the sort of man who wasn't just a couple of moves ahead—he was several entire games ahead of most people. Bergmann realized what had been bothering him subconsciously. How could he, Tommy Bergmann, with two courses in investigation from the police academy under his belt, outmaneuver an old fox who had been *both* an Abwehr and a Gestapo man?

What if Waldhorst himself had killed Krogh? Bergmann had to get him to leave his prints on something somehow. That shouldn't be too difficult. It would be inadmissible as evidence, but it would at least convince Fredrik Reuter that Waldhorst was the killer.

Detective Udo Fritz was easy to spot. Bergmann heard the officer asking for him at the front desk.

He got up from his seat in the bar and was standing at the end of the counter before the receptionist even managed to look him up in the room registry.

"I think I'm the one you're looking for," he said.

Udo Fritz turned around. Bergmann instantly pegged Fritz as a cop, and it was obvious that Fritz came to the same conclusion when he saw Bergmann.

On the drive out to Grunewald, they exchanged some polite small talk. Fritz seemed utterly uninterested in what Bergmann was doing in Berlin, and that suited him just fine. He leaned back in his seat and listened to the chatter on the police radio, even managing to catch a word here and there. Then he started to wonder what life had been like when German was the language of command in his own city. Back when Peter Waldhorst had fallen for Agnes Gerner.

And killed her?

The thought had crossed his mind every so often. *Maybe my hunch is right,* Bergmann thought. But the motive still baffled him.

CHAPTER 68

Sunday, September 27, 1942
Berkowitz Apartment
Oslo, Norway

The young SS sergeant cast a quick glance at her in the backseat. Agnes Gerner looked away and tried to convince herself that her mouth smelled like toothpaste, not vomit. When the maid had announced that a German soldier was at the door, Agnes had bent over the toilet seat and emptied her stomach as quietly as possible. Then she went downstairs to the second floor. The maid had a strange expression on her face, as if to say, "I told you so!" From the next to last step, Agnes could see the German's black trouser legs and understood that he wasn't any ordinary Wehrmacht soldier. She had to grasp the banister more tightly for a few seconds.

She fumbled for her purse. In her panic she hadn't managed to take out the cyanide pill, and now she didn't dare open her purse for fear that he would stop the car and empty out the contents on the backseat.

At the intersection by the Majorstua building, she stared at Helge K. Moen's salon. *Who blew the whistle on me?* she wondered. She said a silent prayer that the sergeant would take a right down Kirkeveien and not drive straight ahead. Heading straight down Bogstadveien could only mean one thing. Agnes watched a little girl doing hopscotch jumps as she crossed the street with her mother. As the soldier stepped on the gas and drove across the crosswalk, Agnes thought of Cecilia and was sure that she'd seen her for the last time.

Victoria Terrasse, she thought. *They're going to lock me up next to the Pilgrim, just so I can hear what they do to him.* Maybe *Brigadeführer* Seeholz himself will torture him. By this time he must know that the Pilgrim was the great love of her life. What was it he'd said? That she should be good to Gustav Lande? And now this? Not merely one, but two murders, on the same day the crazy Brits had recklessly tried to bomb Victoria Terrasse?

When they turned down Frederiks Gate, Agnes was only seconds away from confessing everything. Just before she closed her eyes, she noticed black clouds hovering over the palace, the swastika flag hanging limply, waiting for the first raindrops. None of what she had expected came to mind. No images from her childhood—of her father, her mother, or of all the world's evil—flashed through her mind, not even a vision of the secretary's soundless scream.

The car turned right up Drammensveien.

The next turn will be to the left, she thought. *In just a few feet.*

A jolt passed through the car, and the soldier shifted to third gear at the top of the small hill.

Agnes couldn't help it.

She opened her eyes and spun around in the seat to glimpse the fortified white building of Victoria Terrasse standing undamaged. Black smoke was rising out of one of the collapsed buildings next door.

When she turned back she met the eyes of the young SS sergeant in the mirror and a light blush spread up her cheeks. When the driver turned up Bygdøy Allé, there was no longer any doubt. Agnes thought that she should have said something about how terrible it was, this attack on Victoria Terrasse, that the British would obviously lose the war. But not a word crossed her lips.

"*Kommen Sie, bitte?*" said the SS sergeant when they had parked outside the white apartment building where Peter Waldhorst lived. There was not a soul around. She peered across the street at Frogner Church, thinking that she wasn't even going to get a funeral. That her mother probably wouldn't bother.

The ironclad heels of the SS sergeant struck the sidewalk behind her.

What have you done with the Pilgrim? she thought as he pressed the doorbell. *Why did he drive me past Victoria Terrasse? So I would understand that they know who I really am?*

"*Fräulein Gerner für den Hauptsturmführer,*" he said into the intercom.

The door buzzed open.

The stairwell smelled of soap. She thought it would be the last smell she would ever remember. How she made it up the five floors she didn't know, but she now stood on the sixth-floor landing. The brass plate with the name Berkowitz was still on the door. Waldhorst must have taken a perverse delight in the fact that it hadn't been replaced.

She focused on the door handle when she heard the lock being turned in the massive door. She pictured herself taking a step back into the stairwell and simply letting herself fall five stories onto the granite floor below. But she didn't know if she'd even be able to move her feet. All she could hear was the SS sergeant's heels clacking together when Waldhorst opened the door. He was dressed in a gray suit and looked pale. She managed to think that he looked like he hadn't slept at all last night. Then he dismissed the sergeant, saying something in German that Agnes didn't catch. He was holding a copy of *Aftenposten* in his hand. She knew exactly what the article said. "Blonde woman," she read before the SS sergeant was gone.

Waldhorst placed his hand lightly on her shoulder.

"Strange, I was just now reading the paper. And then you arrive . . ." His voice sounded hoarse, not the way she remembered it. His breath smelled of toothpaste and his cheeks of aftershave, but even that wasn't enough to camouflage the smell of stale liquor on his breath.

Somehow she managed to move one foot in front of the other.

The door slammed shut behind her.

On a low bureau to the left of the door lay a Hitler Youth knife that she'd never seen before. Agnes fixed her gaze on it. The blade looked newly polished, almost unused. She was sure it hadn't been there the last time she was there. She didn't even know why she was staring at it. Maybe because she couldn't get herself to move. She tried to shift her right foot by twisting her heel a bit to the side.

"It's my brother's," Waldhorst said. "My only brother."

Agnes said nothing.

"I don't even know where he's buried. They sent the knife to me. Did I mention that the last time you were here?"

"Yes, you did . . . I'm sorry," Agnes said quietly. Absurdly, the whole exchange made her pulse slow.

"May I take your coat?" said Waldhorst.

She shook her head. Her hands were gripping the handle of her purse.

"The bathroom?" she whispered.

"No," said Waldhorst.

He led her instead through the living room to the library. On the coffee table between two Chesterfield sofas stood a silver tray with a silver teapot and two porcelain cups. She recognized the Royal Ascot emblem. The same image from earlier in the day flitted across her mind's eye. She saw herself on a slow-moving carousel, the horse bobbing up and down, her parents waving to her, on a summer day as warm as it could be in England.

"Since you're half English." He held up a silver creamer.

She could do nothing but nod.

"Why are you holding on to your purse so tightly, Ms. Gerner?" Waldhorst got up and snatched it out of her hands.

She had a sudden realization: there was nothing but the unbearable pain to worry about. Then everything would be fine again.

"I spoke with some friends of yours last night," Waldhorst said as he put the newspaper on the coffee table and opened her purse. The sound of a cortège driving up Bygdøy Allé could be heard through the windowpanes.

Agnes managed to read the headline upside down on the coffee table. "English Fiasco." Beneath it was a photo of Victoria Terrasse completely intact. And a single-column article on the right side of the front page had the headline "Assassination. Blonde woman sought."

She shut her eyes as she listened to Waldhorst taking one thing after another out of her purse and setting them on the coffee table between them.

It dawned on her only slowly. She opened her eyes and looked at Waldhorst as he stared down into the empty purse, whose contents were now all spread out on the table. She had to restrain herself to keep the laughter in her throat from bubbling over. She had obviously been lucid enough to wrap the cyanide capsule in toilet paper and stuff it in her panties. But the sight of the SS sergeant had scared her into forgetting she'd done it. She felt utterly calm now as she felt the coarse toilet paper rubbing against her abdomen. She was overcome with a surge of joy the likes of which she hadn't felt in years. *I fooled you, I fooled you!* she chanted to herself as she looked at Waldhorst and all the trivial things from her purse.

Waldhorst's expression didn't change as he put everything back: makeup, matches, the keys to both the villa and Rødtangen, her ID papers, cigarettes, and a letter from her sister. Then he placed her purse back in her lap, as if nothing had happened, and went back to stirring his tea.

"I am Gustav Lande's fiancée," said Agnes with feigned anger, "and I—"

Waldhorst clapped his hand over her mouth. With his other hand he picked up the paper, keeping his eyes fixed on hers.

The quiet was intolerable. Waldhorst removed his hand and leafed through the newspaper, turning not to the many pages that covered the British attack on Victoria Terrasse, but to the page on which the National Police were interviewed about what they called the assassination of Research Director Torfinn Rolborg and his private secretary.

The calm that Agnes had felt vanished just as rapidly as it had arrived.

"Tomorrow Sipo will offer a reward of twenty-five thousand Norwegian kroner," said Waldhorst. "That's more than enough money to get someone to talk."

Agnes's life flashed before her eyes. She sat on the carousel, waving and waving, but neither her mother nor father was waving back anymore. They weren't there. No one was there.

"What does any of this have to do with me?" she said calmly.

Waldhorst didn't reply. He stared at the shiny parquet floor, the Persian rugs, the oil painting of a dramatic fjord landscape, the heavy bookcases stuffed full of books that the Berkowitz family would never read again.

"So," he said suddenly, rising from his chair. "I will try to . . ." He appeared to be at a loss for words and instead began pacing on the Persian rug by the windows. Finally he stopped and leaned against the windowsill.

"A magician is dependent on an audience that is willing to believe," he said. "Who truly wants to believe. Don't you agree, Ms. Gerner?"

She made no sign of replying.

"That's what the Führer understands. And it's going to lead us straight to perdition . . ."

"I don't know what you mean."

"You wanted to believe in him, didn't you?"

Agnes shook her head.

"The Führer?" she whispered.

"No, not the Führer. Don't you understand what I'm talking about?" said Waldhorst, now almost on the verge of laughter.

"I really don't have time for—"

"The Pilgrim," Waldhorst said quietly. He rubbed his face with his hands before running them through his hair. "Don't you see? The man you want to have a baby with!"

Agnes couldn't stop herself from shaking her head. She had to get out of this madhouse—now!

Waldhorst strode over to his desk.

"Wait," he said. "Wait, I'll show you."

"What have you done with him?" she heard herself say. She was gripping the armrest of the Chesterfield. She stood up, her legs almost buckling under her as she took a few steps toward the huge desk. Waldhorst stood with his back to her, leaning over the mahogany surface. He had opened a file folder and was studying the papers inside.

He didn't hear me, Agnes thought. *He didn't hear what I said.*

If only she'd brought the pistol, she would have shot this madman right then and there.

"What does this tell you?" said Waldhorst in a low voice, without turning around.

Agnes stopped in the middle of the room. With the curtains partly drawn, darkness had almost descended over the room. Only the lamp on the desk gave off any light, shining on the dark wallpaper and the paintings that gaped at her. She couldn't understand what Waldhorst was driving at.

As she took another step toward him, he turned around with a bunch of papers in his hands.

"See for yourself," he said, and dropped all the papers on the floor. "Take a look!"

They stood there like that for a long moment, staring at each other with the papers strewn on the floor between them. Agnes instinctively backed away, even though her feet threatened not to obey.

Waldhorst knelt down and picked up one of the sheets. Then he stood up and silently handed it to her. She merely stared at him. Waldhorst raised his hand to her cheek, gently caressing it. Agnes turned her head away. At last she looked down at the paper. The words swam before her eyes, and she couldn't read what they said. She saw nothing but numbers and letters dancing across the page.

"Why are you showing this to me?"

"These are payments," said Waldhorst. "Receipts. A lot of money. More than you'll ever see. Swiss francs. Swedish kronor. Reichsmarks."

"And?"

"For Santiago," said Waldhorst. Again he touched her cheek. She reached up to remove his hand.

"Santiago?"

"Santiago," said Waldhorst. He turned and went back to the desk to sit down, then took his cigarette case out of his pocket.

Agnes shook her head.

Waldhorst's expression was somber. He picked up a lighter from the desk and lit his cigarette.

He smoked in silence for a moment, then shifted in his chair. Agnes again felt laughter bubbling up inside of her, as if she were about to go mad. What a strange man he was . . .

All of a sudden Waldhorst got up, went over to the window, and drew open the heavy drapes. The boy in the photograph on the desk grimaced at her. Waldhorst's own brother, just a boy.

For a long time he stood at the window, smoking in silence. A light drizzle had moved in over the city. Raindrops ran down the window-panes, forming an elegant pattern.

"Who travels to Santiago de Compostela?" Waldhorst said as if to himself.

He leaned his forehead against the windowpane. Agnes went over to him, unable to comprehend what his question might mean. His eyes were closed.

Santiago de Compostela. The disciple Jacob . . . *Oh God. Oh dear God,* thought Agnes. *Don't let it be him.*

"*Der Pilger.* I think he's going to reveal your name very soon, maybe even tomorrow," Waldhorst whispered in her ear. Again he raised his hand to stroke her cheek. For a moment her panic receded, for just a fraction of a second she wished that he wouldn't take his hand away, that he would save her.

"I love him." Agnes pushed his hand away. "What are you saying? You're sick!" she shouted. "Sick!"

Waldhorst stood there motionless, holding her arms in an iron grip.

"I'm engaged to Gustav Lande. Don't you know that?"

"Why do you want to have the Pilgrim's child?"

A crushing silence filled the room. What had she done?

Waldhorst's face remained impassive, but he let go of her arms.

"Tomorrow we're going to announce a reward of twenty-five thousand kroner. Tomorrow the Pilgrim is also going to attend his regular meeting with his German handler."

He took a handkerchief out of his pocket and wiped his face.

"How do you know that?" Her voice was barely audible. Tears ran down her face.

"Because *I* am his German handler," whispered Waldhorst.

He took her hand. She pulled it away and took a step back.

Waldhorst made no move to stop her. He stood there listlessly, his arms at his sides, on top of all those receipts for money that had been paid to the Pilgrim. He didn't react as Agnes backed away toward the door leading to the other room.

She spun on her heel and strode briskly toward the front hall. She turned the lock, then cast a quick glance at the Hitler Youth knife on the bureau. In a flash of madness she reached out to pick it up, then changed her mind and left it there.

The sound of her heels on the stairs filled the whole stairwell, making it impossible for her to hear whether he was following her. Out on the street the rain was pouring down. When she tilted her head back, her hat fell off and the drops ran down her face.

She started walking toward Solli Plass. Slowly, as if nothing had happened.

She turned around only once.

No, she told herself. Or was that a shadow behind her? The shadow of someone following her?

"No," she whispered into the rain.

CHAPTER 69

Monday, June 23, 2003
Gustav Freytag Strasse
Berlin, Germany

Peter Waldhorst sighed heavily into the intercom when Tommy Bergmann gave his name.

"It wasn't Vera Holt," said Bergmann. He was leaning against the locked wrought-iron gate, trying to detect any movement inside the house.

"Too bad for you," said Waldhorst. "I'm afraid I have nothing to add."

Bergmann didn't know what to say. He exchanged a quick glance with Udo Fritz, who stood beside him, frowning and with his arms crossed, as if he were actually trying to understand the Norwegian words.

"Did you drive to Oslo yourself?" Bergmann asked, speaking into the intercom.

A brief crackling sound was all the answer he received.

He looked over at Fritz again, who looked as though he had too much respect for people living in this neighborhood to be of any help. The detective merely shrugged and frowned again.

"I haven't been back to Oslo since 1945," said a voice some distance away.

Bergmann raised his head and saw that Waldhorst had come out the front door and was now standing there, holding onto the railing, as he prepared to descend the stairs. Moving at a slow, halting pace, he walked toward them along the flagstone path. He was leaning on a cane made of polished hardwood and looked much older than the last time Bergmann had visited. He wore a baggy burgundy knitted jacket, and his light-colored slacks, which were slightly too short, were wrinkled and the wrong weight for the season.

"Don't let the cane fool you," said Waldhorst. "I injured my foot when I slipped on the tennis court yesterday."

He shook his head when he saw that Bergmann was not alone. His face was pale. Not even the glow of the setting sun that had settled gently over the garden could lend a hint of life to Waldhorst's pallid complexion. Bergmann could hardly believe this was the same man he'd seen only a few days before.

"Has something happened?" he asked.

"Not much happens at my age, Mr. Bergmann. Except that you have come here unannounced to conduct an interrogation."

Bergmann was about to speak, but Waldhorst gestured dismissively. "I don't want to have to call the police, Mr. Bergmann. May I remind you that you are a Norwegian police officer on German territory?"

Bergmann pointed to Udo Fritz, who stuck his hand between the bars of the gate and introduced himself. He then had a brief conversation with Waldhorst in German. Bergmann understood enough to realize that Fritz was practically groveling before the old officer.

"Your wife . . . Is she feeling better?" said Bergmann, stopping himself from saying anything more.

"No," Waldhorst said quietly as he shook his head, "Gretchen isn't doing much better, Mr. Bergmann."

"Gretchen . . . Is she Johanne Caspersen?" he asked and then waited for a reaction. *I've got you now,* he thought, unconsciously rocking back on the balls of his feet, like a child who couldn't contain his excitement.

Waldhorst shook his head and frowned, as if he really didn't understand what Bergmann meant.

"What are you talking about?" he said. "Johanne Caspersen? Who's that?"

Bergmann tried for a conciliatory smile, but he could feel his cheeks burning. He'd intended to catch Waldhorst off guard, to expose him with this revelation. Instead, all he saw was an old man looking genuinely puzzled.

"We can come back tomorrow," Fritz told Waldhorst. "It's getting late."

"All right, fine," said Waldhorst. "I'm not in the mood to invite you in." He turned his back to them. "Good-bye, gentlemen."

"Vera Holt didn't kill Krogh," said Bergmann. "That's why I came back here. I need your help."

"Yes?" said Waldhorst. He stopped but did not turn around.

"Why did you say that you loved Agnes Gerner?"

"That was just a foolish remark," said Waldhorst. "Nothing but foolishness."

"So you didn't mean it?"

Waldhorst turned and came back over to them, leaning his hand on the gate.

"I said what I said. I can't very well take it back." A brief smile appeared on his face before his expression again turned somber.

"If you loved her," said Bergmann, "and if it's true that Carl Oscar Krogh killed her back in 1942 . . . Are you sure that the newspaper reports about the discovery in Nordmarka didn't have a strong effect on you?"

Waldhorst's hand trembled as he took his keys out of the pocket of his knitted jacket. For a moment he looked confused, as though wondering what to do with the keys, as if he were senile.

"Were you in Oslo during Whitsunday, Mr. Waldhorst?" asked Bergmann.

"As I told you, I haven't been back to Oslo since 1945, Mr. Bergmann. And the last time I went abroad, it was only as far as Austria. So, if you'll excuse me . . . But do come back tomorrow, after lunch, and I'll try to help you."

"I'm not leaving," said Bergmann.

"And I have no intention of letting you come in."

"You must have driven all the way to Oslo," said Bergmann.

Again Waldhorst turned around and headed back toward the house.

Bergmann turned to face Udo Fritz, who threw out his hands again. That seemed to be the only thing he was capable of. He looked as if he wanted to go home as soon as possible.

"In Lillehammer, you told Kaj Holt that Krogh was the German agent," Bergmann said to Waldhorst. He had a sudden feeling of déjà vu. He was sick and tired of people being difficult.

"The German agent!" Bergmann had to shout because Waldhorst had already reached the front steps. "Was it Krogh who killed Holt?"

Waldhorst had by now climbed the stairs. He stuck his key in the lock and shook his head. The door wasn't locked, but apparently he'd forgotten that.

"No," he said at last, holding on to the doorframe. The old man now looked even older, if that were possible. "Krogh was in a very difficult position . . . His father was teetering on the verge of bankruptcy, and he wanted to help him financially," said Waldhorst. "But Krogh didn't kill poor Kaj Holt."

For a moment none of them spoke.

"It was the Swedes," said Waldhorst, raising his hand to his head and running his fingers through his hair. "The Swedes killed Kaj Holt."

"He was killed because you told him something he wanted to know," said Bergmann.

"Only a fool runs off at the mouth," said Waldhorst. He gasped for breath, as if talking from a distance of ten yards was nearly killing him. "If Holt had let the Swedes have their way with Krogh, he might still be alive today."

"Krogh was a traitor. A traitor who allowed the Swedes to get rid of Holt."

"I've seen worse," said Waldhorst. "Much worse. And don't condemn him because of what happened to Holt. Krogh had no idea. Holt was his boss but also his friend, a friend he really did betray."

"Was that why Krogh was so upset by Holt's death?" asked Bergmann. "But his wife was sent to reinforce the idea that Holt was suicidal."

Waldhorst smiled wanly, as if he suddenly felt sad. He came back down the steps and walked toward the gate, waving his hand. When he reached them, his face was even paler than before, and beads of sweat had formed on his forehead.

"Karen Eline Fredriksen was the mistress of Håkan Nordenstam, a Swede in what was called the C-Bureau. He was one of Kaj Holt's best Swedish contacts." Waldhorst fixed his eyes steadily on Bergmann to show that he was speaking the truth.

"So, was it this Nordenstam who killed Holt?" asked Bergmann.

Waldhorst shook his head.

"If there's nothing else, I really need to rest," he said. He leaned on the wrought-iron gate as he said something in German to Fritz. Bergmann understood only two or three words and didn't even try to assemble them into something coherent.

"I need you to tell me if you know who killed Kaj Holt."

"Why?" said Waldhorst. He was so pale now that Bergmann was afraid he might die right before their eyes.

"Because I might have gotten it all wrong," said Bergmann.

"The man who killed Holt died a long time ago. There's no point in trying to track him down. All of this is pointless, Mr. Bergmann. As for Krogh, he was like a fish you catch and then release. That's what war is like. Everything is for sale—life, death, loyalty, truth, everything. It's true what they say: money can buy anything. Except for doomed love."

Waldhorst turned on his heel and once again walked back to his house. It was obvious that the old man was making an effort not to look upset. The heavy door slowly closed behind him.

"Who killed Agnes Gerner?" Bergmann shouted so loudly that it could be heard all the way down the street. He noticed the German policeman shift nervously from one foot to the other. "Who killed Agnes?" he shouted again, even louder this time. "Was it you, Mr. Waldhorst?"

CHAPTER 70

Sunday, September 27, 1942
Villa Lande
Tuengen Allé
Oslo, Norway

Agnes Gerner put her hand on the door handle but didn't open the door. A shiver raced down her spine, but she shook it off. It was just her soaking wet clothes making her feel cold. Then the same thought occurred to her again. Why had she come back here to Villa Lande? Couldn't she simply leave? Disappear?

But where would she go?

She heard a sound behind her and turned around. The cab had long since driven off, and the street was quiet, almost deserted.

It's nothing, she told herself. *Just my imagination.* There were no shadows behind the tree, no strange cars on the street. All she saw was the rain pouring down. She had no idea why not, but she had to accept the fact that Waldhorst hadn't followed her.

"But where?" she murmured to herself. "Where can I go?"

She didn't know where Number 1 was. Maybe he too had been taken to Victoria Terrasse. Could she go to the apartment on Kirkeveien, to seek refuge with the old couple who lived there? The man had put his hand on her shoulder and given her hope that all of this would someday be over.

She felt her stomach knot up. Without warning, in a flash of hope, she imagined the Pilgrim helping her get to Sweden. Then in a few weeks' time, they would meet in Stockholm. Maybe they could even celebrate Christmas together. Just the two of them. They could run away together, away from this war, this . . . It couldn't be . . . It was a lie. Waldhorst was nothing but a liar! He had faked those papers. He was trying to tighten the noose around her neck, but he wasn't going to get away with it.

The door opened before she pressed down on the handle. Shivering and confused like a fledgling bird, Agnes found herself staring into the face of Johanne Caspersen. She tugged a bit at her apron but didn't say a word.

Agnes brushed past her and took off her coat, tossing it on the floor behind her as she went into the living room. The maid followed close behind, merely stepping over the discarded wet coat. Agnes continued on to the library and went inside, slamming the door behind her.

A pack of Turkish cigarettes that *Brigadeführer* Seeholz had left behind lay on the table. She shook one of the few remaining cigarettes out of the pack. It landed on the table, and she could barely manage to pick it up. She rummaged through her purse for a lighter, then sat down and stared straight ahead. What Waldhorst had said about the Pilgrim couldn't be true. It wasn't possible. Things like that didn't happen to her. She wasn't easily fooled, or she never drew the shortest straw. She'd never been like that. And she refused to let that happen now. *No,* she thought as she went over to stand by the windows and took a deep drag on the strong cigarette. Last night not a soul in this room would have believed that she was working for the Brits, so she wasn't about to let that little *Hauptsturmführer* believe it either. Feeling numbed, almost intoxicated by the strong tobacco, she suddenly felt sure that this whole nightmare would simply pass, that she'd find a way out at the last minute. She would talk to Gustav when he came back from Berlin, and Waldhorst would find himself on the Eastern Front before he could say "Pilgrim."

The door opened. Agnes ignored the maid.

"Aren't you supposed to go out to Rødtangen, Ms. Gerner?" said Johanne.

"Do you think I'd go out there all alone?"

Agnes walked back through the living room and into the kitchen, with the maid following her. She sat down at the kitchen table and stared out the window at the front gate, half expecting to see Waldhorst arrive at any moment.

"No," she told the maid. "There will be no trip to Rødtangen today."

"Mr. Lande will not be pleased. October starts next week, and Rødtangen is always closed up before October."

Agnes stared at the maid for what felt like several minutes.

"I am Mr. Lande's future wife," she heard herself say, "and I alone know whether he will be displeased or not. And if he is displeased, there are ways to please him." She touched the ring that Gustav had given her, turning it around and around on her finger, as if it would protect her from evil—from Peter Waldhorst, who was certain to come after her once he'd collected himself. An awful thought whirled through her mind: How could Waldhorst know that she was pregnant with the Pilgrim's child? They could have found out his code name by torturing someone who'd been arrested. They could have even found out his real name. But not the fact that she was pregnant.

She pushed the thought away.

"I am Gustav Lande's future wife," she whispered to herself. She repeated those words five times in a row, as if speaking them out loud might make them true. "I am Mr. Lande's future wife."

Johanne stared at her as if she were an animal that had strayed into the house.

"Cecilia has been looking forward to going to the woods," she said.

The woods, thought Agnes. It might clear her head to go out there.

"We'll take the car up to Nordmarka instead," she said. "A walk in the woods would do us all good."

She went out to the front hall and picked her wet coat up off the floor. Bewildered and unable to think rationally, she stood there listlessly. How could Waldhorst know? She pictured the Pilgrim's face, how it had grown hard over the past few months. The maid said something to her, but Agnes couldn't make out the words. She turned to look at her. Had Johanne just said something about Waldhorst? Agnes couldn't tell. She wasn't hearing a single sound. She could have screamed and not even heard herself.

They stared at each other for a long moment. The maid's lips were moving, but Agnes heard nothing. But it looked as if the maid's lips were forming that name.

Waldhorst.

Followed by a whole sentence: "Mr. Waldhorst has asked me to keep an eye on you."

No, thought Agnes. *That can't be what she said.*

She turned on her heel and went up to Cecilia's room, first stopping by her bedroom to put on a dry coat. The child was sitting by the window, leafing through a photo album full of old pictures of her mother.

Agnes noticed that her hearing had now returned. She could hear the sound of the thin album pages turning. She went over to Cecilia and stroked her hair. She said they were going to drive up to Nordmarka and take a walk in the woods. They'll go to Rødtangen some other day.

"But it's raining," said Cecilia. She had stopped at one of the photographs of Gustav sitting next to his wife. It had been taken sometime in the early thirties.

"Rain is nice," said Agnes. Only now did she notice that Lande's wife was very pregnant in the photograph. She and Lande were sitting on a big rock, smiling at the photographer. Cecilia ran her finger over her mother's stomach. Then she touched her mother's face.

Cecilia must have gone downstairs, because when Agnes turned around, the little girl was no longer in the room. Agnes looked at the white walls, the bookcase, the countless porcelain dolls on the two dressers, the small canopy bed, the old teddy bear sitting on the wicker chair in the corner.

Without thinking about what she was doing, Agnes picked up the footstool from in front of the desk and carried it over to the wardrobe. She opened the middle door.

The Welrod was still there, untouched, just where she'd left it, behind the piles of old toys on the top shelf. Quickly she unwrapped it from the towel and stuck it in the left sleeve of her coat.

At the door she paused and cast one last look around. In a few strides she crossed the room, picked up the photo album with pictures of Cecilia's mother, and stuck it under her arm.

In the doorway she paused once again. The album suddenly felt too heavy. What was she thinking? She opened it and turned the pages until she came to the photograph of the young Gustav Lande and his wife, smiling and pregnant, sitting on the rock. It felt like the world split apart when she tore the picture from the page and stuffed it in the inside pocket of her coat.

CHAPTER 71

Tuesday, June 24, 2003
Hotel Berlin
Lützowplatz
Berlin, Germany

Tommy Bergmann felt like he'd been through all this before. But this time he really did think that he'd been awakened by an air-raid siren. The remnants of a dream abruptly vanished from his mind. For a fleeting second he remembered everything, and then it was gone.

It took him a minute to realize it wasn't an air-raid siren after all. It was his cell phone vibrating on the nightstand. Swearing under his breath, he fumbled for his watch.

"How's it going with that guy?" said Fredrik Reuter in his ear. "Did you oversleep?"

"You know me too well," said Bergmann. He sat up in bed and pulled up the covers. An image flashed through his mind of Hege coming out of the bathroom, dripping wet, to kiss him on the forehead and say she loved him. For a moment he imagined that he'd never done anything wrong.

"Have you made any progress?" asked Reuter.

"He admitted that Carl Oscar Krogh worked for him during the war, but that's all. Maybe it was old Waldhorst himself who hacked him up," said Bergmann, putting a cigarette to his lips. "If Krogh killed Agnes Gerner and Waldhorst loved her, he at least has a motive, even though the murder happened so long ago. I'm going back out there today to get his fingerprints."

"Maybe I can spare you the trouble," said Reuter.

"What do you mean?"

"I've got a guy sitting right here in front of me in the office."

Bergmann dropped some cigarette ash on the sheets. He swore and then brushed it onto the floor.

"A guy?"

"A suntanned roofer from Poland."

"What are you talking about?"

"He was working on the roof of the house next door to Krogh's place when Krogh was killed. He left for Poland the next day," said Reuter. "Anyway, he saw a car drive away from Krogh's house."

Bergmann stopped smoking and held the cigarette distractedly between his fingers.

"Why hasn't he mentioned this until now?"

"I told you. He was in Poland. They don't have *Dagbladet* over there, Tommy. They just have crucifixes above their beds and outhouses in the yard. So he hasn't read any of the Norwegian newspapers. In fact, he doesn't even speak Norwegian. But when he came back home, he saw the pictures from the case in the papers and recognized the neighboring house."

"Let me talk to him," said Bergmann.

After a short pause he heard the man say on the phone in heavily accented English, "A car."

"A car?"

"A car, for rent."

"A rental car," Bergmann murmured to himself. There might be bloodstains in the car. "What sort of car?"

"Red."

"Red?"

The man on the phone fell silent. Bergmann felt his pulse pounding in his temples and noticed that he was more tense than he wanted to be.

"Newspaper," said the Pole, using the Norwegian word, *avis*.

"Newspaper? What newspaper?"

"Avis . . . car."

It took Bergmann a few seconds to realize the Pole meant the Avis rental-car company.

"What type of car?"

"A small Ford or Opel."

"Why that car? There must have been other cars on the street."

"Not many cars," said the man on the phone. "Not many. This one drove very slow, almost not moving. Like the driver not paying attention. I don't know . . ."

"An old man?" said Bergmann. "Was the driver an old man?"

Silence for a moment.

"I don't know. I was up on roof. I couldn't see, but I think two people."

"Two?" said Bergman. "Two people?"

"Yes, two people."

Bergmann closed his eyes for a moment. "Shit," he murmured between clenched teeth. "Great. That's all I need," he said to the man. "Please give the phone back to Inspector Reuter."

Reuter came back on the line.

"Call all the Avis rental-car offices," said Bergmann, "and get copies of the driver contracts issued for all cars that were turned in on Sunday, June 8. Start with the office at the train station, then Oslo Airport and Lillestrøm."

Reuter paused, as if for effect, before he said, "Do you think we're complete idiots up here?"

Bergmann considered replying in the affirmative but decided not to.

"And fax everything to me here in Berlin."

"Tommy, now that . . ."

But Bergmann had already picked up the information booklet on the nightstand and was rattling off the hotel's fax number. Reuter reluctantly wrote it down. Bergmann could picture him: his face flushed, his reading glasses perched on the tip of his nose, his shirttail untucked, writing down the number on an old scrap of paper at his desk.

"And you're not to do anything at all without Fritz," said Reuter.

In the end, Bergmann grudgingly had to agree.

He was sitting in a shady sidewalk café on a side street off Kurfürstendamm when Reuter called again. Without making a move to pick up his phone, Bergmann downed the rest of his schnapps and studied the light shining through the golden beer in the other glass. After Reuter gave up, he lit another cigarette, thinking that the case was over. One way or another, it would be over in less than an hour. Then his phone rang again.

"Are you at the hotel?" asked Reuter.

"No."

"Well, there's a big stack of papers waiting for you when you get back, since you insisted on having copies." Reuter's voice sounded so resigned that Bergmann felt a growing disappointment replace the tension of the past few hours. It seemed that instead of wrapping this case up, the only thing he had to look forward to was more weeks of groping in the dark. Maybe it was too good to be true for a Polish roofer to provide the ultimate breakthrough in the case. An old drunkard, a crazy woman, and now a Polish roofer were all they had so far.

"So," said Bergmann. "No Waldhorst? No Peter Ward?"

"No."

"He may have used another ID, or taken the car back to another Avis office."

"Possibly," said Reuter. "Or taken it back the next day. I'll do a hotel search too." It didn't sound like he thought that would prove fruitful. If someone committed a murder in a foreign country, there was only one important rule: to get across the border as quickly as possible. "Take a look yourself," Reuter said. "But I can't see anyone in those papers who bears any resemblance to an almost ninety-year-old German."

CHAPTER 72

Sunday, September 27, 1942
Nordmarka
Oslo, Norway

After they'd been walking in Nordmarka for ten or fifteen minutes, the sky overhead turned almost black.

Cecilia was leading the way, a few steps ahead of Johanne Caspersen. Agnes Gerner walked a few paces behind the maid. She had her eyes fixed on the back of Johanne's anorak. Then she turned around to see if anyone was following them. Had Johanne really said that about Waldhorst back at the house? She must have imagined it.

"I'm tired," said Cecilia.

"A little exercise will do you good, Cecilia," said Agnes. She glanced down at her boots to avoid tripping on the wet, slippery tree roots. At one point, the muddy path gave way beneath her feet and sucked her right boot into the ground—she had a fleeting fear that the earth was trying to pull her down into it. It took all her strength to yank her foot back out. The knapsack she had insisted on bringing felt as if it were filled with rocks and not with the waffles they'd made with the last of the butter Gustav had obtained from his German contacts.

Agnes stopped and stared down at the mud, looking for her boot. The ground was bubbling and soon filled up with murky water. She kept picturing herself shouting in the dark library of Waldhorst's apartment.

How could she have lost her head like that?

Well, I just did, she thought.

A stabbing sensation pierced her stomach, way down, close to her pelvis. Then the pain shot up to her left breast. Only now, deep inside this silent forest, did she grasp the truth. Maybe it was the baby inside of her kicking—as if the child knew everything about her.

She turned around again, as she'd already done countless times since they'd started on the path near Frognerseteren. She studied the woods, convinced the dark eyes of Peter Waldhorst were following them.

No, she told herself. *There's no one else here.* Not on the path and not among the trees. Not a soul. She turned once more to inspect the slope they had just descended, peering into the dark trees. A couple of raindrops struck the tip of her nose. She closed her eyes, which stung from exhaustion. She needed to stop thinking like this. She needed to calm down and accept that Waldhorst wasn't following them. She reminded herself that only three cars had been parked near the trail, and they'd only run into two other people on the path, an elderly couple carrying empty berry buckets. No one wanted to go out walking in weather like this. And because so many people had been frantically picking berries because of this insane war, the woods were virtually stripped of them.

By now both Cecilia and Johanne were a good twenty yards ahead. Agnes stopped and watched them continue along the path.

What had once seemed impossible was now inevitable.

Would they notice if she suddenly turned around and began running back to Frognerseteren? Of course. And Johanne would report her at once. And where could she go? Where? She'd be arrested before the day was out.

She forced herself to start walking again. After a few steps she stopped to glance over her shoulder.

Was that a sound?

Was someone following them? In the shadows? Among the trees?

"No," she whispered to herself. Three cars and two people. That was all. She started walking faster and soon caught up with the others. Because of Cecilia's injured hip, it was easy to reach them. Much too easy.

Agnes stroked the child's wet hair several times. Each time her hand shook harder.

They soon reached a small area that had been cleared of timber. Agnes stopped. At the end of the clearing she saw a narrow path; the forest around it appeared even more dense than it was along the main path.

"Over there," she said, pointing in the direction of the path before she could change her mind. All three looked at each other in silence.

"We need to go home before it gets dark," said Johanne. Her green anorak looked almost black, soaked through with rain. "Cecilia won't be able to walk much farther."

Agnes glanced up at the sky. In an hour or so it would be so dark that they'd have trouble getting home if they took the narrow path.

"Sure she can," said Agnes. "Right, Cecilia? Doesn't that look like an exciting path?"

Cecilia looked up at Agnes and gave her that special smile that only the two of them shared. Agnes turned away. She didn't want the child to see that she couldn't bear to smile back.

Without waiting for the maid, Agnes and Cecilia crossed the clearing and started down the path. After only a few steps, Agnes heard Johanne behind them, taking short, hurried steps. She slowed down and placed her hand on Cecilia's shoulder. The girl had a secret little smile on her face, her determination clearly evident under Agnes's hand. The stupidest thing the maid could have said was that Cecilia couldn't go on. They should have done this more often; it would have made the child strong and healthy and happy.

Agnes suddenly felt that if she turned around now, she wouldn't see Johanne's face but instead all the greenery down by Westerham Ponds. Then she regretted thinking about that. Bess's shattered skull flashed through her mind and then merged with the soundless scream of Torfinn Rolborg's private secretary. Agnes tightened her grip on Cecilia's shoulder. Overhead the black spruce trees seemed to be reaching for the sky, blocking out the last of the daylight.

After they'd walked for about ten minutes, the path seemed to be leading them toward another clearing. Agnes thought she could see a grove far ahead. She paused to let the maid walk past. Her boots sank into the ground as she watched Cecilia lead the way, with Johanne just a few steps behind her. Then she directed her gaze to the clearing up ahead.

Johanne was waiting for her. She had her arms crossed, as if to block her entrance. Cecilia was standing just behind her. Agnes tried to move past, but the maid stood in her way.

"We need to turn around," Johanne said in a low voice. "Unless you want to carry her all the way back."

Agnes didn't reply. *She's probably right,* she thought. And if they were going to do it, it had to be now.

The maid's eyes narrowed. Her pointed nose looked bigger than ever.

Agnes opened her mouth to speak, but no words came out.

"Where are you taking us?" asked Johanne.

Agnes didn't know what to say.

"I know what you are. Don't you realize that?"

Cecilia poked her head around the maid to find out what was going on.

"Are you trying to take us as deep into the woods as possible?" said Johanne.

Don't be afraid, thought Agnes. She took a deep breath and exhaled slowly. Only a faint quaver at the end revealed her fear.

"Herr Waldhorst asked me to keep an eye on you," the maid said again, as if the very words were dangerous. An almost imperceptible smile appeared on her face.

Agnes slowly shook her head. It was too late. It was all too late. There was no way back.

"I'm not scared of you. Do you think I am? It was you, wasn't it? In the newspapers? But Mr. Lande won't be in the dark for long. Just wait until we get back."

But Agnes was no longer listening. Through the rain she was staring at Cecilia, who was holding on to the maid's anorak. The barrel of the Welrod was jabbing into her left breast. The rain must have made the gun visible through the sleeve of her coat.

She had never intended for it to end like this.

My little girl.

"You should have been my little girl," whispered Agnes.

His and mine.

The Pilgrim's and mine.

"Run, Cecilia!" Johanne cried. "Run!"

CHAPTER 73

Tuesday, June 24, 2003
Hotel Berlin
Lützowplatz
Berlin, Germany

The rain was coming in through the open windows of his hotel room. Tommy Bergmann lay in bed for a few more minutes, staring up at the white ceiling. It took him a moment to remember what day it was, what city he was in, and what he was doing there.

He must have fallen asleep earlier, either from exhaustion or disappointment. As soon as he arrived back at the hotel, he had dutifully picked up all the faxed documents, which the desk clerk had stacked up on the counter for him.

"I don't really need these," he'd considered saying. But he'd taken them to his hotel room anyway without so much as a word of thanks.

Then he'd briskly leafed through the fifteen pages that Avis had faxed over to police headquarters in Oslo. The quality left something to be desired after being sent through two fax machines, but it was good enough for Bergmann to conclude that no Peter Waldhorst or Peter Ward had rented a car from Avis and then brought it back to the train station, the airport, or the Lillestrøm office on Sunday, June 8, 2003.

He lit a cigarette and went over to the window that faced the broad avenue. He held his hand out the window for a moment, allowing the rain to soak his skin.

Then he stared back at the stack of papers on the desk. He trudged over to it, feeling defeated, as if there was no point in expanding their search to rental cars returned on any of the next few days after the murder. When he reached the desk, he leafed through the pages once more. None of the names got his attention.

He dropped the whole pile into the wastepaper basket under the desk. A few pages landed on the floor, and he resisted the impulse to tear them into tiny pieces and toss them out the window.

He had a sinking feeling inside, a heavy, black stone of disappointment weighing him down. Maybe it was the sense that he'd wasted so much time and effort on this case. Maybe it was the thought that old Waldhorst had managed to wrap him around his little finger.

Bergmann tried to push that thought to the back of his mind and accept the fact that he was going to have to start from the beginning.

He stood at the window by the desk and tried to locate the Bendlerblock, where Claus von Stauffenberg of the German Resistance had been shot in July of 1944. He could at least stop by to take a look before he went back home. But he eventually gave up—there were just too many buildings in this town. He stared down at the papers he'd tossed in the wastebasket. He bent down and picked up the three or four pages that had landed on the floor. The first two contained information about a forty-year-old Brit who had rented an Opel Astra at Oslo Airport on Friday, June 6, and brought it back to the airport on Sunday. The first page showed a copy of his driver's license. The next page was the form he'd filled out with the car's license-plate number and starting mileage, as well as his personal information. Bergmann studied the photo on the driver's license. Just as fucking uninteresting as all the other twenty-four individuals who had rented cars that weekend. He tore the two pages into strips and dropped them on the floor.

Just as he was about to head out the door, he paused for a moment, rocking back and forth on the balls of his feet. For several seconds he was overwhelmed by the feeling that he'd forgotten something important. But what was it?

No, he said to himself, shaking his head. *It's nothing.*

As he waited for the elevator, the feeling came back.

What the hell have I forgotten? he wondered as the doors opened down in the lobby.

The feeling was still there, lurking at the back of his mind, when he opened the umbrella he'd borrowed from the hotel and tried to settle on a route to the Bendlerblock based on the directions he'd received from the desk clerk.

When he reached the canal, he saw it: the yellow building was situated between two others about three hundred feet to his right.

Paradoxically, the rush of traffic on the wide avenue behind him actually made it easier for him to concentrate. He fixed his eyes on the canal. The sound of the rain steadily striking the water helped him to gradually formulate a clear image in his mind. That was when he realized what he had forgotten.

Three people were killed, he thought as he avoided the worst of the puddles on the sidewalk.

A little girl, a woman, and a man.

And that's what I don't understand, thought Bergmann.

He pictured Peter Waldhorst's face when he'd asked whether Gretchen was Johanne Caspersen. It had been nothing more than a wild guess, but Waldhorst looked as if he'd been waiting for that question for years. For decades.

Waldhorst met his second wife at Tempelhof Airport in the summer of 1963. Several months later, a woman starts phoning Krogh at home. Late in September, maybe on the anniversary of the very day when Agnes Gerner, Cecilia, and an unknown male were killed.

Suddenly it came to him.

There *was* a name that had caught his eye when he was scanning the list of car-rental customers at Oslo Airport.

What an idiot I am, Bergmann thought.

Gretchen.

Gretchen was a nickname. A *real* nickname.

CHAPTER 74

Monday, September 28, 1942
Kornsjø Train Station
Norway–Sweden Border

The sound of ironclad heels could be heard throughout the train car. Then there were a few seconds of silence before a compartment door was opened.

She paused as she raised her hand and stared into the flame from the silver lighter. She saw her reflection in the window and was just barely able to make out her facial features under her hat, the white cigarette hanging from her lips.

The boots stomped onward, approaching her compartment, then stopped. She heard the hollow thud of another door opening. Then muffled voices, nothing like the harsh sound of German. The door closed, and the German soldiers moved on.

She lit her cigarette, inhaled deeply, and studied the mark of her red lipstick on the paper. The light on the station wall glared above the letters spelling out Kornsjø and shimmered in one of the puddles on the platform. Three Wehrmacht soldiers stood silently under the arched entrance to the building. One of them was gripping the leash of a German shepherd. The dog tugged at the leash as someone was escorted out of a second-class car toward the back of the train. She couldn't see what was happening, only the soldier, who pulled the dog back. A man was shrieking like an injured animal at the northern end of the platform. She found all this commotion oddly reassuring. For a moment she was able to actually feel something. Maybe one day she would be human again.

She took another drag on her cigarette, automatically knocking the ash into the ashtray on the wall. Then she took her identification papers and border pass out of her briefcase. Though she managed to keep her eyes open despite an overpowering weariness, she once again lapsed into a state of indifference. Never again would she sleep or even close her eyes for more than a fraction of a second. Because when she did, all she saw was the image of herself standing over the child, who lay still, very still, on the wet, muddy ground. Her green coat blended into the ground underneath her, and her eyes showed no fear. They were just wide open and staring, as if it were all a dream.

After a moment the train station grew quiet again. The door to the neighboring compartment was yanked open. Again she heard a German voice, possibly an officer speaking. It was so quiet she could hear him asking for the passengers' identification papers.

It was her turn next. She fiddled distractedly with her cigarette case, as if she weren't in this train compartment at all, but instead on Gustav Lande's terrace, looking at the man seated across from her as he took his cigarette case out of the inside pocket of his tux.

A lieutenant with a soft-looking face tore open the door but said nothing as he gestured toward her. Three soldiers stood behind him. She held out her papers, but only far enough that he had to take a step inside the compartment to reach them. Just to show him that she couldn't care less, she lit another cigarette, her hands completely steady, while the lieutenant looked through her papers. She had memorized everything, in case he started asking her questions, but she doubted he would dare.

"Bitte, Fräulein," he said, handing back her border pass with a nod. Then he cast a quick glance at her new passport and identification papers, which showed she was a secretary at the German legation in Oslo. The border pass stated that the purpose of her trip was to take up a temporary position as office manager at the German consulate in Göteborg. The lieutenant clicked his heels together and handed back her papers.

"Allow me to wish you a pleasant trip, miss."

She got up and placed her hat on the rack overhead, running her hand gently over her hair as she studied her reflection in the window-pane. The platform was now deserted. Only the puddles remained.

As the train started moving, she sat down again and leaned her head back to look up at the netting of the rack. Her suitcase was a threatening presence. If the lieutenant had decided to open it, she would have been dead. Her real papers and a thousand Swedish kronor had been trustingly stuffed under a few pieces of clothing.

She listened to the ringing of the axles over the railroad ties for several minutes. As the cars filled with Swedish police officers, she stroked the cigarette case she had stuck in her pocket at the Østbane railroad station.

P.W., she murmured to herself.

P.W.

After the Swedish police officer had exited the compartment, she glanced at her watch for the first time, thinking that Gustav Lande must have landed in Oslo an hour ago. Maybe he was sticking his house key in the lock at this very moment. Maybe he was walking through the house, calling her name, then picking up the phone to call the summer house, and when he couldn't reach her to call friends.

She stood up and stuck her hand inside her coat pocket to take out the photograph of him and his wife. As if she wanted to speak to the pregnant woman sitting on the rock in the picture, smiling, unaware of everything that was to come.

The next thing she remembered was the loud whistle of the locomotive at a crossing, a cigarette burning her fingers, ash falling onto her lap and possibly ruining her dress. As if that mattered.

The moon shone through the cloud cover, lighting up her face in quick flashes.

She pressed her hand over her stomach, which was teeming with life, a new life.

May God have mercy on your soul.

CHAPTER 75

Tuesday, June 24, 2003
Hotel Berlin
Lützowplatz
Berlin, Germany

Tommy Bergmann swore loudly as he stood in the corridor after trying to open the door three times with his cardkey.

The lock finally clicked open on the fourth try, and he hurried over to the desk. He knelt down and first looked at the shreds of Avis papers lying on the floor. *No,* he muttered to himself. *It's not any of these.* Then he picked up the wastebasket and dumped the contents on the bed. Before he began searching through the papers, he found Udo Fritz's business card among the clutter on the desk.

Where have I seen that name? he thought as he listened to the phone ringing on the other end.

Udo Fritz answered, his voice sounding wary.

"Gretchen," said Bergmann as he started sorting through the papers on the bed, neatly setting aside the two-page documents of people who didn't interest him. *The old woman,* he said to himself as he looked for her. How could he have overlooked that?

"Gretchen?" said Fritz.

"It's a nickname, isn't it?"

Neither of them spoke for a moment. Bergmann was slowly making his way through the pile of papers, putting aside the paperwork of a Japanese woman.

"Yes," replied Fritz.

Bergmann had less than ten pages left to look through.

"It can be a nickname for Greta . . . or Gretel," said Fritz. "But why . . . ?"

Bergmann turned over the last two papers lying on the bed. He stared at the photo of the woman on the German driver's license. He could hardly contain himself as he held the paper in his hand.

Why hadn't he noticed her before? Maybe because her birthdate was listed as 1919 instead of 1918. Maybe because her ID stated that she was a Swedish citizen. And she had given a street in Stockholm as her home address, rather than Gustav Freytag Strasse in Berlin.

"Shit!" he exclaimed. "I'm a fucking idiot."

"Bitte?" said Fritz.

"What about Margaretha?" Bergmann said so quietly that he hardly even heard himself.

A pause. Then Fritz said, "Yes. It could be a nickname for Margaretha."

Bergmann felt the hairs stand up on his arms, which were still wet.

Even on this poor faxed copy, he could see the same look in the eyes as he'd seen in the picture of the young woman in *Aftenposten*, and in the photo taken at Gustav Lande's home on Midsummer Eve in 1942.

"Margaretha," Bergmann murmured. He'd seen that middle name in only one place, and that was in the National Archives, in the missing-persons report from the Vinderen police station from September 1942.

Margaretha Fredriksson was the name on the German driver's license, which had been issued in December of last year. Only now did he see that the birthdate was the same as the one he'd seen in the missing-persons report. Only the year of birth had been changed. That was why Waldhorst took a gift and a flower to the hospital on Thursday.

"How soon can you get here?" said Bergmann. "To the hotel?"

"I don't understand . . ." said Fritz.

"I'll explain on the way," said Bergmann. "We're going to the German Red Cross Clinic in Westend."

They got stuck in traffic along what seemed like endless, rainy boulevards. There were nothing but long lines of red taillights wherever Bergmann looked. In his hands he held the two pages from Avis, which showed that the Swedish woman Margaretha Fredriksson had been in Norway on Whitsunday.

Udo Fritz merely nodded silently, showing only moderate interest in the story. But Bergmann thought he noticed an underlying tension in the German policeman, who swore when he stalled the engine in an intersection.

It was dark by the time they finally reached the clinic. The rain was coming down harder, and the sky overhead was nothing but a dark-gray mass of clouds, relentlessly drowning everyone in its sorrow. Fritz dropped off Bergmann at the entrance before going to look for a parking place in front of the clinic. Bergmann stood under the canopy, looking across the parking lot. This was where Peter Waldhorst had uttered the few words that gave him all the information he needed—if only he'd realized it at the time.

Two white-clad nurses came out of the main building behind him. They gave him a nod and a smile before they raised their umbrellas and set off into the rain.

Fritz shook the rain off his coat and motioned toward the entrance.

Bergmann took two more drags on his cigarette, then stubbed it out and followed.

"Just a minute, please," said the woman at the reception desk.

"We'd like to speak to Margaretha Fredriksson," Bergmann said.

"I'm sorry, but visiting hours are over," she said.

Fritz came over to stand next to Bergmann. He said something in German and placed his ID on the counter. The young woman picked it up and studied it for what seemed like a long time. A phone began ringing in the back room. As Bergmann studied her hand holding the plastic ID card, he had the inescapable feeling that he'd stood here like this before. He raised his eyes and caught sight of the Madonna lithograph on the wall behind the nurse.

"Margaretha *Agnes* Fredriksson," said Bergmann. The phone stopped ringing.

The young woman handed back Fritz's ID. Then her expression turned stern. She cleared her throat.

"Mrs. Fredriksson is very ill," she said.

"Very ill?" said Bergmann.

"She has cancer."

"Since when?"

The young woman gave him an inquiring look.

Fritz motioned for her to answer.

"I can't see why that makes any difference. Mrs. Fredriksson is very ill. And her condition was made worse by a trip she took when she should have been here undergoing treatment."

Fritz said something to the nurse, sounding slightly annoyed. Bergmann understood that he was ordering her to take them to see the patient at once.

In the elevator up to the fourth floor, Bergmann had to lean against the wall. His face had lost all color, and he hardly recognized the man staring back at him in the mirror. How could he have overlooked it all? Waldhorst had held up the answer right before his eyes, but he had refused to see it.

Why had she gone to Oslo? The Polish roofer had said there were two people in the red car. Who was with her?

By the time the elevator doors opened onto the white corridor, Bergmann was no longer able to think clearly.

The narrow room was almost completely dark. Only a faint reading lamp shone some light on the old woman's face. Bergmann paused just inside the door, which had closed behind him, and studied her in silence. Next to him Udo Fritz was breathing loudly through his nose. The white blanket was moving steadily up and down, but too quickly for the gaunt old woman to be enjoying peaceful sleep. Bergmann thought that she might be the sort of person who would ask for the smallest possible dose of painkillers. Someone who wanted to spend the last days of her life on her knees. On the nightstand was a worn icon showing St. George slaying the dragon.

He took a few steps forward. The nurse placed her hand lightly on his arm. The old woman lying in the bed appeared to be more dead than alive. The EKG machine wasn't even hooked up, and she had only a single IV attached to her arm. Maybe she had told them that if she was about to die, there was no sense in dragging it out. Maybe this was what she wanted—to lie there with no one at her side. Her face was so sunken that it was almost beyond recognition. Bergmann recognized only one feature from the missing-persons photo from 1942, and that was her eyebrows. They were still as dark and elegant as a young woman's, giving her face a trace of hope, suggesting that the life force hadn't yet been extinguished.

So we've come full circle, Bergmann thought as he tried to come to terms with the fact that the hunt for Agnes Gerner's murderer had been in vain. He walked across the room to stand by the window. As he looked at the cars down below, he thought about how this whole investigation had been one coincidence after another. If Marius Kolstad hadn't mentioned Kaj Holt's name, he wouldn't be standing in this hospital room right now. Two people close to death, neither of them allowed to take their secrets to the grave—unless of course the woman in the bed happened to die this instant.

For what felt like several minutes, Bergmann stood there lost in his own thoughts—thoughts that ultimately had nothing to do with the old woman.

He heard some faint sounds behind him but didn't turn around.

"I'd almost given up on the idea that you would find me," said the woman from the bed.

Bergmann still made no move to turn around.

"Agnes Gerner," he merely said.

Maybe he was being overly dramatic by staring down at the parking lot outside. Maybe he hadn't yet recovered from the shock that this was, in fact, Agnes Gerner lying in the hospital bed behind him.

"Yes," said the old woman, taking such a deep breath that for a moment Bergmann feared it might be her last.

"I don't understand," he said, slowly turning to face her.

The woman who was once called Agnes Gerner lay in bed under the soft glow of the reading lamp, her eyes closed.

"There's always something a person doesn't understand. That's what my husband once told me."

"I see."

"It was apparently something he'd once said to another Norwegian. A man I held in great esteem. And now . . . Sometimes I don't understand why my life turned out the way it did." She opened her eyes.

Bergmann stayed by the window, leaning on the sill, his gaze fixed on the icon beside her. St. George, driving his spear into the dragon's mouth, was supposed to protect those whose faith was weak. Wasn't that how it went?

"Who killed the three people in Nordmarka?" said Bergmann. "Who killed Cecilia?"

Agnes closed her eyes again.

He opened his mouth to repeat the question.

"Maybe that's why I'm refusing to die," she said in a low voice, the words barely audible. "Nothing good awaits me on the other side."

Her breathing grew fainter.

Bergmann shook his head. He didn't understand.

"Nothing good?"

Agnes raised her hand, grimacing at the effort. The nurse briskly went over to the bed to hand her a glass of water from the bureau. She drank from the glass like a child, with water running down her neck. The nurse tried to wipe if off, but Agnes gently pushed her away.

"Do you think Cecilia's waiting for me there? I haven't slept in years. Am I still human after what I've done?"

"What do you mean?"

Agnes took a breath before she whispered a few words that Bergmann never thought he would hear. He felt as though the linoleum floor might buckle under his feet. *That's impossible,* he thought. *Not this woman.*

"What was I supposed to do? Leave her out there in the woods? Believe me, it's something I think about every single day and every night. That I should have let her live . . ."

No one in the room said a word.

Unaware of what he was doing, Bergmann sank into a chair next to Agnes's bed. After a moment she placed her hand on his, as if wanting to console him.

"Why did you go to Oslo?" he asked quietly.

The nurse motioned for them to leave, pointing at the door, but Bergmann ignored her.

"I wanted to see him again. One last time."

Bergmann shook his head.

"The Pilgrim?"

She beckoned him closer. Bergmann leaned forward, past the smooth face of St. George, toward the dragon's head pierced by the spear.

"I went there to *kill* the Pilgrim," Agnes whispered in his ear. For a moment he thought she smelled as she must have back then, that she was as beautiful as in the photographs. She put her hand on the back of his neck. It felt both soft and cold.

"It was his fault. All of this was his fault. Do you understand? That was why I had to kill him."

With great effort Agnes repeated what she'd said, this time in German. Then she seemed to faint and fell back on her pillow.

Bergmann studied the dying woman. It would do no good to ask her who had been with her.

Udo Fritz was having a quiet but intense conversation with the nurse, who uttered a horrified gasp. Bergmann guessed they were talking about arranging for a police guard. He moved his gaze to the saint on the gilded piece of wood. St. George, *Sankt Göran* in Swedish. The dragon slayer. Then he took Agnes's hand and squeezed it before reaching up to touch her cheek. As if he, of all people, was in a position to grant anyone forgiveness.

Bergmann stood up and placed his hand on Fritz's shoulder.

"Take me to Waldhorst," he said.

CHAPTER 76

Tuesday, June 24, 2003
Gustav Freytag Strasse
Berlin, Germany

The large entryway of the house was filled with the strong scent of fresh flowers. A dozen bouquets of tulips had been placed in crystal vases on the antique sideboards along the walls and on the two massive mahogany bureaus that stood on either side of the double doors leading to the living room.

Udo Fritz stood in the middle of the marble floor. Tommy Bergmann looked at the vases of dark-red flowers. All of them were exactly alike, so they must have come from the same florist.

Someone pressed down the handle on the door to the living room. Bergmann expected to see the old face of Peter Waldhorst, but it was the Turkish maid coming back. She said something in a low voice to Fritz. He nodded to Bergmann, who had no choice but to follow the two of them through the dimly lit house.

Bergmann and Fritz paused just inside the veranda door. A candle was burning next to the photograph of Gustav Lande and his first wife.

Waldhorst was sitting in a chair out on the veranda. He was staring out at the black waters of Hundekehle Lake, the rain coming down in torrents. On the horizon a plane with its landing lights on was heading for Tegel.

"So. Agnes Gerner," said Bergmann.

"I must say you took your time, Mr. Bergmann," said Waldhorst without turning around.

Bergmann ignored Fritz's inquiring expression and went out onto the veranda. Waldhorst motioned toward the other chairs. Bergmann cautiously took a seat two chairs away, looking at the old man in profile. A big wool blanket was covering Waldhorst's legs, and he was holding an extinguished cigar. On the table beside him was a tall, empty glass.

"She doesn't even want me to be with her anymore," said Waldhorst. "She's taken to her bed to die."

No one spoke for a moment.

"I understood the minute I saw that my brother's knife was missing," Waldhorst said at last. "I knew it would end like this. I knew it."

He brushed off the ash from the blanket and fumbled on the table for a box of matches. He murmured something in German, and Fritz proceeded to sit down next to Bergmann.

Waldhorst's face looked pale as a ghost in the light from the match flame. He puffed on his cigar, making the orange glow pulse against Bergmann's retinas. It took a few seconds for his eyesight to return.

"What did you know?" Bergmann asked.

Waldhorst puffed on his cigar, and for a moment it looked as if he were lost to the world.

"When I came down to the kitchen in the morning and saw that the discovery of the three bodies was on the front page of *Aftenposten*, I knew that she would end up going to Norway."

Another pause. Then he said, "She told me that she killed Carl Oscar Krogh for everyone. For herself, for Cecilia, for Kaj Holt, for Vera Holt. For everyone who died because of him."

"Was she in contact with—"

"Vera Holt? Yes," said Waldhorst. "A couple of times, in the past few years. God, how Agnes hated that man. I tried to tell her that's what happens in war, that you have to expect betrayals, but . . . She fooled me. I thought she'd come to terms with what happened." He rubbed his face, then sighed heavily and gave a resigned laugh. "'The Pilgrim got me in the end,' she said when she came home on Sunday evening. And well, you know . . . she won't last much longer."

Bergmann lit a cigarette. Fritz sat motionless next to him. Both stared at the horizon. Another plane emerged from the clouds and slowly descended toward the city.

"How . . ." Bergmann began but then stopped. He didn't know what to ask.

Again all three men lapsed into silence.

"She came to the door," Waldhorst said finally. He nodded to himself several times, looked down at his cigar, let it burn out.

"She rang the doorbell," he corrected himself. "It was such a lovely apartment, you know, Mr. Bergmann. Quite lovely. At the top of Bygdøy Allé, right across from Frogner Church . . ." He let the words die away. "I opened the door without saying a word."

Bergmann waited.

"And there she stood, right before me. Tears were running down her face, and she was holding a gun."

Waldhorst fixed his eyes on Bergmann and gestured with the burned-out cigar.

"An angel. She was like an angel."

"Why? Why did she come to you?"

"She knew that I'd had her surrounded long ago. She wanted me to have her arrested. All she wanted was to die," said Waldhorst. "She had killed a child. A child that she loved."

"What did you do?" asked Bergmann.

"I convinced her that I could get her out of Norway. That her own death wasn't going to bring Cecilia back to life. I went over and took the gun out of her hand. A gun made by the Brits. I'd never seen any like it."

"And?"

"Then I took the engagement ring off her finger and stuck it in my pocket. She told me where the two bodies were. All I had to do was follow the main path until I came to the logging area on the left-hand side. A good flashlight was all that was needed to find the place. I took the keys to Gustav Lande's car and drove to Torshov, where one of my informants lived. A lonely and embittered little devil of a man from up north somewhere. Someone I knew nobody would miss, at least not until the war was over. It took us an hour to dig a grave in the woods, in utter darkness and a hell of a downpour. First we threw in the poor child. Then the maid. She had been working for me, but I was the only one who knew that. At least she took to her death an engagement ring from Gustav Lande. Then I pulled out Agnes's Welrod and shot the poor informant in the head. He never even knew what happened. He never saw me point the gun at him. He was leaning on the shovel, staring down at the two bodies. And he was crying. 'Just a child,' he said. 'That poor little girl.' When he said it again, I pulled the trigger and rolled him down into the grave. I drove the car back to town, parked it on Madserud Allé, and then walked back to my apartment, where she was waiting."

"So that's why the car was found on Madserud Allé," said Bergmann. Waldhorst nodded.

"I knew where all the checkpoints were in town, so I drove around them. Besides, who looks out the window in a dark city with blackout curtains? No, Mr. Bergmann, the car was the least of my problems."

Bergmann lit another cigarette. He tried to think of something to say, but then thought it best not to say anything at all.

"Do you remember what I said to you the first time you were here?" asked Waldhorst.

"No," said Bergmann.

"I said that in war, only one thing matters."

"Survival?" said Bergmann.

Waldhorst nodded.

"Agnes survived," Bergmann said.

"At that moment I held her life in my hands. I wanted her to survive," said Waldhorst. "That was the only thing I cared about." He reached for the matches and relit his cigar.

Bergmann got up and went over to one of the pillars. He leaned against it and watched yet another plane descending toward Tegel.

"I think you're lying," he said and turned around to face Waldhorst.

The two men stared at each other.

"Every word I've said is true," he replied.

"About the war, yes," said Bergmann.

"So?"

"There were two people at Krogh's house that day," said Bergmann. "Two people drove down Dr. Holms Vei in a red rental car. One of them was Agnes Gerner, but who was the other person? Who had she turned to for help?"

Waldhorst's lower lip quavered. He opened his mouth to speak, but changed his mind. He stared out at the dark lake, at the falling rain.

"Carl Oscar Krogh was killed with tremendous force. More than sixty stab wounds. More than a dying, eighty-year-old woman could manage. And why would she kill him with a Hitler Youth knife?"

Waldhorst made an attempt to answer again. Bergmann had all the time in the world. He let the old man take his time.

"Have you ever wondered why I never asked?" Waldhorst finally said.

"Asked what?" said Bergmann.

"Who you talked to in order to find me?"

Waldhorst grasped the armrests of his chair and slowly got to his feet. Then he went inside.

Bergmann lit another cigarette and waited on the terrace without exchanging a single word with Fritz. Waldhorst came back a few minutes later. He paused just inside the terrace door. In one hand he held a photograph. Bergmann motioned to him, but the old man didn't move. A tear spilled from his left eye. Bergmann went over to him, holding his cigarette in his right hand. He held out his left. Waldhorst handed him the photograph.

"Without him you would never have found me, and without me you would never have found your way back to him," said the old man in a low voice. "He turned sixty a few weeks before Whitsunday. We weren't there, of course, but Gretchen, Agnes . . . She just wanted to see him one last time and tell him the truth about what happened in Nordmarka back then. She gave him all the money she had . . . And I gave him my brother's knife."

Bergmann took a deep breath before he turned over the photo.

There were three people in the picture, a relatively recent color photograph. It took him two or three seconds to comprehend the connection, to grasp why the landscape looked so familiar and that he had not been mistaken. He really had seen this man standing in the middle before.

"I thought you said that you hadn't been to Norway since 1945," said Bergmann, handing the photograph back to Waldhorst.

"I said I hadn't been back to Oslo." Waldhorst looked past him at the lake.

"I'll need to ask you to contact him," said Bergmann.

"She said that she'd already killed one child too many."

Bergmann nodded.

"But after a few weeks she gave him away to an orphanage. Ten years ago she found him again."

"I understand," said Bergmann. He placed his hand on Waldhorst's shoulder.

"I want you to believe that she was a good person, Mr. Bergmann. A good person."

CHAPTER 77

Wednesday, June 25, 2003
Steinbu Lodge
Vågå, Norway

Tommy Bergmann signaled to turn left and began driving up the final steep incline. The last rays of sunlight that reached down into the valley glittered on the surface of the water on his right. Chet Baker's trumpet on the car radio competed with the sound of the windshield wipers. Bergmann turned off the radio and glanced in the rearview mirror. The music reminded him of something he didn't want to remember.

The photograph that Waldhorst had given him was stuck in the edge of the mirror. As he shifted into second gear, he looked at the three people in the picture. They were standing in this landscape, surrounded by magnificent mountain formations, more peaceful than anywhere else on earth. The big man in the middle and the two old people on either side of him—Peter Waldhorst and Agnes Gerner—were smiling at the photographer. As if the world had never caused them any harm. Bergmann shifted his gaze to the mirror to check on the two patrol cars from the sheriff's office following close behind. It wouldn't take much for them to switch on the sirens. The Vestoppland police chief had even given the sheriff—who was one of the drivers—permission to carry a gun. Bergmann had merely shaken his head at their overeagerness, but there was nothing he could do.

The place looked deserted. Only three cars were parked next to the building where he had stayed two weeks ago. No lights were visible in any of the windows. Only a single light above the carved sign telling visitors that they had arrived at Steinbu Lodge. The two setters scratching at the fence in the dog run on the north side of the main building were the only sign of life.

Bergmann stood in the middle of the yard, staring at the water, smooth as a mirror, below the main building. Then he tipped his head back and looked up at the evening sky.

Why the hell did it have to be you? he thought.

Five uniforms were now standing next to him, all wearing Kevlar vests. The sheriff, an ambitious new hire from Østfold, had already taken out his gun. Bergmann's only protection was the same GANT shirt he'd been wearing in Berlin over the past few days. The last thing he wanted was a bulletproof vest. He motioned for the sheriff to put his gun back in the holster.

Finn Nystrøm's wife was in the lobby. She was just about to bend down behind the counter when Bergmann stepped inside. At first she gave him a welcoming smile of recognition. Then, as the uniformed officers quickly filled the small lobby area, her expression changed to what looked like deep sorrow. The last traces of the young girl she had once been seemed to disappear from her face for good.

"He's in the kitchen," she said quietly.

Bergmann nodded. The sheriff was following so close he almost stepped on his heels.

Nystrøm's wife bowed her head toward the wide pine counter.

"Do you have to do this?" she asked.

Bergmann wanted to respond, but he couldn't think what to say. He chose to remain silent and started down the stairs to the dining room, holding out his hand behind him to keep the sheriff at arm's length. Out of the corner of his eye, he saw two other officers run along the side of the building to secure the doors to the terrace and the kitchen. *As if there were any place to run up here in the mountains,* thought Bergmann. He paused on the bottom step. Three people—a middle-aged couple and a young girl—were eating dinner in the spacious dining room on the right. The man noticed the shadow of the police officer who had taken up position outside. One by one the guests put down their forks and knives and turned to look at Bergmann and the two officers behind him.

Bergmann heard the muted sound of a radio coming from the kitchen on the left. He stepped quietly down onto the terracotta tiles and peered through the round window in the white swing door. Nystrøm was bent over several saucepans on the big stove. He had cut his hair short since the last time Bergmann had seen him. All that was left was a thick mat of gray hair above his weather-beaten face.

Finn Nystrøm, Bergmann thought, realizing that he'd done a bad job. If only he'd bothered to check—just done a simple search in the National Registry—he might have been suspicious. He would have found out that Nystrøm had emigrated from Sweden at the age of nineteen, and a year later changed the spelling of his last name from Nyström to Nystrøm so he fit in. He also should have realized that faint, barely discernable accent he'd heard was a remnant of the man's native Swedish. But even so, that might not have done much good. He pushed open the door. Nystrøm hadn't ever used the last name Gerner either in the Swedish orphanage or with any of his foster families. And Agnes had supposedly been dead for what amounted to two generations. Yet Bergmann nonetheless felt that he'd failed in some way when Nystrøm raised his eyes from the saucepans to look at him.

"Why did you lead me to Iver Faalund and Peter Waldhorst?" asked Bergmann, taking two steps forward on the white tiled floor. He held his hand behind his back to signal to the sheriff to wait outside the kitchen. "If you hadn't done that, I never would have found out you . . ." He stopped. It all seemed pointless.

"Otherwise you never would have found me," said Nystrøm, turning his gaze back to the pots. "Wasn't that what you said?" A strong aroma of stewed meat and gravy filled the air.

Bergmann didn't know what to say.

"I knew you would come," said Nystrøm, reaching up to the shelf to turn off the radio. "You must be hungry after traveling all the way from Berlin and then driving so far." He took off his blue apron and laid it on the kitchen counter.

"The footprint," said Bergmann. "Was it hers?"

"Agnes—or rather, my mother—went back inside after I came out, covered with his blood."

Nystrøm stepped toward Bergmann with his hands raised, as if to show that his intentions were peaceful.

"But why?" said Bergmann.

"Why?" Nystrøm snorted. "Because I knew what he'd done during the war. And because he was my father. Because . . . I really never understood it until that Whitsunday. Because I was ashamed of myself. He'd bought me off, you know. More than twenty years ago, when I finally came home from Stockholm, right before I took off from the University of Oslo, the Pilgrim gave me two hundred thousand kroner. By way of consolation, as he put it. And I took the money without saying a word. He wasn't stupid. He knew from the first time we met that I was his son and that I already knew too much about him. But I was basically a pitiful bastard who needed money. Money to buy booze." Nystrøm leaned one hand on the stainless-steel counter. He raised his other hand to touch the pots and pans hanging from a metal pipe above the counter. The movement caused a strange clattering sound.

"If Agnes hadn't come from Berlin and driven me all the way to Oslo, it never would have happened. Maybe I felt sorry for her. I don't know. She was so depressed after reading about the discovery of the bodies in Nordmarka. But she didn't want me to think that it was the Pilgrim . . . Krogh . . . who had killed them."

"Agnes told you that she killed Cecilia and the maid?"

Nystrøm nodded.

"Yes. She wanted me to know. She said she was pregnant with me at the time. She also said that she had been used, that the assassination of Rolborg had never been cleared by London. It was something that Kaj Holt and the Pilgrim had decided on their own. They took credit for the whole thing, while she ended up paying the price. She should never have made the trip from Berlin earlier this month. She was actually too weak for such a long trip, but she was dying and said she wanted to see her sixty-year-old son. She brought along the knife that had once belonged to Peter's brother. She knew how obsessed I was with the war. She called me the last pilgrim, you know . . . She wanted me to have the knife, and apparently Peter did too." A faint smile appeared on his face. "I even went back to Oslo with her. Agnes wanted the three of us to reconcile before she died."

Nystrøm rubbed his face.

"Look at me," he said. "Look how much I resemble him . . ."

"Then what?" said Bergmann. "What happened?"

"I . . . I regretted it as soon as we arrived. We would never . . . It would have been better if she'd never found me again, Tommy. Do you understand? Nothing good ever comes of such things."

"Was it something he said? Krogh, I mean?"

Nystrøm took the last few steps toward Bergmann. He laughed quietly, but Bergmann saw that his eyes filled with tears, as if the child inside him were trying to get out.

"He didn't even invite us in, that traitorous old fucker. And the things he said to Agnes . . . to my mother . . . and to me . . . I don't know. He was afraid someone would see us. 'Bastard child,' he called me. He was practically shaking with rage because we'd come to his house. I had the knife in my pocket, and I actually thought of killing him on the spot. But I told my mother we should just leave. So we went back to the car, but when she got in she started crying. She was inconsolable. That was when I realized he had to die. He had locked the front door, so I went around back. First I cut the throat of that damned dog of his. I couldn't stand the thought that he owned a setter. The terrace door stood open . . . and, well . . ." Nystrøm fell silent.

"And?" said Bergmann.

"I should have cut him right down the middle. That was the only thing I could think of. Cut that fucking man apart so nothing was left of him. Do you understand? I've always hated him for what he did, and hated myself because he was my father, and because I took his blood money."

For a moment neither of them spoke. The swing door behind Bergmann opened slightly, but he signaled that everything was fine.

"Do you think I'm going to kill you too?" said Nystrøm. He raised his hand, as if to place it on Bergmann's shoulder.

"Don't do that," said Bergmann. "You'll get us both killed."

Nystrøm nodded and took two steps back, holding his hands up in front of him to show the sheriff on the other side of the door that he had no intention of doing anything other than talking.

"And Agnes went back inside?"

Nystrøm nodded.

"I came out, covered with Carl Oscar's blood, and after I got in the car, she went around to the back of the house. As we drove back to town, she told me that she—of all people—had forgiven him!"

Nystrøm laughed, but it quickly turned to sobs.

The sheriff came in. Bergmann motioned for him to stop.

"I need to tell you this," said Bergmann. "I'm sorry it turned out to be you."

"Really?" said Nystrøm. He looked down at his big hands, as if he couldn't understand how they could have hacked his own father into pieces.

Bergmann nodded.

"You're going to have to come along with me, Finn," said the sheriff quietly.

But Nystrøm wasn't listening. He simply walked out the swing door and through the dining room, where the three people were still sitting, seemingly frozen in place. The sheriff went next, keeping his hand on the hilt of his gun in the black holster. Bergmann came last, moving slowly, almost reluctantly. Through the open terrace door he could see Nystrøm heading for the lake. The sheriff went after him, with one of the young police officers a few feet ahead. Nystrøm started to run toward the water but was soon caught by the policeman. He fell to his knees at the edge of the lake, bowed his head, and buried his face in his hands.

ABOUT THE AUTHOR

Photo © 2014 Charlotte Hveem

Gard Sveen is an award-winning crime novelist who divides his time between writing and working as a senior adviser to the Norwegian Ministry of Defense. *The Last Pilgrim*, his debut novel, was originally published as *Den siste pilgrimen* in Norway and is the first in the series featuring troubled police detective Tommy Bergmann.

The novel was an instant hit with critics and readers, and it went on to win the Riverton Prize in 2013, the prestigious Glass Key in 2014, and the Maurits Hansen Award, also in 2014. Sveen is the only author to date who has received all three honors for a first novel. The only other author who has managed to win both a Riverton and a Glass Key for their debut novel is Jo Nesbø.

Sveen is currently working on his third book in the Tommy Bergmann Series.

ABOUT THE TRANSLATOR

Steven T. Murray is an American translator from German, Swedish, Norwegian, and Danish. He translated the bestselling Millennium series by Stieg Larsson, three crime novels and two African novels by Henning Mankell, three psychological suspense novels by Karin Alvtegen, four police procedurals by Nele Neuhaus, and works by many other authors. In 2001 he won the Gold Dagger Award in the UK for his translation of *Sidetracked* by Henning Mankell. He was born in Berkeley and now lives in Albuquerque with his wife, Tiina Nunnally, and their two cats.